Praise for *Net Force: Dark Web*

"*Net Force: Dark Web* is a tightly woven, expertly crafted story with a finger on the pulse of the overwhelmingly clear and present danger of cyberterrorism. A riveting read."

—Marc Cameron,
New York Times bestselling author

"*Net Force: Dark Web* is a thriller tailor-made for our perilous times. Jerome Preisler gives readers a global thrill-ride with dire and deadly consequences—the action is relentless."

—John Gilstrap,
author of the Jonathan Grave thriller series

NET FORCE
FORCE
ATTACK
PROTOCOL

NET FORCE ATTACK PROTOCOL

A NOVEL

SERIES CREATED BY
TOM CLANCY and
STEVE PIECZENIK
WRITTEN BY
JEROME PREISLER

HANOVER
SQUARE
PRESS

HANOVER
SQUARE
PRESS™

Recycling programs
for this product may
not exist in your area.

ISBN-13: 978-1-335-08078-3

Net Force: Attack Protocol

This edition published by arrangement with Harlequin Books S.A.

Hanover Square Press
22 Adelaide St. West, 40th Floor
Toronto, Ontario M5H 4E3, Canada
HanoverSqPress.com
BookClubbish.com

Printed in U.S.A.

For my parents,
Thea and Sam,
with love.

All warfare is based on deception. Hence, when able to attack, we must seem unable; when using our forces, we must seem inactive; when we are near, we must make the enemy believe we are far away; when far away, we must make him believe we are near.

—Sun Tzu, *The Art of War*

PART ONE

WAR DRIVING
NOVEMBER 22–23, 2023

1

The first snowfall of the season was dusting the banks of the Somes River when a catastrophic failure struck the power grid, plunging the western third of the country into darkness.

Nicu Borgos was just an hour into his midnight shift when things went wrong. An operator for Satu Mare District's Electrica Power Distribution Center, he was tired from caring for his daughter, who was seven and sick with the flu. His wife, Balia, a sales clerk at a clothing store, was also miserably under the weather, and he had been doing his best to help her as well. But money was tight and, like him, Balia needed to work and bring in a paycheck.

The night before, she had come home from the shop, put chest rub on Angela, tucked her in, showered, and climbed into bed with her dinner untouched. Nicu normally slept until 9:00 p.m. or even a little later, but the sounds Angela was making in her room concerned him. He had lost his dear mother to the pandemic three years ago, and the outbreaks still could be vicious.

Taking no chances, he'd resolved to stay up to check on the child, poking his head through the doorway every fifteen or twenty minutes. It was a while before she settled in.

So Nicu was worn out and bleary, which might have been why he doubted his eyes when he saw the cursor suddenly drifting across his screen. The computer was networked into the energy grid, and the numbered blue buttons on its display controlled the circuit breakers for ten substations throughout the county—an area of almost seventeen hundred square miles, with some three hundred thousand residents.

The cursor landed on the switch for Substation One. Clicked. A dialogue window opened below the button:

Warning: Opening the breaker will result in complete shutdown. Do you wish to proceed?

YES NO

Reaching for his mouse, Nicu tried to drag the cursor out of the window, thinking its driver might have developed a minor glitch. But it remained there…and slid to Yes.

He quickly swiped the mouse across its pad, wanting to move the cursor to No.

It stayed on Yes. Clicked. The dialogue box vanished, and the button for Substation One changed from blue to red.

Nicu inhaled. He had been an operator at the distribution center for half a decade and did not need to bring up a map to see the region each substation covered. The map was already in his head.

Substation One was Lazuli, a rural commune of six villages to the extreme north, near the Ukrainian and Hungarian borders. Its six thousand residents had now gone off-line. Even as Nicu registered this, the on-screen cursor jumped to the Substation Two button.

He snatched up the mouse in desperation, lifting it above the pad. It made no difference. The cursor clicked. Opened another dialogue window requesting confirmation. Went to Yes again.

Click.

Blue turned to red, and Nicu Borgos watched Substation Two go down in an instant.

"Draga meu Domnezeu," he rasped. "My dear God."

Substation Two was the city of Satu Mare itself. With a population of one hundred thousand—a full third of the county's inhabitants—it was now completely dark.

Nicu tried to think clearly. During the day, the operating station would have two people on shift. There was a second computer to his left, with a separate monitor. Possibly the problem was only with his machine. If he could log in to the system using the other computer, he might prevent more breakers from tripping open.

He rolled his chair in front of it, tapped the keyboard. The computer came out of idle showing the operator log-in screen. He entered his username and password.

A *Wrong Password* notification flashed on-screen.

He slowly retyped the password, thinking he might have entered a wrong character in his haste.

The notification appeared again. He was locked out of the system.

Nicu sat up straight, his spine a stiff rod of tension. His original machine showed that Substation Three, which provided power to Negresti Oas's twelve thousand citizens, was down. He glanced at its screen just in time to see the cursor move to Substation Four… the distribution station for the commune Mediesu Aurit's seven villages. The two stations combined served more than twenty thousand customers.

He remembered that tonight's temperature was forecast to drop below freezing in the mountain areas, and felt suddenly helpless. Whatever was causing the shutdowns, he could not deal with the growing emergency himself.

His heart pounding, he reached for the hotline to call his supervisor.

The black BearCat G3 bore north on the unmarked strip of macadam that linked Satu Mare City to the tiny farming village of Rosalvea in the Carpathian foothills. Its windshield wipers beating off fat, wet flutters of snow, the vehicle moved smoothly and quietly for a big four-tonner armored with hardened ballistic steel panels.

At the wheel was Scott Dixon of the CIA's elite manhunting Fox Team, recently placed under operational detachment to Net Force. Kali Alcazar sat beside him. In her late twenties, she had short silver-white hair and wore a black stealthsuit and lightweight plate vest. They were standard organizational issue. A Victorian English adventurer's belt and a vintage film-canister pendant hanging from her neck were personal additions.

"How we doing timewise?" Dixon asked.

Kali looked at her dash screen. On it was the same controller's interface Nicu Borgos was struggling with at the power distribution center. A moment ago she had seen the circuits trip in rapid succession.

"Pickles," she said. Using the unfortunate name given to the vehicle's AI by its architect, Sergeant Julio Fernandez.

"Yes, K?"

"Outlier," she corrected. Using the dark web handle she had long ago created for herself.

"Yes, K."

"Bring up the Satu Mare power grid."

"Yes, K."

She clicked her tongue. Fernandez had infused the AI with one too many of his stubbornly aggravating personality traits. But the upside was that, like Julio, it was also smart, nuanced, and intuitive. She could live with it.

In front of her now, the panel on-screen was re-placed by a sector-by-sector map of the region, its cities and towns numbered according to the sub-stations that supplied their electricity. The five al-ready off-line were black, the rest red.

She watched as a sixth went dark.

"Over half the stations are down," she said. "Total blackout in about five minutes."

"Bitter cold out, a quarter million people with-out light or heat," Dixon said. "Women, children, seniors. All for the sake of bagging one guy."

She glanced over at him. "The hackers—the *technologie vampiri*—are the local economy. The government protects them. The *polizei*, the citizens, everyone."

He shrugged with his hands on the wheel. She was right. Suspicions definitely would have been raised at the syndicate's current headquarters—the Wolf's Lair—if they only cut power to its surrounding village.

"I get it," he said. "Still tough."

"Tougher than it was on New York?"

Dixon didn't answer. Four months ago the *vampiri* had launched a cyberattack that left the East Coast a shambles, killed hundreds, and almost took out the President. Now his team's pursuit of the Wolf had led them out here to the Romanian boonies, making them key players in the first fully integrated opera-tion conducted by the various elements of America's new Department of Internet Security and Law En-forcement. Net Force, in bureaucratic government shorthand.

He really *did* get it.

The BearCat rolled between the gigantic ever-greens standing sentinel on either side of the road. In the rear compartment, Gregg Long, Fox Team, sat with a small detachment on loan from Task Force Quickdraw—six men in tactical gear with Mark 18 CQBR carbines strapped over their shoulders and short-barreled Mossberg 590 combat shotguns racked to the sides of the passenger compartment.

"Distance to the target?" Dixon asked after a few minutes.

This time Kali skipped the AI, tapping her computer keyboard for the GPS sat map. "Thirty-two miles."

Dixon nodded and checked the speedometer. He was doing about fifty. So a little over half an hour.

Taking his hand off the wheel, he adjusted his earpiece and hailed Carmody on the ground-to-air.

Raven winged over the Romanian countryside at her top cruising speed of 280 knots, her tilt-rotors angled down for forward flight. She had maintained an altitude of 6,000 feet, slightly below the low, heavy ceiling of clouds. Faye Luna and Ron Cobb, Net Force Cy-Eye Surveillance and Aviation, occupied the pilot and copilot seats. Mike Carmody, Fox Team, stood behind them in the cockpit's dimness, facing its wide wraparound window, peering down through the gauzy veil of snow.

One after another, the rows of homes on the streets and lanes below went dark. He thought suddenly of Christmas lights. Strings of unplugged Christmas lights.

"Preacher, you copy?" It was Dixon over the Radio over Internet Protocol, or RoIP. He was using Carmody's call name for the mission.

"Yes," he said. His hands were meshed together behind his back. "What's up?"

"The precip's heavier than expected," Dixon said. "Want to confirm you're still tracking us."

Carmody moved up to the touch-screen interface spanning the width of the avionics board. It was, as his training instructor put it, a giant smart tablet. *Pinch, zoom, swipe.* External sensors on the outside of the aircraft—its PDAS, or Pilotage Distributed Aperture Sensor suite—gave the multifunction display a fully integrated 360-degree view of earth and sky.

Set for night flying, the screen's background was a fused infrared/low-light magnification terrain map of Satu Mare. Its radiance washed the cockpit in green and gray.

Raven was a bespoke version of the Bell V-280, and Carmody saw her as tricked out like something straight from a sci-fi flick. At a cost of fifty million dollars, she was expensive but worth it. He'd proposed that Net Force order twenty. Its Director of Operations, Carol Morse, requisitioned a fleet of ten. Congress had approved funding for two.

He selected a tracking window for the two Bear-Cats and widened it with his thumb and forefinger. The SUVs appeared inside it, along with the GPS latitude, longitude, altitude, and speed coordinates.

"Rover One, I see you fine," he said.

"Nice being the only things with lights."

Carmody wished he could have lit a cigarette. "Okay. Keep it rolling."

He signed off and glanced over at Luna. Dark-haired, round-faced, she looked about fifteen. But he knew her quals and reputation as an ace among flying aces. US Air Cavalry, Task Force Viper, Afghanistan. Then college on the GI Bill and a stint with the FBI Critical Incident Response Group. She and Cobb had crewed the only chopper allowed in the air over New York in the hours after the attack, their actions earning the express gratitude of POTUS herself.

"Better run my checks," he said.

"Yes, sir." She kept her right hand on the joystick, pointed to the screen with her left. "The bird's picked up quite a tailwind. We could beat our own ETA."

The aircraft rocked and trembled on an air pocket. Carmody turned toward the cockpit door, grasped the handle. He thought about Drajan Petrovik, the Wolf, and their first encounter in a dark Bucharest hallway. About squeezing his wounded arm and feeling his blood well up between his knuckles. Carmody had smelled the hacker's blood in a corridor splashed with the blood of dead men, and thought he could smell it now, taste it at the back of his tongue like copper.

But that was his imagination. He paused and breathed through his nostrils as if to prove it to himself. *Nothing.* Just the sterile, filtered scentlessness of the recycling cockpit air.

After a moment, he pushed through the door and joined his men in the troop cabin.

2

Four hundred fifty miles southeast of Satu Mare, the Midnight Runners were gathering for their nightly meetup. Organized by physician Lavonne Hughes at Forward Operating Base Janus, the group had grown from Lavonne and her two staff nurses to about a dozen regulars. Tonight they were short a few members, several of them on assignment with the Satu Mare hunting expedition.

As she did her warm-ups near the south perimeter fence, Lavonne saw three late arrivals hurrying over from their barracks. She straightened from a calf stretch and waved, steam puffing from her mouth into the cold, snow-flecked air. With almost a third of its personnel up-country, and only a thin detail left behind, the general mood around the installation was anxious. Scalpel was FOB Janus's first official operation since its transfer from US Army command to Net Force Quickdraw. It was dangerous and politically sensitive.

Lavonne wasn't sure how much the Romanians knew about it, but she'd heard through the grapevine that it wasn't half what they were supposed to know. Meaning that if the task force ran into trouble, they could face major consequences from their host government in addition to whatever the hackers threw at them—and the *technologie vampiri* weren't your stereotypical keystrokers. They were violent criminals, armed to the teeth and ready for a fight.

The latecomers reached Lavonne and the others at the fence. Sergeant Pierce and Privates Ryder and Berra were all on Colonel Howard's staff and had just completed their shift.

"Evening," she said to Pierce. "How's it going in Command?"

"The colonel's been stuffing his pipe with tobacco all night," he said. "And stalking the halls."

"Must be pure joy working under him."

"Totally."

She looked at Pierce through the snow. "Any news on the team?"

"It's still early," he said, then hesitated. "Can't say much more, y'know."

He sounded half-apologetic. Everyone on the post had a top-secret security clearance, but the details of tonight's mission were under sensitive compartmented information—i.e., need-to-know— restrictions.

Like it or not, Lavonne understood.

"Check," she said. "You guys should get loose. The rest of us are way ahead of you."

He nodded past her, tilting his head slightly toward the right. "Spree doing glute stretches, too?"

Lavonne glanced over her shoulder at the 'hog gliding toward them along the fence, its rubber tracks imprinting the newly fallen snow cover.

"Nah," she said. "That robot gunslinger's got a butt of steel."

Pierce smiled, and Lavonne smiled back. There were four lethal autonomous weapons systems, or LAWS, sentries guarding the compound's perimeter— Spree patrolling its south line, Nash the north, Earl the east, and Walt its western boundary. Colonel Howard had been the first to call them hedgehogs, though in her mind their squat, hardened chassis, sensor pods, and weapons arrays said R2-D2 on steroids.

"Okay, Sergeant. Unlike Spree, I need to finish warming up," she said.

"And my boys need to get started," Pierce said. "Give us three minutes?"

"Take five."

"You're the best, Doc."

He and the two privates walked off toward the fence, where the rest of the group were warming up. After five minutes, they buddied up into two lines and jogged off along the compound's perimeter.

A minute later Spree followed.

Robotics and Autonomous Systems Specialist (24 Delta) Mario Perez saw lights on in the mess hall as he drove by in the flurrying snow. He went on for another dozen yards, then stopped his JLTV Jolt in front of the glorified trailer that passed as the base exchange store. Getting out, he trotted up to the door, found it locked, and leaned his head against its glass to peer inside. The overhead fluorescents were off, but he could see a dim glow behind the counter, where Laura was counting the day's receipts.

He rapped on the glass. She glanced up from the register, saw him outside, and came around the sales counter to let him in.

"Mario," she said, opening the door. "*Dónde has estado?* I was wondering when you would show up."

His face was puzzled. "I thought you said to come at midnight—"

"Midnight was *fifteen minutes* ago. Didn't your shift end at eleven thirty?"

He looked at her contritely.

"I suck," he said. "I apologize."

She frowned, waving him in.

"Okay, hurry up," she said. "It's been a long day."

Mario entered as she switched the lights on.

"I really *am* sorry, Laura," he said. "With the time difference, it's four in the afternoon yesterday back home. I did a FaceTime call and must've lost track of things."

"Oh?" She tried to sound casual. "Must be somebody special."

"My mom," he said. "Dad died a couple of years ago. So I never forget to call for Thanksgiving. Actually the Wednesday before. It's kind of a tradition for us. So we can talk a while before she gets busy cooking."

Laura looked at him. Besides being relieved, she felt her heart melt a little. Mario, who had told her he was from El Paso, Texas, was the nicest guy she'd ever met, possibly even the guy of her dreams. She liked his sense of humor, his warmth, his sincere brown eyes…and his buff, muscular arms.

She sometimes imagined those strong arms around her waist, drawing her close against him.

"When they found out you were open late tonight, everyone at the barracks kept adding stuff to our order," he said and took out his phone. "You wouldn't know half the base is on deployment from looking at it."

She leaned closer to read the shopping list.

"True that," she said.

He felt his heart skip a beat. Five feet five inches tall, dark-haired and dark-eyed, Laura Cruz, whose father was Venezuelan and whose mother was American, had been raised between Caracas and Dayton, Ohio. She was in his humble opinion the prettiest, sexiest, most amazing girl ever to walk planet Earth.

"So," he said, "think you have everything?"

"I stocked up on chips, pretzels, soda, and beer— especially beer—for the long weekend," she said and looked up from the phone. "I hope the team gets back in time to celebrate."

"Same," he said. "It's a top-secret op, so I'm out of the loop. But I think they're still up-country."

Laura nodded slowly, pulled a shopping cart

from the small row near the door. "Come," she said. "It will be faster if I help."

"Hey, thanks. Anything you get for yourself is my treat."

She smiled. "You're a doll. But I've got a new chest freezer, and it's loaded up with food. I just want to get back to quarters, shower, and put on my pj's."

He started up the aisle with her, imagining she would smell like a garden full of sweet-scented flowers after a shower, and look very clean and pretty in her pajamas.

A few minutes later, they wheeled the fully loaded cart up to the checkout counter, both pushing it by the handle.

"I'll pack," he said. "I'm an expert packer."

Laura smiled. "I will enjoy letting you prove it," she said, going around to the register.

Mario neatly transferred his items to the counter as she rang them up, thinking she was beyond the tiniest doubt his dream girl. He had known it from the day she started working at the exchange a month or so back, which was also when he noticed she wasn't wearing a ring on any critical finger. But though they hit it off at once and things got sort of flirty between them, he'd still hesitated to ask her out.

Maybe it was fear of a turndown. But he wasn't afraid of a turndown right now. He didn't know the reason for that, either. He just wasn't.

"Laura, well…there's this concert in Bucharest next Saturday night," he said, carefully bagging some chips, pretzels, and marshmallows. "It's at the college. A battle of the bands—"

"Yes," she said.

"Yes, you'll come *with me*?"

"Yes," she repeated.

Mario stood there smiling at her, his eyes shining like stars. He thought she was as beautiful as the autumn moon.

"Why the big smile?" she asked.

"Because," he said.

"Because *why*?"

"Because I can tell you really want to kiss me," he replied to his own astonishment.

A second passed. Another. She looked directly over the counter at him. Mario opened his eyes wide, feeling a sudden dread. What could have possessed him to say what he'd said? To let those words escape his lips…putting aside that he actually *meant* them?

He was thinking he'd just made a terrible mistake, utterly blown things with her, when she at last broke her silence.

"A woman wanting a man to kiss her isn't enough," she said. "She must invite him."

He swallowed hard, his throat suddenly dry. "How will he know the invitation?"

She smiled.

"If he's the right man for her, he'll know," she said and went into the office to get her coat.

Neither said anything at all as they wheeled the groceries outside into the snow and arranged them on his Jolt's back seat. But as he hefted the last bag inside, Mario realized—again to his surprise—that he was no longer feeling the slightest bit uncomfortable or self-conscious. In fact, he was totally at ease with himself. And with Laura.

"Can I give you a lift back to quarters?" he asked outside the vehicle.

"That's okay," she said. A snowflake landed on the tip of her nose, and she brushed it off. "I like to walk. And I have to make a pit stop at my neighbor Emily's place. I'm looking after things while she's home for the holiday."

He nodded. "Okay," he said. "See you at dinner tomorrow?"

"*Desde luego*. I can hardly wait."

She turned toward the mess-commissary. The small multiple-unit dwelling reserved for non-military personnel was a five or ten minute walk beyond it on the east side of the compound.

Mario watched her move out of sight in the snow and darkness, then slid into the Jolt and took out his phone. He started to put on some music but remembered that he'd been listening to the latest episode of Alex Michaels's *Net Talk* podcast, and decided to play the rest of it over the sound system.

Driving away from the exchange, he noticed one of Janus's four hedgehogs bearing toward the mess from the nearby perimeter fence.

He'd already reached his barracks when it struck him the robot had no business being there.

Information Systems Operator-Analyst (25 Bravo) Dwayne Reese said he was calling his latest off-the-top rap "Midnight at the Mess," though it was already *half past* midnight, and he was technically not on volunteer mess-hall duty but assisting at the scullery with trash disposal and hauling the big, bulging bags out to the dumpsters.

Walking beside him with his own garbage bag in tow, Signal Support Specialist (25 Uniform) Nick Savarino knew what was in store. They had been buddies for a while.

Reese heaved his load into the dumpster, then began clapping out a beat under the security lights behind the building. "Midnight at the mess hall, my game be dumpin' out the trash, yo. I know it late, but it ain't gonna wait, I got to give it to ya straight…"

Savarino rolled his eyes heavenward. "Please, spare me."

Reese ignored him. He bent his knees, giving his rap some bounce. "Come on, my brotha," he said.

"C'mon *what*?"

"Come on, *come on*." Still clapping, Reese got up on the balls of his feet and worked in a slide step. "Thanksgivin' tomorrow, don't talk 'bout no turkey sorrow—"

Savarino broke into a helpless grin and dropped his bag. *If you can't beat 'em.*

Getting into Reese's bounce vibe, he pushed at the air with his hands. "I tell my baby, we gonna fine dine—"

"So pass me that wine, gonna lay it on the line—"

"I want what you got, like my dressin' sweet 'n' *hot*…"

They both cracked up. Neither of them really knew what was so funny, but they were dog-tired. With a quarter of the base personnel off on a classified mission, everyone left behind was concerned. So any excuse to blow off tension was a good one.

Besides, it *was* the night before Thanksgiving. Even at this late hour, they could smell the aromas of baking apple and pumpkin pies from the vents in the kitchen's rear walls and hear the racket of bowls, utensils, and electric appliances inside. The cooks were working their tails off and would probably stay at it till daybreak. But all their activity was generating mountains of scraps, peelings, grease, eggshells, and other assorted kitchen waste. The heavy-duty bags each held forty pounds of recyclables and compostables, and somebody needed to clear them out.

Which was why Reese and Savarino had offered a hand. The scullery was as understaffed as the rest of the outpost, and its crew needed all the help they could get. The two technical specialists had waited till after the midnight meal, assisted with the cleanup, and then started to bring the bulging trash bags out to the dumpsters. There were nine or ten bags altogether, and they were on their first run when Reese the Rapper launched into his freestyle improvisation.

And now they were pushing up, pushing down, pushing left, and pushing right, rhyming and slide-stepping in the snow between the back of the long, low, prefab mess-scullery building and the dumpsters lined near the compound's western perimeter.

Stuck here at Janus on the night before Thanks-giving, they figured they deserved to give them-selves a little holiday-season head start and were dancing like drunken elves.

Some fifteen yards to their right, the hedgehog known as Walt noticed their movement and devi-ated from its routine patrol pattern along the fence.

All four of the 'hogs at Janus were arrayed with nonlethal and lethal armaments. The nonlethals included smoke and tear-gas launchers and laser-induced plasma-effect weapons. Each lethal-arms suite consisted of a .50-caliber heavy machine gun with eight hundred rounds of ammunition, two gre-nade launchers, with a total six-grenade capacity and a lightweight recoilless rocket launch system. The laser-guided, 84 mm bunker-buster rocket rounds could travel a distance of over a mile and deploy multitarget armor-piercing warheads de-signed to take out light tanks.

Walt tracked quietly toward the two dancing sol-diers. Its machine brain full of noise, it stopped ten feet away and took their range. Reese was show-ing off his rag-puppet move, his arms up and out, loose and bent like they were hanging on unseen strings, when he spotted the hedgehog with his peripheral vision…and realized its machine gun was rotating in their direction.

He froze. Nick looked at him. He was still danc-ing on his toes.

"What's wrong?" he said, a little breathless.

That was when the 'hog opened fire. The first rounds blew off most of Reese's lower jaw. A split second later, the top of his face exploded. It was as if two swipes of an eraser had made his head disappear.

Nick felt a surge of fear and horror as the gun recalibrated slightly for his position and discharged again. Bullets tore into his body. He saw chunks of himself fly through the snow, recognized scraps of his uniform clinging to them. He felt pain rip through him and died.

Inside the kitchen, the racket near the dumpsters sounded like a backfiring motorcycle, but not really. One of the cooks had seen Reese and Savarino lug the trash out the door minutes before, and he wanted to know what the hell was happening. He dropped his pie tray, ran over to the door, and pushed it open. The rest of the men and women on the scullery crew hurried after him.

The hedgehog turned toward the building. Its thermal sensors had picked up moving heat presences gathering behind the doorway. It instantly measured the ratio between their temperatures and the temperature of their ambient environment. Then it gauged the difference between their moving velocities and the static environment. Their combined heat-and-motion characteristics told the robot the presences were human, a background subtraction calculating there were seven of them. They were moving at attack speed.

The hog's poisoned brain rapidly characterized the threat as lethal to base personnel and initiated its response, firing a single 84 mm rocket from its launch tube.

As the scullery's back door swung out into the snow, the cook who had dropped the pie pan heard the pop of the rocket leaving its delivery tube. He barely had time to glimpse its conical warhead as it jetted toward him, trailing a long rope of white smoke.

The bunker-buster shot through the doorway, plowed into the cook's chest, and knocked him backward off his feet. Traveling at a speed of five hundred miles an hour, it shattered his rib cage and pulverized his internal organs, killing him at once. The cook's limp, broken body flew into the kitchen staffers crowding the entrance behind him, carried into them by the projectile's momentum. A few of them screamed. Most didn't have a chance. The warhead detonated fast. There was a flash and a roar and then the searing heat of the blast wave. The humans inside the mess-scullery were incinerated instantly. The sink, stove, and refrigeration units flew through the air as if they weighed nothing at all. The building's walls bulged outward like the sides of a cardboard box. An expanding fire-ball punched a ragged hole in its ceiling and roof, rising high into the night sky.

In the red-orange glow of the flames, Walt concluded it had neutralized the immediate threat and went tracking off through the snow. Its state of alertness raised to maximum defense emergency, or Cocked Pistol detection mode, the 'hog did not return to the perimeter fence. It was now on free-roaming patrol and actively seeking out potential hostiles.

Behind it, the ruin of the mess-scullery burned steadily in the night.

* * *

The unwieldy military abbreviation was C4ISR, which stood for the even more unwieldy Command, Control, Communications, Computers, Intelligence, Surveillance and Reconnaissance center. Situated at the north side of Janus, the narrow concrete structure was the base's operational hub, the place where information was gathered and integrated, key decisions were made, and mission orders given.

Base personnel simply called it headquarters.

Five minutes before the explosion at the western perimeter, Colonel John Howard was stalking its halls and stuffing his pipe bowl. The pipe was a handmade Savinelli briar imported from Italy. The tobacco was Escudo Navy Deluxe, a coin-cut perique cultivated in Virginia and aged in Scandinavia. Both were gifts from Carol Morse, Net Force's D/O and his former CIA liaison. Howard had received them after accepting her offer to join the president's new cabinet-level cybersecurity organization as lead officer of Quickdraw, its global rapid-response arm.

Janus was Morse's baby. The model for a projected network of semicovert and covert outposts hosted by allied governments in all seven continents. Four months into Net Force's existence, the base was still an unrefined template, a work in progress. But it was vital to launching the search for the hacker who had masterminded the cyberstrike on New York.

Morse knew her stuff. Professionally and personally, she paid attention to the fine points, Howard thought. The Escudo, his favorite blend, was damn good quality. Its taste reminded him of grapes, the fat, round green ones his grandmother would pick wild during all his summers with her in Oklahoma. Scuppernongs, she called them, and they were nothing like the store-bought grapes back home in Baltimore. Their skins were as thick as olive skins. When you ate one, you turned it so the stem scar was over your mouth, and squeezed it between your fingertips so the sweet, soft pulp would burst out onto your tongue. Howard would devour them in the field outside Nana's farmhouse, the juice running down his chin, getting on his T-shirt, making a sticky mess of him. They were not for eating in polite company, like when the pastor came over for Sunday supper. Pastor John Joseph Cotes of the Bixby Memorial Church, his wife, and their daughter, Rose.

Rose Cotes, with her almond-shaped eyes, knee skirts, and smooth brown legs. He'd shared them with her a few times, the scuppernongs, when they sneaked off to the barn after dessert.

In the corridor outside his operations room, Howard abruptly stopped pacing to refill his pipe, remembering the scents of drying hay and Rosey's hair and the taste of the grapes on her lips. Taking two medallions of the Escudo from his tin, he rolled them into balls and tamped them into the bowl, gently, because he wanted to leave some air underneath. The air pocket was the secret, keeping the tobacco lit. Pack the balls too tight and they would keep going out.

When the bowl of his pipe was full, he struck a wooden matchstick, held it over the tobacco, and put the stem in his mouth, drawing in air to get it started.

Damn good.

Morse, she knew him inside out. He no longer bothered wondering how, just accepted that knowing people was one of her skills, possibly an instinctive thing. And what she didn't know, what she couldn't see for herself, she made a point of learning. Howard had met her face-to-face—what, twice? Three times? The rest of their communications were long-distance, Washington, DC, to Baneasa. Yet she understood what made him tick…and how to get to him.

It was Morse who had sent him Carmody and his wild boys, and he couldn't quarrel with the outcome. Without them, there would have been no tracing the Wolf to his hideout in Rosalvea. But the Outlier, Kali? Someone who was still an international fugitive? Morse had given her clearance exceptions. Access to base facilities. A free pass to fly aboard *Raven*, the most guarded aircraft in the military. It seemed crazy given her list of hacking offenses.

Howard knew what she could do. He knew what she did to help Carmody's Fox Team pull off the data heist in Bucharest. But he still didn't know *why* she helped or where their common goals ended.

He puffed steadily as he moved the match around the bowl. The tobacco glowed under its flame, and he held in the smoke.

Scuppernongs, he thought and exhaled through his mouth. The cloud of smoke held its shape a second or two and then dissipated in front of him.

He liked clear-cut lines, borders with straight edges. And Kali…she was like smoke. Despite her actions in Bucharest, he couldn't get a fix on her. She made lines blurry and indistinct, and that bothered him.

Tonight it bothered him more than most nights because of the mission. It had been entirely Morse's call to send her with Carmody, against his objections. For all her arguments about it making operational sense, he hoped they all wouldn't live to regret her decision.

He looked over at the swing door to Ops, puffing steadily on his pipe. Abrams, Berra, and the new kid, Wasserman, were inside watching the screens, but they would have next to nothing for him in the way of updates. The Scalpel team was keeping radio silence, and it wouldn't be the first time. The operation had to be kept covert to all appearances. If things went wrong, the White House could have some distance, claim it wasn't involved, insist no international laws were broken with its knowledge. Bent, maybe, but loans and foreign aid would candy-coat the bullshit enough so the Romanians would swallow. That was basic geopolitics, and Howard got it. But he wasn't a politician. He was a soldier. A dozen of his men were with Fox Team, and he disliked being in the dark.

He was about to resume his uneasy pacing when he heard a loud, sharp cracking sound like a thunderclap outside the building. He guessed it might be connected to the snow, although the forecast hadn't made him expect much of a storm. Just a light accumulation and slightly higher than average winds. Otherwise, he would have kept *Raven* wheels down and delayed the grab. But the closer you came to winter in this corner of the world, the more changeable and unpredictable the weather.

He stood listening for several seconds, heard nothing. Still, he wondered about that noise.

Howard started toward the entry door, meaning to take a quick look outside. He took exactly two steps before the sirens went off and stopped him cold. Then the swing door flew outward, and he saw Abrams standing in the entryway, his eyes enormous.

"Sir, we're—"

They were the only words to leave his mouth before Howard heard another deafening crack, this time all around him. He saw a bright flash of light, felt a sudden vibration and terrible, blistering heat on his face. He shouted for Abrams to get down, but it was too late, he was gone, dissolved into a blinding orange brightness.

Then everything turned into fire and smoke.

"Hey, Sarge! Thought you were catching some shut-eye."

Sergeant Julio Fernandez, Net Force Quickdraw, glanced up from his tablet to see Private Glenn Wasserman approaching from the stairwell. He held a finger up to his lips.

"You never saw me," he said. "I told Howard that I was heading back to quarters."

Wasserman passed Fernandez's table, veering toward the coffee maker. They were in the basement level of HQ that was known as the Pit once upon a time, back in the bad old days of the CIA rendition program and black detention-interrogation facilities. Nowadays the hardened sublevel—its walls were steel-reinforced concrete, and its air came through a nuclear-biological-chemical filtration system—served primarily as a high-tech conference room, with this small recreation/coffee area spurring off one end.

It was four minutes and nine seconds before the explosion in Ops.

"Any word from the Scalpel team?" Fernandez said.

"Nothing yet, sir. The colonel's on pins and needles. And turning us into pin *cushions*. You know how he gets."

Fernandez's laugh turned into a tired, sleep-deprived yawn halfway through. "Why do you think I'm hanging around after an eighteen-hour shift?" he said. "I figure you guys might need protection from him."

"So it isn't because you're as anxious as the rest of us."

"*Of course not*, bro."

Wasserman smiled a little and reached for the coffeepot. "Reading one of your e-books?" he said, nodding toward the sergeant's tablet.

"Yeah," Fernandez said. "*Chasing the Millennium Prize*. By Dr. Martin M. Lewy."

"What's a millennial prize?"

"Millennium," Fernandez said. "See? The problem with millennials is you can't stop thinking about yourselves."

"I'm borderline Gen Z, sir. Born twenty-oh-three," Wasserman said. "Respectfully, you would fall squarely in the millennial age group, being twenty years older than me."

"Which is the reason I know how you so-called borderliners think! Plus, when did I ever tell you my birthday?" Fernandez lifted up the partly drunk coffee cup in front of him and made a face. "Mud's cold, bleh."

"I'll pour you a fresh cup. Black, no sugar, right, sir?"

Fernandez stared at him. "What the hell *don't* you know about me?"

Wasserman grinned and poured. In his view, the sergeant was cool enough to be microwave safe. Barely forty, standing five foot eight in thick-soled boots, he had recently updated his haircut from a modified mohawk to what he called a brushback fade—thick on top, shaved on the sides, plus a full, neatly clipped beard to round things out and totally irritate Colonel Howard, who hated fades and facial hair even more than mohawks. Being technically off duty, he was wearing an army-green tank top over his broad, hairless chest, which sported a single tattoo picturing a man and woman that looked like trees—or trees that looked like a man and woman—facing each other with their roots and branches tangled together. Wasserman thought the man looked a lot like Fernandez, though he'd never commented on it. He also thought the woman was damn hot stuff, though he'd never said anything about that, either.

Now he carried the coffees to the table, put one down beside Fernandez's first cup, and took a seat opposite him. In the corridor above them, Howard was filling his Italian pipe while thinking about Rose Cotes, her hypnotic brown eyes, and her smooth, coltish legs. It was four minutes and fifty-one seconds before the explosion.

"Anyway, it's *millennium* prize," Fernandez said, picking up the conversation where he'd left off. He sipped the hot coffee and grunted with pleasure. "Back around the year two thousand, when, um… *borderline* millennials like you were popping out of maternity wards in droves, a board of scientists at a place called the Clay Mathematics Institute—it's in Massachusetts, near Cambridge, naturally—was granted seven million dollars to solve the hardest math problems of the time. They decided to hold a contest, listed the top seven, and offered a cool one-mil prize for every solution. Hence, the book title, Wassy."

Wasserman looked at him. "A million bucks? Seriously?"

"Seriously," Fernandez said. "But it isn't like any of them were cinches. To give you an idea, one of 'em, the Reimann hypothesis, was from *an older* list somebody put together around nineteen hundred. And only a single problem on the Clay list's been solved so far."

"Was the Reizman one of them?"

"Reimann," Fernandez corrected. "And no, it was actually the Poincaré conjecture."

"Oh. Sounds like an episode of *Star Trek*."

"Which would be right up my alley," Fernandez said. "Actually, it's a geometric problem about three-spheres and three-dimensional manifolds." He noticed the confounded look on Wasserman's face. "Better skip the details. What's important about Poincaré is that a Russian genius came up with a mathematical proof."

"And won the million?"

"Yup. Then turned it down. Go figure."

Wasserman mouthed a silent *wow*. It was ninety seconds before the explosion. Upstairs, Howard's pacing was interrupted by a thunderous noise across the compound.

Down in the former Pit, meanwhile, Fernandez and Wasserman heard nothing through the foot-thick walls and ceiling.

"So, is this contest still a thing?" Wasserman asked, sipping his coffee.

"You bet," Fernandez said. "In fact, I'm shooting for one of the prizes."

"No." The private searched Fernandez's face for any sign of a put-on. He didn't see one. "I mean… really?"

"Absolutely," Fernandez said. "It's high time my computational science degree was worth something."

"Wait. Didn't you just get your intelligence designer rating, like, last month?"

Fernandez flapped a dismissive hand. "Small potatoes, dude. I'm trying to solve the P Versus NP problem."

Wasserman stared at him over his steaming coffee. "Sounds amazing. I think."

"It would be, if I can prove the theorem." Fernandez lowered his voice to a confidential tone. "If I can *prove* it, it could change the field of computer security. Revolutionize it. First, by making most current encryption applications obsolete. Second, by opening the way for better methods."

"No shit," Wasserman said. "I mean, no shit, *sir*." He lowered his cup to the table. "Y'know, you ought to be a guest on *Net Talk*."

Fernandez looked at him blankly. "What's *Net Talk*?"

"You know. *Net Talk*!"

"I'm sleep-deprived, not *deaf*." Fernandez frowned. "That a game show or something?"

"It's the official Net Force podcast, Sarge. Hosted by Alex Michaels."

"Wait." Fernandez looked at him. "You mean *Professor* Alex Michaels?"

"That's right, sir."

"Our boss?"

"Right," Wasserman said. "He does an episode a month and has great guests. Like the latest show. It's about that cloud-computing deal everybody's arguing about. You know the one I mean—"

"CloudCable. Worth ten billion bucks—"

"Right. The topic's usually internet security…"

"Which is what *we* were just talking about…"

"Which is exactly why I brought up the podcast, sir. He had Adrian Soto on the show I just mentioned."

"Soto? Wow. The dude's kind of my hero."

"No shit."

Fernandez nodded. "I grew up in San Diego, which, come to think, you probably already freaking know," he said. "Anyway, a computer geek like me from the city's toughest neighborhood didn't have many guys to identify with. But Soto's the Man. In fact, I've been hoping to meet him in person. You know, with us becoming part of Net Force, and *him* also becoming part of it." He scratched his chin and hmmed. "Now that you mention that podcast, I wonder how I would—"

He never finished the sentence. There was a sudden, booming noise, closer than the last, and this time both men heard it clearly. It came from right above them, muffled by the foot-thick ceiling, but still loud enough to make everything in the room vibrate. The table, chairs, everything. They trembled, shook, and shuddered like crazy. Like in a severe earthquake. A seven-point Richter-magnitude earthquake. Coffee sloshed in Fernandez's cup, though he was holding it steadily in his hand.

He looked at his dripping knuckles for a second, put the cup down on the table. A split second later, a second rattling, shuddering vibration tipped both his cups over on their sides.

Fernandez stared across the table at Wasserman,

meeting his stunned, uncomprehending eyes with his own. His mind on overdrive, he hardly noticed the coffee dripping all over him. Two sets of stairs connected the sublevel to the main floor. One led directly from the rec room to the Operations Center. It was the stairwell Fernandez had come down a few minutes ago, its entrance just a few feet away. The other was in the adjacent conference room and led up to a corridor on the far end of the building.

The boom seemed to have come from directly overhead. From Ops. Fernandez wasn't about to lead Wassy straight up into the middle of whatever caused it. They would take the farther set of stairs.

"We better hurry," Fernandez said, jumping up off his chair.

He ran for the conference room, Wasserman close on his heels.

3

Carmody was back in the crew compartment prepping for the drop when Cobb's voice sounded in his earpiece.

"Zero minus fifteen, Preacher," the copilot said. "Thought you might want a look below."

He quickly went on with his inspection. He wore a two-gun harness with loops for his H&K MP7 and a nylon shoulder holster for his sidearm, a custom Sig P225 15 + 1 chambered for .40 S&W rounds with reduced trigger pull, a flared magazine well, tritium/fiber-optic front and rear sights, and a rail-mounted Foxtrot night light. The knife in his leg sheath was a Microtech Combat Troodon with a titanium-coated, steel-alloy blade. The flipdown digital night-vision assembly on his helmet would provide a panoramic view of his surroundings and was jacked into both *Raven* and the Sentinel drone for multispectral visual, radar, and data scans. The contents of his lightweight backpack were standard demo and survival gear—a couple of C-4 charges, a CamelBak hydration pack, some Frog Fuel shots, and a blowout kit for first aid.

The last thing on Carmody's checklist was the smartphone-size device on his forearm. He powered it on and off, then made sure the strap was securely fastened. Kali's sniffer-spoofer digital lockpick would be vital to his success.

Satisfied, he moved up beside Cobb in the cockpit. Glancing at the touch screen, he instantly recognized the estate's upper stories and rooftop bastions.

Fox Team's practice mock-up back at Janus, where they had conducted weeks of rehearsals, was nearly identical.

"We're live," Cobb said. "Sentinel's at fifteen thousand feet. The night vision's color-enhanced for clarity."

Carmody studied the aerial images.

Drajan Petrovik's estate was nested amid the forests and widely scattered farm plots of the mountainous countryside along Romania's extreme western border. While planning, Carmody had scratched up old documentation that told him it was once the fortress of the spectacularly paranoid Count Anton Graguscu the Poisoner, a sixteenth-century royal who'd honeycombed it with secret escape routes and was said to have executed his wife and twin sons after dreaming they would someday conspire against him.

It was an enormous hundred and fifty acres shaped like a horseshoe, with the fortress at the bottom of the curve and the front gate stretching across its open southern side. Between were outbuildings and stables, manmade and natural ponds and streams, and wide, rolling fields of grass where noble generals had once trained in the saddle. The castle's front and flanks surrounded by a wrought-iron fence, its rear rimmed by thick deciduous and evergreen woods, it was best reached by road via a serpentine drive that ran four looping, curling, curving miles from the main gate to its wide front plaza.

Not part of the original landscape, the drive was graded and paved during World War II, when Nazi occupiers used the castle as a Wehrmacht headquarters and officers' billet...until Soviet tanks rolled in and blasted them out and left it abandoned and falling to pieces for the next seven decades.

The drive, however, had remained in good shape, as did some of the outbuildings that Drajan Petrovik now used as guardhouses.

He'd owned the property for several years, purchasing it at auction for three and a half million euros. Repairing, renovating, modernizing, and building upon its walls, towers, and baroque spirals was an entertainment that had gone on for many months. The available photos of the castle interior all dated back before the renovations, but there was nothing of recent vintage. Carmody had combed through the online records of Rosalvea and Salta, the villages comprising the nearest commune, and come up empty-handed.

The lack of search results didn't surprise him. The estate's extensive rehabilitation would have required construction and electrical permits, and the floor layouts needed to obtain them were typically kept in online databases. But he knew the score. The combined population of Rosalvea commune's two villages was six thousand—the same number of residents as fifty years back, and fifty years before that, and fifty before that. It was the sort of place where nothing much changed and people were desperate for work and wages. A place the Wolf could run like the feudal lord who built the estate. His renovations would have been a financial windfall for local builders, tradesmen, and suppliers of construction material.

Carmody assumed he had bribed some town clerk to circumvent the permit laws—or to wipe out whatever official records were on file.

"Trapdoors, hidden passages," he said. "We're going into a trick box. And you can bet Petrovik's added some new ones."

Cobb nodded. "I hate that there's no way of knowing what they are, sir."

Carmody suddenly remembered something he'd heard way back. He was on a base near the Iranian border that wasn't supposed to exist, ramping up for a mission that never officially happened.

How do you rehearse for the unknown?

It was on Armed Forces radio. A talk show. Someone was listening in an officer's tent, and he'd heard a snippet of conversation as he walked past. The person on air had posed the question rhetorically. He hadn't sounded like a soldier. He might have been a musician, an actor, a writer. A politician for that matter. Even so, he easily could have been asking about Carmody's upcoming mission, which was full of dangerous unknowns.

How do you rehearse?

Carmody supposed that if anyone wanted to know that of him, he would reply that you couldn't. Would say that if you were good enough, capable enough, experienced enough, if you had properly honed skills, you didn't waste time worrying about unknowns. All that counted was what you brought into a situation. What came at you from outside was hardly a consideration.

He moved up between Cobb and Luna to the virtual window. "Okay if I use this thing?" he asked.

"Sure." Cobb leaned sideways to give him some room. "Better do it quick."

Carmody reached for the screen, drew a box around a section of the roof with his thumb and forefinger, and zoomed in. The fortress's main entrance looked eastward toward Rosalvea proper, about ten miles away over an unmarked country road. Its fully restored bastions projected from the roof in three directions, the largest extending to the north. Solid stone with a heavy wrought-iron rail, the semioval lookout was wide enough for a dozen people to stand atop. A stone staircase twisted down from the bastion to an arched entry tower one story below.

Probably the three bastions were part of the estate's original structure. Western Romania was a historically quarrelsome region. There had been floating civil wars between princes and governors and ethnic tribes. There had been successive waves of invasion from Dacians, Wallachians, Visigoths, Moldavians, Turks, Hungarians, and Austrians. Count Graguscu, a Goth, lived in an era filled with conflict and would have kept a watchful eye on his neighbors.

Bringing his fingers together, Carmody pulled out for a high overhead view of the entire fortress. It had windows on all sides—sixty-seven windows. Despite the blackout, he saw lights in about a third of them. Predictably. The Wolf would have emergency generators on premises. His intruder alarms were likely online and would signal his personal guards. But they wouldn't connect to the Rosalvea police department or any other local gendarmes or militia that might be protecting him. Kali's outage was too widespread. Too many electrical distribution centers were down. The decrepit power grid in this backwoods territory would not have the built-in redundancies of modern networks. He was isolated.

"We didn't see guards on the rooftop," Cobb said. "Nobody outside the building, either."

Carmody mulled over that a second. "It only looks like medieval times around here," he said. "They don't need to climb the ramparts. They'll have monitors inside."

"You think they suspect something's up?" Luna said.

"What do you think?"

"The Wolf launched a cyberattack on New York. He's responsible for hundreds of deaths," she said.

"They'll be on the alert. Maybe even waiting to spring an ambush."

"Potentially. That's why we blacked out the whole area. Or part of the reason. So they don't feel too special and threatened."

"And if they do?"

"Worst case, there'll be some extra helpings of turkey in the mess tomorrow."

Luna didn't answer. Carmody looked at the avionics display. The mission countdown clock read zero minus ten minutes.

"Bring my team down," he said. "We'll take care of the rest."

She glanced over at him.

"Sir?"

"Yeah."

"The more the merrier at Thanksgiving dinner."

Carmody nodded.

"I can't argue with you there," he said.

Five thousand miles to the west in Teaneck, New Jersey, Stephen Gelfland pulled his Toyota Corolla into his driveway, turning its tires neatly into a blanket of unraked autumn leaves. It was 6:00 p.m. on the Wednesday before Thanksgiving, and he was returning from the supermarket with his groceries.

Gelfland planned to spend the holiday at home, and had bought some things for fixing himself dinner. A small frozen turkey, packaged stuffing mix, canned cranberry sauce, and a couple of sweet potatoes. For dessert, he'd found a packaged pumpkin pie and some whipped cream to dollop on the crust. Though he wasn't much of a drinker, he had also picked up a six-pack of microbrewed India pale ale. Gelfland enjoyed having a bottle or two with his college football.

He walked around to the rear driver's side door, opened it, and leaned inside for his grocery sack. It was a chilly night and he had his car coat open. Up until three years ago, Gelfland had always gone to his father's place on Long Island when ashore for Thanksgiving. The year after his passing, he celebrated on a tanker vessel off the coast of Australia and then, last year, went to visit a married cousin in Pennsylvania. A nice and fairly short drive away. He liked his cousin, her husband, and their two kids. There was a spare bedroom and plenty to eat and he'd enjoyed spending the weekend with them. But he preferred staying home nowadays. It wasn't that he was antisocial, not in his eyes. When he was at sea, he was constantly around other crewmen. He just liked keeping his own company, and doing things in his own time.

Now Gelfland hefted the reusable grocery bag off the seat, slung its strap over his shoulder, and shut the door. The Toyota's lights flashed to indicate it was locked up tight.

He turned toward his lawn, the dry, brown leaves underfoot piled over an inch deep. He was thinking he really needed to haul the blower out of the garage. Clearing the driveway would be a good start on his long to-do list. With the CloudCable cruise just five, six weeks off, he would be shipping out before he knew it. Time flew by.

Gelfland stepped onto the front walk, motion lights turning on around it. There weren't many leaves scattered on the grass. Those on his driveway had mostly fallen from his neighbor's property, the rest drifting in off the street. His few shrubs and trees were all evergreens—junipers on each side of the walk, a hedge of tall arborvitae across the lawn, a couple of blue spruces out front. Low maintenance, which only made sense. He spent four out of every six months at sea.

He took out his keys. The street running past his house was quiet. It was always quiet the night before the long holiday weekend. Although people were off from work, everyone was either away or busy with preparations. Cooking and cleaning and getting their guest rooms tidied and set up.

"Steve, hi."

Gelfland stopped and turned toward the voice. It had come from the far end of the lawn. A male voice, somewhere near the row of arborvitae.

He peered into the darkness. He didn't see anyone, or know who it possibly could be. The neighbor on that side was a single mom, and the voice for sure wasn't hers. Which wasn't even the strangest thing about it...

"Hello?" he said. "Who is it?"

A moment's silence. Then the voice again. But from a different spot. Off to his left, in the shadows near the bottom of the lawn.

"Hello??"

Repeating his words like an echo. Except it wasn't an echo. A second ago, when it called his name, he'd thought the same thing—that it sounded like *him*—but realized that was ridiculous. This second time, though, he was positive.

It sounded *exactly* like him.

Confounded, he stood looking down the lawn. The spruces were about thirty feet high, with fairly thick trunks and long, outstretched limbs. He'd pruned their lower branches to seven or eight feet above the ground to create some shade.

He didn't see anyone standing under them.

The back of his neck prickled.

"Who's there?" he asked. "Where are you?"

"Who's there? Where are you?" said the voice.

Gelfland was still. Now it wasn't just his neck tingling with gooseflesh. It was his arms, his back, even his chest.

The voice, *his* voice, hadn't come from anywhere near the trees. It had moved again. Come from behind him. The driveway, seemingly.

He turned a complete hundred-eighty degrees and stood facing his Toyota, his grocery sack hanging from his shoulder. He could see the car clearly from here. The driveway, too. The motion lights around the walk brightened it so there were barely any shadows.

"Look, this isn't funny," he said. "What do you want?"

Silence. He stared up ahead toward the driveway. Then looked around. "Hello?" he said. "Tell me what you…?"

The question dropped off his lips. He'd glimpsed

the slightest flicker of movement from his right side, near the front door. And not just movement, a shape. A tall, thin silhouette of a man.

He was spinning toward the door, toward the flickering shadow, when a hand clamped over his mouth from behind. It was gloved and large and covered the entire lower half of his face.

Gelfland was strong and physically fit. He'd been an able-bodied seaman on dozens of commercial tankers, carrying heavy tools and loads, climbing and descending ladders. He handled deck machinery and cargo, and was trained in emergency lifesaving procedures. Between cruises he worked out and jogged. He was no weakling.

Yet he was helpless to break free. He brought both hands up to the one smothering his mouth but couldn't pry it away. He struggled to get his elbows into whoever was behind him and was unable to gain any leverage. The hand didn't budge. Its grip was unyielding. Groceries spilled from his bag. He heard the clatter of the beer bottles on the ground.

The hand didn't budge.

"I'll be a fine version of you, Steve," his own voice said behind him. "Promise."

Gelfland felt something hard and circular press into the nape of his neck and immediately knew what it was. Before he heard the click of the pistol's hammer, he knew.

Then it discharged twice. Two muted pops, two bullets in his brain, and he thought and felt nothing more.

4

Baneasa/Satu Mare District, Romania

At first, Howard didn't know who or where he was.
Didn't know if he was upright or horizontal. Didn't
even know which *way* was up or down.

Then sensation slowly began to return. He realized he was down on his right side.

He lay still, his senses flooding back to him.
Identified his own ragged breaths. Felt his elbow
underneath him, bent uncomfortably under his
upper body and the floor. He wondered why the
floor was so cold and what was pecking at him.
After a moment, he remembered Abrams in the
entryway, the bright flash of light, the explosion.

The blast must have knocked him off his feet.

Then what?

He didn't know.

He didn't know.

He didn't know.

Why was everything so goddamned cold?

A hand fell on his left arm. It was a big, strong hand. He could feel its strength. He jerked reflexively.

"Easy, sir."

A hushed voice. Howard recognized it.

He turned his head a little and saw Sergeant Julio Fernandez's broad, square face looking down at him. Specks of white swirled around it, dusting his hair and beard.

Snowflakes.

He felt confused.

"Julio," he said, "where the hell am I?"

Howard shifted his weight so he could half roll and half flop over onto his back. His side hurt. His neck hurt. His face was burned and throbbing. He blinked the snow from his eyes. He was outside in the night, Sergeant Fernandez squatting beside him, looking down at him, wearing a charcoal-gray service uniform with the Net Force patch on its right breast pocket. A ruggedized mini tablet was strapped over his shoulder.

"Sir, take it slow…"

Fuck slow, he thought. He pushed his hands and elbows against the hard, icy ground, managed to sit up, then tried getting to his feet. The sergeant's big, strong hand went to his chest, fingers outspread. His tattooed forearm applying a counterforce to hold him down.

"Just give it a second," Fernandez said. His palm firm against his chest. "I pulled you out. Got you over here. I think you'll be okay, but—"

"For the second time, where's *here*?"

"Behind headquarters. Janus Heights."

Howard looked up at him. Blinked again in the falling snow. "Thought I ordered you off to bed, Sergeant."

"Good thing I didn't hear you, Colonel."

Howard said nothing. *Janus Heights*. The north field between HQ and the compound's long-vacated original barracks.

"Abrams?" he said.

"He's gone. Berra, too. Ops took a direct hit."

Howard brought up his head some more and saw Private Wasserman standing about a yard behind Fernandez. The sergeant caught the look at once.

"Wassy was downstairs with me," he said. "Getting coffee. We heard the blast, came up right away, found you in the hallway."

"What the hell happened?"

"It's the 'hogs."

"What?"

"The hedgehogs. They've been compromised. All of them."

"How?"

"Not sure. Yet. They're set on Cocked Pistol attack protocol. Free-roaming lethal defense of the base. I think they've been fooled into recognizing base personnel as hostiles."

Howard sat processing that a minute. "The rest of the base," he said. "What's the damage?"

"The mess was hit hard—"

"Casualties?"

"We don't know. The whole kitchen staff would've been on tonight. Thanksgiving prep."

Howard grabbed the sergeant's wrist.

"Help me up off my ass," he said.

"Sir—"

"*Now*, Sergeant."

Fernandez shot Wasserman a glance and went around to his right side, the private stepping over to his left. They took hold of his arms and helped him up, Fernandez with a bracing hand on his lower back.

Howard took two deep breaths, a third, as he steadied himself on the dry, crisp, frozen grass. Then he touched his fingertips to his face, taking a damage assessment. There were cuts and scratches. His cheeks felt singed. One eyelid was swelling up. He turned toward the blazing headquarters building with just the slightest wobble in his legs. Its windows were blown out, and he could see tongues of flame lapping and curling inside through jags of broken glass.

"Any clue where the 'hog went, Julio?" he said. Not looking at the sergeant, still staring across the shriveled brown grass at the fire.

"No," Fernandez said. "It's on the prowl."

"For targets of opportunity."

"Yes."

Howard finally turned to him. "The west barracks. You hear from anyone there?"

"It was quite a few minutes ago, but the situation could've changed," Fernandez said. "I ordered radio silence. The 'hogs can scan and intercept our communications."

"*All* of them?"

"I can answer your question, sir," Wasserman said. "We've been testing out a spread-spectrum system for emergencies. It transmits across a wide range of frequencies to—"

Howard looked at him. "English," he said.

"The message hides in the bandwidth noise that's always clogging the air. A needle in a stack of needles. But two cell phones with a proprietary app can code and decode it."

"And nobody told me about this shit?"

Wasserman cleared his throat.

"Sir, I did. Last month."

"And?"

"You told me you didn't want to hear about it again till we *finished* our tests," Wasserman said. "Which we haven't."

Howard frowned. "All right, go on."

"Some of our personnel have the required app on their phones as part of the trials," Wasserman said. "And there are wireless boosters in the underground shelters. So theoretically we do have an open channel."

Howard thought for a minute. With two-thirds of his personnel out on Scalpel, the barracks were partly deserted. That meant there were fewer defenders—and they would be at a severe disadvantage. As base commander, he had exercised his prerogative to loosen the standard military outpost/gun-free-zone rule at Janus. But that only went for sidearms and carbines. The 'hogs were loaded up with rockets and grenades and heavy machine guns.

No contest.

"How about the vehicles? Their AI network?" he said. "If somebody's hacked into it…"

"I'm betting they're all clean, Colonel," Fernandez said.

"How much you ready to put down on the table?"

"The whole bank. They use Argos. Adrian Soto's firewall. The same encryption that bucked the Hekate virus."

"And the 'hogs?"

"Their upgrades are pending."

Howard automatically reached down for his pipe roll. *Pending*. While the Washington pols went playing games with Quickdraw's operating budget.

"We have to get ourselves mobile," he said. "And we'll need firepower."

Fernandez nodded. "The trucks give us both if we can reach them. Onboard weapons, rifles, grenade launchers. And with Argos, a protected AHEF channel so we can get messages out."

Howard regarded him for a long moment. He unsnapped the roll, felt for his Savinelli, and realized it wasn't there. Then he remembered dropping it in the explosion and let his empty hand fall to his side. The vehicle depot was near the southern perimeter. Opposite HQ and across the 'Burbs, or south field—three hundred fifty yards of open ground, the equivalent of almost four football fields. But he was unarmed. The same for Wasserman. And he could see that Fernandez was only carrying his service pistol. If they tried to reach the vehicles on foot, they would be easy targets for the 'hogs. The idea was a nonstarter.

"Safer if they come to us," he said at length. "We head for the depot, the damn robots will pick us up. Nail us before we get anywhere near it."

"Agreed," Fernandez said.

Howard looked at him.

"All right, Julio," he said. "Call us a ride. An escort, too. And do it *quick*."

Mario Perez stamped down on the Jolt's brake pedal, bringing it to a halt outside the Quonsets that housed the compound's nonmilitary personnel.

A second later he pushed the door open, sprang out into the night, and glanced quickly back the way he came from. Two huge globes of flame glared in the distance. One was straight behind him, to the west, around the concession and mess hall. The other fire was off toward Command headquarters, near the northern perimeter. They corresponded to the explosions he'd heard while speeding toward Laura's quarters.

Mario gazed at them with bewildered horror. There was an orange glow above the burning buildings, the firelight refracting off the frozen snow crystals in the air in a kind of scattered, rippling aura. He didn't know what was going on. But he couldn't stop thinking about the hedgehog he'd seen after saying good-night to Laura. He was sure they were only supposed to leave their rounds in an emergency and had felt concerned enough that he'd decided to make sure she got back to her housing unit okay.

The two apparent detonations occurred as he was driving here. One closely following the other. When he heard them, Mario had immediately radioed the watch but gotten no response. Absent explicit orders from Command, he was thinking he would go investigate the fires. But not until he found Laura Cruz.

He turned toward the long aluminum huts. Six of them stood in a row behind a small dirt parking area, ten or twelve feet apart, separated by narrow alleys. Two had cars out front.

Mario didn't know if Laura owned a car. Didn't even know which unit was hers. But only one of them, the second from his right, had lights spilling from its front windows. And she would have gotten home just minutes ago.

It stood to reason she was still awake.

He hurried up to the Quonset. The shades were drawn shut in all its windows, the light escaping their sides and bottoms in pencil-thin yellow lines. There was a rubber welcome mat, a glass storm door, a buzzer in the inner door's metal frame. The light seeping from the window next to the door was bright enough for him to read the printed adhesive label underneath it: *L. CRUZ.*

Mario pressed the buzzer.

No one came.

He pressed again, holding his finger steadily down on the button, listening to the grating buzz inside the hut.

No one came.

He knocked on the storm door, got no answer. Knocked again a little harder, four quick raps. No answer. He opened the storm door, knocked on the solid inner door. Nothing.

Mario sidestepped to the window, cupped a hand over his eyes, and tried to peer through the pencil opening on one side of the shade. But he couldn't see anything besides the thin strip of light and the reflected glow of the distant fires in the glass pane.

His heart thumped. What if Laura wasn't home yet? Didn't she say she was stopping at her friend's unit?

It was possible she was there. But he couldn't help thinking about the sentry robot. The hedgehog that had strayed from its patrol area in the darkness. It was also possible she had run across it on the way home.

He returned to the front door and called her name. Nothing.

Again, louder. "Laura!"

"Mario...I'm over here!"

Her voice, from his left. Then the sound of a door slamming shut and footsteps scraping on the ground.

He turned his head, saw her hurrying over from the last Quonset in the row. She had carried something out the door with her. Initially Mario thought it might be a pillow, but after a moment he realized it was kind of wriggling and squirming around in her hands.

Pillows didn't wriggle and squirm.

He ran toward Laura. She ran toward him. They stopped, facing each other.

"Gracias a Dios!" she said. "Are you all right?"

He nodded, his eyes dropping to the agitated little creature in her hands. It was black and white and plump and furry. Twisting and squirming and thrashing in her grasp, pawing and clawing at her sleeves.

"This is Buttons," she said. "He's a cat."

"I can see that," he said. "Laura—"

"Emily's cat."

"Laura, listen—"

"I was feeding him when I heard the noise," she said. "It was like bombs went off."

"They weren't bombs, Laura. At least I don't think so. I saw a hedgehog back at the concession. Out of its patrol box—"

"Did you hear those blasts?"

"I heard them."

"I thought the first one might have been thunder. But when I heard the second, I knew it wasn't," she said breathlessly. "Buttons panicked and hid, and I had to dig him out of the closet. Once I found him, that is. He—" She abruptly interrupted herself. "Wait. A hedgehog."

He exhaled, guessing she was pretty upset and must have needed a few seconds to register what he'd told her about the robot. "Yeah," he said. "I know it's wild. But—"

"Mario, listen…"

"We can't stick around here—"

"Mario…"

"We have to—"

"Mario, *listen to me.*"

He stopped. "What is it?"

"I told you," she said. "A *'hog.*"

Mario abruptly realized she wasn't looking at him at all but past him into the near distance. He snapped a glance back over his shoulder, following her gaze.

The sentry robot's squat, low-slung outline was unmistakable in the glow of the parking area's pole lights. It was about a hundred yards off…and gliding silently in their general direction.

He turned back to Laura, standing stock-still in the snowy darkness. If they hurried, they could make into his JLTV before it got too much closer. But that wouldn't help if something strange was going on with the 'hog. If it was sniffing around for them, its sensors would lock onto their thermal signatures. And onto the heat of the vehicle's engine. And onto its motion. *And* it would have rocket-powered grenades that could take it out before he put any distance between them.

"The robot," she whispered. "You think it knows we're here?"

He watched it move closer. "I'm not sure," he said. "I think it's very possible."

"Then what do we do?"

He looked quickly around for a place to take cover. The aluminum walls of Laura's Quonset might mask their body heat. But there was a door in front. Possibly a back door, too. And even the thinnest spaces between door and door frame would leak heat from inside. Mario didn't know if it was enough heat for the 'hog to pick up their readings, but he suspected it would be. In which case the hut would become a death trap.

He looked around some more, acutely aware of the 'hog's continued gliding approach. Then his eyes seized on the space between her hut and the next in line. He saw a bicycle leaning against the side of the hut on one flat tire, and the trash bin shared by both Quonsets. Right in front of the bin was a rectangular chest of some sort. It was about four feet high and twice as long.

"Laura, what's that over there?"

She followed the urgent jab of his finger.

"It's my freezer. I dumped it when I got the new one. You think it would hide us?"

Mario was thinking it would have built-in side-wall insulation, a sheet of thick fiberglass foam between its outer and inner panels. And rubber stripping on the edges of the lid.

"It should," he whispered. "But we gotta lose the cat."

"No."

"Laura—"

"This is nonnegotiable."

"What?"

"Nonnegotiable."

He stared at her. She stared back defiantly, pulling the cat against her body.

The 'hog was no more than sixty yards away from them. They couldn't stand out in the open any longer.

"You win," he said, tugging at her elbow. "Now, *please* let's hurry up."

And with that, they ran for the gap between the huts, Buttons cradled deep in Laura's arms.

5

Satu Mare District, Romania

Dixon and his follow vehicle reached the Wolf's Lair at half past midnight, killed their lights, and drove along its wrought-iron outer fence toward a high, ornamental entry gate.

The second BearCat stopped just before reaching the gate and pulled parallel to the road. Moving on ahead, Dixon halted, shifted, and reversed across the blacktop and shoulder onto a wide, flat farm field lying empty and still under a thin sheet of snow.

He looked across the road at the gate. Kali sat beside him in the passenger seat, her night-vision smart glasses defining the world outside in varied shades of rose. Though less effective than the DNVGs worn by the entry team, they allowed for greater freedom of movement. She thought it a worthwhile trade-off.

The Cat's engine ticked. She watched the snow fall steadily outside.

Dixon turned to her. "Your show."

Kali's fingers pattered against her tablet. Behind her, the farm field was a vast, featureless expanse running back toward the southern Carpathian foot-hills. There was a fine cover of snow over every-thing—the dirt shoulder; the dry, frozen grass; the stacked, rectangular bundles of cut, tied grass. Somewhere in that distance there would be a small Magyar farm cottage with stone walls and a roof of orange or brown clay tiles. It would have a barn outside for storing the potato and sugar-beet crops, a shed for the farm tools. A stable with a couple of strong, broad-backed mules or workhorses inside. Possibly a henhouse. With the power grid out, the local homesteads would not have electric lights or heating tonight. But most had woodstoves and fire-places, and there would be candles and oil lamps. They would not freeze.

In the Romanian countryside, the people lived much as they had for centuries. The encroachment of technology was creeping and tentative, and they had not yet become altogether reliant on it. To many who tracked the evolution of cybercrime, it seemed paradoxical that the *technologie vampiri* had origi-nated in this remote corner of the world. But Kali understood.

The internet was a magic portal. Distances meant nothing in the space. Governments and territorial laws were of little consideration. The youth of these remote villages explored and connected over its boundless pathways. They could shape worlds without physical constraint, and it empowered them. And with that great power came temptations.

Kali understood. She especially understood Drajan Petrovik.

She sat tapping on her device. Drajan had replaced the security and surveillance cameras around the estate after the raid on his Bucharest stim club. But once the Sentinel drone surveillance images disclosed the new system's manufacturer, she had been as good as in. She hoped to someday stand eye to eye with the imprisoned Chinese hacktivist, Mad Dragon Butcher, and thank him for the backdoor exploit.

"Done," she said. "I have the camera feeds on a thirty-minute delay."

Dixon glanced at her and nodded. "Just like Munich."

Silence. *Not just like.* In Munich, she was the hunted, and he one of the hunters. She had not forgotten.

Dixon was looking out to his right at the second BearCat. "Rover Two, you're on," he said over the RoIP.

The Cat's rear door swung open. Kali watched a man in jeans and a hooded parka exit and then lean back inside. After a moment, an enormous tan Belgian Malinois followed him out, bounding from the troop compartment on a short leash. The man led the dog over to the fence and stopped in front of it. His name was Joe Banik. A translator/interpreter and K-9 handler, he was on loan to FOB Janus from the Army's Third Special Forces Group. Banik spoke fourteen languages fluently and several more with a high degree of proficiency. Hungarian and Romanian were just two of them.

The BearCats had passed only a few scattered homes on the road—the nearest a third of a mile back—and it was a dark, snowy night. There was perhaps a fifty-fifty chance of any locals showing up to investigate when they heard a commotion. But if curiosity got the better of them, Banik would represent himself as one of the Wolf's security guards and send them off.

Dixon waited until he and the dog were positioned outside the fence. Then: "Whiskey, your turn."

This time his vehicle's rear door opened. In full assault gear, E4 Adam Warren, Quickdraw, hopped out. He carried a silenced MP7 over his right shoulder and a black leather sling bag under his left arm.

Warren hurried across the road. There were no guards stationed at the gate; its cameras, electronic lock, and telephone entry system—presumably Wi-Fi/Ethernet—were designed to keep it secure from intrusion. A breach at the fence or gate would bring men down from the estate's secondary access-control point, a guardhouse twenty yards beyond the fence.

By then, Kali knew, it wouldn't matter.

Approaching the gate, Warren reached into his sling bag and extracted an object about the size and shape of a kitchen sponge. Kali and Dixon watched him attach it to the electronic lockbox and then walk quickly back across the road to their vehicle.

Dixon waited until he was back inside to contact Carmody.

"Preacher, we're ready and set," he said.

"On my go," Carmody replied in his earpiece.

Raven was the sneakiest aircraft Faye Luna had ever piloted. Its composite rubber-panel skin was shaped and angled to deflect radar beams, sunshine and earthshine—but that was a countermeasure that her old-school Army flight instructors would crow about in the cockpits of aging Apaches. The tilt-rotor's extreme stealth was really the product of three major innovations. First, its outer panels were colored with carbon nanotube blackest black, a material engineered at MIT that was ten times blacker than any other substance known to man and absorbed nearly a hundred percent of all incoming light. Watching *Raven* fly in broad daylight was said to be an unsettling experience—like looking at a huge hole in reality, a winged, dark-as-the-void shape cut out of the sky.

Hardly as dramatic, but equally essential, were the bird's secondary and tertiary stealth elements, an integrated network of electronic radar jammers and sound dampers, as well as a state-of-the-art infrared-emissions-distribution system that ran the entire length of the fuselage, remixing and cooling the hot air and gases produced by its running temperatures.

With all that going for her, Luna was confident

she could avoid detection en route to the target. But things were sure to get dicier once they reached it. She and Cobb needed to be on top of their game.

She banked and dropped down, then banked again and dropped more steeply over the Wolf's Lair, its towers coming up large and aggressive in her naked eyes. Finally, she straightened into a flat, stable hover some thirty-five feet above the north bastion.

Crouched at the door in the troop compartment, Carmody slapped a round into the chamber of his pistol, then put on leather fast-rope gloves like the rest of the men.

The line was two inches thick, forty feet long, and tied into the aircraft with an eyehole splice. Carmody tested it with a hard jerk and nodded to Schultz, the broad-chested man behind him.

Schultz checked the mission clock displayed on his night-vision lenses. It was 0128 hours. "Ready and set!"

The others gathered at the door. Schultz and Long belonged to Carmody's Fox Team. The remaining three were on loan from Janus Base.

Carmody grabbed the coil of rope, leaned out, and looked down at the bastion thirty-five feet below. *Raven*'s wings reduced the wash of its rotors so there was almost none of the push on the back of his neck that he would feel roping from a chopper.

He tossed the line and watched it uncoil, making sure the end of the rope touched on the bastion's stone floor.

"Go!" he shouted. Then he was around and out

the door, sliding down, the rope trapped between his feet to control his drop. Long followed, and the next man, and the next, less than six inches of line separating them, Schultz going last in the rear-guard position.

Thirty seconds later, they were all down.

Carmody's *Go!* came over the RoIP at precisely 0130 hours.

Dixon straightened behind the wheel. Glancing into the rearview mirror, Kali saw Warren tap his phone to trigger the breaching charge he'd affixed to the lockbox.

The packet's detonation was instantaneous, its C-4 core igniting an envelope of pyrotechnic thermite. Steel typically melts at two thousand five hundred degrees Fahrenheit. Within three seconds, the burning thermite reached a temperature of four thousand degrees, reducing the lockbox and its guts to molten, white-hot slag.

Droplets of liquefied steel spat into the air. Kali's NV-enhanced smart specs registered their color as fiery magenta. She braced herself, the gate looming in front of her.

Dixon floored the accelerator. "Okay, okay, we're on!"

The Cat surged forward, bumping from the frozen dirt field onto the flat, paved road, then shooting toward the heavy gate. Midway up its height, the lockbox flared between its metal bars like a trapped nova.

A moment later, Dixon smashed through to the other side.

* * *

On the castle grounds, it did not take long for the emergency generators to kick in, with priority given to the estate's guard stations and alarm systems.

In the front guardhouse, three black-clad men were thawing out over hot coffees when they heard a crash at the bottom of the drive. All of them glanced up at their monitors simultaneously.

The video feeds showed nothing unusual. There was no sign of a disturbance. The grounds were empty and still.

But their readiness did not hinge on what they saw on the screens. Two of them were former Constellis operators—top flight SpecOps-for-hire. Their group leader was a recent poach from Braithwaite Global, the new big gun in executive security. These were highly skilled specialists. The blackout had triggered their alertness, and that crash was very loud.

Wearing soft-armor vests, they abandoned their coffee cups and snatched their ballistic helmets and Steyr automatics from the weapons rack. The two Constellis men raced through the door to investigate. The remaining guy paused briefly at his console to notify the rear-guard station and manor house.

The shooting started outside as he was reaching for his carbine. When he heard the noise, he quickly changed his mind and grabbed something else.

There were several secret entries to Castle Graguscu's vast, honeycombed complex of cellars, chambers, and underground passages, all hidden from plain sight behind false wall panels and other clever contrivances, some modern, others predating the Wolf's renovations by many centuries. For mobile communications, he had originally installed the same type of radiating cables—or leaky coax— used by miners and large, modern metropolitan subway systems. Later he added a network of wireless sensors and subsurface radio relays to provide uninterrupted internet access and connect to his intruder-detection system.

Although the entire space below the castle served as his command center, he would not have tolerated anyone using that term to his face, smacking as it did of the governments, armies, and agencies he scorned and despised. Nevertheless, he had divided it into two functionally distinct sections that, together, constituted his lair in the truest sense. Deep underground, and most elaborately hidden, was the computer room from which he oversaw and coordinated the activities of his global hacking syndicate. The primary monitoring station for the estate grounds was closer to the surface, nested among the old count's wine cellars, armory, and cavernous torture chamber.

It was to this room that his head of security, a man called Matei, came shortly after the blackout hit. He hadn't initially linked it to his boss's enemies; after all, the power failure extended beyond Satu Mare to the southeastern fringe of Marmures. While a localized disruption would have seemed suspicious, it seemed a freakish, random, widespread occurrence. But he had thought it best to err on the side of caution and check out the grounds.

All that had just changed dramatically. Now he sat upright in his chair as an alert flashed onto his desktop monitor. It was a Code Red from the front guardhouse. But the attached voice-to-text message was even more stunning—and confusing to him. How could there be a security breach at the gate? The images on his video wall showed that it stood intact. Yet the motion and RFID sensors confirmed the alert. According to them, at least one vehicle had passed through onto the grounds and was moving toward the castle.

Moving fast.

Matei jabbed the intercom button and felt a sharp pain in his wrist. On the best days, it felt tight. Most days it ached, and sudden motions could be pure agony. The thought of a surprise attack raised unsettling memories of the female demon who had shattered it, ruined his handsome nose, and left him with a broken windpipe. For two long months he had been incapable of speech. Despite tracheal reconstruction surgery and endless rounds of therapy, he was left with a voice that cracked and scraped like gravel. Worse, his breaths were accompanied by wheezing, whistling sounds when he exerted himself physically, an embarrassment.

He had to press the button three more times before getting a response from the master suite. The delay was not unexpected. Its occupant had one of his women up there tonight.

"Yes?"

Finally. Matei's wrist throbbed. "We have a problem," he said.

A moment's silence at the other end of the line. Then:

"Talk to me."

* * *

Clinia Ranor worked as an insurance agent in the city of Cluj-Napoca, a few short kilometers from her hometown of Rosalvea. She loved good times and dressing up, found the city's wired-in nightlife an irresistible lure, and when feeling especially adventurous would slip off to the underground hot spots for some exotic kicks.

It was while partying at the scandalously in-vogue stim club Orbital that she was invited to the Wolf's estate. She had found her host's sexual cravings novel and fabulous… Certainly more fun than being stuck in tonight's blackout.

But a minute ago their feast had been interrupted by the buzzing of his intercom. Now, after getting out of bed to answer, he was hastily putting on his clothes.

Stark naked, Clinia pushed herself up against the headboard with her elbows. "Is something wrong?" she asked.

"I'm stepping out a while."

"What? In such a hurry?"

He sat on an ottoman and slipped on his boots, then went across the room to his closet. His overcoat was a retrofuturistic tuxedo cut, with a long swallow tail and textured jacquard silk pentagrams on solid black velveteen.

"I won't be long," he said.

Clinia heard the faintest of creaks, seemingly from the middle of the spacious room. She cocked her head, listening. Then her eyes widened. A large, square section of the parquet floor was *rising* between his closet and the bed…opening like the lid of a hinged box.

Her jaw dropped as two men in dark clothing emerged from a winding metal staircase beneath it. One turned toward her, his gaze roaming up and down. She pulled the sheet up to her neck as her host shrugged into his coat.

An instant later he plunged down the stairs with the others, the panel lowering back into place, once again becoming part of the hardwood floor before her astonished eyes.

And then she was alone.

It was as if he'd vanished. Or was never there at all.

Leaving her alone, confused, and frightened in his cooling bed.

Dixon roared onto the estate grounds in Rover One. The second BearCat swung in through the blown, crookedly leaning entry gate behind him, peeling off hard to the right and heading off-road as it looped around toward the back of the manor.

He saw Kali glance intently at her tablet, checking that the manor's security cams were still on delay.

"We good?"

She nodded, and he fed the Cat some gas.

The drive ahead of him was dark. So were the trees and shrubs along its borders. Everything in shadows. The outside floods were dimmed or doused, probably to go easy on the backup generators. Dixon would rely on the roof cameras feeding heat imagery to his dash screen and head-up display.

"Pickles, wide pan."

"Got it, Dixie."

He shook his head. *Dixie.* Maybe Pickles thought

it was his *bestie*. Fernandez was a prize assclown designing an AI that assigned its own nicknames to people. Or had Pickles's annoying personality developed without his input?

The Cat's engine growled as he steered around a curve toward the guardhouse. It was still about two hundred feet from the low brick structure when his roof cams caught two guys with rifles dashing from inside. Splitting up the instant they hit the drive, they ducked behind the shrubs to its left and right, their heat signatures making them look like radiant ghosts.

Dixon glanced in his mirror. In the rear section, six of the men were in their bucket seats, three on each side, their weapons poking out the gun ports. The seventh, Emerick, was on the shooter's platform behind a roof-mounted M110 AI sniper rifle, his head and upper body up through the hatch.

He could see the two operators in the bushes, the Cat's roof cameras streaming their thermals to his HUD. Though the mesh of twigs and branches cut the images into slivers, it would have taken a solid object like a boulder or tree trunk to block them entirely—and he figured they knew it. But there was no better cover available.

Emerick swiveled his gun toward the radiant ghost on the right, adjusting its angle to compensate for the Cat's rapid, jarring movement. The rifle coughed in his hands, the shrub twitched and shuddered, and the ghost fell backward to the ground.

He swung his weapon toward the second one. But before he could lock in, the guy rolled from behind the bush, sprang partly upright, and triggered his gun. Bullets clacked against the front of the hatch.

Emerick returned fire. Ghost Number Two was wearing a plate carrier, but his rifle's black tip aero-shells could pierce Type III armor like hot needles through butter. The guy went down, spraying ghost blood, the droplets glowing white sparks in Emerick's night-vision goggles.

Then someone new emerged from the guard-house. Emerick instantly identified the weapon against his shoulder by its boxy shape. It was an H&K Punisher, the proverbial shiny object—equipped with a laser range finder and program-mable rocket-powered grenades, it had been field tested by his Delta unit in Afghanistan. Did well in a controlled environment, but get it out in the sand and dust and heat or match it against composite armor, and it became a forty-pound hunk of steel.

Unless whoever was firing it knew not to target armor. Then it could be deadly.

The third ghost was aiming high.

Emerick reacted quickly, but he was jolting along in the hatch, and Ghost Number Three was on firm ground. It made him a little quicker. There were two pops from his weapon, then a loud whis-tling whoosh as the spin of its electronic projectiles ranged their target. Emerick tried to drop down into the hatch but never had a chance as the grenades blew a foot above him, scattering stainless-steel fléchettes in all directions.

He heard himself scream. His face and scalp ablaze with agony, he folded down through the hatch and spilled from the platform to the BearCat's floor.

At that same instant, one of the men at the right-hand gun ports finally got a bead on the ghost with the rocket launcher. His name was Max Spencer, and Emerick was his best buddy.

He fired, saw the guy go down, and shuffled to Emerick's side, groping for a Sacred Heart medal he wore on a chain around his neck. Jimmy Singh, the medical corpsman, was already working on him, pulling one thing after another out of his blow-out kit. Singh exchanged glances with Spencer and shook his head. Emerick wasn't going to make it. They could see part of his brain through his skull.

Spencer tried to remember a prayer. But his mind was blank, and he just clenched his medal, cursing himself for being too late.

"I'm sorry," he said. "I'm sorry…"

Dixon pulled a breath through his teeth. He couldn't slow down. More lives were at stake, and Carmody was depending on him. He couldn't slow down.

His foot hard on the gas, he suddenly heard a click from his left, and glanced at Kali to see her shrugging free of her harness.

"I'm going back there," she said.

He looked surprised.

"Singh's got it," he said. "I don't see how you can help."

She pushed off her seat.

"I have to try," she said.

6

Carmody's entry team ran down the wide stone stairs from the north bastion, stacking up in a T formation. He took the point, his flankers abreast of him—Doug Wheeler at ten o'clock, and Joe Begai, a Quickdraw sapper, at two o'clock. Schultz and another of Howard's E4s, Stafford Sparrow, were bringing up the rear at five and seven.

The wind and snow blew around them. Their rubber soles slapped down on the worn stone steps hugging the wall. The manor's exterior lights were out, but they had their quad DNVGs flipped down and could see perfectly in the darkness.

The wall to Carmody's right led through a series of curves to an arched wooden door. Fifteen feet high, thick vertical oak planks, wide iron bands bolted across the top, middle, and bottom. The rust-scabbed, discolored hardware looked ancient and hand-forged and depicted a dragon with a wolf's head, gaping jaws, and three serpentine tongues looped around the hanging door ring. Its outspread wings formed the lock plate.

He grabbed the handle, pushed, felt no give in the door. Begai got a signal from him and moved up to it. Producing a thermic lance from his vest, he palmed a cartridge into its grip and depressed its firing button. An iron vapor jet hissed out, burning at over five thousand degrees Fahrenheit. The dragon glowed red, then white, then started to melt off, its wings curling into themselves, its triple tongues dripping down over the circular handle.

A second later, the handle clanged onto the steps.

Carmody motioned for Begai to stand clear and stomp-kicked the door, driving in his heel under the smoking, dripping lock plate.

The door swung open heavily. It was reinforced on the inside, a modern addition, the solid steel liner attached to the wood with smooth, flush riveting. The steel popped and bubbled where the lance's vapor jet must have penetrated.

Carmody stormed through into a lightless, narrow passage, the men falling into single file behind him. It was a tight squeeze and came to a dead end on the right. But looking to his left, past an interior arch, he saw a descending staircase blocked by a mesh gate.

He sprinted toward it, noticed the sliding tracks. There were biochip readers on the wall, like at Club Energie, one on his side of the gate, one on the stair side. But Kali's lock hack wouldn't work twice;

their man would have changed his biometric database after the Bucharest raid.

It was nothing Carmody hadn't foreseen.

He shot a glance around at Begai.

"We need a big hole," he said.

The sapper nodded. "Big hole coming up."

He reached into his pack, his hand coming out with a C-4/thermite breaching charge like the one Dixon's element used at the perimeter fence. He affixed it to the gate's upper track and placed a second on the lower track and waved for the others to back down the passage. Joining them, his arm in the air, he ticked off a countdown with his fingers: five, four, three, two, little finger down.

A sharp crack, and the charges flashed into flame, blowing the gate off the tracks. It hung from the ceiling a second, teetering precariously in a cloud of smoke and masonry dust. Then gravity tore it free of the upper track, and it clanged down the flight of stairs.

Carmody led the men past the toppled gate and down to the pitch-dark hallway below.

But his eyes didn't see a hallway. They saw a linear, narrow, dangerous piece of terrain—and a potential killing ground. Longer and wider than the upper passage, it doglegged to the right some fifty feet ahead. Its floor was covered by a plush carpet runner, and the right-hand wall was draped in tapestries of ancient battle scenes—armored warriors, swords, and galloping horses. There were a couple of closed doors on the left.

He waved his men toward the side that was opposite the doors. They lined up behind him single file, heads up, eyes up, weapons at their hips, moving, moving, moving through the corridor. Their assault plan was to clear every room.

Carmody was still three or four feet short of reaching the first door when he heard footsteps up ahead—coming from the intersecting hall. Then the muzzle of a rifle angled around the corner of the wall.

The shooter opened fire, his gun chattering.

Carmody yanked a grenade from the hard-shell trigger pouch on his vest. He'd used flashbangs in the 22nd Special Tacs, but this was a different species. Thermobaric, rectangular instead of round, it didn't roll away from the target but stayed where it landed. Nor did it blow outward so everyone around, including the thrower, felt the effects. When the grenade went live, an interior computer scattered a combustible cloud around the bad guys and then ignited it. The noise and light were directed inward.

"Coming out."

The men averted their eyes as he released the spoon and lobbed his grenade up the hall.

The *flash* part of *flashbang* was a brilliant 10,000 candelas, five hundred times brighter than a police spotlight. It would cause rapid pupil constriction and photobleaching of rhodopsin, or retinal purple, the same pigment Fox Team's NV-capable smart glasses exploited for light amplification. The effect was full but temporary blindness.

The type of *bang* it made depended on where you were, relative to the detonation. To Carmody's men, the noise was a mildly startling thump like someone slapping his palm down on the hood of a car. But within the five-foot cloud radius, it exceeded 180 decibels. That was louder than the roar inside a 737 jet turbine, and louder than a pound of exploding TNT. At 180-plus decibels, glass shattered, balloons popped, and the atmospheric PSI jumped ten percent from the compression wave. At 180-plus, vision blurred, and it became hard for a person to breathe or swallow. He would get nauseous, dizzy, and disoriented.

Carmody raced up to the turn and swung around it with his bullpup at his hip. There were two hostiles in the intersecting hall. Both held assault rifles and wore body armor and night-vision goggles. They were staggering, out of it, and probably seeing spots and sparkles. But in seconds they would recover enough to become lethal threats again.

One of the prime rules he'd learned as an operator was to never give an enemy extra cracks at you.

He shot them between the eyes, clean double taps. Blood misted onto the wall from the backs of their heads as he turned and looked back around the corner. Thumbing Schultz and Sparrow toward the first door, he signaled for Long and Begai to follow him, then broke into a fast trot along the branching hall.

It ran straight for about forty paces. Halfway down its length, a niche in the thick fortress wall displayed antique suits of armor resembling those pictured in the tapestries. Mounted behind them on the wall were lances, pikes, maces, and swords. Immediately to the right of the niche, a flight of carpeted stairs climbed to an upper story or tower. To the left at the far end of the hall was another staircase.

Two to choose from.

Carmody gazed at the ancient battle array, noting a metal crest mounted on the wall above it. The wolf-jawed dragon with three tongues again.

He blinked his right eye twice to snap a photo with the goggles. Then, "Pickles, identify."

The AI searched its web of databases. A moment later Carmody's head-up showed the results:

Dacian Drago. The Wolf-Dragon. Standard of the ancient Eastern European Dacian army. Seen on Trajan's Column in Italy. Word origin: Drago derived from the Greek gazing *or* to watch with a sharp eye.

Carmody gestured toward the right-hand set of stairs. Easy bet.

He dashed up the eight or ten steps to the landing, the others close behind him. At the top, a short hallway curved toward two doors, one on the left, another straight ahead at the end of the passage. The first was stainless steel, a biometric reader alongside it. The door that faced them was old, high, and arched, with large wood panels. A lever-type handle and thumb latch. Carmody saw a pencil-thin strip of light underneath.

He squeezed Long's shoulder and pointed to the wooden door. Long nodded, went to the hinge side, Carmody and the others stacked up behind him. Shifting to the opposite side, Begai reached across for the handle, pulled it open, and made first entry. Long moved in next.

Carmody went last, dead center through the doorway. The extended stock of his MP7 pressed against his arm, he scanned the room, quick sweeps of his eyes.

It was a large, oval parlor. No one inside. A lofty,

raftered ceiling, wide casement windows, and antique furnishings: an oriental rug, wing chairs, side tables, sconces, elaborate curtains and wall hangings.

Then Carmody saw an interior door across the room, arched like the entry door, but narrower.

He sniffed the air. A sweet fragrance hung in it. Resinous, musky...

Incense, he thought. *Oud*, the expensive stuff. Iran, Sudan, Birhan. Arab royals liked using it as an aphrodisiac.

He gestured toward the door, and they moved fluidly over to it, Wheeler taking the left-flank position, Begai going right, Carmody hanging two steps back with his gun upraised. This one had a knob, and Begai reached for it, turned it, and pushed.

As he stepped through the open door, Carmody saw a woman spring out of a chair near the bed, a shocked, agitated expression on her face. She was in her late twenties or early thirties. A long fur coat unbuttoned over a short black bodycon dress that hugged her like a second skin and showed plenty of leg. Spike heels, dangle earrings, she was sitting there alone, looking like that, at one o'clock in the morning.

What was wrong with the picture?

His gaze flicked to an incense burner on the night stand. It was polished brass, a half-burned clump of the dark, tarry *oud* in its bowl.

Alone now, yes, he thought. But she hadn't been.

Carmody strode over to her, faced her, fingers wrapped around his submachine gun.

"Hands up. *Manaile in aer*. Now."

She raised them stiffly over her head. Wheeler

shifted over to her, did a hurried pat-down, shook his head to indicate she wasn't carrying anything.

"Do you speak English?" Carmody said.

She said nothing.

"Do you speak English? Yes or no."

She hesitated. "Yes. A little."

Carmody nodded. "Drop your hands," he said. "Go on."

She slowly brought them down to her sides.

"Now take a deep breath. In and out."

She inhaled. Exhaled.

"Again."

She breathed. Carmody saw her posture relax, some of the tension draining from her shoulders.

"Okay," he said. "Tell me your name."

"Clinia."

"Are you from right around here, Clinia?"

"I live in Cluj."

"That's to the south, yes? *Este spre sud?*"

"Yes."

"And that's where you met him? In Cluj?"

"Yes. Just tonight. At a club."

"A stim club?"

"Yes. How do you know?"

Carmody didn't answer.

"Clinia," he said, "where is he?"

She said nothing.

He took one hand off the gun barrel and flipped up his goggles, wanting her to see his eyes though the opening in the balaclava.

"I'm asking you to tell me where he went, Clinia. It's very important."

The woman looked hesitant again. "I'm afraid," she said.

"Don't be. We'll protect you."

She said nothing.

"He left you behind," he said. "Tell me."

She still said nothing. But her eyes broke away from his for a split second.

He caught their trajectory at once. They didn't go left or right. They went straight down to the floor.

Carmody immediately looked where she'd looked and felt his stomach harden up.

"Shit," he said.

Even as Carmody and his team reached the Wolf's tower, the four men descending its long hidden staircase got to the bottom, where they turned down a lighted passageway with bare walls and a hard granite floor.

The passage would divide in about twenty yards. On the left, it ran a few short feet to an automatic steel door. The right branch went coiling through many long yards toward Castle Graguscu's ancient wine cellars, armory, and torture chamber…and by stages to the main computer room.

The group bore right, following the shorter passage to an automatic steel door. One of the guards held an RFID card to a scanner, and the door whispered open, and they all went through. Emergency power was flowing to this part of the fortress, and overhead lights came up instantly around them.

The multimillion-dollar climate-controlled garage had elicited comments of different types among the Wolf's chief lieutenants. While most were impressed, a few thought it excessive, joking out of earshot that he had seen too many spy movies. But Drajan Petrovik viewed it as a sensible escape hatch, and tonight's events were proof of his foresight. He was a big fish, and his enemies trolled deep.

Sunk fifty feet beneath the castle, the garage was shaped like a Y, with concealed exits at each end of the fork on the east and west sides of the castle, and a third exit at the base of the vertical stroke, beyond the estate's rear gate. Inside were a Mercedes G-Class SUV, two Rezvani Tank X's, a reflective silver-blue Rolls-Royce Black Badge Ghost sedan, and a hybrid *rosso corsa* Koenigsegg Regera. Two metallic black Kawasaki Ninja H2R motorcycles stood together in a corner. No one had ridden the bikes since the day they had been tested and tuned.

The man from the Wolf's tower turned toward the Swiss-built Regera. Among the fastest cars in the world, with a top speed of two hundred fifty miles an hour, it looked like liquid mercury in the wind.

"I'll drive this beauty," he told one of the guards.

The guard looked uncertain. "It's bound to draw their notice."

He dismissed the question with a shake of his head.

"I'm playing against expectations," he said, eyeing the car. "Let's see them catch me if I'm wrong."

It was 1:00 a.m. when the drones took flight from the extreme western border of Mihail Kogălniceanu Airfield, joint headquarters to the Romanian Air Force's 863rd Helicopter Squadron and the United States Army's skeletal Black Sea Area Support Team.

The swarm was composed of a hundred inexpensive cylindrical, 3-D printed, mergeable-nervous-system aerial robots. It had two brain units, the Monarch and its backup possessing higher adaptive and decision-making capabilities. Mixed together in formation were surveillance, radar-jammer, and communications drones, although nearly two-thirds of them carried an explosive payload and were essentially stupid kamikaze bombs.

They deployed from concealed LOCUST II launch tubes with a rapid series of pops, like the sound of a hundred and thirty champagne bottles uncorking two at a time. *Pop-pop, pop-pop*, they hopped up into the darkness, opened their wings, and climbed high into the sky. The noise startled a flock of cold, sleeping crows in the brambles and sent them swirling up into the snowy night sky, shrieking and cawing in agitated complaint.

Expanding their foldable wings, the drones soared due west over the Wallachian hills.

The launch took under three minutes from start to finish. Besides the distressed crows, its sole witness was the occupant of an unmarked brown Uro KOVAK military vehicle sitting with its left tires on the cracked, heaving old roadway and its right tires on its lumpy dirt shoulder.

When the last pair of drones was airborne, the woman in the driver's seat transmitted a coded message and started up her engine.

As she pulled away, a smaller flock of seventy-five sleek, flying-wing VTOL Romanian drones took off from a hangar roof at Camp Turzii Air Base near the blacked-out city of Cluj-Napoca, in the central Transylvanian Balkans. They jumped straight up into the air from their launch stands as if on springs, each carrying five and a half pounds of high-yield EPX-1 plastic explosive in its nose for a combined three-hundred-pound payload.

Turzii hosted several rotating Romanian and US squadrons and had been upgraded in recent years to deter the Russian MiG-41 hypersonic stealth fighters and Beriev A-50Us that were aggressively violating Romania's sovereign airspace with forays over the Black and Caspian Seas. Ironically, the drones were manufactured by the Saint Petersburg–based Kronstadt Group and originally ordered by the Russian client state Iran, which in turn bundled and shipped them to Romania, one of its leading trade partners, as a component of a multimillion-dollar weapons and technology deal. In the complicated landscape of global geopolitics, the arms market was often a circular firing squad.

Be that as it may, the ascent of the little drone cluster was being closely monitored from a place near the Black Sea, seven hundred long miles from Camp Turzii. The observer's dark eyes fixed raptly on a computer display, he lifted a cup of sweetened Turkish coffee to his lips, drank it in two deep gulps, and followed it with a shot of chilled raki, the anise-flavored spirit sometimes called Lion's Milk for its strong bite.

He felt the coffee and raki heat up his cheeks, his throat, his chest, his stomach. With his window slightly open to freshen the room's air, he could hear the tumble of waves against the fortified breakwater. The sea was high and rough tonight, but his lover wasn't timid. She had gone out on the rocks facing the ocean, walking out near the old Cold War submarine pens.

The entire area was under curfew, and an ordinary citizen might have been stopped by the military police. But Quintessa Leonides was a woman of high status and strong will. The daughter of Bratva's boss of bosses, she held control of Eastern Europe's most powerful bank and cryptocurrency exchange. She did as she pleased.

He pictured her out there, the waves crashing at her feet in the darkness. And then unwillingly, he thought of two ravens in flight.

His hand went to the small tattoo behind his ear, a symbolic wheel of ancient origin.

It was exactly 1:40 a.m.

At one forty-two, the Mihail Kogălniceanu swarm came within twenty miles of the village of Baneasa, its Monarch drone making first contact with the renegade hedgehogs at Janus Base. Seconds later, it absorbed their AI into the hive mind, making them its own, placing them under its full control.

Camp Turzii's swarm, meanwhile, was nearing its destination over Rosalvea.

Separated by hundreds of miles, the drones were ready to strike.

7

New York City, United States

Stepping from the shower onto the bathroom tiles, Sergei Cosa looked down at himself with a fair measure of satisfaction. His pectorals layered with thick slabs of muscle, his abdomen flat and rippled, he was as sturdy and hardbodied at fifty-seven as he'd been in his midtwenties. Father Time, with his scythe and hourglass, might be an implacable adversary, but Cosa's conscientious diet and rigorous weight-lifting program had thus far kept the Old One's cruel cuts to a minimum.

Now he donned a lightweight Turkish morning robe, stepped into his leather slippers, tossed a fresh towel over his shoulders, and went over to stand by the sink, carefully studying his reflection in the mirror. With his high, blunt cheekbones, full black hair, and prominent ridge of brow, Cosa conformed to the classic East Baltic phenotype—and proudly so. He was a nationalist to his core and held a powerful contempt for those who would live in a homogenized contemporary society, all genetic and cultural heritage thrown into the blender. Though a proud and dedicated Russian, he took equal pride in his Romanian lineage…in having the blood of Dacian warriors in his veins. His ancestors had lived in the Carpathian mountains since prehistoric times, fighting off Alexander the Great, the Celts, and the Gallic Boii in succession, driving their armies from the steppes to make the Danube run red.

Yes, Sergei Cosa was proud of his familial steel, proud of the strength and endurance of his line. His long diplomatic sojourn in New York had only reinforced that feeling, while increasing his disdain for America's soft, boneless cultural stew. It was, in his view, too weak to stand the test of centuries.

Still, he enjoyed certain aspects of the city. There was an energy. A pulse. And, for those of status, an unparalleled luxury. Even during last summer's cyberattack, with the rest of Manhattan dark, there had been no power outages here on prestigious Beekman Place…at least none affecting the high-rise where he occupied a large duplex condominium with wraparound windows overlooking the river to the east, and the United Nations complex to the south.

Rubbing a hand over his dark growth of beard, Cosa ran the tap, lathered up with his shaving brush, reached for his straight razor, and applied the blade to his cheeks with short, deft strokes. The water was warm, the light above the mirror bright and even.

He had almost finished shaving when he heard the faint ringing of his landline through the bathroom door. Then the voice of his housekeeper, Edelle, answering the call.

Turning from the sink, he dabbed off his face with his towel and went out into the hallway. Graceful and light-footed for a man of his imposing frame, he moved quietly over the hardwood floor in his slippered feet.

The living room was open and expansive, its antique lamps and Impressionist canvases orbiting a hand-knotted Persian carpet, silk-cushioned sectional couch, and a custom, gold-ornamented walnut cocktail table.

Edelle stood by the circular table holding out a cordless handset.

"Mr. Cosa," she said, "it is your cousin."

Precisely on time, he thought. Dependability was one of the baseline traits that made Grigor an outstanding agent. Elite even within the SVR. The same had been true of Anton Ciobanu, which was why he was chosen to plant the bomb at the U.S. president's rally in Zuccotti Park. But Ciobanu was dead, killed by the Americans. Grigor, on the other hand, continued operating at will in the shadows. A product of Ivan Mori's multigenerational breeding program—a science-city child—his inborn aptitudes, education, and wide range of skill sets put him in a category of his own.

As he strode across the carpet, Cosa noticed Edelle was looking out his southeast windows toward the East River, a contemplative expression on her face. He glanced in that direction and saw the lights of the newly repaired and reopened Brooklyn Bridge twinkling in the night like strings of crystalline beads. Three months ago, he had stood at the same windows, watching gray smoke spiral up from a burning police helicopter into a cloudless blue sky. The aircraft had been caught in the suspension cables like a winged insect in a spiderweb.

There had been more smoke, ash, and airborne grit to the south from the explosions at Zuccotti Park, where the president had announced the formation of her Net Force; Cosa could still recall the downtown area fading into the haze like a desert mirage.

Hours after the explosions, Ciobanu was tracked down by law enforcement. But for all the thousands of news reports about what happened that day, Cosa had never seen one that asked whether the same man who planted the explosive charge near the president's podium was also responsible for bombing the office building across the street. He was sure America's investigative agencies— including Net Force—were pursuing answers to that unresolved question in secret…

But Cosa was one of the small handful of people on earth who knew of Grigor's role as accomplice.

Now he took the phone from Edelle and looked closely at her face.

"What troubles your thoughts?" he asked.

She shrugged a little. "I have served you here for many years," she said. "Everything is going to change."

He looked at her in silence.

"Be soothed, *mamă*," he said after a moment. "Change simply means we are alive. Come what may, you are under my steady protection."

Edelle smiled, giving him a small nod. Then she turned and left the room without another word.

Cosa waited until she was out of sight to raise the phone to his ear.

"Hello?" Grigor asked. "Are you there?"

"Yes. I was speaking to my servant. She is Magyar. My childhood sitter could have been her double." He paused. "Okay, talk. And watch what you say."

"Always," Grigor said. "I've taken care of the bird, 'cousin.'"

Cosa was silent. It had been a long day, and he'd planned an early bedtime. But his weariness was suddenly gone.

"When was this done?" he said.

"Earlier tonight. Outside his New Jersey nest."

"And where is he now?"

"Packed in marinade," Grigor said. "Well and thoroughly, I might add."

Cosa thought a moment. "This is excellent news. We should talk in person."

"Sure," Grigor said. "When?"

Cosa glanced at his wristwatch. It was 7:00 p.m. There was no reason to wait. The call had energized him.

"Tonight."

"So soon?"

"Yes, why not?" Cosa said. "I'll see you in an hour. You know the place."

He disconnected. Deep in thought, he stood

holding the phone for a long moment after the call ended. Then he put it down on the cocktail table and turned back toward the windows, staring out into the night.

Russia's ascent was finally coming. The pandemic of a few years back had crippled her economically. And she was still struggling to recover while the irresponsible Chinese skated past the consequences. *Change simply means we are alive.* Cosa believed that to his core. Master chess players, his people in Moscow had taken the long view even as they endured dreadful sickness and hardship.

Cosa stared out the window. Again he remembered the helicopter and the fire and the carnage of last summer's strike. But all that was mere prelude. An opening move. Drajan Petrovik, the Wolf, had spawned an electronic hydra, and it was a deadlier creature than America realized. Still growing, *spreading*, through the country's digital infrastructure, it would soon lock its jaws around the very heart of Western power.

Chimera...

Chimera was the game changer. The great realigner. Once it started nothing would be the same. There would be before, and there would be after. And the motherland would stand alone in the new world order.

The antiques shop was on Eighth Avenue and Twenty-Sixth Street in Manhattan's Chelsea district, an amalgam of restored row houses, tenements, factories, and warehouses a short distance from the Hudson River and the High Line park.

Walking crosstown, Sergei Cosa reached the shop at 7:48 p.m. and entered with his key, hearing the chimes jingle softly as he opened the door. He did not reach for the overhead light switches but instead moved carefully toward the counter and turned on a standing brass boom lamp alongside it.

In the lamp's muted radiance, he could see his way around the shop without drawing attention from the street.

The place was tiny, with framed vintage travel prints on one wall, shelves displaying cobalt and Depression glassware on another, and only a few choice items of furniture arranged on the sales floor—a mid-nineteenth-century military campaign chest, a rosewood Napoleon III escritoire, an ornate Victorian corner chair, an Italian Chippendale dining table, and, in the back opposite the entrance, a large oak wardrobe with mirrored doors that covered nearly the entire wall.

Cosa sat down on the corner chair and waited, checking his wristwatch only once. At eight o'clock on the dot, he saw a tall, exceedingly thin man peer through the front door's glass.

His hair cut short, his sunken eyes a pale, almost transparent shade of blue, Grigor wore a heavy wool sport coat that hung loosely off his arms and shoulders and looked almost too large for his frame. Cosa thought he resembled a cardboard skeleton, a two-dimensional Halloween cutout, something made to dance on strings and frighten the neighborhood children.

"Right on time," he said.

"In fact, I was early and decided to enjoy the fresh air—it's a nice evening," Grigor said. "I was right outside when you arrived twelve minutes ago."

"Really? I didn't notice you out there."

"No one sees me unless it's my wish," he said. "You know that."

Cosa regarded him from under his shaggy brows. Grigor did not exaggerate. He could stalk a ghost undetected.

"Yes, it's partly the reason we're here," he said and nodded toward the armoire. "Come with me."

Grigor bowed his head slightly in deference, waiting.

A moment later Sergei strode to the rear of the shop, where he pulled open the armoire's double doors to reveal a large entryway behind it. Stepping through, he reached through the opening for a wall switch, spilling light over an office with an oak rolltop desk, some chairs, and little else.

He went to the desk, slid out a drawer, got his smartphone out of his pocket, and dropped it inside. Then he looked around at Grigor.

"Yours, too," he said. "And whatever weapon you're carrying."

Grigor's phone was already in his hand. He deposited it in the drawer, reached under his jacket, and a slipped a matte black Walther P22 Q from a concealed carry holster underneath it.

Cosa watched as he set it in alongside the phones.

Then he shut the desk drawer, turned to a plain door to the left, opened it, switched on more lights, and stepped onto a spiral staircase winding down to the basement.

Grigor followed silently behind.

Years ago, Cosa had received a tour of the property from an acquaintance who dealt in real estate. Its history as a Prohibition-era speakeasy run by Owney Madden, the notorious racketeer and bootlegger, intrigued him, and he had purchased it through cutouts.

With his minimal restoration, the saloon looked just as it had almost a century before—brick walls, exposed pipes and ducts, a well-stocked mahogany bar with stools and hanging globe lights. There were small round tables and chairs around the room and comfortable divans against the walls.

"Would you care for some *Pálinka*?" he said, going around the bar counter.

Grigor noticed the absence of a label on the bottle. "Well, now…this looks like some fine moonshine."

Cosa grinned slightly at his Southern drawl. He could replicate regional dialects in a snap. "The only spirits worth the name are made in home distilleries. But I think you know its origin. I'm stocked by the owner of a guesthouse in Darjiu. Hardly Kentucky, like your accent."

"It's Western Tennessee. There's an Appalachian twang," Grigor said. "Still, I'm glad you're amused." He nodded toward the bottle. "And yes, I'll have a drink, thank you."

Cosa took two tumblers off the rack, poured them nearly full, brought them over to a table, and motioned for the other man to sit. Then he settled into the chair opposite him.

"Prostym udovol'stviyam," he toasted, raising his glass. "To simple pleasures."

They clinked and drank the colorless plum brandy, Cosa taking a moment to enjoy its sweet, strong kick before he spoke.

"First things first," he said. "I'm pleased that you've completed your assignment."

"I love the ocean blue," Grigor said. He'd switched voices. "It's going to be an interesting cruise."

"Is this Gelfland now?"

"Yes…and you should have been there when I spoke to him in his own voice," Grigor said, back to sounding like himself. "The looks on their faces—I always enjoy that part."

"I'm sure." Cosa drank. "In all frankness, I hadn't expected you to get the job done this quickly."

"I can't help it. I'm gifted."

Cosa was silent, his hand around the tumbler of *Pálinka*. "I leave for Crimea very soon," he said. "I thought it best that you know."

Grigor looked at him. "Respectfully, I'm surprised."

"Why is that?"

"One gets used to the bright lights of America."

Another silence.

"You aren't wrong," Cosa said after a moment. "My status here has its creature comforts…but that's not the point. To stay is to put the mission at risk."

"And the mission is to dim those Western lights."

"Exactly." Cosa drank. "I want to make sure all our recent business has been put to rest. And discuss your new assignment."

Grigor nodded, waiting.

"Let's begin with the Ilescu family," Cosa said. "They're clumsy Romanian hotheads. But I needed them to distribute Zolcu's white plastic last summer, and knew they could do it quickly. And I knew they had contacts with other organizations. Bratva, the Asians, the Macheteros. The black gangs and what's left of the Italians."

"They did the job," Grigor said.

"Yes," he said. "But they also created a mess for us. Giving those brothers cards."

"The Waleks."

"Yes."

Grigor shrugged. "I cleaned it up to the best extent possible. It was shortly after Manhattan went dark, and the city was hot with investigators. I couldn't move their bodies from the apartment without undue risk."

"Understood," Cosa said. "But did you notice there was almost nothing about them in the press?"

"They were nobodies. Clowns."

"Still, two dead men. Someone must have put a hold on the story."

"You think it was the police?"

"The police, the FBI, Net Force...all three, possibly. You, yourself, said it. The city was crawling with law enforcement. And keeping quiet the details of a crime is typical during an open probe," Cosa said. "You see, Grigor. We have too many dangling threads. The explosion at One Liberty, for example. By now it must have dawned on investigators that Ciobanu couldn't have planted the bomb there. Not unless he was in two places at once. Do you agree?"

Grigor looked at him. "Yes," he said. "I do."

"And the garage attendant," Cosa said. "Yalin. I personally gave him the Jumpdrive that passed along the computer worm."

"You could have assigned that to a messenger."

"It was too important to delegate. Besides, it's long done. And in his case your cleanup had unintended consequences."

"I saw that the car and his body were destroyed."

"That destruction involved the FBI's top New York Cybercrimes man. Someone who saved the President of the United States. Net Force's Director of Cyber Investigations."

"Harris."

"Yes," Cosa said. "I do not raise any of this to be critical of your work. The circumstances were what they were. But the Western lights you mention… You see why it's time to leave them behind." He spread his arms expansively to indicate his surroundings. "Enthralling as they might be."

Grigor's eyes met his. "You said you wanted to discuss my present assignment."

"Yes, Grigor. Or is it Mr. Gelfland?"

"Whatever."

Cosa grinned.

"There's great friction here about the Cloud-Cable initiative. In political circles, at least. As might be expected when the CIA and National Geospatial Agency—two primary sources of American intelligence—enter into a partnership with Olympia, the largest e-commerce company in the world."

"Owned by James Yates, a trillionaire who also owns newspapers, television networks, and social media," Cosa said. "People here mistrust such alliances. They see a blurring of lines. The government and the private sector. Surveillance and civil liberties. All that immature nonsense. In fact, Cloud-Cable is an American capitalist venture at its most definitive—and technologically state of the art." He paused. "One thing they've kept secret is ONI's involvement. There's more to the deal than a new computing cloud."

"As if that weren't enough." Grigor laughed a little. "Anyway, yes. I understand. The Office of Naval Intelligence is responsible for keeping an eye on submarines."

"With other subordinate agencies," Cosa said. "But its current monitoring system is archaic and slapdash. Some fiberoptics, some mobile arrays, and seventy-year-old hydrophonic cables that are a step above cups on a string. There's nothing close to consolidation." He paused. "CloudCable is partly designed to remedy that, and completion of ONI's piece of the network has already advanced beyond the rest. It's well ahead, in fact."

"Yes, I know," Grigor said. "I'm not surprised Naval Intelligence is a player behind the scenes."

Cosa regarded him over the rim of his tumbler.

"ONI is the *main* reason the Americans have poured a fortune into the underwater cable system," he said. "But they're less concerned with us than China. Or Chinese ambition and underwater stealth capabilities. That's behind their haste to complete the project." He took another drink. "Have you ever really thought about the crucial nature of sea power? Specifically, why the strongest nations on earth are always competing for *command* of the sea?"

Grigor looked at him and shrugged.

"It has fish," he said. "You can piss in it when you're swimming and no one notices."

"Ha! Good start!" Cosa laughed and regarded him another moment. Then his face turned serious. "Grigor, I think it's time you learned more about how you fit into the big picture. About the real purpose of Operation Chimera. It's been strictly need-to-know to this point. But with your ship setting sail in just a few weeks, you *do* need to know you're going to have some help."

"Specifically?"

Cosa drained his glass.

"Specifically," he said, "a marine task force of Spetsnaz's best. Black berets. And all the lethal weapons they can carry."

8

Satu Mare District, Romania

Carmody tapped the wearable on his forearm while Wheeler and Begai kept an eye on poor, confused Clinia from Cluj. She sat, fur coat and all, in an antique chair behind him and across the room.

She had been cut loose and left stranded by tonight's boyfriend. Tossed aside like she was worthless and disposable. She was scared and leagues out of her element, and Carmody felt sorry for her. But Clinia wasn't his problem. He already had enough problems. Like getting through the trapdoor his quarry had slipped through, so he could get after him.

Even then, catching up wouldn't be easy. Their man had a solid lead and was on his home turf. He knew what was around every turn, while Carmody didn't even know where the turns might lie.

It was a disadvantage he'd anticipated, and Kali's wireless protocol sniffer-spoofer was his best means of overcoming it. His only other option was to blow the trapdoor, but that might take the rest of the floor down with it. So it wasn't really an option at all. He needed her app to work. She had timed its key emulation speed at between one and two minutes, two being the outside measure, which by most calculations was lightning fast. But right now it felt like an hour.

Carmody waited, a silent clock in his head chewing through the precious seconds. *Fifty-six, fifty-five...fifty-three.* His touch screen was populating with RFID tags, their bit patterns racing across it in clusters of zeros and ones as the computer grabbed them out of the air for analysis. *Forty-eight, forty-seven...*

He was good with technology. He got it, embraced it, applied it to his work in countless changing ways. But he was a classic, out-of-the-box user, and Kali Alcazar the Outlier could not have been more the opposite. Aware of the castle's secret passages, and the millions of dollars Drajan Petrovik spent on renovations and upgrades, he had asked Kali to help him prepare for the unexpected. Like his present quarry escaping through a trapdoor escape hatch and vanishing like a ghost in a haunted house.

Kali's snoofer was configured to do two things. One of them was to scan every known wireless platform used in smart-building automation. The networks that controlled doors, lights, climate-control systems, window blinds, and other Internet of Things gadgets. The other was to inject the scanner with a machine-learning algorithm—an AI ghost in the machine—that would synthesize millions of fingerprints, handprints, and retinal characteristics and fool any biometric authentication.

"Every fingerprint is unique," she had explained, "but the attributes stored in biometric systems are not. They can't be. There are constant daily micro-changes in every print. Scratches, burns, cuts. Scanners detune themselves to be less accurate, or they would never find matches."

Kali had reverse-engineered the software, built her own reader hardware with spare parts scavenged from around Janus, and used both to study the biodata and cryptography on several radio-frequency ID cards. She explained to Carmody that there were different RFID platforms and encoding formats, but most used the same standard for tags.

He got lost right about there. Which was okay. He hadn't cared about the technical ins and outs of the thing. He still didn't. He just needed to know it would work.

He waited another ten seconds that felt much longer.

"American…what will you do to me?"

Carmody kept his eyes on the screen. It was Clinia from Cluj, behind him. An unwanted distraction right now. He told himself not to waste a second answering her.

"American, please. What will you do?"

He told himself again not to answer.

"You should've probably asked your friend that question," he answered with a backward glance.

She looked at him, her eyes red from crying. "I am afraid."

"I said we wouldn't hurt you."

"No. Afraid of *them*."

Carmody was silent. He understood her fear. She would be in trouble if the Wolf's men suspected she had cooperated with him. Maybe she'd liked flirting with the danger those people represented. Maybe it was an edgy lure. But he knew what they would do if they felt betrayed. And so did she. Or at least she had an inkling. Suddenly her thrill ride wasn't fun anymore.

He snapped his gaze to the almost indiscernible seams where the trapdoor was set flush with the floor, camouflaged so it almost completely disappeared against its surface. It had been over a minute since the snoofer blew through its first binary sequences. Going on a minute and a half. And waiting wasn't his strong suit under any circumstances.

He was about to consider alternatives to the trapdoor when the wearable beeped. A coded binary tag was highlighted in green on the display. The snoofer had identified a protocol for the nearest source of common IoT radio emissions—the trapdoor—then searched its database for a range of possible key tags to activate its controller. Right now the app was like somebody standing outside a door with a huge clutch of keys, knowing one of them would fit its lock...just not which one. But while a person with a hundred physical keys might take as many minutes to test them all, Kali had claimed the snoofer could try fifty thousand possible digital keys in two seconds maximum.

It only needed one second to find a match, beating her outside estimate by more than half. Car-

mody saw a hinged square panel lift from the floor
to reveal a flight of descending stairs.

He stepped over to the opening and reached down
for the handrail. Then he motioned to Wheeler and
Begai and called Schultz and Sparrow from the ante-
room over the RoIP. They stacked up behind him
and waited as he lowered himself into the entryway
and his booted feet found the stairs. He was already
several steps down, his head and shoulders barely
above the floor, when he glanced back at Clinia.
She hadn't budged from the chair. It was as if some
inertial force had settled over her.

"Did you come in through the Great Hall?" he
asked.

"Yes."

"Wait down there, and I'll come back for you."

She looked at him. He wasn't sure if what he saw
on her face was hope, relief, or both. It was an expression understandably restrained by skepticism.
She had already gotten burned once tonight.

"I will wait," she said.

Carmody nodded and flipped down his goggles.
A moment later he was gone, racing downstairs,
his men pouring through the trapdoor behind him.

"Faye, I just saw three vehicles shoot right out
of the ground." Cobb enlarged a sector of the topo
map on *Raven*'s cabin-wide touch-screen window.
"They must be kidding."

Luna glanced over from the pilot's seat. Their
aircraft was hovering at a height of 6,000 feet, close
to its ceiling in this bad weather. It was a non-
stop battle keeping it on its sweet spot through the

strong, shifting winds and extreme fluctuations in atmospheric pressure.

She rolled her neck to loosen a crick. "Everybody's a James-freaking-Bond wannabe," she said. "Bring us up to max zoom. With coordinates."

Cobb spread the screen wider. Their SPDD's intelligent, multispectral imaging not only provided crystal-clear video through a seemingly impenetrable curtain of snow between them and the earth, it gave it in perfect high-def color, using an object's heat emissions and light-wave reflectivity to fill in the visual gaps of what the heavy snow conditions blurred out.

The flame-red car Cobb had just seen emerge from the grass beyond the estate's rear gate was streaking northeast toward the Ukrainian international border, beyond which Quickdraw had no license to operate. The two black vehicles—SUVs judging by their large, boxier shapes—were still within the borders of the estate, driving off in opposite directions, east and west.

"Check out the car," he said, reading his digital speedometer. "Baby's juiced."

Luna nodded. It had shot from zero to a hundred in under six seconds. Nobody on the ground was catching up to it. Not without an assist.

"Carmody needs to know," she said. "Patch him in."

Old slowpoke me, Cobb thought.

"On it," he said.

Carmody was almost at the bottom of the stairs when he heard Cobb's voice over the comlink. "Preacher, do you read me?"

"Yeah."

"We have three FMVs."

"Pictures?"

"Stand by."

A second later, Carmody saw a tiny streaming video image appear at the upper right-hand corner of his goggles' display.

"You run a vehicle recognition?" he asked.

"Affirmative," Cobb said. "The black wagons are Rezvanis. Red's a Koenigsegg Regera. Twin turbo, fifteen hundred horses. The electric motors give it instantaneous power off the line. Like lightning. And it's already outside the grounds. Bearing north, number four-two road."

"I need you to stop it," Carmody said.

"What?"

"Stop the car and turn it around. Can you?"

"I think so. But we don't have the legal auth—"

"Just do it. Inform Duchess. We'll need her to run cover."

Carmody descended the final few steps and saw a hallway or tunnel winding out ahead of him. A vaulted ceiling, ancient masonry walls, cool white LED droplight panels on overhead suspender cables. His men following close behind, he ran down the passage at a hurried trot.

A few paces in, an arched entryway on his left opened to a deep, brick-wall chamber. He motioned to Wheeler, Begai, and Sparrow, tapped his middle and index fingers to his eyes, and extended both toward the arch. The three men broke away and sprinted through it.

Then Cobb was in his ear again. "The sports

car's practically screaming for us to chase it, sir. What if it's a deke and the target's in one of those Rezvanis?"

Carmody paused a beat.

"That's what they expect us to think," he said. "Think what they *don't* expect. Those wagons are the decoys. He's in the Regera. Bet on it."

The Regera's tires bit deep into the snow, grabbing it up and spitting it back in white clumps and wads. Glancing into his rearview mirror, its driver saw the castle grounds recede into blurry oblivion behind a curtain of windblown flakes. As he sliced past the 180–miles per hour mark, a rapid surge of g-forces whumped the breath from his lungs. The car hummed and pulsed with turbocharged power and acceleration. He felt at the razor's edge of control.

Three miles north of the castle grounds, he came up to the crossroads—its left leg running off into the western Transylvanian foothills, the right toward Satu Mare proper, the snow-dusted blacktop ahead stretching through miles of empty hayfields and scattered woods toward the borderlands.

He shot forward, staying on the main road, optimistic he could reach the nation's outer margins in an hour. As long as the storm didn't worsen. An hour, ninety minutes at the outside. There he would weave his way west and south along the lonely, zigzagging line between his country and Ukraine, eventually turning down through Moldova to the Crimean Peninsula. Even with occasional rest stops, and the weather potentially creating obstacles, he estimated it would take under a day to reach the secret city.

At Okean-27, he would be safe. Untouchable. Reunited with Drajan Petrovik, the man whose role he'd played to perfection at the Wolf's Lair. Lured to it by a perfectly conceived and executed charade—a plan of genius, really—the Americans responsible for the problems and disruptions of the past four months had been deceived into thinking he was the Wolf himself. They would stay close behind. But they wouldn't dare follow him onto Russian federal territory.

Besides, they were about to find themselves with more pressing concerns.

Gustav Zolcu drove on. It seemed ages since he, Drajan and their boyhood friend Emil had done their first hacks. Small-time scams—wire fraud, identity theft, stolen test answers. But the three of them were the nucleus of the *technologie vampiri*. The core group of what was now a vast global operation. Though Zolcu supposed he could include Emil's sister Stella, who had seemed peripheral back then but would become instrumental to last summer's strike at America.

He toed the gas pedal a little farther down and the car responded with a quiet, purring sigh.

Which somehow reminded him of Clinia. He wished he hadn't been forced to cut her loose so soon and get out so fast tonight, but he felt no regrets. Everything had been calculated. Everything was part of the setup. His time in Romania was at an end. There were new worlds to conquer.

He whipped past a derelict farmhouse on his left, the car's traction controls keeping it perfectly stable even at his extreme high speed. There were no lights in the windows, no lights anywhere. The blackout was still eerily complete. With the trees around him flocked with snow and the road pitch-black except for his headlights pushing out ahead and nothing else in sight, it was almost as if he was speeding through an abandoned movie set. A replica countryside unspooling on both sides and behind him.

New and better worlds were ahead. Time to say goodbye to the old.

Glancing into his mirror as if to confirm it was all behind him, Zolcu sped on north through the cold, wind, and snow.

In *Raven*'s cockpit, Luna and Cobb saw the Regera go streaking past the spot where the road divided, the imagery beamed to their HUDs from the Sentinel drone flying out beyond the fork.

"Ready and set," Cobb said in the gunner's seat.

For him this was fun time. He did not intend to hit a moving object. This was, moreover, not a strike against a building standing in proximity to other buildings and innocent civilians, a situation where he wanted to avoid collateral damage. His target was a section of deserted country road in the middle of a remote nowhere. Nothing else around for miles. No other factors to consider. Not even snowplows.

Luna nodded as he got a radar lock on the segment of road they were about to blow. She had based their choice of a target on a single criterion. Actually, a criterion and subcriterion. The criterion was that it lay between the Regera and the next possible turnoff, which would severely limit its driver's options. The subcriterion was that it was far enough ahead of the driver for them to demolish it without injuring him. There were questions only he could answer about the strike on New York, among many other things. Carmody wanted him bagged and out of the country in one piece.

"Go!" she said from the pilot's station.

Cobb gripped the fire-control handle. His HUD's radar overlay showed multiple sets of targeting coordinates, all of which the AI was repeating in his ear. He could have released the Hellfire III with a virtual button on the cabin-wide touch screen. He could have done it with a verbal command, giving the AI a mission-specific firing code. But he was a certified Army sniper and preferred the tactile reassurance of a physical trigger.

He pressed the button to initiate the missile's launch sequence. A millisecond later, its solid propellant fuel ignited, the gases produced by its rapid burn generating five hundred pounds of thrust.

Cobb and Luna both felt *Raven* shudder from nose to tail as the Hellfire III shot from its rail, hissing off toward their target at Mach 13, a fiery plume of exhaust trailing behind it into the night.

At Mach 13, a missile was traveling about a thousand miles per hour, a hypersonic velocity many times exceeding the speed of sound. The section of road Luna and Cobb had tagged for destruction was a half mile to their north.

The Hellfire III took 1.8 seconds to reach it. Two blinks of their eyes.

At launch, the Regera was roughly midway between Cobb and his target, therefore midway between the Hellfire and its designated target. And while the car was streaking forward at a hundred thirty miles per hour, which was extremely fast for a vehicle on the ground, it might as well have been standing still relative to the missile.

Gustav Zolcu never heard it pass overhead. Its contours were designed to avoid creating a loud sonic boom, and the whooshing roar of its rocket engine would take a while to reach him. In fact, he never glimpsed its brilliant exhaust trail scratching through the clouds. Nine-tenths of a second after its launch, a single blink of his eyes, the missile soared over and past him and then slammed into the road a quarter of a mile to the north.

The initial flash of the explosion took a spherical shape, like ball lightning. Momentarily blinded, Zolcu felt the entire car shake. The column of flame that rose at the point of impact looked like a blazing arm punching up through the ground. The road there was completely obliterated in the detonation, leaving a ten-foot crater that stretched from one embankment to the other. The asphalt at the edges of the crater broke into sizzling black chunks of pitch that spattered the trunks and branches of the roadside trees and clung, gummy and burning, to their dry outer bark. Many trees were incinerated as pressurized, superheated air washed over them. Others ignited more slowly, blisters of hot sap popping and sizzling on their trunks as the fiery globs of road material lit them up like torches.

Stunned, Zolcu hit his brake pedal hard. The Regera's tremendous horsepower was directed from its V-8 engine to two electric-drive motors mounted over its rear tires. At his rate of speed, the enormous torque generated by a short stop would have sent almost any other car into a forward rollover, the stresses on its frame instantly making it crack up. But its robotic stabilizer system kept it intact with all four wheels to the road.

The blast crater's rim still sixty feet in front of him, Zolcu came to a halt and stared silently out at a solid, pulsating wall of flame.

"Cacar in palarie," he swore under his breath. "Shit in a hat."

In *Raven*'s cockpit, Cobb glanced over at Luna. "Bull's-eye," he said.

A full minute after the blast, Zolcu was still staring out into the conflagration. The snow had gotten lighter, at least for now, but he kept his windshield wiper on to bat off the persistent flurries. What had just happened here? His first thought was that he'd tripped a mine, but the detonation must have occurred twenty yards up the road from him. A mine wouldn't be planted so far ahead of its intended target.

No, he decided at once. It wasn't a mine. A planted explosive would have been set to go off directly beneath his car. More importantly, how could anyone have predicted he would be driving this road? This was no random hit.

He took a deep breath. The wall of flames throbbed and crackled up ahead. Could it have been a rocket strike? He didn't think it all that far-fetched. A shoulder-launched rocket or even a missile fired from a drone seemed possible, even plausible, given who he believed was behind tonight's raid.

The Americans would have the resources and the balls. And there were certainly precedents for it. Like when they hit the Iranian general in Baghdad. Soleimani had not been the first. Nor would he be the last.

He stared into the fire and considered that a minute. The more he thought about it, the surer he became it was a missile. In which case he might have gotten very lucky. Even the most accurate ones could be off by a few yards in poor weather; it could have been a near miss. Then again, maybe the strike hadn't been *meant* to take him out. Say their primary intention was his capture, and their target was the roadway in front of him. With the northbound road impassable, he would have no recourse but to double back toward the castle. Or otherwise abandon the car and set out on foot. But he wouldn't get far. There was nothing around for miles in either direction. Nothing but deep woods and empty fields. He would freeze to death in the snow and darkness. He knew it. His enemies knew it. They wouldn't expect him to try it.

Their goal, then, was to turn him around. It had to be. That would send him right into their hands.

Unless…

Lifting his foot off the brake, he shifted into Reverse, turned his wheel sharply to the right, backed onto the gravel shoulder, and spun around toward the crossroads he'd left some miles behind him. He needed to reach it before his pursuers. He had no idea how close to it they might be, but he would soon find out. Getting there first was his only chance.

If this had turned into a race, he was driving the right car for it and had no intention of betting against himself.

* * *

Carmody stood a couple of paces inside the garage, Schultz to his left with his gun at the ready, covering the door. The snoofer had gotten them through without any problems.

The silent underground space was probably half-empty. Carmody saw a Mercedes SUV, a Rolls… and two motorcycles leaning on their kickstands somewhat apart from the four-wheeled vehicles.

He stared at them, his eyes very still behind his goggles. They were identical Kawasaki Ninja H2Rs. Onyx-black shiny metallic finish. Supposedly the fastest bikes in the world.

His molars clicked.

His and hers. Charming.

"Pickles," he said into his headset. "Rover One."

The AI opened a channel to Dixon's BearCat.

Kali had seen people die violently before, seen her own parents murdered when she was only a girl of nine, and she knew Dixon was right. Emerick didn't have long.

Crouched between the two front seats, facing the BearCat's crew compartment, she realized at a glance that he was in seizure, his back on the metal floor, his right arm and leg thrashing as if flooded with voltage. Though the men had elevated his feet under a rolled up field jacket, they seemed undecided about whether or not to restrain him. They didn't want him to suffer the indignity of the paroxysms, but they also didn't want to make his pain any worse.

She shuffled toward him on the balls of her feet, swaying with the vehicle's rapid motion. The dressing Jimmy Singh had applied to his head and jaw, a loose cravat, was already soaked through with blood, and she saw a runny red puddle on the floor under the bandages. At the back of his head, the wrapping had been sucked in and wadded up like a saturated paper towel. It explained why they hadn't lifted him onto one of the stretchers that were anchored, flat and unused, against the side of the vehicle. Nothing was left of his skull there. It was entirely blown away. If they had tried moving him, his brain would have spilled out of the wound.

The Cat shifted suddenly to the right, and something rolled against the side of her boot—a discarded auto-injector. She scanned the label and nodded to herself. Ketamine: good, better than morphine. The drug was a bronchodilator as well as a painkiller. It would make it easier for him to breathe and was less likely to deepen his trauma.

Jimmy Singh was kneeling over him, bracing his head gently between his hands to steady it against the vehicle's jerky side-to-side movement. He saw Kali edging closer and nodded. She nodded back. Jimmy was among the few people at base she had allowed herself to become friendly with in the past four months. She had been on one of her predawn walks when she first saw him doing his yogic asanas out in the field behind headquarters, facing east toward the sunrise in the traditional manner. They had soon started doing their morning practices together.

Now their eyes connected over Emerick. His spasms were worse, his heel rhythmically banging against the vehicle's floor.

"Let me help," she said.

Jimmy nodded. No hesitation.

Kali moved up closer to Emerick. *Bang-bang bang bangbang.* Spencer was kneeling over his lower half, a medal clenched in his fist. Each time the dying man thrashed he started a little, as if they were joined on a string.

"I need you hold him steady," she said.

Spencer nodded, let his medal fall over his shirt, and placed both hands on Emerick's right ankle. Pushing it down as gently as he could manage, he succeeded in restraining him.

Kali unlaced his combat boots, tugged off his right, then his left. She reached into her jacket for a Swiss Army knife, cut the right pants leg up along its inner seam to his thigh, and tore it away from him. Bending over him, she put her left thumb over a point below his kneecap, then placed her right index and pointer fingers an inch to the outside of the femur.

His leg jerked and twitched. Spencer held it down. Kali gave him a small nod of encouragement and applied direct, even pressure with her fingertips, slowly increasing it, concentrating on the slight pulsations under Emerick's skin. She couldn't let the vehicle's rocking and swaying affect her. She needed to be focused and precise.

After fifteen seconds she felt the leg start to relax. It was as if hard little knots of tension were dissolving under her fingertips. But Emerick's hands were still clutching at the air, and she could see reddish-blue blotches on his knees. His heart was no longer pumping adequate blood to his extremities. She had more to do, and quickly.

She looked at Spencer.

"You'll have to take over for me," she said.

He stared at her. "I'm not sure I can."

"This isn't magic. I promise."

He looked down at Emerick. After a beat of silence, he raised his eyes back to hers. "All right," he said. "Show me."

She motioned with her chin. "Put your hand next to mine. Position your fingers like this. See?"

"Think so...yeah."

"Good. Now we switch. On my nod."

"Okay."

Kali allowed another second, nodded. She watched as his fingers replaced hers on Emerick's leg.

"Keep them on the points," she said. "Don't turn them. Count to thirty, increase the pressure, decrease it. Then repeat."

He glanced up at her face. "Got you."

Kali edged farther toward the rear hatch. Emerick's blood was all over the floor, his uniform everywhere. Still crouched over him, Jimmy Singh was holding his head between his hands. They were smeared red.

"Open his vest," she said. "His shirt. Hurry."

Singh nodded. Keeping Emerick's head in a stable position, he gestured for one of the other troopers—an E9 named Jamal Carter—to open the zippers, clasps, and straps of the dying man's uniform.

Kali leaned in. She put a hand on his bare chest below the rib cage and felt a wiry, shivering tension. He was in pain despite the ketamine shot.

Then Dixon, over the crew radio: "Kali, we're out of time!"

Before she could reply, automatic fire rattled outside the BearCat, and it hauled forward with a jolt, its engine roaring like a jet plane. Emerick let out a long, deep moan, his spine arching up off the metal floor. His lips were blue, his mouth wide open. He was panting rapidly. Shallow, explosive breaths. It didn't resemble normal respiration, because it wasn't. His autonomic nervous system had taken control of his vital functions even as they shut down.

Kali steadied herself against the vehicle's acceleration. She looked down into Emerick's eyes, and they stared back at her, wide and glassy and barely present. But she saw the fear in them. Whatever shred of awareness he still clung to, he was terribly afraid.

She couldn't save him. She knew that. But she could ease his way.

Kali spread her fingers over his abdomen, placing one on each of the five points running in a vertical line between the ribs and navel. She applied pressure and leaned closer, feeling the absolute calm that had come upon her at certain moments nearly all of her life. It was neither inside nor outside her, a space without interiority or exteriority.

Long seconds passed. Emerick gasped, a deep, slow breath, different from the rhythmic panting. Kali slid her left hand down off his forehead and took hold of his hand. Its fingers were cold, weak and rubbery. He gasped again, pulling in air. She brought her lips close to the blood-soaked bandages around his head and whispered to him.

There were more shots outside. Kali was peripherally aware of them as the BearCat rumbled along at high speed. She stayed focused on Emerick, whispering, holding his left hand in hers, pressing the points beneath his ribs with the fingers of her opposite one. He breathed again and raised his head. Jimmy Singh cradled it in his hands, and blood and lumps of pale gray brain tissue spilled out into them. He looked at Kali, his dripping hands under the back of Emerick's head, holding it up off the metal floor.

After a moment the dying man sighed—a long, quiet expulsion of air from deep inside his chest. Then he shuddered softly, and his head sank back down in Singh's hands, and everything went out of him.

Kali glanced at Singh and turned toward the front of the vehicle, nodding at Spencer as she scrambled past him into her seat.

The BearCat was still rolling fast.

"Emerick?" Dixon said from behind the wheel.

"He's gone."

He nodded, staring straight ahead. "We have a change of plans," he said. "The target's slipped off."

"Where is he?"

"In a car heading east. That's all I know. Except for one more thing."

"What?"

She silently listened to his answer.

Matei could feel the tension crackling off his men as he hastily gave his instructions. They were professional security personnel, fifteen of his best, and had been elite soldiers in one army or another before going private. Coiled tight in their readiness for action, armed to the teeth, they already knew what to do. They were prepared. But he was in charge. So they listened to him. Or pretended to listen.

He knew how they thought, knew well, because he was very much the same.

The monitoring station where he'd assembled the men could be reached in two ways. From above, one would simply take the stairs behind a false wall panel in the castle's Grand Hall. The twistier route led through the cellars and then through a door disguised to look like part of a regular wall made of gray masonry. In each case, Drajan Petrovik had chosen to leave the original mechanisms, restoring them to pristine working condition rather than replacing them with electronics. Out of respect, he said, for their ingenious design—and their wily designer, Graguscu the Poisoner.

But Matei suspected Drajan had another unstated reason. This was his seat of operations. Or current seat. The Wolf had many properties here in Satu Mare. Many lairs. Respect for a long-dead count would not factor into his security considerations. When had he shown respect for anyone of aristocratic stature? A master hacker, he knew any electronic security system could be penetrated by another system. As the embarrassing fiasco in Bucharest had proven last summer. It would not surprise Matei to learn that the Wolf had grown to mistrust the sophisticated tools of his own trade and ultimately put greater stock in creaking counterweights, pulleys, and hinges.

That sort of speculation could wait, however. Even as Matei gave his orders, he was keeping a close eye on the video wall to his left and plotting his next moves. Because of his size, people assumed he was slow and dull, a large blunt-force instrument, and he was fine with it. Let his enemies have that impression. Let them underestimate him. It gave him a tactical advantage.

The video wall consisted of twelve sixty-inch high-definition flat-panels, four rows of four, extending from floor to ceiling so its images were easily seen from anywhere in the room, including the presently vacant computer stations along its three other walls. Each of its panels could give multiple views of the castle and its grounds. It was like a huge compound eye.

One section of the display showed the intruders that had gained access to the underground garage. Another showed the group that had splintered off from them. The remaining screens provided views from cameras everywhere around the grounds. These could be automatically displayed through preset sequences or switched over to an operator's control.

Matei saw the two speeding Rezvanis on the east and west access roads. He saw the armored vehicles in which the intruders had crashed through the front gate. He saw the girl that had come down from the tower room, and he saw the American posted outside what was left of the gate, standing guard with his gigantic shaggy brute of a dog. Interiors, exteriors, everywhere the wall was a moving mosaic of video imagery.

"Okay," he said. He looked at one of the men, Krask, a thick-bearded former Spetsnaz operator with a portrait tattoo of Vladimir Putin on his neck. The radiance from the monitors made it look almost phosphorescent. "Are you clear on your instructions?"

"Yes."

Matei's eyes went from one man to the other.

"And the rest of you?"

Brisk nods from all of them. Probably they were just glad he was nearly finished talking.

"Let's do our job," he said.

They hefted their rifles against their sides and fell in line behind him. But Matei was not yet through giving orders. As he led the group up the short passage to the wall panel, he radioed the Rezvani on the east drive over his headset. He was certain of what the bastards in the garage were up to and wanted to arrange a little surprise for them.

At the false wall, Matei turned and reached for one of two stone posts in front of it. The wall slid back on unseen tracks, opening up a passageway that ran on straight ahead through the dimness for several yards before bifurcating like the tongue of a snake. At the split, the group broke into two teams, Krask racing off to the left with his group, and Matei veering to the right with his, leading them down the corridor at a full run.

One hell of a night, he thought. And it wasn't even close to being over.

The immense torture chamber of Count Graguscu smelled of dampness, mold, and infused mineral deposits. Long gone were the breast rippers, *cavaletto*, and Judas cradle with which the count once inflicted horrific pain on the wives, lovers, and many others he suspected of a thousand different betrayals. Gone too were the rack, breaking wheel, and thumbscrews he had used to extract confessions from his accused enemies. But there were still thick, rusty chains of indeterminate age hanging from the high, vaulted ceiling, and round iron gratings on the floor still covered the entrances to three deep cells, or oubliettes, where prisoners were once left to rot at the old aristocrat's suspicious whims. Scabbed with whitish deposits of sediment, the chamber walls were originally done in rough-hewn granite. But if Wheeler's information was right, not all *were* original, and some weren't actually walls.

The question for him was only which were which?

He pressed his Wally through-the-wall-sensor device against the chamber's stone side like a doctor holding a stethoscope to a patient's chest. He'd picked the wall to his right going through the archway, only because he needed to start somewhere. But he could just as well have started on the left. Back at Janus, Carmody had insisted that the inside of their castle mock-up be rearranged before each mission rehearsal. Walls, corners, halls, and stairways were repeatedly moved from one place to another. The interior layout of the real place had loomed as a dangerous unknown, and he hadn't wanted the men getting false ideas of what to expect. If a member of the team thought for a moment that something was where it wasn't or wasn't where it was, he could get himself and his teammates killed for a simple misstep.

Wheeler stayed very still, aware even a small slip of his hand could throw his results out of whack. Resembling a tablet computer with two nubby antennae, the device transmitted and read a wide cone of radar pulses in the one-to-ten gigahertz frequency range—bands that could penetrate wood, glass, and concrete barriers and were sensitive enough to pick up the slightest motion, the softest intake of breath, even the presence of a breeze or buzzing fly on the other side of the wall. Wheeler knew the unit had certain limitations. Its Doppler pulses couldn't penetrate walls more than a foot thick. Nor could they pass through sheet metal. But they hadn't used steel construction in walls this old, and running into it would be its own kind of giveaway, a sign of some later renovation.

He checked the Wally's readout screen, suppressing a flicker of impatience. Its scan took about a minute, and the results would display on his screen as both numeric values and Doppler imagery. Meanwhile, the two Quickdraw guys who had accompanied him into the chamber were concentrating on their own specified tasks.

E4 Begai's was to sniff for things that might blow other things to smithereens, his next-best skill to blowing things up himself.

In the middle of the cavernous room now, he stood waving a terahertz scanner that resembled the spectrographic wands used by airport-security personnel. Its T-rays inhabited the so-called terahertz gap—a bandwidth region that sounded as if it had been named by Anakin Skywalker and fell somewhere between microwaves and infrared light. Whereas TTWS pulses could travel fifty or sixty feet through most walls, terahertz beams went a bare fraction of that distance before becoming absorbed by chemicals and gases at different and differentiable rates, making the wand just right for close-range bomb detection.

Begai had entered the chamber ahead of Wheeler, leading the way with the wand, sweeping for hidden explosives that could bring the walls and ceiling— real or false, original or not—down around their heads. But the space was the size of an auditorium, and they had no way to know how much time was available to them. The Wolf's security personnel might or might not be aware they were down here. They might show at any moment or not at all. That uncertainty put pressure on Wheeler and Begai to make haste, but they were also being careful not to make mistakes. The trick was just to stay focused on the job that had to be done.

It was up to Sparrow to provide his teammates with cover. Wearing a balaclava sewn with the patterns and colors of his ancestral Seminole war paint, he stood facing the archway with his back to them, his rifle pointed out toward the curving passage they had just come from. Handpicked for the mission by Carmody, he was good at handling firearms of every type, and no wonder. His father ran a firing range on the Big Cypress Reservation near Lake Okeechobee, and while other kids were shooting hoops in the high-school gym, Sparrow had been shooting at silhouette targets and eventually beating seasoned three-point aces in local tournaments.

Now he carried a pair of his personal firearms in addition to Quickdraw's standard-issue MP7. Specifically, an Mk 12 SPR designated-marksman rifle in a back sling, and a side-holstered Glock 34 pistol. Both were combat modified.

"This room's clean," he heard Begai report to Wheeler. "I didn't pick up any traces."

Wheeler grunted in acknowledgment. It was a distinct positive to know the floor wouldn't blow up underfoot. But he also had yet to find evidence that the rock walls were anything but walls and that the Wolf's computer room was in fact where Carmody's top-secret intel source indicated it was.

He went deeper into the shadowy chamber, stopping every few feet to hold the TTWS unit up to the wall, waiting the requisite sixty seconds for each reading.

"Sparrow?" he said and glanced over his shoulder at him. "How's the passage?"

"All quiet, sir."

Wheeler grunted again and kept scanning. The wall was fairly straight. The room more or less rectangular. *Clean and quiet.* It seemed too good to be true. He couldn't help wondering about the complete absence of guards.

He reached the end of the wall and started on the rear of the chamber. After a minute, Begai joined him. They had gone about halfway along the width of the rear wall when he noticed Wheeler looking at his Wally's display with perked interest.

"Find something?" he asked.

Wheeler held up his free hand in a wait-a-second gesture. His attention went from the screen to the wall.

"Something, yeah," he repeated vaguely and ran his eyes over the stones. The radar wasn't picking up any objects behind the wall. It wasn't finding any people, either. Only space. A whole lot of space.

And what seemed to be breezes.

"I don't see normal dimensions for a room here," he went on. "It's like…I dunno…like the other side isn't just empty. More like it's big and *hollow*."

Begai didn't know what to make of that. He watched Wheeler fiddle with his unit's controls, checking and rechecking its readings.

After a long minute, Wheeler shoved the Wally into its harness pocket and slipped a Maglite out of a leather holster on his belt. He shone it on the wall in front of him, gliding its beam over its bulges and cracks, probing with his gloved fingers. His hand went to a seam between two large irregular stones. Then went to the stone itself.

He pressed one of them with three fingertips. Nothing happened. He slid his hand onto the stone on the opposite side of the seam. Pressed again. And felt it give slightly under his touch.

"What the hell's going on?" Begai said beside him.

Wheeler didn't answer. He pressed the stone harder, and it gave some more. A moment later there was a grinding noise, a shifting of weight, and the wall to his right moved outward.

Begai took a reflexive step back. "It's a door," he said, answering his own question. "A God almighty door."

They were both silent. The stack of rocks that composed the moving section of wall was rotating on a central axis. Begai thought crazily about the *Hardy Boys* mysteries his grandfather had kept dustily boxed away in his attic on the reservation.

Within seconds, the pile of stones had swiveled perpendicular to the rest of the wall, creating openings on its left and right. Each was large enough for one person to enter at a time.

Wheeler hoisted his carbine, slipped cautiously through one of the openings, and sucked in a breath of damp air. His mouth a wide, amazed O under his balaclava, he glanced back over his shoulder at Begai.

"You'll want to see this with your own eyes," he said.

Begai slid through the door, came up next to Wheeler, and stopped cold.

"Whoa," he said. "What is this place?"

Wheeler shook his head. He was at a complete loss. They were on a circular ledge, actually the rim of what looked like a huge cylindrical well shaft, its mouth thirty or forty feet in diameter. The cellar's vaulted ceiling rose high above them. The surface of the rim underfoot was fairly level and flat, the stones worn and smooth. A couple of yards to their right, it curved down into a sort of channel that resembled a water sluice, then ran another few feet counterclockwise to a helical staircase. The stairs wound along the walls of the shaft, descending through a continuous series of arches supported by narrow, carved piers.

Wheeler aimed his Maglite into the mouth of the well but realized he wouldn't need it. There was a soft, cool, diffuse radiance coming from under the arches. Electric lighting. Probably LED panels.

He guessed the shaft plunged two or three hundred feet into the ground, the stairs and arcade running all the way to its bottom. The walls were mortared stone. The arcade was mortared stone. The columns and stairs and landings were mortared stone. All their surfaces were patchy with moss. Except for the stairs. The stairs looked clear and clean.

Wheeler had noticed that the bottom of the shaft had a smaller circumference than its mouth. Looking straight down into the well shaft was like peering into the wide end of a funnel. The floor was tiled and had a faded red symbol in the center. He recognized it at once. As a CIA man, he should have.

It was a compass rose—this version with four triangular arrows pointed in the cardinal directions.

"Do you see what I see?" Begai peered into the well. "We hit the jackpot."

Wheeler grunted his acknowledgment. The kid reminded him of the guys on his old SFOD-D unit. No fear, no low gear, everything full speed ahead. But he was right. They had found what they came for. There was a computer workstation on each arrow of the rose. Setups like the ones used by floor traders in stock exchanges. Or by serious hackers. Horseshoe desks with multiple terminals, multipanel flat-screen display rigs and freestanding acoustic partitions.

No one was at the stations. The desk surfaces were bare. The monitors were all dark.

Wheeler felt inclined to hurry up and grab whatever he could out of the computers. But he also wanted to know more about what the hell he and Begai might be getting into down there.

He suddenly visualized Carmody outside the tower room, asking Pickles to identify the dragon crest hung above the armor and weapons. During their haunted-house mission rehearsals at Janus, the boss had stressed thinking of the AI as a full-fledged teammate. He might have trouble typing on a keyboard with his big, clunky fingers but he was good at utilizing technology. Wheeler figured it was time to get with the program.

He looked straight down into the shaft.

"Pickles, tell me what I'm seeing," he said. Then, using Begai's call name, "Patch in Four-Boxer, proximate data sharing."

The AI synched their helmet terminals, accessed Wheeler's helmet camera, and tracked the position of his head and eyes to determine where he was looking. It took just three seconds to run a successful image recognition and project its findings onto their HUDs.

Initiation well. Circa 11th century CE. Cross-reference: Inverted Tower of Sintra, Quinta da Regaleira, Portugal. Origin: Order of Knights Templar.

Wheeler exhaled heavily. *Knights Templar.* They were way, way through the looking glass here.

He stayed put another moment, studying the bottom of the well. There were more arches around the rose, one at each of the four cardinal points.

"Pickles, zoom in," he said.

The AI tracked and zoomed. Each arch framed a wooden door with steel bands and rivets and hardware that looked exactly like the one Begai had blown up on the rampart.

"Can you tell me what's behind the doors?"

The Sintra comparison suggests a high likelihood of radial passages. No other data is available.

Which wasn't good. Once they were down at the bottom, he and Begai would be surrounded. By those doors, and the passages behind them, and potentially anyone laying an ambush inside the passages.

But the computers were why they had come this far. They couldn't access them from where they were right now. They had to go down there.

He looked over at Begai. "Give me a minute," he said.

He turned back toward the rotating door and stepped through to the chamber where Sparrow was standing lookout. He didn't like leaving him. But there was no getting around it.

"Stand your post," he said and quickly explained what he'd found on the other side of the door. "Keep your eyes open. We won't take long. Signal us if you get a whiff of anyone getting close."

Sparrow nodded.

"Questions?" Wheeler said.

"Only one, sir. What if they don't come at you from up here?" He pointed at the door opening with his chin. "What if they come from down there?"

"Then listen for my orders. If you don't hear from me, get out of this hellhole."

Sparrow was silent.

"Don't be a hero," Wheeler said a bit more firmly. "Okay?"

Sparrow looked reluctant. But he was, above all, a soldier.

"Yes, sir," he said.

Wheeler clapped him on the shoulder. Then he turned and hurried back to the well.

9

Mario Perez hunkered with Laura Cruz in the cramped darkness of the freezer chest, his ear pressed to its sidewall, listening carefully to the hedgehog's swift approach. It was returning from the far end of the row of Quonsets and sounded like it had almost reached the alley between Laura's hut and the one next to it.

This would be its third probe in exactly twenty minutes. Mario had timed its comings and goings with his smart watch; he wasn't sure why, not altogether, but he thought that might turn out to be important.

He heard the robot swing around into the alley. There wasn't much here for it to inspect—the hobbled bicycle, the trash bin, the kitchen chairs, and the discarded freezer where he and Laura were hiding out. That was all. Even so, it had returned twice after prowling off down the line of huts.

Searching.

Searching for *them*.

He kept an eye on his watch. Fifteen seconds passed. Thirty. The 'hog was theoretically designed for stealthy surveillance, but in reality it was a big, wide, heavy contraption with a lot of moving components, and the alley was a tight squeeze. If somebody knew what to listen for, it was easy to picture its movements out there.

Mario knew. He could hear the metallic clatter of the 'hog tilting the trash bin for a third inspection. He could hear it lifting the bike from against the side of the hut to search behind it. He could hear the click of metal bearings, the hum of servos and battery-powered drives, the high-pitched whine of torque manipulators, the soft slide of its pincer arm extending and retracting, and the crackle of its treads rolling over the frigid, snow-covered ground. He could hear the combined, complementary actions of its different mechanical parts and visualize the 'hog probing, testing, and identifying the objects around it.

Whirrr. Click. Whirrrrrrrrr.

He checked the time again. Almost two minutes had ticked by. Beside him, Laura sat with her hand protectively covering the small lump in her peacoat that was Buttons the cat. She had tucked him under its front flap to keep him calm, and so far it had worked. He was still and quiet. Mario hoped to God he stayed that way.

Two minutes now. He heard a clattering racket outside. The 'hog moving the trash bin around again. Inside the chest, meanwhile, it was getting very warm, very fast. Laura's breathing had become arduous, and that wasn't good. Mario also felt the lack of air.

He listened and waited and thought. Sweat trickled down his forehead. The 'hog kept searching. It stopped and started, edged this way and that, circled, advanced, backtracked, about-faced...

There was a sudden, loud knock against the freezer. The 'hog had bumped it hard, possibly an accidental collision, hitting the outside of the metal panel Mario was leaning on. He felt it quiver against his cheek, felt Laura tense against him, and glanced over at her without turning his head— a hard, quick flick of his eyes that cautioned her not to move or make a sound.

She stared back at him. Her face was barely two inches from his own, its features pale and ghostly in the bluish radiance of his watch. He saw tension in it, and he saw fear. But he didn't see panic.

They waited together in silence, neither of them moving a muscle.

Click, sssst, click.

Twenty seconds passed.

They waited.

And then, finally, they heard the 'hog withdraw, the sounds of its mechanical functions growing fainter and fainter as it once again left the alley to range off along the row of Quonsets. Five seconds later, it was out of earshot.

Mario rolled his neck. It felt wet and slick against his collar. He tapped the screen of his watch for the digital thermometer and saw it was seventy-eight degrees. When they had first taken cover, the chest's interior was the same temperature as the night outside, cold enough to make him shiver.

Before too long the 'hog's sensors would pick up the heat differential, and they would be in serious trouble. His immediate concern, though, was the sound of Laura's breathing. She was really starting to labor. And it wasn't just Laura. So was he.

And it wasn't just them.

So was Buttons.

Mario heard the cat panting a second before Laura opened her coat to give it some air. As its head pushed up between the flaps, Mario saw in the glow of his watch that its mouth was open, its tongue lolling out and sort of trembling, like a tiny leaf.

"Do cats usually do that?" he said.

"I'm not sure." Laura stroked its head. "It doesn't seem normal."

He touched his fingers to the animal's chest and felt it rising and falling. Buttons's respiration was very fast, and he didn't think it was only because of the rising temperature. The freezer couldn't have held much oxygen to start, and they had been inside it almost thirty minutes.

Mario knew their air supply was running out. At the same time the carbon dioxide level inside the chest was steadily elevating. It was almost like being in a closed garage with the motor on. They would eventually pass out and suffocate.

"We can't stay here," he said. "We'll get carbon monoxide poisoning. Before we even use up the oxygen."

"That doesn't sound good."

"It isn't."

"How long will it take?"

"I don't know exactly," he said. "But I have an idea about how to get away."

Laura stroked the cat's head. *"Sigue,"* she whispered. "Tell me."

"The 'hog's looking for us. I think it patrols from here to the last hut, then doubles back. The timing's always about the same." He wriggled his watch. "I've kept track. Five huts. Three minutes a hut. Fifteen minutes for the full patrol. It's stuck in a behavioral loop."

"So…it's got robot OCD?"

He smiled wanly in the darkness.

"Kind of." He reached into his pocket for his JLTV's ignition fob, felt for her hand, and slipped the fob into it. "You drive, right?"

"Yes."

"Good. When the 'hog comes back, we wait. Let it snoop around. Once it leaves, we wait some more. Fifteen minutes. Till it's at that last hut."

"But what if you're wrong?"

"About?"

"The patrol. Maybe it doesn't go up the line. Just pokes around next door or something."

"I'm not wrong," he said. His chest felt heavy. Talking used up too much precious air. "Laura, please listen."

A pause. "Okay," she said. "Go on."

"When the 'hog's at the far hut, I'll jump out of here. Draw it away. It'll buy you time to get to the Jolt and drive off base."

"Wait. What about you?"

He didn't answer.

After a second, she said, "Mario, *que no*! We stay together."

"If we do, we'll all die."

"But maybe it won't come back."

"It will. In seventeen seconds."

He saw her shake her head. "How are you so sure?"

"I told you. I know. I'm a robotics specialist."

"Honestly?"

"Yeah. A systems architect. I—"

He stopped.

Whirrr. Click. Whirrrrrrrrr.

Their eyes locked in the faint glow of his watch. Mario heard Laura pull in a breath. Felt her shoulder and arm tensing against him.

The mechanical sounds grew louder outside the freezer.

The 'hog was coming back. Right on time.

The armored wagons approached front on, lights off, in a tight wedge formation.

Colonel John Howard stood in the field watching them come closer, a Puma 6x6 optionally manned fighting vehicle flanked by three four-wheeled variants, the 4x4s hanging slightly back, reminding him of muscle-bound bodyguards.

He looked over at Fernandez and Wasserman.

"We still could have people at the barracks," he said. "We do, we're pulling them out."

Fernandez glanced up from his tablet. He was thinking that nearly all the permanent structures at Janus had been built on existing foundations left by its original Romanian Land Forces occupants... and the troop-housing center was no exception. Its basement was essentially a concrete bunker like the underground sublevel at HQ—but without the cosmetic upgrades and technical frills. If they had taken cover inside it when the 'hogs hit the building, they could have found themselves trapped.

"I can get us there fast, sir," he said. "But we better roll."

Howard watched the vehicles halt about five feet in front of him. One big happy family.

He strode over to the Puma, his feet crunching into the newly fallen snow. Then he opened its right hatch and lifted himself in. As he folded slowly and stiffly into the crew seat, he realized Fernandez and Wasserman were staring at him from outside the vehicle.

"What're you two looking at?" he said.

Fernandez shook his head. "Nothing, sir."

"Then let's move."

An instant before the sergeant shut the hatch, Howard thought he heard a faint humming or buzzing noise somewhere out in the night. It was like a helicopter, high up and far off, but not so high and far it didn't arouse his curiosity. Helicopters didn't usually fly in bad weather.

He was still wondering about it when the hatch's hydraulic actuators lowered it smoothly into position, and the sound was blocked from his ears.

Windowless and sunk low in the hull, the Puma's forward crew section was a compact, steel-walled, fully functional version of the operations center that had been wiped in the headquarters explosion—for all practical purposes, a mobile command center.

Sergeant Fernandez was at the wheel, Wasserman riding shotgun. In the jump seat, Howard tried to find a position that didn't make his shoulders, arms, ribs, ass, and just about every other part of him hurt. But all the moving around just increased his discomfort, and he finally sat still and waited impatiently to get rolling.

It took less than thirty seconds. The authentication system read the unique digital token on Fernandez's wristband, prompted him to tap in his ID code, and the control panels lit up.

"Pickles," he said. "Have we got Argos online?"

"Yes. Satlink signal at ninety percent."

"Okay. Back-door into the hedgehogs. Give me visuals on their positions."

"Handshaking in progress."

Howard saw the overhead monitor light up with a realistic 3-D visualization of the base. Then the four hedgehogs—their graphic icons—appeared on-screen. Two were already outside the barracks. The others were converging on it fast from the base's northern and southern quadrants.

The Puma kicked into gear and lurched forward. Howard winced.

"I thought the robots' trackers were disabled," he said.

"They are, sir."

"But?"

"I installed Argos-shielded chips a while ago," Fernandez said. "As fail-safes." He glanced back over his shoulder at the colonel. "I took a few other precautions while I was at it. In case the 'hogs got hacked."

"And you didn't ask my permission?"

"Actually, sir, I did."

"And what'd I say?"

"That I should stop asking questions and do it," Fernandez said. "Told me you don't know what the hell I'm talking about half the time anyway."

Howard frowned but said nothing. The sergeant accelerated, the unmanned escorts hanging several feet back on his left and right flanks. The little triangular convoy continued across the field at a rapid clip until it reached the paved transverse running parallel with the southern fence. Then the two autons fell in behind the Puma, and all three rumbled west in an arrow-straight line, their wheels digging deep into the snow.

Fernandez had only driven a short distance west when he came to sudden, jarring halt. Howard and Wasserman looked at the screens.

There were at least ten people on the ground near the perimeter fence. Men and women in outdoor exercise clothes. Sweaters, mufflers, leggings, sneakers.

They were covered in blood. The clothes saturated with it.

"It's Doc Hughes," Fernandez said. His voice shook. "Her runners."

Howard snapped open his safety harness. "I'm getting out."

Fernandez tore his eyes from the windshield to glance at the base map. "Spree…the southern 'hog, it's still close by."

"I don't give a good goddamn."

Fernandez gave Wasserman a quick glance, nodded for him to take the wheel, then disengaged the hatch lock. By the time he got out of his straps, Howard was halfway outside.

The two men approached the inert bodies. Or what was left of them. They had been cut to pieces, and there was blood everywhere. It dripped wetly from the fence linkages. It seeped from their wounds in red streams and runnels. It ate away at the snow on the ground, soaking in and mingling and pooling and making the ground slippery underfoot.

Howard saw dozens of shell casings scattered around the 'hog's track marks like metal seeds. He saw Andy Benslow heaped near the fence. He saw Doug Ryder on his back, the fine white dusting of snow on his contorted face giving it the look of a plaster mask. He saw Jason Pierce and Lavonne Hughes, his mauled body partly covering hers, as if he'd tried to shield her from the gunfire. He saw one of the nurses—her name was Donna Apple.

Apple of my eye, he'd always ribbed her during his checkups, knowing she must have heard the line a thousand times. There was a soldier named Jameson who had just volunteered for Quickdraw the month before, and two civilian staffers named Brennen and Tovias. There were a few people lying on the ground who had been so badly torn apart by bullets they were unrecognizable.

The wind picked up, and the snow fell harder. Howard was barely aware of it. Then he noticed Fernandez coming up on his right with a flashlight in his hand.

"They were slaughtered," Howard said. "This was planned. All of it."

The sergeant aimed the flash at the caterpillar tracks. They ran in a continuous west-to-east line and then ended about ten feet away and doubled back on themselves. "The 'hog must've followed them here, opened fire, and turned around," he said. "Tread marks run toward the barracks, sir."

Howard turned to him, his upper lip curling back over his front teeth.

"Somebody's gonna pay," he said savagely. "I swear to you. *I will make somebody pay.*"

Fernandez felt a shiver run though him. He wasn't sure if it was the horror of what he saw on the ground, the look in Howard's eyes, or a combination of both.

"What makes you think those Argos sats can get word out without an intercept?" Howard said.

"Different reasons," said Fernandez. "They use concentrated beams—spot beams—to relay their signals. Sat to sat, sat to earth, no ground stations. There are antijamming measures. And there's Soto's firewall. I'd be amazed if they were hacked."

"Then we need to give Duchess a sitrep," Howard said. His jaw muscle worked. "Nothing we can do here. I want to get the hell over to the barracks. We'll come back for these people later."

The sergeant nodded his understanding. The living took precedence over the dead. They had to be sure there was room in the Puma for anyone they evacuated.

Howard turned toward their vehicle, took a step or two forward, then stopped. He listened, looked up, and listened some more, squinting into the windblown snow.

The buzzing in the sky again. How could he have missed it after leaving the Puma?

"You hear that?" he said.

Fernandez nodded. He was also listening closely. "Yeah," he said. "Heard it before, too."

"Back in the Heights?"

"Right, sir. Figured it for a plane."

Howard kept looking up. And he'd thought it might be a helicopter. But now it didn't seem like either. Somehow it was too...

He didn't know the right word. *Wide*, maybe.

He lifted a hand over his eyes to screen them from the snow, but it was coming down harder now, the flakes dipping and darting and spinning under his palm and between his fingers to peck coldly at his cheeks. As he stood peering into the sky, the sound seemed to first strengthen, then gradually fade out, and then strengthen again, as if whatever was up there was in a repetitive, elliptical flight pattern, with the gusty wind drowning it out at the more distant points in its trajectory.

Which explained why he hadn't heard it immediately, he thought. But he still couldn't see anything overhead.

"I don't like this, Julio," he said. "Not one bit."

They trundled back to their idling vehicle. Howard's entire body felt sore, and there was a pressure in the middle of his chest that seemed to clamp down hard around his lungs. He didn't so much sit down as spill back into his seat, breathless and dizzy, hoping the others wouldn't notice.

Up front and on the move again, Fernandez noticed.

10

Dixon thundered forward in the BearCat, the high, long-limbed trees crowding close on either side. His GPS showed Castle Graguscu several hundred yards up around a wide bend in the access road.

Carmody's idea seemed half-crazy to him. Which he supposed made it fifty percent less crazy than most of Carmody's ideas.

"We're almost there," he said to Kali. "You sure you're all right?"

"Yes. Why not?"

"Look, I've seen you in action. I know what you can do. But a man just died in your arms."

She pulled on her balaclava, leaving the bottom down under her chin.

"Everyone dies," she said. "He moved on. He wasn't afraid."

Dixon nodded. "Carmody was right."

"About?"

"The whole world wanted you locked up," Dixon said. "He knew you weren't what they said you were."

She reached into a jacket pocket for her gloves.

"I'm what I need to be," she said. "What people say isn't my concern."

Dixon took the cue and shut up. Kali slipped on the gloves and they turned the bend. The outline of the castle came into view against the darkness of night. It was about fifty yards away, all towers and turrets and crenellated battlements thrusting into the sky.

"Okay," he said. "They're on the way."

She clicked open her seat harness.

"I'm ready," she said.

The lift platform climbed evenly up from the buried garage, a horizontal sliding door retracting overhead as it rose to the surface.

Carmody and Schultz stood atop it with the two Ninja motorcycles. As it stopped its silent ascent, they realized they were in the middle of an artificial pond that had been drained of water, probably for the winter season. The platform had replaced its bottom and come up level with the surrounding lawn.

They looked around them. It was no longer snowing, but the temperature must have plunged ten degrees since their drop from *Raven*, freezing and solidifying the lingering airborne moisture into microscopic needles of ice. The particles flicked and spun into the lenses of their DNVGs, blurring them with a thin crystalline film.

Schultz snapped his goggles up over his helmet with a gloved hand. He was looking south toward the main gate, hoping to spot Dixon's BearCat amid the trees and hedges.

"I don't see them," he said through his balaclava. "You?"

Carmody raised a hand and gestured to his right, eastward, where the walls and turrets of Castle Graguscu loomed high above them. He'd heard the low grumbling surge of an engine.

He stood looking out across the front of the castle. Lights shone from many of its casement windows, and for a moment they were the only things visible in the pitch darkness. Then he saw a hazy glow coming on about a hundred yards beyond the castle. It intensified and coalesced and then divided amoeba-like into two distinct circles of light.

Headlights. They were high off the ground, pushing their long bright beams across the snow. Behind them, Carmody saw the shadowy outline of a large vehicle.

It was moving fast, barreling toward them from the east.

Wrong direction.

He flicked a glance at Schultz.

"That isn't Dixon," he said.

The Rezvani's driver, a veteran security guy named Lazlo, leaned over the wheel and hurtled toward the two men standing up ahead near the

Ninja motorcycles. In the passenger seat, a recent addition to his detail named Bogdan sat straight as a lamp pole.

"They have guns," he said. Which was unquestionably true.

"And we have armor," Lazlo said. Which he felt was equally true but of greater consequence.

He disliked being saddled with Bogdan. In fact, once things settled down, he would recommend Matei either cut Bogdan loose or transfer him to another team. Preferably somewhere off the estate. Lazlo sensed he was the sort to fold when it really counted. Personal security wasn't for chickenshits.

He was far more confident of the two men in back, Andre and Khasan. Both were with him when he'd driven the Wolf out of Bucharest months ago. The Wolf and his icily beautiful cryptobanker friend Quintessa Leonides. They had escaped the city with half its streets and boulevards cordoned off, and the *polizei*'s helicopters whirling overhead, and their cruisers and tactical wagons closing in from all sides.

It had been a tricky spot. Very tricky. By comparison, this one wasn't even close. In fact, Lazlo knew he easily could have been free and clear of it. He had been well outside the east gate when Matei radioed. But when he was summoned back to the estate to deal with the intruders, back he came. The job was the job.

He rumbled forward in four-wheel drive, both hands on the steering wheel, his Sig MCX Rattler resting beside him on the center console. Not that he expected to need it. The intruders were no more than a hundred yards ahead, standing on the cobblestones between him and the bikes on the wide, semicircular court that served as the manor's parking apron. The pair had spotted his Rezvani's headlights and heard the animalistic howl of its V-8 as it came on like a battle tank. But they weren't budging.

Lazlo was thinking they had balls. Huge brass balls just staring him down. Give them that. But they didn't stand a chance. His bumper, grill, and engine block combined for over a thousand pounds of metal. They couldn't just stand there much longer. If they made for the hedges around the apron, he would swing off-road and jam his front end up their asses before they went ten feet. If they tried shooting through his windshield, its ballistic glass might shatter on the outside, but would stop their bullets cold. If they aimed for the Rezvani's tires, his run flats could keep it rolling for miles. They would know all that. They couldn't possibly be stupid enough not to.

There were now fifty or sixty yards between him and the apron. Then about the same distance across to where the intruders stood facing him.

He would run them over, flatten them on the cobbles, balls and all.

He gritted his teeth, bracing himself as he neared the apron. Built for horse-drawn wagons centuries ago, it was raised several inches above the surface of the access road. At his speed, he was in for a jarring bump.

"Hold on, we'll feel this!" he warned.

Hoping Bogdan wouldn't piss his pants, he gripped the steering wheel as if to shatter it with his large, bare hands. And hit the gas.

Their guns upraised, Carmody and Schultz stood motionless as the Rezvani charged toward them on the access road.

It was now fifty or sixty yards from the apron. Maybe eighty total yards off, its headlights almost blinding in the digitally enhanced vision of their quads.

Carmody tasted adrenaline at the back of his tongue. His reptilian fight-or-flight response had kicked in, but he wasn't a reptile. He could think rationally. Even with his nerves and glands and reflexes telling him to run. *Think*.

Running would do no good. He and Schultz might make it off the apron, but they wouldn't make it very far before the driver plowed into them.

The Rezvani got closer and closer, its headlights smacking their faces with glare.

"Aim high and steady," he said. "Above the lights. On my word."

Schultz nodded once. He knew exactly what Carmody was thinking.

They kept their legs planted apart, their assault rifles shoulder-high, and pointed at the oncoming vehicle. They had maybe four seconds before the Rezvani reached the apron. Another one or two before it reached them.

And they had fresh sixty-round magazines in

their guns. At a firing rate of 950 rounds per minute, they knew they could empty the mags before the Rezvani struck them down. Its windshield would deflect a single bullet. Even a scattered spray of bullets. Its outer layer would fracture and spall but disperse their energy, so they didn't penetrate. But Carmody and Schultz were using high-velocity, low-recoil black-tip ammunition. If each of them poured it on, hit a single spot multiple times at close range, they might weaken it enough to punch through the glass.

They waited. The Rezvani was about twenty yards off.

Carmody prepared to squeeze the trigger.

Then, at the edge of his vision, he abruptly saw a new set of lights ahead and to his right, racing up from the south on the main access road.

Without turning his head, he flicked a glance in its direction to confirm his hunch.

This time it *was* Dixon.

And he was coming on in the BearCat.

Dixon rounded the curve and saw the Rezvani up ahead. It was fifty yards to the right of Carmody and Schultz, on the west side of the apron, and bearing toward them in a straight line. He was likewise to their right, perpendicular to the apron, roughly midway between the motorcycles and the Rezvani. But he was also twenty yards south of the apron, giving him extra ground to cover. He would have to step on it.

He manually disengaged the airbags and warned

the men in the crew section over the comm. *"Brace for impact! Brace! Brace!"*

Beside him, Kali bent slightly forward and planted her feet on the floor. She felt the vibrations from the Cat's rapid increase in speed traveling up her legs.

Dixon pulled in a breath and held it. Like Carmody, he assumed the Rezvani was armored. But the Cat was, too. Plus, it was designed for tactical offense, and the other vehicle wasn't. Plus, he knew what he intended to do, and the other driver didn't. Plus, he'd done his Crash/Bang with the Company boys at Blackstone. And didn't give a damn whether the other guy had or hadn't.

The BearCat shot over the final few feet of road leading up to the apron. As the other vehicle came on from the right, Dixon lowered his accelerator nearly to the floor, closing the gap between him and the apron's rim, bouncing up over it and coming down heavily onto the cobbles. Then he was shuddering over them at a high rate of speed, the Rezvani crossing his path dead ahead, long and dark, its grill, hood, windshield, and front-passenger door blurring through the brightness of his headlights.

Dixon timed his move perfectly. When you were going to deliberately ram a vehicle, you didn't aim for is centerline, where its weight was balanced between the front and rear. You didn't T-bone it. What you did was go for its rear end, so *it* took the brunt of the hit, and caromed away from you, and the rest of the vehicle's disproportionate weight spun counterclockwise in a fishtailing skid.

Pushing the gas pedal all the way down, he bashed into the Rezvani inches forward of the tail-light, right about where its fuel-tank door would be located. He heard the crash of metal on metal and rocked back and forth in his seat. His next move was automatic and instantaneous. It was a burst of synaptic sparks firing through his neural pathways to trigger a muscle memory. It was what the Blackstone course had embedded in his reflexes.

As the Rezvani spun to the right, counterclockwise, toward the castle steps, he immediately cut his wheel to the left, turning in the direction the other vehicle had been going, veering away from its spinning trajectory.

Which left him hurtling toward the spot where Carmody and Schultz had stood moments ago. They had scrambled off the apron into the bordering hedges, leaving behind the two motorcycles. They leaned on their kickstands almost directly ahead of him.

Dixon knew it would be tight. He slashed the wheel to the right again, an instant before he would have smashed head-on into the bikes, shaking and bouncing and jolting over the cobbles as he slid his foot off the gas and applied it to the brake pedal. The Cat rumbled on for several more feet as its brake pads clamped over its rotors and finally ground to a lurching halt.

A moment passed. Dixon exhaled, a long slow stream of breath. To his left, Carmody and Schultz were hurrying back to the motorcycles. He was still on the apron, the castle's western bastion five yards or so to his right, his headlights pointed toward the open field behind it. The main entrance was another five yards off to the right. A colossal arched doorway made of tall wooden planks, it was recessed deep in an ornate stone portico. A set of wide low oval stone stairs scalloped down from the door to the apron.

The Rezvani was partly overturned on the top step. Though the snow had subsided to flurries, the cobblestones were coated with whiteness. He could see wildly looping skid and yaw marks where the vehicle had spun out toward the castle and rolled up onto its stairs, crashing and bouncing off the arched entry door before coming to a halt in front of it. Flipped partway over, it was tilted almost completely on its passenger side, its right wheels off the ground, its front end facing east. With its high center of gravity, it probably would have rolled over completely if the big wooden door hadn't stalled its momentum.

Dixon gave it all a quick glance, then turned to look at Kali. "Your stop."

She dropped her hands to her harness buckle, undid it, and shrugged off the straps. Then she gave him a fractional nod, pulled her balaclava up over the lower half of her face, and sprinted off into the darkness, deliberately leaving her door wide open.

"Good luck," he said to her receding back.

Kali and Schultz dashed in opposite directions, crossing each other's paths like relay racers, Schultz running straight for the BearCat's open door as she ran past him toward Carmody and the bikes.

He stood with his night goggles flipped up over his helmet, an MK7 AI carbine slung over his shoulder, another across his chest. The motorcycles were behind him. They stood side by side, facing north, warm and idling on their kickstands. Kali felt her shoulders stiffen.

"They're for us. A shared gift."

"No. They are only toys for your ego."

"You're wrong, Kali. I love you."

"Boy. You do not even know me."

But that was long ago. Now she heard Dixon gun his engine behind her and broke her eyes away from the bikes. Carmody was approaching her.

"All yours," he said, and dropped a key fob into her hand. "Take this, too." He slipped the carbine off his left arm. "It's Schultz's."

"I don't want it."

"Take it anyway," he said. "We have no time. I need you to ride like you did in Germany. But not unarmed. You trained with one of these for a reason."

Kali didn't reply. She took the gun from him and slung it over her shoulder. Carmody unfastened a spare magazine pouch from his rig, stepped closer, and passed it across to her.

"There's sixty and sixty," he said "Okay?"

"Okay."

She clipped it to her belt, and they mounted the bikes. Kali got hers out of its lean, pushed up her kickstand, and clicked into first gear with her heel.

Their headlights came on and speared the darkness. The north access road was just around the west bastion. They could see it running straight back from the castle through the tall trees behind it.

"Let's do this," Carmody said.

Kali nodded.

He revved up and sped off toward the access road. A split second later, she opened her throttle and followed.

Dixon shifted into Reverse, gunned his engine, and backed up with Schultz still climbing through the door into Kali's vacated seat.

"You in?" Dixon said.

Schultz grabbed his harness straps. "Barely."

"Barely's cool," Dixon said.

He wrenched his wheel to the right and made a K-turn, pointing the BearCat at the castle and the flipped-over Rezvani. Its driver was trying to exit in a rush, but the vehicle had stopped with its front end angled high in the air, and he was struggling to get his door open against the tilt. Dixon saw another guy pushing up through its right-rear door.

He stepped on the gas and lunged across the cobblestones. The man in the Rezvani's rear tumbled from the door to the ground, slipped in the snow, and dropped his weapon, a Sig semiautomatic. Then he was groping for it on his knees.

Dixon rolled straight at him. The guy stared up into his headlights, his hands around the weapon. But the Cat was on him before he could bring it up to fire. As Dixon struck the guy, he saw the gun fly from his grasp, then saw his hands come up and go down below the Cat's hood. There was a flat thud and a bump and a drag under the tires as the guy was caught underneath them.

Dixon backed up two or three yards, swinging his wheel to the left to bring his front grill perpendicular to the Rezvani. The guy he'd hit dragged brokenly along for several feet and at last spilled free of his spinning tires. A crushed, shattered heap, he crabbed across the ground on his stomach, leaving a smeary wet trail in the snow.

"Hang tight in back!" Dixon ordered over the crew intercom. "Turret and gun ports shut! Got me?"

"Yes, sir!" Carter answered.

Schultz breathed in. He saw two more men coming out of the Rezvani. Then Dixon pushed the shifter into Drive, and the BearCat lurched forward, running over the guy in the snow again as it rolled straight toward the vehicle on the stairs.

"Here goes," he said.

"What's he doing?" Bogdan screamed. He'd partly hoisted himself through the driver's door of the Rezvani, his fists pushing up against its frame.

Lazlo stared silently across the short distance between their vehicle and the oncoming BearCat. He was already outside, squatted precariously on its right-rear door, his Sig Rattler clenched in his fist. Its third remaining passenger, Khasan, was unconscious in the back seat, his head and face covered with blood. He'd gotten badly knocked around when they tipped over against the castle door, and that was too bad. Like Lazlo himself, he was a Chechen and tough as nails.

"I need help getting out of here," Bogdan said. He was waist-high out the door and straining to get the rest of the way up. "My leg's caught on something."

Lazlo didn't answer. He glanced over his shoulder at the castle entrance and noticed that its wicket door had been slammed inward by the impact of the Rezvani's collision. Suddenly, he had an idea. It was a gamble, but he had seconds to live unless he took it.

"Do you hear me?" Bogdan gasped. He was pushing up with his fists. "I need some fucking *help*."

Lazlo sprang up from his crouch and took a wide stance atop the rocking, unstable vehicle.

"Sure," he said, and kicked him hard in the face to knock him back down through the Rezvani's door. He'd had enough of his frightened squeals but wasn't going to waste a single bullet on him.

As Bogdan crashed heavily back inside, Lazlo balanced himself upright and watched the BearCat come on big and loud with its headlights hurling brightness across the apron. His pupils were dilated from a rush of adrenaline and alarm pheromones, and he could see as clearly as a hawk.

He waited until the last moment before he turned away from the advancing lights, spread his arms, and leaped toward the castle's door.

Dixon saw the guy outside the Rezvani drop-kick the guy climbing through the door but had no time to think about what the hell it meant.

"We done yet?" Schultz said.

"Almost," Dixon said. He was thinking the thinnest armor on any armored vehicle was always on top. He was also thinking the stairs ran up from the apron at about a thirty-five degree incline. There were six in all, and while they were wide, they weren't particularly high or deep.

He had made higher and steeper climbs in vehicles with lower suspensions and much less horsepower.

He radioed the crew to sit tight and clicked the shifter into Drive, his foot going down on the gas.

The Cat thrust forward again. It rumbled over the cobbles, slow and inexorable, climbed the stairs in a series of thumping, jarring little hops, and struck the partially overturned vehicle at sixty miles per hour. The physics of the collision turned his front end into a high-speed fulcrum. The Rezvani flipped up onto its passenger doors, listed and swayed and rocked for the briefest of moments. Then its center of gravity shifted all the way, and it rolled over completely on the wide top step.

Dixon reversed and braked halfway down the stairs. The upended Rezvani reminded him of a turtle rolled over on its back. The guy who'd been drop-kicked by his friend was still squirming around inside. Dixon could see him through the Rezvani's passenger window.

Shifting the Cat into first gear, he jockeyed it up the steps again and uppercut the front of the rolled-over Rezvani just behind its left-front fender. The Rezvani bounced up and down and spun halfway around in a circle, its front end slamming into the already-splintered castle door. Sparks flew as the vehicle's roof scraped over the top step and caved inward. The outer panes of its bullet-resistant front windows and windshield spider-webbed, puckered, fragmented, and spilled out onto the cobbles in pools of crumbled laminate glass.

Dixon backed down the stairs and stopped with his headlights beaming on the overturned wreck. No one inside would be in any condition to pose a threat.

"Everyone okay?" Dixon glanced over his shoulder into the crew section.

"Affirmative," Spencer said. There were nods from Singh and the others.

Dixon faced front and peered out the windshield.

"Did you see what happened to the guy that jumped?" Schultz asked.

"No," Dixon said. "But he didn't go left or right across the plaza, and he didn't run toward us."

"So he must have ducked into the castle."

"So we forget him and move on," Dixon said. "We can't exactly bulldoze the front door and drive around in there looking for him."

"You sure?"

Dixon smiled a little. Carmody was rubbing off on them. They had all worked together for a very long time.

He sat there taking stock. Emerick was dead. Carmody and Kali were off chasing the target through the hills, and Wheeler's squad was somewhere deep under the castle, very possibly out of radio contact. Nor had he heard anything from

Long in Rover Two, but he would break his silence if things got hairy at his position.

Unless ordered otherwise, Long's job was to keep his eyes open for hostiles and be ready to extract Wheeler and his boys when the moment arose.

Dixon thought quietly for another minute and turned away from the stairs, arbitrarily pointing the vehicle eastward. Dealing with unpredictability was part of the action plan. But he'd already lost the poor kid in back, and it concerned him that the teams were so divided. He was only hoping to ride out of Transylvania without the mission taking any more unexpected turns.

He would not come close to getting his wish.

If the heart of a medieval castle was its Great Hall, then the Castle Graguscu's heart was a joyless chasm, its murals chronicling generations of brutal and bloody tribal warfare; the swords, shields, and pole arms along the walls giving coldly tangible emphasis to these graphic renderings of siege and conquest. Carved in the shape of grinning human heads, the stones that supported the massive wooden roof beams seemed to look down upon visitors with their own secret amusement. Opposite the main door was a yawning fireplace where the flames were once occasionally fed by the bodies of the mad count's real and imagined enemies; even the balcony overlooking the hall, typically occupied by musicians at balls and banquets, contributed to the sinister ambience for those familiar with Graguscu's infamous practice of calling nervous guests to the waltz while his victims sizzled and burned.

Lazlo had been unaffected by these bleak surroundings moments ago, after racing into the hall through the bashed-in wicket door. The violent visions on the walls were nothing compared to what he'd seen and done in his line of work, and he was only glad he wasn't in pitch darkness. There was a hierarchical system by which different parts of the estate received juice from the standby generators during a blackout. Priority was given to the monitoring stations, computer rooms, garage, gatehouses, and of course the tower suite. Then the other rooms and halls and exterior lights would come online in order of importance.

Lazlo didn't know where the Great Hall fell on the list. That was all Matei's business, and none of his. That the lights were on was the only thing that counted.

He looked around a minute, standing a foot or two inside the archway, his Sig Rattler still in his right fist. Though the hall's lighting appeared to spill from crystal chandeliers and electric sconces, he knew LED panels had been discreetly installed to augment their output. To his left, a flight of narrow stairs climbed to the balcony. To his right, a more elaborate spiral staircase wound up to the castle heights. What was it he'd once read? The spiral stairs were designed to slow down raiding parties and make it easier for defenders to hide in wait around each turn.

The question for him was basic, if not quite simple:

Should he stick around and defend the premises or take off for someplace safe? Matei and his men were either scrubbing the computers down below or preventing the intruders from accessing them. The rest of the premises were being evacuated. Moreover, there was no way operations could resume here. The estate was compromised. This was the end of the road for the Wolf's syndicate in Castle Graguscu, Rosalvea, and probably all of Romania. In fact, it had been over months ago. Tonight Drajan Petrovik was calling his own last waltz.

When he reviewed things thoroughly and rationally, Lazlo didn't see any real choice. He needed to make a getaway.

He stood inert for a long moment, thinking and listening. He heard nothing outside the door. Nothing at all. Which told him the men in the armored vehicle must have moved on. It made total sense. The Americans weren't going to waste their time and resources on him. Weren't going to divide their manpower in his pursuit. They wanted their man and whatever intel and information they could extract from his computers. He, Lazlo, wasn't the object of their hunt. He wasn't in their main sights. They would be focused on Zolcu, thinking he was the Wolf, never knowing Drajan Petrovik had quit the premises weeks ago.

Still, if he were going to escape the estate grounds, his problem would be one of evasion. And it couldn't be minimized. Tonight's raid would have required careful and extensive planning. It would not have been undertaken without some sort of aerial surveillance and support. An eye in the sky. Or several eyes. Meaning he couldn't just run off like a scared rabbit and think he would avoid capture. It was one thing to know he wasn't first in their sights. It was entirely another to make himself an obvious, easy target of opportunity.

No, he—

Lazlo's thought was cut short like a snipped thread. He felt his abdominal muscles tense into two tight lateral bands.

He'd heard something. Not outside the castle. Inside. With him.

He stood listening, his carbine down against his outer thigh, pretending he hadn't noticed anything. Though he was sure the sound had come from the spiral staircase, he did not glance over at it. He had been looking neutrally across the room at the fireplace, and that was where he kept his gaze. He looked unbothered, not at all focused on the stairs.

But he was studying them closely out of the corner of his eye. The upper curve of the staircase, especially. A person in his line of work naturally grew alert to certain warning sounds, and what he'd heard was the click of a heel.

Sharp, clear, slightly hollow.

Not a man's shoe, he realized with a flicker of surprise.

He listened, watched…and soon saw what he was looking for on the staircase. At the top step of the curve leading to the floor above.

The bottom of the fur coat falling almost to

her knees. The lower part of her legs. The pointed stilettos.

Lazlo pivoted hard on his left foot, bringing the right side of his body around with one swinging step, snapping his weapon upward in his fist.

"Nu fungi...stai unde esti!" he said in Romanian. Warning her not to run, to stay right where she was, as he took a broad stride, then another, then moved forward so he got closer to the stairs.

She didn't retreat. Didn't budge. She was too terrified to move a muscle.

Lazlo stood there looking up the stairs, the snout of his Rattler aimed squarely at the young woman above him. He had brought her here earlier that night. Driven her from some loud Cluj pickup spot with Zolcu. She was looking worn and tired, her hair a bit disheveled, her eyes...

But it had been long night.

He searched his recent memory for her name.

"Clinia," he said, "what are you doing here?"

She didn't answer his question. Not that time. But it was all right.

He had barely gotten started on her.

11

The George Bush Center for Intelligence, Langley

CIA Director of Operations Carol Morse was driving her black Lexus RX up Dolley Madison Boulevard when her satphone rang. It was 7:00 p.m., an odd time for her to head into the office, especially on the night before Thanksgiving. But with Scalpel underway in Romania, she'd thought it best to be here in case any contingencies arose. She didn't want her tension infecting the kids right before the holiday. Jackson and Tricia were better off just being with their father.

She glanced at her dash and saw the caller ID letters J2R JH on the display. It was Howard at Janus. That couldn't be good. All parties involved in Scalpel were on strict orders to preserve opera-

tional silence while the mission was in progress…
unless something major had occurred to warrant
her immediate attention.

"Colonel?" she answered on the hands-free.

"Duchess. You at home?"

"On the Campus road," she said. "What's happening?"

"I can call back once you're in the office," he
said. "We won't want to be interrupted."

"No, stay with me. I just have to get through
security."

Morse reached the checkpoint and showed her
credentials. Her cell was a Cognizant Model 21, the
most secure satphone in the world. But if she went
on to her office, she would have to temporarily end
their call or route it to her landline and risk losing
it in the transfer. Agency policy prohibiting mobile
devices inside the complex left no room for exceptions—there couldn't be even a slim chance of a
compromised GPS signal being used to map the
facility. This applied equally to high-level officers
and visitors. Everybody on the compound was required to leave their phones in their cars or lockers.

Morse drove through the guard station and
turned past the Mi-17 helicopter on display near
the headquarters building. The parking area outside
HQ was nearly empty at this hour, and she pulled
into the first in a long row of open slots. Her office was farther up in one of the complex's newer
steel-and-glass buildings. But Howard would not
have called without an urgent reason. She wasn't
going to wait.

"Colonel," she said. "Are you still with me?"

"I'm here."

"Tell me what's going on," she said.

FOB Janus

Whirr. Click. Ssssst. Click.

Mario checked his watch again. The hedgehog's latest search of the alley between the Quonsets had gone on for nearly three minutes.

Two to go, he thought.

He listened and waited inside the chest, sweat pouring down his face and making his shirt cling damply to his chest, back, and arms. According to his watch's digital thermometer app it was eighty-three degrees, an uptick of five degrees in the last four minutes. When they had climbed in to hide, it was the same low temperature as the night air, cold enough to make him shiver.

That wasn't good, but Laura's labored breathing was more worrisome. And his own breaths were even heavier than hers. Under her peacoat, meanwhile, Buttons's panting had grown fluttery, irregular, and so faint he could barely hear it.

He realized somewhat guiltily that the cat's weakened condition was part of the reason he and Laura were still alive. If it had been strong enough to carry on the way cats normally did under stress, meowing and clawing and squirming around, the 'hog would have picked up the sounds and gone into attack protocol. But it was hardly moving or breathing at all. The poor thing was fading away.

Dying from a combination of overheating, oxygen deprivation, and CO toxicity, like a canary in a coal mine.

And that, Mario realized, meant he and Laura would be next.

Whirrrrrr. Click.

He kept his eyes on his smart watch. Laura had asked how long it would be until they lost consciousness, and he'd told her he wasn't sure. But that was a lie. Or at least only halfway true. He had a very good head for measurements and ratios. If he estimated the cubic space inside the freezer, he could easily figure out the amount of air it held empty, and about how much would be displaced by two average-size people, and how fast they would use it up, and how much carbon dioxide they would exhale into the space in a given time. But he hadn't even tried doing the math. He didn't see the point. He knew they needed to get out of the chest, and soon, or they never would.

He checked his watch. They had a minute and a half until the 'hog moved on again. Assuming it didn't break the search pattern it was stuck in and use its claw arm to lift the freezer's lid and peek inside. If that happened, he and Laura were goners.

But so far it hadn't happened. Though that surprised and puzzled Mario at first, it also clued him into what Laura had called its robot OCD. Before coming to Janus, when he was with the five Cs—Command, Control, Communications, Computers and Combat Systems—at the Aberdeen Proving Ground, his job had been to put bots through their

paces in simulated operational conditions. He'd
worked with all types, from the dumbest Pack-
Bots used for inspections and bomb disposal to
the smartest robot soldiers, and had helped to de-
velop the huge fleet of mechanical sentries that
patrolled over two hundred square desert miles of
Army ammunition-storage facilities in Hawthorne,
Nevada. They were in the midrange of artificial in-
telligences and never deviated from a limited set
of behaviors and responses. They were also mostly
unarmed and programmed to alert human guards
if there was a security breach.

The hedgehogs' adaptive AI was much more advanced, and their electronic senses and weapons
systems matched their bigger brains. They could
detect and target you at a distance, choose from a
dozen ways of taking you out, and lock, load, and
fire before you knew what hit you. But they were
still machines and had certain machine traits. Like
a lack of experience and common sense. It was the
biggest hurdle for C5 programmers. They had to
input algorithms for robots to perform the simplest
tasks, like teaching them the difference between
using their claws to pick up straight or round objects, something human babies naturally learned
before the age of one.

But a robot wasn't born and raised in the real
world. It didn't have years to grow and mature and
learn through experience. If nobody gave it an algorithm for recognizing a stick as a stick or a ball
as a ball and other algorithms for how to grip and
manipulate them, a bot ran into problems. That

was why robots excelled at repetitive tasks in controlled conditions. Put a robot in an automated factory, where its surroundings were orderly and predictable, and it would run fine. But take it out of those sterile environments, and strange things happened. Like when the robot sentries Mario initially field tested in Aberdeen were deployed to the Nevada ammo dep. He'd spent a month there to work out any crimps with the fleet. Everything went smoothly the first couple of weeks. The robots carried out their tasks the same as they had in trials. Until one of them came across an ordinary desert tortoise on the ground while on patrol.

Its reference database was loaded with animals. Birds, rodents, deer, thousands of different species. Except nobody in Maryland had input data for turtles and tortoises. It was a simple oversight. An omission. There weren't many of either plodding around the Aberdeen range. So the bot didn't recognize the tortoise as a tortoise or any other kind of reptile or living creature. For some reason, though, it mistook the tortoise for a rifle. Nobody could figure out why. Maybe something to do with its shape, but that was a stretch. The robot just stood there signaling *rifle* to its human handlers. But what really threw it into fits was that the rifle didn't conform to any make or model of rifle in its memory. It was a complete unknown as far as rifles went. An anomaly. And besides that, it was *moving* across the ground. Which no kind of rifle in its database could do.

The robot was in a logic trap. Mario had observed it remotely for hours. Not that there was much to see. It never budged. For hours. It couldn't resume its patrol until it worked out the contradiction of the walking gun that could not be a gun. But it didn't have the necessary tidbit of data. For all its computing power it was paralyzed, stuck in place.

The hedgehog was a close cousin of that sentry bot. It had access to more onboard and cloud-computing power, but the architecture of their artificial intelligence was more similar than different. And Mario recognized that it was now in the same kind of unbreakable logic trap.

It had seen its human prey run into the gap, where there was almost nowhere for them to hide. It hadn't seen them emerge, but couldn't pick up their biological readings anywhere inside the gap. And since it likely had no concept of what a freezer was, it was unable to deduce that those heat readings were masked by its insulated walls. The 'hog was programmed to patrol the outer margins of a military base, where freezers weren't ordinary features of the environment. Probably nobody ever input a reference for horizontal freezers into its memory. A simple omission, understandable even, but it had totally screwed up the 'hog. The freezer was its tortoise in the field. The cause of its obsessive-compulsive behavior.

Since it had identified two humans, and humans were capable of speed and stealth, it wasn't totally stalled like the Hawthorne sentry. Mario figured its electronic mind allowed that they might have slipped into one of the other closely aligned

Quonsets or alleys, so it was ranging up and down the line. Over and over. But it wouldn't range any farther. It had concluded that if the humans had tried running in the open field behind the huts, or the parking area in front of the huts, or onto the paved road leading across the base, it would have reacquired them as targets. That they still had to be somewhere in or around the line of huts.

Whrrrrrr. Whrrrrr...rrrrrrr...rrrr...

Mario glanced at his watch, listened. The mechanical sounds grew fainter. He brought his eyes up to Laura's again and held them, a finger to his lips. *Fainter and fainter.*

Five seconds later, he couldn't hear them at all. The 'hog had left the gap between Laura's hut and its neighbor.

Mario inhaled, exhaled, rolled his neck to loosen a knot. Let another ten seconds pass to give the 'hog time to roam up the line.

He slipped off his watch, held it out to Laura.

"Here," he said. "Take it."

"I don't need it."

"You will." He lifted her hand from where she was holding it on top of Buttons, placed the watch in it, and closed her fingers around it with his own. "When I jump out of here, wait fifteen seconds. Then make a run for the Jolt. There's a system that'll protect you from things. Just drive to the south gate and don't stop."

"Mario—"

He looked at her. She looked at him. Their eyes held for the briefest of moments. And suddenly she leaned over and pressed her lips against his, a hard, fierce kiss that was somehow also soft and yielding and almost stole whatever breath remained in his lungs.

"Wow," he said, when she finally drew away. "Was that the right time?"

"It was for me." She gave him a strained smile. "Don't get hurt, Mario."

He nodded but said nothing.

A second later he reached up with both arms, placed his palms flat on the underside of the freezer door, and pushed, breaking its seal's magnetic hold, slamming it up and back and open. Frigid air swooped into the chest and instantly displaced the stale warmth inside.

With a final glance at Laura, Mario sprang to his feet and leaped out of the freezer. As he ran off, his footsteps crunching in the snow, she remembered his instructions, looked at the watch in her palm, and began to count down the seconds.

Revived by the cold, Buttons started kicking and clawing and meowing under her coat.

Mario launched from the alley toward the front of Laura's Quonset, then turned sharply right and sprinted along the row of vacant huts. It was snowing lightly but steadily. Vapor puffed from his nose and mouth. Up ahead of him toward headquarters, and off to his left now at the western perimeter, a pinkish-red glow bled eerily into the sky.

He ran past the second hut, spooked, thinking it looked like the whole compound was ablaze. Then he saw the 'hog outside the fifth hut in line, its sensor arrays turned toward the arched front wall.

"Yo!" he yelled, waving his arms in the air for good measure. "Over here!"

The robot instantly rotated toward him, its .50-caliber machine gun swiveling on its mount so the barrel thrust out in his direction.

Mario hooked into the alley mouth as the gun erupted with fire. Ammunition slapped the ground behind him, hurling billows of talc-white powder up over his footprints in the snow.

The alley was clear. Waste bins empty, no cast-off junk scattered around. Probably the civilians who lived here had tidied up before leaving for the holidays.

Mario flattened himself against the side of Quonset Three and peeked around the corner to the right. The hedgehog was on the move, coming in his direction.

"Oye!" he yelled. *"Aqui!"*

The 'hog fired another salvo, high and tight. Bullets clattered and banged against the hut's corrugated front wall, hitting it almost level with Mario's head. He'd bet the robot wouldn't expend one of its rockets on a single human target. So far, it looked like he was right.

"Hey! Soup can! Come on! *Aqui, aqui, aqui!*"

He was shouting at the top of his lungs, wanting to keep the 'hog's attention directed at him, hoping desperately to gain Laura some breathing room.

So far, it looked like his plan was working. The robot advanced on him at a steady clip, bulky, squat, low to the ground, at once beetle-like and nearly human in its appearance and articulated movements. Like a hybrid life-form that had evolved in a cave on Jupiter. At first it retraced the path that its three earlier patrols had left in the snow cover. Then it veered sharply toward the mouth of the alley, its caterpillar tracks shoving and pushing and piling the snow on either side of them into loose, crumbly banks. Mario guessed it was doing thirty to forty miles an hour, probably close to its top speed. No match for his Jolt but faster than he could run. And bristling with weaponry that would extend its killing power well beyond whatever distance separated them.

Then an idea popped into his head. It was a desperate ploy and might only buy a few seconds. But that was better than nothing.

He took his phone out of his pants pocket. The lock screen still showed his podcast app's Play-Pause-Skip controls. He pressed the Play button and thumbed the slider all the way up to max the volume.

"—like to thank my friend and colleague Adrian Soto and CloudCable's Jim Yates for presenting different sides of the controversial plan to—"

Mario waited till the 'hog had almost reached him before he pitched the phone into the trash bin. Then he turned and hurried down the short length of the alley.

The Quonsets were the standard twenty-by-forty-eight prefab dimensions, and as he emerged behind them three seconds later, glancing back over his shoulder, he saw his ploy had worked. The 'hog had paused to investigate the voices, tipped the bin on its side, and plucked out the phone with its claw. Mario could still hear the podcast blaring from its speaker.

"—be happy to return as the project advances, Dr. Michaels. This is a transformative moment in web connectivity—"

The 'hog held the phone up to its optical lenses, examining it much as a person might study a curious new object. Mario almost stumbled looking back at it. There was something strangely fascinating about its approximate human inquisitiveness.

But the inspection only lasted a second. The 'hog confirmed the voices did not belong to a present threat and then was finished with it.

Mario was already outside the alley as it dropped the phone into the snow and started after him again. He had gained several seconds—and the longer he kept the 'hog away from Laura, the better.

He raced to his left behind Quonset Four and hurried on toward the fifth and last hut in line, crossing behind it, wanting to cut around its north side and put the hut between himself and the robot. Only as he neared the corner of the wall did he risk another look back.

The robot was emerging from the alley mouth between Quonsets Three and Four. It turned behind Quonset Four and unleashed another volley from the machine gun just as he rounded the corner of Quonset Five. The hut shielded him from the fire, but he was at the end of the line. All the huts were behind him and there was nothing but open field in three directions.

He was out of cover.

Mario ran west over the snow and frozen grass. He had been listening for something else, and now, finally, he heard it. The sound of an ignition turning over.

Glancing to his left, he saw taillights wink on outside Quonset One. Laura's hut. She had reached the Jolt. In a matter of seconds she would be headed off toward the south gate—and then hopefully out to safety.

He kept running to lure off the 'hog, hoping to God he could buy her all the time she needed.

Laura was wrenching open the JLTV's door with one hand and desperately trying to hold Buttons against her body with the other when the cat shot from her arms.

Her eyes wide open, her heart clutching in her chest, she watched him run off. There was nothing she could do. No time to even think. In a second, he was gone. Lost in the darkness.

Shaken up, she opened the door the rest of the way, got in, and started up the engine.

Her hands trembled around the steering wheel, but not from the cold. She was barely even aware of the cold.

She shifted into Drive and put her foot on the accelerator and leaped forward. Mario had left the vehicle facing south. She could speed from the parking area to the north–south transverse and reach the gate in minutes. Then turn east on the road to Bucharest.

But she did not head for the road. Instead, she turned right, swung another hard right to make a full U-turn, and sped north across the fronts of the huts.

Away from the gate and in the direction Mario had led the 'hog.

Her foot heavy on the accelerator, Laura prayed silently under her breath. A prayer she learned from her mother as a little girl, for when she was alone in bed and the lights went out. *Angel de mi garda, dulce campaia, no mi desampares, ni de noche, ni de dia.*

Guardian angel, sweet companion, don't forsake me, not by night or day.

She refused to let that heartless, soulless metal *thing* hurt Mario. Refused to let it take him from her.

Wrapped around the wheel, her hands continued to shake with angry determination.

Mario was in the field north of Quonset Five, scampering west through the snow, when he heard the low rumble of the JLTV speeding toward him from the left. He looked over his shoulder and saw the bright circles of its headlights growing larger and larger and realized to his horrified surprise what Laura intended to do.

She was coming back for him. She had to know it was suicide. But she was coming back.

The 'hog's .50-cal chattered behind him. He'd put about seventy-five yards between himself and the row of huts, close range, but the bullets struck the ground to his right, muffled beats in the snow. The robot's bumping movement over the frozen, uneven turf had thrown its aim off the mark: two inches closer, and the burst would have torn off his arm and half his torso.

Mario ran forward, his knees and hips working overtime in the ankle-deep accumulation.

He gulped cold air into his lungs and ran. Ten feet. Twenty. The hedgehog was catching up. It probably weighed seven hundred pounds. That massive weight compressed and flattened the snow underneath it, and its tread belt gave it solid traction. And it was a machine. He already felt himself getting fatigued, but machines wouldn't fatigue. They had no muscles to stiffen up. They never got tired.

Mario ran, his throat raw, snow sucking at his boots. His legs were getting tired. His elbows were stiff from pumping. He thought he could hear the 'hog's servos whirring faintly behind him as it edged closer and closer.

It was no more than thirty yards back when the headlights flooded over him, coming straight on from his left until they were almost on top of him. Their horizontal beams momentarily dazzled his eyes and then abruptly swung out and away as he watched Laura scrape around in a hard left turn and grind to a halt, nosed in the same westerly direction he'd been running, the right-rear door hanging wide open.

"Stop staring and get in!" she said through her lowered window.

Mario dove into the back seat as she jammed her foot on the gas and the JLTV bucked forward with his door still open, its tires spinning up a cloud of fine white snow crystals.

"Cut the lights and zigzag!" he yelled, sprawled on his stomach.

"What?"

"The lights! Cut them! Then zigzag!"

Laura cut the lights and veered left, right, left, right, ice, dirt, and frozen grass rasping and rapping against the Jolt's undercarriage. Mario pushed up in his seat, swayed violently, braced himself with both hands, and looked back through the rear window in time to see a rocket-powered grenade blaze an orange trail through the night between the 'hog's angled launcher and their vehicle. The projectile smashed into the ground a few feet off to the right and detonated with a loud booming blast and a churning orange fireball.

"Keep going!" Mario shouted.

She veered left and sliced right, putting more distance between themselves and the 'hog. A second RPG landed behind them and exploded with a bright flash, but it was farther off its mark than the previous one. They braced for a third round, but it didn't come. The rocket fire had stopped. The robot could no longer draw an accurate bead.

"What's next?" Laura said.

"I'm not sure," Mario said. "We'll figure it out."

"Will it follow us?"

"I don't think so. It's too slow to catch up. It understands that."

She drove through the darkness in her deliberate zigzag. Mario felt his weight shift this way and that.

"I lost Buttons," she said after a minute. "I feel awful."

He nodded. "I'm sorry, Laura."

"I was opening the door, and he jumped."

"When I didn't see him, I kind of figured. But I'm pretty sure he'll be okay."

She was silent a moment. "You really think so?"

"I do," Mario said. "Cats can take care of themselves."

She nodded.

"I just hope—" She broke off abruptly, cocking her head to one side. "Mario, do you hear something?"

He listened. "Yeah. A buzzing…that what you mean?"

She nodded. "Like a helicopter," she said. "I wonder if it means help is on the way."

Mario listened some more but said nothing.

"Do you think it might?" Laura asked. "Mean we're getting help, that is?"

Mario hesitated. It didn't sound all that much like a helicopter to him. But he didn't want to alarm her. "I'll try to check it out when we can stop," he said.

Laura was thinking that Mario's vague response was kind of odd. Like he didn't want to scare her. Which scared her a whole lot.

Doing her best not to show it, she rolled on across the wide, snowy field, orienting herself by the diffuse red glow above the horizon, headed west.

Five minutes earlier, Sergeant Julio Fernandez had driven his Puma 6x6 over the same snow-

sheeted field and in the same westerly direction as
the Jolt. Now he was stopped three hundred yards
to the east of what once had been parade and assembly grounds for Romanian land troops. He sat
carefully monitoring his display consoles, a sensor tower atop the vehicle's hull transmitting multispectral images of the barracks to its cabin.

The visuals were clear and chilling.

Erected on about half an acre of land at the far end
of the parade grounds, the building had been wider
than it was long, with gray concrete walls, a flat tar-
paper roof, and rows of square windows on each of
its three stories. But the hedgehogs had left very
little of it standing. The side walls had been blown
outward and the roof collapsed inward. Fernandez
saw flames dancing and leaping above their shattered remnants. Streamers of black smoke, flecked
with red and orange, gushed from the broken front
windows and rose skyward in sooty columns.

There were two hedgehogs in the yard—Spree
and Nash according to their radio-frequency identification tags. A third 'hog was in back, out of
visual range and represented by a graphic icon. All
stood unmoving in the glow of outside light poles,
CIA-era upgrades with flat, shoebox-shaped LED
fixtures designed to give off a smooth, cool white
radiance.

"Check out the 'hogs' RFIDs," he said, glancing
around at Howard. "Spree's over to the south. Nash
is on the north side of the yard. Walt's behind the
building in the parking lot."

"Where the bunker exits."

Fernandez nodded. The small concrete maintenance shed at the far western end of the lot was a
Romanian Army holdover. It stood about a hundred
yards from the perimeter fence and had a steel door
that could be opened with a simple key card issued
to all official base personnel. He'd used it once or
twice out of curiosity and guessed there were ten
or fifteen metal steps inside leading down to the
subsurface bomb shelter.

It would be Walt that normally passed the shed
while making its rounds. Multiple times a day, in fact.
So it made a certain kind of sense that the 'hog was
back there guarding it right now. Which confirmed
a little something about the bots' current behavior.

"They're sticking to their quadrants," Fernandez
said. "Interesting."

Howard looked at him. "Fuck if I know what
you're talking about, Julio."

Fernandez paused a second. "If you're a hacker
who seizes control of a system, you want *total* control. The ability to move the hogs anywhere on the
board." He shrugged. "That's ideal."

"And?"

"Seems to me they're on leashes. Longer ones
than we gave them, but leashes."

"So you're saying they've been *duped*?"

"More like they're delusional," Fernandez said.
"I'll explain later. But I'm guessing they still think
they're guarding the perimeter."

Howard inhaled. "Okay," he said. "How's that
help us right now?"

"Short-term, it means we probably don't have to

worry about Earl coming up on our rear." Fernandez pointed to the display. "It's near the civilian Quonsets at the east end. More or less where it belongs."

"And long-term?"

"It'll be useful when we get to sorting out what's happened here tonight. And when——"

"Sir?"

It was Wasserman. Urgency in his voice. Glancing back at him with a hand on his left earpiece.

Howard sat forward with a wince. His ribs felt like jagged glass. "What is it?"

"I have contact with the bunker," he said.

"Who?"

"Captain Jeffries, sir. We have thirteen men and women down there. And some are in pretty bad shape."

Back east across the field, outside the row of civilian Quonsets, Earl stood motionless in the snow. White flakes corkscrewed around it, formed a thin white skin on its metal surfaces, and filled in the tracks it had left between the huts like a connecting rope.

Still and silent, the hedgehog showed no sign of visible activity. But it continued to function without interruption.

As the JLTV carrying the two human threats inside sped off, it had received an algorithmic data transmission from the Monarch drone. A bit of malicious deep-learning code that fit neatly within the framework of its original programming.

The drone swarm was descending to protect the base.

George Bush Center, Langley

A short while after Howard had gotten off the phone with her, a pale and dismayed Carol Morse sat in her office preparing to make a difficult call of her own. She would have preferred taking some time to digest what the colonel reported but could not allow herself that luxury. The call could not be delayed. She was in all but title an adjunct to the Director of Net Force, Alex Michaels. Formally, she remained a CIA operations officer. But from Net Force's inception as a cabinet-level cybersecurity arm, President Fucillo had wisely understood it would not be able to fulfill its mission as a siloed entity. She had worked closely with POTUS getting the organization off the ground and was given broad powers relating to its operational integration with the Company and every other mainstay law enforcement, intelligence, and military body.

Morse took a deep breath, gathering her thoughts. With the base under siege from its own robot sentries, and kamikaze drones incoming from Mihail Kogălniceanu, and over a dozen confirmed casualties so far, it appeared the Wolf was once again hitting them where it hurt…almost certainly uncoincidentally on the very night Janus had sent a team into his Satu Mare hideaway.

Scalpel was a so-called special-technique information-collection operation. A snatch-and-bag against the *technologie vampiri*, authorized pursuant to Executive Order 14301 issued by President Fucillo, which was an amendment to President

George W. Bush's Executive Order 13470, itself an amendment of a prior order signed in 1981 by President Ronald Reagan.

Reagan's EO had extended the CIA's power to order cooperation and the sharing of information from other federal agencies. Bush's order gave the Director of National Intelligence, a cabinet-level official, expanded power to order and approve clandestine activities abroad and overseas, establishing a chain of command that pointedly did not require the direct involvement or sanction of the president, giving him or her plausible deniability should things straddle the lines of legality...or go south.

Fucillo's recent EO had brought Net Force into the mix. Its purpose was to give the organization the same authority as the CIA to require cooperation from other agencies, and to put DNF Michaels on equal footing with the DNI in planning and ordering clandestine ops.

Michaels had only green-lighted Scalpel after consulting with Morse. In fact, she had been the one who convinced him to proceed with it, against his reservations.

And now it looked like the Wolf had anticipated the operation and taken advantage of the base's vulnerability on a night Carmody and his support team were hundreds of miles away in Western Romania. Maybe that would prove untrue, and the timing *would* turn out to be coincidental. But Morse doubted it. Which opened up some profoundly unsettling questions about *how* that top-secret information might have been compromised…and left Morse very concerned that Scalpel was itself a trap.

Divide and conquer. If that was the enemy's stratagem, and her people had fallen prey to it…

POTUS had to be looped in. Net Force was her signature initiative, and she'd pushed it through against a shitstorm of political and bureaucratic opposition. She needed to know about the Romanian situation while it was developing, not after word leaked out. And it would on the Hill. At near light speed. It always did in spite of all precautions.

Morse picked up her receiver and pressed the speed dial for Fucillo's secure cell.

She answered on the second ring.

"Carol, hello." She sounded like she was already bracing for trouble. A phone call on Thanksgiving eve wasn't quite as dreaded as a 3:00 a.m. call. But it rarely brought good news. "Is everything all right?"

"Marie," she said, "we have a problem…"

12

Senior Sergeant (MOS) 09L Joe Banik heard the sounds of a motor and snow chains, turned to his left, and saw a pale smudge of light out past a hump in the cracked country blacktop. A full two minutes passed before the truck came bouncing into sight.

"Hee'sha'er," Banik said, giving his dog, Ellie, the Hebrew command to stay. The Malinois was one of the select few bred and trained by Alex Michaels, who used stringent Israeli K-9 certifications.

Banik waited at his post near the blown, crookedly leaning castle gate. The vehicle was an ancient double-cab Dacia pickup, its yellow, rust-spotted paint job reminding him of nothing so much as a bruised banana peel. The truck rattled and clattered down the slope, pulled over to the gravel shoulder on his side of the road, and then halted about ten feet off.

After a moment, the driver's door opened and the cab lights went on. Banik glimpsed its occupants through the windshield, a couple in their sixties or seventies, probably husband and wife. The woman in the passenger seat was wide and thick and wrapped in a heavy shawl. The man behind the wheel was wider and thicker and wore an old-fashioned flatcap and car coat. He laboriously pushed through his door and approached Banik with stiff-legged difficulty, his baggy brown pants tucked into knee-high winter boots.

The sergeant waved him back. *"Margeti mai departe, bunicule,"* he said in Romanian. "Go home, grandfather. It's unsafe out here."

The old man disregarded him. He walked up to within two or three feet of Banik and stopped, looking warily down at the dog, then up at his face. His coat was ratty and threadbare and about two sizes too snug.

Banik was thinking he looked as desperately in need of maintenance as his truck.

"The lights are out," he said, steam puffing from his mouth. "We have no electricity. No phones."

"More reason to stay off the road."

The man's gaze went briefly to the MP7 on Banik's shoulder, moved past him to the blown gate, then returned to Banik's face.

"What happened there?" he asked.

"Nothing to worry you."

"We live nearby. We hear guns. Other things. How can we not worry?"

Banik didn't answer. There had been rattles of

gunfire from the estate just before he'd seen the pickup's headlights. A loud bang. The sounds traveled a long way in the hills.

The old man nodded toward the estate grounds. "Who are you?" he said. "Are you with the Wolf?"

Banik didn't answer.

The old man looked straight into his eyes. "I do not think so," he said. "*Si tu nu arata ca un Rus…* I do not think you are Russian, either. They have a certain look about them."

There was a long pause. Banik didn't know what being or not being Russian had to do with anything. But he couldn't worry about it right now.

"Grandfather, please—"

"When the lights went out and we heard the shooting, I told Lati, 'I wonder if they come tonight.' The gendarmes have told us to be ready."

Banik stood silently in the falling snow. He still had no idea what he was talking about. "Go back to your wife," he said. "Take her home."

"There is no invasion?"

"Not tonight."

The old man looked down at the Mal, then back up at him. "Who are you?" he asked again.

Banik said nothing. He heard more noise from the estate grounds. Unmistakable stitches of gunfire and what he guessed were racing engines. The old man listened with heightened interest, as if wondering what it all meant.

They had that in common, Banik thought.

The man stayed where he was another few seconds. If he was sixty, he would remember living under Communism and the dictator Ceaușescu. In his time, he had probably accepted and ignored a lot to stay out of trouble, probably buckled under plenty of men with authority and guns.

Finally, he dipped his head, a long, low nod like a tired mule. His submissiveness left Banik feeling crummy. He was another powerful outside force asserting itself on the old man's life without so much as an explanation. Banik didn't like it, but he was, ultimately, exactly that.

"Noapte buna," the old man said, his head down but his eyes on Banik's eyes. After a moment he lowered them to the Mal. "A good and safe night to you, too."

He turned toward his pickup without another word. Banik watched him walk back to it, listening to the harsh noise from the estate grounds. Then another sound caught his ear. Separate, distinct, high overhead. Pausing outside the truck, the old man also heard it. He turned his eyes up to search the snow and darkness, the cab lights washing over him through the half-open door, ribbons of fine white powder blowing dustily over and around his boots. In the passenger seat, his wife looked initially impatient for him to get inside with her. But an instant later, she heard something, too. Looking puzzled and nervous, she tilted her head to peer through the windshield.

The buzzing was loud, dense, and collective, like an assembled cloud of wasps. Banik felt Ellie tense slightly against him as she sniffed the air, her short, black fur rippling, smooth as oil, over her muscular flanks and shoulders.

He looked up toward the humming noise but was blinded by the pulses of snow overhead. Then the pickup's door slammed shut. Back inside with his wife, the old man pulled a U-turn and struck off toward home, his engine wheezing and knocking, his tailpipe burping exhaust as he climbed the hump in the road.

When the rattletrap was out of sight, Banik lifted his gaze back toward the dark, trembling sky. He still couldn't see anything through the snow. But he didn't like that noise, not even a little.

Whatever was up there, he needed to inform the entry teams about it in a hurry.

It was just shy of 2:00 a.m. when *Raven's* PDAS radar, infrared, and laser detection systems acquired the objects. They were flying in from the south-southwest at eleven o'clock, traveling a touch over thirty miles an hour, and a hair under the tilt-rotor's hovering altitude.

In the copilot's seat, Cobb saw Luna straighten with alarm as he threw the imagery from his HUD onto their huge, shared multifunction display.

"Crap," she said. "I think that's a drone flock."

Cobb had already reached the same conclusion. "I'll alert Carmody," he said.

North of the castle, Ray Long, Fox Team, was pulled to the shoulder of the road in Rover Two, his front end facing the crossroads a quarter mile ahead. His vehicle idled quietly, its lights extinguished. The snow had stopped, the outside temperature dropped, and the wind kicked up. Cold blue starlight pierced the thinning clouds at the higher levels of the troposphere. Lower to the ground, it was scattered by a fog of frozen moisture hanging over the trees and fields.

Not yet having heard anything unusual up above, Long sat there per Carmody's orders and checked his visuals. Two of his sources were video-game stuff. A central dashboard screen gave the big picture of what was happening around him, and coming at him, with high-def aerial images relayed from the Sentinel drone by way of *Raven*. His digital rearview mirror showed the curved, narrow stretch of road he'd taken from the castle grounds. He could watch the fork up ahead the old-fashioned way, through the windshield with his naked eyes.

"They're coming," said the big, dark-skinned E-3 in the passenger seat. One of four Quickdraw guys with Long in the BearCat, his name was Reggie Fults. "Just behind us."

Fults was at that moment looking at the dash screen. Long was watching the digital rearview. He saw a silky, white fan of light advancing over the roadway about fifteen yards back. It slid around a bend and swiftly resolved into two circles of brightness a few feet off the ground. Behind it was another twin headlight.

The two supercharged motorcycles sped along in single file, their LED headlights shafting out ahead of them. Sleek, compact, cowled in black, they shot up on Long's right and went humming past him. Carmody was in the lead, Kali following him closely, their heads and bodies tucked in behind the curved glass of their windscreens.

They rode on ahead toward the crossroads and passed straight through, staying on the wide main road, their taillights zipping off into the darkness like red meteors.

When he could no longer see or hear them, Long glanced at the dash screen for a bird's eye view of the road above and below his position. He immediately picked up the bikes again. And the Regera bearing toward them from the north.

"Okay, this is it," he said.

Shifting into Drive, he eased from the shoulder onto the snow-covered two-lane, drove slowly past the crossroads, and pulled across the road to block it off.

He had no sooner come to a halt than he heard the noise in the sky.

He looked over at Fults. "You hear that?"

Fults nodded. "It's close. *Whatever* it is."

Long sat listening in silence. He thought it almost sounded like the Sentinel UAV. But louder. As if there were more than one in the air.

He listened some more. The noise got even louder. It reminded him of the swarming cicadas he'd heard as a kid on the farm. He was pretty sure it was being made by multiple drones.

Everyone in the BearCat listened quietly. They were thinking along the same lines as Long, guessing there were drones up overhead, a whole *lot* of them.

Then Cobb radioed and confirmed they were right.

* * *

Kali blew past the crossroads on the Ninja. She was close behind Carmody, doing seventy miles per hour, her headlights tunneling through the darkness.

She sensed more than saw the emptiness of the frozen, expansive pastures to her right. On her left, the soaring trees were a solid black wall, a natural buffer against the ferociously cold alpine gusts. Speed slowed things down for her, and she was moving fast.

Toward the place where two roads met.

"Hekate of the Three Forms. Guardian of the crossroads. Mistress of heaven and hell."

"Virgil. The Aeneid.*"*

"I memorized it. For you, Kali. Though, I still don't understand your fascination with this place."

She and Drajan. Long ago amid the temple ruins in the gathering dusk. They had traveled to Western Turkey on holiday from school in Madrid.

"The ancient Greeks were first with the concept of free will," she'd said. *"Of taking responsibility for our lives. This temple speaks to it."*

"Yet they came here to beg favors of a goddess? I call that hedging a bet."

"Then you don't understand. Hekate carries a torch and key. The torch lights the way for souls in transition. The key opens doors to the under- world. But she doesn't decide which they take. She protects them in dangerous places. The in-between places. The choice is theirs."

That familiar look on his face. That hard smile.

"A good lady," he said, and nodded up at the sky. "If the stars ruled my fate, I'd be doomed."

The memory came and went, sweeping over her like the wind. Kali realized she'd lost sight of Carmody as he took a curve up ahead. Three seconds later she swung into it, and he was back in her lights.

They sped up. She saw no sign of the Regera with her unaided eyes. But the relay feed from *Raven* showed it in her HUD speeding south.

The road curved and straightened and rose and fell without apparent landmarks to help her distinguish one span from another. In the daylight, she knew, it would be easier. But at night the countryside seemed unvaried and unchanging. The snaking blacktop. The wide open, featureless farm fields. The solid ranks of towering pines and deciduous trees. Nothing to make one empty mile look any different from the next.

No Regera.

They were three or four miles north of the castle when they first smelled smoke. It was slagged asphalt, charred wood, and bubbling sap, commingled with the acrid stink of burning fuel.

They sped up. The tarry smoke got thicker. It made their eyes sting and their chests tight. More curves, dips, and rises, and Kali saw the orange stain of the flames in the sky up ahead. And lower, closer, oncoming headlights. Bearing directly toward them.

In her ears over the drumming of the wind, Carmody's voice on the RoIP.

"It's our man," he said.

"Yes," she replied.

He sped up again without another word. Kali throttled fuel into her engine and raced after him.

Zolcu recognized the Ninjas the moment he spotted them shooting up from the south. He had been wrong about the Rezvani leading his hunters off his tail. They must have started after him at once. On the Wolf's own cherished motorcycles.

In hindsight, it should have been no surprise. Nothing tonight was going as predicted. Not for a minute.

The question now was what he would do about it.

His immediate impulse was to run the riders down. Just plunge right into them and leave them for dead. It would be risky. All three vehicles were moving at high rates of speed, and his car was lightweight carbon fiber. And he had hundreds of miles to travel before he reached the Crimean Peninsula. Long, desolate country miles. He did not want to jeopardize his ability to drive that distance with serious crash damage. If the car cut out on him, he would be in bad shape. Trying to make it anywhere on foot in the pitch darkness was out of the question. The temperature outside was falling. The farms and villages here were widely separated. While his phone's GPS would orient him, it would lose its charge within hours. He might freeze to death before coming upon civilization.

But he needed to reach the crossroads. He would get nowhere otherwise. And the riders were in his way. There was really no decision to be made.

Bracing himself, Zolcu slammed on the gas and shot toward the lead bike.

Carmody broke radio silence to tell Kali to pull off, resisting the urge to do the same as the Regera swelled out of the darkness. Instead, he roared directly toward it, lining himself up between its headlights, reaching across his body with his left hand to draw his Sig. It was his weaker hand by far, but with his throttle on his right side, he could either take his chances or wind up a smear on the car's front fender.

He had less than a second to choose his target. He could aim for the windshield, but it was probably ballistic glass. The driver might slow down a little, but a few shots in passing wouldn't do much to stop him.

Trying to take him in a single swoop wouldn't work. He would need several passes.

The Sig balanced in his fist, he held its barrel over his handlebars and angled the gun toward the car's left headlight, taking quick aim. Two shots, right on the money, and the headlight disintegrated in a spray of glass. But the Regera kept belting toward him, snarling like an angry cyclops.

Riding one-handed, Carmody veered to his extreme right to avoid it, leaning hard in that direction. The car shot by to his left, missing him by inches as he roared past its passenger side, eased off the throttle, and swung back around behind it, staring at its taillights now, facing north, ready to make his second run.

Then its driver did something unexpected.

* * *

What Zolcu did was make another snap decision based on limited options. The Ninja's rider had improbably aimed, fired, and blown out his headlight. Fired accurately with one hand from the back of a speeding motorcycle. And now he and his gun were right on his tail.

But Zolcu had certain skills of his own, and one of them was knowing how to handle a car. He would shake off the driver and make sure he stayed off.

Cutting the wheel sharply left with one hand, he pulled his passenger-side tires onto the gravel shoulder, lifted his foot off the gas, and engaged his e-brake with his free hand to lock the rear tires. Then he cranked the wheel hard to his right so the Regera began to spin like a propeller, its front tires scraping for traction, the weight of the engine under its hood whipping it around clockwise. He breathed in as it turned ninety degrees in a controlled skid, breathed out, and lowered the emergency brake to release it, restoring traction to the front tires with his foot still off the gas, letting the rotation continue until he turned a full one hundred eighty degrees into the left lane and was again heading north.

Zolcu's reversal of direction took under three seconds. He could now see the rider about thirty yards up ahead, facing him from the Ninja's saddle, coming straight toward him. Less than a mile farther on behind the rider, the sky bled orange and red from the flames raging alongside the blasted roadway.

He stared out his windshield. The bike kept rushing at him. He could hear the throb of its engine. He could see its rider leaning down over the handlebars, his black-gloved hand still wrapped around the gun. He was getting ready to fire again.

Cursing under his breath, Zolcu jammed his foot down on the gas and went at him head-on.

When the distance between them shrank to six or seven yards, Carmody opened his throttle hard, extending the Sig over his handlebars in his left fist. Then he took aim and pulled the trigger.

Three things happened as a result.

The right headlight blew to bits and pieces, spraying outward in a jagged constellation of glass. The Regera's driver instinctively wrenched his wheel to the left, away from the shots, swerving toward the road's soft shoulder from the south. And Carmody sliced to *his* right, onto the same dirt shoulder, from the north.

Neither vehicle slowed. They were still rushing toward each other, this time at the extreme edge of the road, a scant few yards separating them.

Carmody knew he had no chance of surviving a head-on collision. But if he tried swinging away from the Regera's turn into the southbound lane, he would slam into its angling right flank and probably wind up dead anyway.

He had time for just one move.

As the Regera came within inches of him, he cut his handlebars abruptly to the right and veered off-road onto the bordering pasture. His front wheel jarred over the lip of the frozen grass. His rear wheel tagged along, and then he was completely on uneven ground, heading east, cross-country, rocking and bouncing and swaying astride the motorcycle. His headlight beams cast a silvery shimmer over the snowfield, reflecting off the colossal haystacks scattered ahead and around him like a village of high, white igloos.

He heard the furious pulse of an engine and glanced into his rear-camera display. The Regera. It was fifteen yards or so behind him. Following in a taper-straight line. In the pitch darkness and without headlights.

Carmody knew immediately that its driver could not only see him but see the whole pasture around them. And not with his naked eye. The Regera had a two-million-dollar price tag. It would have something better than the Ninja's rearview camera onboard. Probably long-range night-vision cameras. Forward and rear.

He checked his side mirror and saw the car gaining on him. Checked his digital speedometer and saw that he was pushing eighty. Fast for riding off-road on snow and ice. Too fast. The Ninja wasn't built for it. It was too low-slung. Its wide, smooth tires weren't designed for gripping and quick turns. It was light for a street bike and had a good engine, probably over a hundred horsepower, but the Regera's engine could generate ten times that. And it would have all-wheel drive and suspension, giving it balance and traction he lacked.

He sped forward. Glanced at the mirror again. The Regera was getting closer. He estimated that his own headlights gave him four hundred feet of visibility. The optics on the Regera's cameras would reach much farther, but the driver would find it hard keeping his eyes on the dash for more than a few seconds. Cars weren't like planes. They weren't meant to drive on instruments. There were obstacles on the ground. There was glare and spatial distortion. And it would take getting used to the angle of sight. To the awkward posture. That wasn't the sort of thing anyone practiced. It would slow his reactions.

Carmody looked up ahead. The cluster of haystacks he'd spotted from the road was about sixty yards off and slightly to his left. He would reach it in seconds. Time for his cat and mouse to end.

"Outlier, you in position?"

"Yes."

His molars clicked.

"Good," he said. "Coming right at you."

"Eyes on the road," said the Regera's canned feminine voice.

Zolcu swore aloud as he bumped over the field. The driver-alert system had read the bent position of his head and determined he was either nodding off or paying unsafe attention to his dash screen. As if he were a stoned-out teenager mucking with his stereo settings.

The stupidity of a commercial AI could never be underestimated. Bad enough being without headlights, he could barely stand that badgering, repetitive voice. How had Drajan failed to disable it?

He kept his focus on the screen and did his best to block the alerts from his mind. The motorcycle's lead was down to a handful of yards. Directly ahead of it were three stacks of hay made up of dozens of large, compressed bales. Zolcu had grown up in this farm country and guessed each of the bales weighed five hundred pounds. In this brutally cold weather, they would be frozen and dense. If the bike struck one of the haystacks going at its present speed, it would be like hitting a solid wall.

He lowered the gas pedal, watching the dash screen.

"Eyes on the road," the AI warned.

"Go fuck yourself," Zolcu said and kicked forward behind the motorcycle.

As the Regera came speeding up behind him, Carmody suddenly remembered the cartoons he would watch as a boy. The cat chases the mouse around a room. The mouse finally runs straight at a wall and dashes into its mouse hole. The cat smacks against the wall and gets flattened.

Mouse wins.

He squeezed his throttle. The triangle of haystacks was dead ahead. Black humps in the night, looming like three small hills. And the car was right on his back. He could feel its weight and power as a palpable force. Hear the huge noise of its charging engine.

He had seconds. That was it. The space between the pair of nearer haystacks was wide enough for him to get through but not wide enough for the car.

Its driver probably thought he would try slipping between them like the mouse into its safe haven, then weave a path around the middle stack, the one set slightly behind the others. The driver also probably figured he could beat him at his own game. The Regera was bigger and faster and all well-tooled muscle. He could catch up to the bike before it reached the outer two haystacks, smash it into one of them, then veer off before running into them himself.

Carmody waited until he'd almost come up to the haystacks and they were the only things he could see with his headlights. Waited until the front end of the Regera was on top of him. It nuzzled his rear fender, bumping him forward so he felt a rough, stomach-jerking jolt of acceleration. And precisely at that instant, knowing the next hit would be full-on, that it would send him flying through the air and plowing into the middle haystack with enough force to shatter every bone in his body, Carmody hammered the back brake with his foot to lock the rear wheel, snapping his handlebars to the right-hand side. As the Ninja started fishing in that direction, he squeezed the hand brake, keeping his foot heavy on the back brake, freezing both wheels as he simultaneously leaned hard to the left and dropped the bike onto its side.

Carmody released the handlebar grips, letting go with both hands, staying loose as he rolled from the saddle, pulling his left leg out from under the bike before its five hundred pound mass could land on top of it. He twisted to his right as the pancaked bike went skidding sideways to his left, his elbows pulled up and into his side, his fingers balled into relaxed fists, sliding several feet clear of the bike, clear of the haystacks, letting his momentum carry him away from them.

He was still flat on his back in the snow, a few feet to the right of the two front stacks, as the Regera side-swiped the one nearest him, its headlights sweeping around in his direction a split second before it would have slammed into the stack head-on, its right flank raking against the piled bundles of hay with a crunch of metal and shattering composite. The impact pushed several bales in the stack's lower and middle layers backward, undermining its vertical stability. It bent, and it bowed, and then it leaned halfway over, bales falling onto and around the car, pounding down on its hood and roof in a small avalanche.

Carmody heard the crashes, propped himself on his elbows, and saw the Regera backing away from the haystack. It was a battered wreck, the left side of its roof sagging under a fallen bale, its right-front fender crunched and mangled. The door on that side hung off the frame like a broken and partially detached wing. Its driver had turned barely in time to escape wiping out. The car reversed for several feet and stopped parallel to the toppled haystack, facing him, its headlights dark, empty pits. The bale that landed on its roof had smashed all the way through to the cockpit's passenger side. Its weight had caused the roof frame's front crossbar to buckle over the windshield. The glass on that side was fractured and bulging out over the hood. Carmody stared through into the car's interior and saw a pale, watery blue radiance, maybe from the dash screen. The driver was in clear silhouette, his arms stiffly outstretched in front of him, his hands still gripping the wheel. A rigid posture, far from ideal for handling the car. It looked like he'd pushed his seat back to give himself a better angle for watching the screen.

Carmody got to his knees in the cold snow. His body felt like a single large bruise, but he hadn't lost or broken any limbs and was sure he was in better condition than the car. He saw it shiver a little as the driver changed gears. Probably putting it into Forward. Probably intending to run him over.

"Outlier," he said into his throat mike. "Now."

Her headlights flashed on about twenty yards to his left, brilliant and white, lancing out from behind the middle haystack. Then her Ninja woke from its idle with a full-throated growl and spurted into sight, swinging a wide hook around his flipped-over bike.

He was already on his feet as Kali came to a dead halt inches to his left. He mounted the seat behind her, one hand going to her hip. The other went to his holster and drew the Sig.

"Here we go," he said.

Kali nodded and slashed around toward the Regera, speeding toward it even as the car charged at her. She waited until they were within six feet of each other and then sheered abruptly to her right, buzzing by its left flank.

Riding piggyback in the saddle, Carmody thumbed on the Sig's rail light to cast a wide circle of brightness onto the Regera's front tire. He aimed between the dots of his sight and shot three times at the sidewall in quick succession. The tire exploded with a loud bang, shreds of rubber flowering from its rim.

Kali went straight ahead for four or five feet. She glanced over her shoulder, applied weight to her right foot peg, and leaned the bike to the left, giving it a little fuel, slipping the clutch to control her speed as she swung around in a tight, spin-the-bottle U-turn. She was clipping along to the Regera's right, back toward its front end, moving in the same direction it was.

Carmody pointed the gun at its rear tire and triggered another three. The tire exploded, but the car kept hobbling forward. He had suspected it would have run flats, and that proved he was right. It might continue to roll for a good distance. But it could not go faster than forty miles per hour on the hard, smooth emergency rims, especially over snow and ice.

Now Kali pulled another tight, sharp U, turning back to its left for her second pass. Carmody got ready for his next three shots. As they reached the tail end, he took aim and fired at the left-rear tire, blowing it to bits and pieces that went flying in all directions.

She spun around again, facing the car's rear. It continued to flounder along, heading away from them. Its driver had lost interest in running anyone over and was trying to limp off like a wounded animal.

"One more time," Carmody said to her and added his hurried instructions.

He returned his Sig to its holster and put his hands on her hips. Kali raced past the crippled Regera on the driver's side and quickly overtook it, tooling on ahead for fifty or sixty feet. Then she hit the front brake so the bike's nose dipped down and the rear wheel bucked up six inches off the ground, spun around on her front tire, dropped the end of the bike, and came to a stop facing the car.

Carmody jumped off the saddle, went around the front of the bike, and planted his boots apart in the snow. The Ninja's headlights were upped to their brightest setting, and he stood in their wash staring straight ahead at the Regera, backlit like an actor ontsage. The effect was deliberate and purposeful. He wanted the moment to stay with its driver a long time. Wanted him to picture it later on in an interrogation room.

The car started turning to the left, toward the road. Battered and maimed, hitching jerkily over the bare, bumpy ground. Unless he was in a blind panic, the man at the wheel had to realize he was going nowhere.

In case he didn't, Carmody raised his MK7, thumbing the fire control to its third position. Four red bullets in a row, full auto mode.

He opened fire, seeing clearly in the Ninja's lights. He started with the Regera's low front grill, angling the weapon downward, pouring a long, continuous stream of steel-jacketed penetrator rounds into it. He raised his weapon to the bumper, pounded it with bullets until it cracked and split and fell to the ground in chunks. He saw the driver duck down and cover his head with his hands, and brought the gun barrel up higher, sheeting the hood with parallel bands of fire, riddling it with holes, working his way up from the nose toward the bottom of the windshield.

A moment passed. He ejected his spent magazine, slammed in a fresh one, and took two giant steps closer to the car. The driver was still hunched over in his seat with his head buried in his hands. Carmody aimed to his left and hammered the windshield, his grip firm around the weapon, holding the barrel steady against its kick. Ballistic glass cracked and chipped off into hundreds of tiny granular particles, spilling onto the torn up remnants of the hood. He saw a hole appear in the center of the web-shaped fracture and pumped a long salvo through it into the contoured passenger seat. Flakes of chewed-up leather and foam fluttered like confetti inside the cockpit.

Carmody took another extended step toward the car, moved about three feet back of the front seat, and poured a stream of rounds into the radiator and engine block. The engine popped, hissed, and gagged, gushing fluids into the snow.

Finally, he peered through the driver's window at the man ducked with his head under the steering column. He was just on the other side of the door.

Tilting the weapon's muzzle slightly upward, Carmody fired a long burst at the window. It disintegrated in a shower of glass, the bullets flying two inches over the driver's back and shoulders. He still had his head beneath the wheel.

Carmody stepped up to the door and pointed the gun through the crumbled window at his back.

"Sit up," he said.

The driver didn't budge.

"Now," Carmody said. "I won't tell you again."

The driver straightened. He was tall, thin, and dark-haired and wore a flashy overcoat Carmody thought would have looked right on Merlin the magician. Stim-club chic, he'd seen it before. Seen the guy wearing it, too. Last summer, in Bucharest. At Club Energie.

"Not much car here for a couple of million bucks," Carmody said. "Probably won't even get decent trade-in value."

The guy's lip trembled. "You wanted the Wolf, but he is long gone," he said. "Everything you've done is wasted. I'm not your man."

Carmody stared at him over the barrel of his gun.

"Zolcu," he said, "that's where you're dead wrong."

Cobb and Luna were roughly above the crossroads when Carmody radioed up to them. *Raven*'s cockpit was dim, and they were keeping a tense watch on the drone swarm nearing Castle Graguscu from the west.

"How fast can you get here?" Carmody asked after making his request.

"Three minutes." Luna's hands were on the sticks. "We're already on our way."

"Okay, what kind of prep time do you need?"

"Talon's rapid-deploy, sir," Cobb said. "It's ready to rock."

"Okay."

"Sir?"

"I'm listening."

"ETA on the drone arrival is zero two hundred hours. We have ten minutes to evac the castle grounds."

"You hear from the rest of my team?"

"Negative, sir. Not a word. And there's something else." Cobb paused. "We haven't been able to raise Janus."

"What do you mean?"

"Just that, sir. We called in the hourly sitrep, and there's been no response."

"You try all available channels?"

"Yes."

"Including the Argos net?"

"More than once, sir."

Carmody was quiet a full ten seconds.

"Could be a technical glitch," he said finally.

"Yes, sir."

"But none of us really think it."

"No, sir."

"Which bothers me."

"Same here. But we'll keep trying."

Another silence.

"All right, one thing at a time," Carmody said. "I'm standing by."

"Look up in about thirty seconds and give us a wave," Luna said.

"Look down close enough, you'll see me wink," Carmody replied.

13

Raven arrived ten seconds early, a shadow that would have folded seamlessly into the night if not for the pinpoint star clusters outlining its sleek black form.

Carmody heard only the barest hum as she glided in over the treetops across the road, the downwash of her blades lashing and contorting their crowns and whisking soft lumps of snow off their uppermost branches. Then the air began to churn around him as the aircraft settled into position overhead, its searchlight flashing on with a brilliance of 75,000 lux, bathing the field in the equivalent of midday sunshine.

"What is this?" Zolcu was squinting out his blown-out window. "I can't see anything."

"Right," Carmody said. "You're probably better off."

"Better off *how*?"

Carmody looked in at him. He stood three feet to Zolcu's right, his MK7 in his hands. Kali was still straddling the motorcycle a few yards from the front of the car.

"I think you should shut up," he said. "Maybe grab hold of your seat."

"Why? What are you planning to do?"

Carmody stood there as the aircraft shed altitude, her rotors stirring tiny cyclones of snow around his boots.

"You're getting repetitive," he said.

"You haven't answered me."

"I haven't shot your head off yet, either," Carmody said. "No man knows how bad he is till he's tried very hard to be good."

"I don't understand."

Carmody stared at him, raising his rifle barrel a little higher. "I'm saying you shouldn't tempt me," he said.

The aircraft dropped down to about a hundred feet. Carmody bent his head back into the glaring light, shielded his eyes with a hand, and saw a panel in its belly slide open.

The Talon was in fact a thousand-pound clamshell gripper assembly, built of welded pipe sections, each with eight steel tines. It lowered smoothly from a remote-controlled winch inside the *Raven*'s cargo bay, its high-tensile smart cable transmitting data and commands between the gripper and cockpit, where Cobb would be at his instrument cluster monitoring the telemetry.

Carmody watched as it descended over the car. There was nothing too complicated about its operation. It was like working a crane that gave constant feedback about the wind, ground conditions, and whatever it might be lifting up into the air.

From the corner of his eye, Zolcu saw the Talon's shadow fall over him in the lights, its long, flat tines spreading open like gigantic saurian teeth. His eyes grew wild with sudden realization.

"No," he said. *"Please."*

Carmody didn't reply. He folded his arms across his chest and watched as the Talon came down and down, its jaws wide open. They hit the ground with an audible thunk and immediately began to clamp shut around the car, scooping through the shallow snow. Within a minute the gripper had the Regera in its clutches, Zolcu still inside, its tines fully interlocked under the car's flattened tires. Cobb lifted the Talon into the air, the winch in *Raven*'s cargo bay quickly winding in its cable. Loose fragments of the car spilled off between the tubular bars of its cage as it rose toward the aircraft.

Zolcu was screaming overhead. A high, shrill, tattered cry of horror and fear. When the gripper was fifty or sixty feet beneath the aircraft, its ascent abruptly stopped. It hung from the cable, swaying a little in the wind, Zolcu shrieking away inside its tubular bars.

Carmody strode over to Kali. "He should consider himself lucky. If those jaws had clamped shut any higher, there wouldn't be enough of him left to kick and scream."

She looked at him. "You need him alive."

"Right. He's got that going for him, too."

They watched *Raven* bank toward the east, Zolcu's cries trailing away into the wind. Carmody guessed the flight back to Mihail Kogălniceanu Airfield was about six hundred miles. He would have plenty of time to enjoy the trip.

Carmody walked across the field to his bike. It was on its side with the handlebars turned down toward the ground. He turned his back to it, took hold of a handgrip and the passenger backrest, bent his knees, and leveraged it up onto its wheels. Then he stood it on the kickstand, brushed the snow off, and gave it a hasty inspection.

The cowling was cracked in places but seemed mostly intact. The lines, frame, and tires looked good, and no fluids had leaked out into the snow.

Carmody climbed on and tested the levers. They moved easily. Finally, he put the bike in Neutral, rolled it back and forth, and started it up.

The engine revved smoothly.

He rode over to Kali. "Seems okay," he said.

She nodded and he got on the RoIP to Rover Two.

"We're heading back," he said.

He wasn't telling an outright lie. But it was close.

Long lowered his window as Kali and Carmody pulled abreast of him on their motorcycles. With their grab made, he had moved the BearCat onto the two-lane's gravel shoulder to reopen the crossroads.

The noise up above had been muted with the window shut. But now it was unnervingly loud and clear. The sky was humming and vibrating like the head of a snare drum.

Long reached an arm out and motioned toward the rear hatch.

"Get in. I'll take us out of here."

Carmody shook his head. "Not yet," he said. "Not me."

Long looked at him through the lowered window. "Did I miss something?"

"I'm riding back to the castle."

"Boss, we need to evac." Long nodded his chin skyward. "Those drones are headed right where you want to go."

"I hear them." Carmody paused. "There was someone with Zolcu."

Long said nothing.

"A woman," Carmody said. "Her name is Clinia."

Long said nothing.

"I promised I'd come back for her," Carmody said.

Long stared out the window a second or two. Then he scratched under his ear. "Guess I did miss something," he said.

Kali turned to Carmody from atop her bike.

"I'm going with you," she said.

Carmody looked at her. She met his gaze, her shoulders very straight.

He exhaled through his mask. Not hard, and not

visibly, just quietly breathing out. The sound in the sky had become loud and low and constant, like ocean waves. They had no time to lose.

"Okay," he said. "Stay close."

She nodded.

"Wait here for my orders," he told Long. "Be ready in case things get hot."

"Will do."

Carmody slipped a little fuel into his engine and eased in front of Kali. They throttled up, their Ninjas bucking forward with shudders of awakened power.

An instant later they were streaking south on the road to Castle Graguscu.

The sky throbbed with the sound of the approaching drone swarm as Carmody and Kali emerged from the woods behind the castle on their motorcycles, bore right off the two-lane, then swung left around the soaring western bastion. The only sign of the storm system that had passed through earlier that night was a light accumulation of snow on the ground.

At the drained artificial pond, they again turned left and rode straight across the band of open ground between the pond and cobblestone apron. The wreck of the Rezvani was ahead of them on the castle's scalloped outer stairs, flipped over on its roof and nested in broken glass. They could see blood in the snow around it.

About six feet from the apron, Carmody signaled a halt.

She pulled up alongside his bike. The phased, fluctuating white noise in the air seemed to envelop them. He raised his voice so she could hear him.

"Stay here," he said. "Someone has to stand lookout."

"I'll wait outside the entrance."

"Here's better."

Kali didn't speak. She could hear drones swirling and buzzing overhead.

"Listen," he said. "I'm disabling my AI link. The RoIP, too."

"We'll be out of contact. You can't be sure what's waiting in the castle."

"Clinia, hopefully."

"You know what I mean."

Carmody looked at her. "They break into our link, they can map our relative positions. Pinpoint your whereabouts out here."

"I'll be fine."

"I know," Carmody said. "But if I'm not back in five minutes, get out of here. Just in case."

Kali was quiet a second. The clear, star-encrusted sky overhead looked deceptively settled and peaceful. There was no visible sign of the drones. Only the pulsing sky to warn of their coming.

"I think it's wisest that we stay together, Mike," she said. "But that won't change your mind."

Carmody throttled a little fuel into his engine.

"Not this time," he said. "Stay alert."

Then he broke his eyes away from hers and rode off toward the apron without a backward glance.

Crimea

Drajan found her standing on the stone jetty running out from the seawall to the unsettled chop of the surf. Her back was to the shore, the whitecaps slapping up against the large, kelp-draped rocks under her feet.

He glanced down from atop the wall. A short jump below him, a narrow beach of sand and wet, wave-polished pebbles ran between the base of the wall and the perpendicular jut of stone. Crouching on his toes, he held on to the wall with one gloved hand, lowered himself a little over its ocean side, then dropped onto the beach.

The jetty was several yards ahead to his left. He strode lightly across the pebble beach to its landward side, then climbed up onto the rocks. She continued to face the ocean, standing above the shallows, a fur-lined hood drawn up over her pale blond hair.

He walked up behind her. The water lapped and slurped at the rocks to either side. The wind sounded like breath inside a throat. When he was almost close enough to touch her, she turned to face him.

As always, Quintessa Leonides had chosen her moment.

"Drajan," she said, "I'm surprised to see you out now."

He looked at her face. It was like finely cut crystal. Sharp-edged and beautiful, with striking glacial-blue eyes.

"You've been gone over an hour. It's cold."

"No colder than inside," she said. "How goes it in Romania?"

"I haven't heard from Zolcu. He's vanished. In my custom Regera."

She smiled thinly.

"Naturally," she said. "Do you think they've taken him?"

"I don't know. I'm not too concerned yet." He paused. "The rest goes as planned."

"In Baneasa as well?"

"Yes. Our fliers are in the air. The Americans will be crippled. Even if they choose to rebuild, their attention will be diverted until it's too late for them to interfere with us."

She nodded, her gaze turning northward. There was a bright smudge of light about a quarter mile up the unseen curve of the shoreline. A constellation of smaller lights surrounded it, sprinkling the darkness of the harbor water with red, blue, and white.

"The men work on the boat round the clock, and the Americans and their allies are blind to it," she said. "Their satellites, their drones, their spy planes. Blind. More incredibly, they see what isn't there. I don't know how you do it. I don't have a head for it."

"Koschei provides the tools. Resources unlike any I've ever had at my disposal."

"No matter. It is still sorcery to me."

He shrugged.

"I manipulate data, you manipulate currency. Each in our own way, we trigger events and capitalize. Our skills are complementary."

She looked into his eyes, nodding. "And here we are in Crimca."

"You sound unhappy."

"I am not fond of solitude. The peninsula is dreary and gray. But if I were unhappy, I would be elsewhere."

Drajan was thoughtful. The breeze flapped his raincoat and whipped his hair around his head. The strands framed his thin, pale face like a dark, fluid crown.

"What is it, Quintessa?" he said. "Talk to me."

Her gaze wandered. This time her eyes did not go toward the lights but to the rocks beneath her feet. After a moment, she looked back up at him.

"I have done something stupid," she said at length. "I took you to bed for my pleasure and fell in love."

Drajan did not speak. A response eluded him.

"You've had dreams lately," she said. "Who is Kali?"

He still did not speak.

She reached a hand out, put a gloved finger to the tattooed wheel on his neck.

"Who is she?" she said. "When you say the name in your sleep, your hand goes to this spot."

Silence. The waves lapped and gurgled around the stones below them.

At last Quintessa nodded to herself. Her hand slowly retreating to her side.

"Please return to your affairs," she said. "Rest assured, I won't fling myself into the sea."

Drajan stood there looking at her for a long moment. Then he turned without another word, walked the short distance back to the beach atop the rocks, and retraced his steps along the seawall to the edge of the secret city.

PART TWO

TERMINAL INTELLIGENCE

14

Six minutes before he got the call, Alex Michaels was on the neatly groomed front lawn of a Sacramento cottage sealed off with yellow crime-scene tape and guarded at the door by uniformed officers. His attention was divided, and that was an unfamiliar, even an alien, feeling to him. As a researcher and educator, he always maintained a perfect focus, cutting himself off from distractions. He was the noggin. The absent-minded professor. Clichés, stereotypes, of course. But he'd understood the subjective perception, and it wasn't really objectively wrong. He believed at his core that there was a solution to every problem. When working to solve one, he could always home in and make the rest of the world scarce.

It wasn't like that anymore. Being chairman of Columbia University's School of Computer Science had been a weighty responsibility. But he was now Director of Net Force, a position he had accepted because he knew he had the essential capabilities it demanded and because President Annemarie Fucillo asked…and because he loved her dearly, although it had been years since they were romantically involved. Michaels had been hoping to grow into the dual roles, but three months along, he felt oddly suspended between them, pulled in two directions at once, neither here nor there. That had never been truer than this morning, with Operation Scalpel underway in radio silence.

But these thoughts were distractions in themselves, and Michaels made an effort to push them away. He needed to see how the new kids handled things.

He faced forward, looking across the lush fescue at the driveway, where two Fair Oaks police cruisers and a county forensics van were parked nose to tail outside the garage. The narrow county road running past the property was blocked off in each direction by another two cruisers with bright red-and-white roof lights. Pulled parallel to the lawn was a long sleek white vehicle with a sliding cargo door on its passenger side. On the outside of the door was Net Force's departmental logo: a stylized *NF*, with an integrated circuit pattern inside the *N* and patriotic stars inside the horizontal bars of the *F*.

The van was one of a growing fleet of SEEKERs—mobile cyber-triage labs that Net Force Cyber Investigations deployed to assist local law enforcement in cases involving high-level cybercrime or technological threats to national security. The lab allowed for the on-site extraction, processing, and archiving of digital evidence while a mission was in progress. In doing so, it sped up crisis-response times and reduced the possibility that vital clues or evidence might be lost or deliberately purged from seized devices before their transport to a conventional lab facility.

Michaels quietly watched a small group of five Net Force instructors and trainees step from the van onto the grass. All wore black jumpsuits with the organization's shoulder patch, black boots, and sterile latex gloves. The lead instructor was Natasha Mori, a tall, wisp-like woman of thirty with skin the color of cream and choppy white hair. An albino and tetrachromat with heightened perception of color, she wore dark sunglasses to protect her exceedingly sensitive eyes.

Alex's brightest student when he arrived at Columbia, Natasha had later become a paid employee of his research lab. Then she left, and came back, and left again, in and out the door for her own reasons. Recently he'd gotten her to return on a provisional basis, convincing her to stay on through Net Force's first nationwide college recruitment push. Her specialty was predictive modeling, a cutting-edge discipline that used computational data to chart the probability of future outcomes.

Bryan Ferago, her assistant, was the professor's other best wirehead. With sandy brown hair pulled up in a high, tight bundle, he had the long, lean muscles of a swimmer or track-and-field runner and had in fact been a qualifying Olympic finalist for both sports as a college senior. His field of expertise was forensic systems and network analysis.

The trainees were the first of several groups that Michaels wanted to observe today. Two of them, Chris Way and Jase Hudson, were graduates of his digital forensics program at Columbia. Emily Sherron had recently earned her master's in cyber defense at the Naval Postgraduate School in Monterey.

Outside the mobile triage now, Natasha and Bryan briefly addressed their trainees and then led them up the gravel path toward the cottage. As they neared the spot where Alex waited on the lawn, he began walking alongside them at a steady, easy pace.

Not a single member of the group gave him so much as a passing glance. No one acknowledged his presence.

They reached the front door. There was a cop standing just to its right. An hour ago, the Fair Oaks police had raided it as the home base for an Iranian hacker cell, which had been responsible for penetrating the computerized operations system of Shasta Dam, the largest in the state. When they were caught, they had been days from seizing control of the water levels, flow, reservoir storage, and hydroelectric-power infrastructure for all of Sacramento. Over three million people.

Natasha was first up to the door. The cop reached for the handle and pulled it open.

"You can go right in," he said.

She nodded and entered. Then the new kids, single file. Last through the door was Bryan Ferago.

Michaels reflexively hung back a few paces. The cop didn't notice him. After a second, he followed the group into the cottage.

It was now four minutes before he got the call.

The cottage had an open, single-story layout—a living room/dining area just past the door, two bedrooms, kitchen, a bath and a half. County forensic technicians were milling around in their coveralls and gloves, tagging, bagging, dusting, marking, and snapping photographs.

There were about two dozen evidence bags on the dining table. Each showed a serial number and its collector's name. Each bore a notation about where the evidence was being sent for analysis. Each was marked with a police case number, date, time, item description, and case type. They were organized by destination, with those on the right side of the table marked *SFIU*—the Sacramento Forensics Identification Unit—in black Sharpie ink. Fewer than half were on the left side of the table and marked *NF*.

Natasha went for a closer look, motioning for Sherron and Way to come along while Hudson stuck with Bryan in the living room.

"What do you see?" she asked the trainees.

They studied the evidence bags a moment. Over half were transparent plastic. The rest were opaque Faraday, or radio-frequency shielding bags, variously sized nylon pouches lined with metallic fabric to prevent the captured electronic devices inside them from transmitting or receiving Wi-Fi, Blue-tooth, or satellite signals.

Sherron read the descriptions on the Faradays. "They're ours," she said. "Two phones…a tablet… three laptops. A few Jumpdrives."

"That was quick," Natasha said. "Again, what do you see?"

Sherron did not miss her abrupt tone. She shifted her attention from the Faradays to the clear plastic bags earmarked for the SFIU.

After a long moment, her eyebrows came up.

"Eew," she said. "Gross."

Unseen, Michaels smiled a little. In his white-paper evaluation of the botched Shasta Dam hacker prosecution, the piece of digital evidence Emily had just noticed was one of several to largely slip past investigators.

"What do you see?"

Sherron's cheeks reddened. "A rubber vagina," she said. "A sex toy."

"Not exactly realistic," Way said under his breath.

Natasha gave him a sharp look. "You're sure?"

Way cleared his throat.

Natasha faced him another moment, then turned back to Sherron. "Okay," she said. "What caught your eye about it? Creepiness aside?"

Sherron lifted the bag off the table between her thumb and forefinger, using them like tweezers.

"There are power and Wi-Fi switches," she said. "It's intelligent."

"Interactive suits me better. But you're correct,"

Natasha said and paused. "Mr. Way…what can an IoT pocket pussy tell us about its user?"

More throat clearing. "Well, he'd use it for web-cam sex."

"How? Be specific."

"The guy would log in to a chat room—one with a live model—and give her its password. So she can control its, uh, actions during their session. While she talks dirty to him. Or, you know, does things like…"

"I know," Natasha said. "Emily? Anything else?"

"The sessions aren't free," she said. "He would pay for them with a credit card or cryptocurrency. Either method is traceable, even if he's using an alias or counterfeit plastic."

"We can also find out *when* he was online. What times. And for how long," Way said. He was plainly angling for redemption. "That would put him at the computer, and here in the house, during certain periods that might coincide with other information we have on him."

"Also," Emily said, "I think the model could have information to share."

"Again…*specifically.*"

"Say he has loose lips. He might have blurted something out while he was getting a virtual f—"

Michaels turned back toward the living room. Natasha's group was fine. He wanted to see how things were going with Bryan's trainee.

The Hudson kid hadn't been an outstanding student by most academic standards. He didn't shoehorn easily into conventional measures of intelligence or do well on standardized tests. But he

tried hard and showed good instincts, a dogged-
ness that reminded Michaels of Leo Harris. He was
rooting for him to succeed.

He drifted into the room just as Bry and the kid
were entering from a connecting hallway. They
stopped near the open front door, where the crime-
scene techs were filtering out of the cottage to their
van. Michaels could hear their evidence trolleys
rolling and clattering over the lawn path.

"They're done," Bryan said to the kid. "Taking
off. And they missed something big."

"Do we know what it is?"

Bryan shrugged. "*I* know," he said. "But I've
been to this scene, like, twelve times. It's you that
counts."

Hudson looked around. The room was almost
bare. Cleared of everything but a sofa, some chairs,
and a coffee table. He seemed stumped.

"Want a tip?" Bryan asked.

"I sure won't say no to one."

Bryan stood next to him. "Be Gumby. Not a
Blockhead."

Hudson's face was confused.

"Obscure cartoons-on-cable reference, sorry,"
Bryan said. "The thing's to be flexible. Don't zero
in. Just soak up what you see."

Hudson looked around some more. Rubbed
the back of his neck. Then looked around again,
his eyes wandering the room. After a minute, he
stepped toward the front wall. There was a smart
thermostat about five feet to the right of the door.
It was small and round with a digital LED window.

Michaels followed him over to the thermostat. It was two minutes before he got the call.

"Wow," the kid said. "Smart therms work on adaptive learning. They have all kinds of sensors for reading the environment. Like near- and far-field motion detectors that record when somebody's home. And when the place is empty."

Bryan nodded. "What else?"

"Ambient-light sensors. They measure electric-light usage in the house and link on/off patterns to people's everyday routines. Say, when they wake up and go to sleep." Hudson thought for a second. "Don't they use Wi-Fi and cellular signals to communicate with people's devices? So they can adjust the temperature settings remotely?"

Bryan nodded again. "Tell me why that's important."

"When two devices communicate, you never know exactly what incidental data's exchanged. It's like a stream picking up sand and depositing it somewhere else. There might be info on the therm's microprocessor that can help us." He paused. "The hackers didn't own this cottage, right?"

"It's an Airbnb rental," Bryan said. "How does it matter?"

The kid shrugged. "I just can't see them bothering to download a thermostat-control app on their phones. They had other things on their minds."

Bryan looked at him.

"So?" he said. "Think."

He thought. Michaels waited. Hudson was within

a hair's breadth of finding another of the original
case probe's fatal omissions.

The kid stood there thinking ten seconds longer.
Then his eyes lit up.

"IoT devices have hidden internet ports," he said.
"They send data back to their manufacturers without users ever knowing it. Then add it to information from other users' thermostats or whatever
device it might be. That's how they aggregate data
about their customers. Put it all together and turn
it into *metadata*. They use it for product develop-
ment, ad campaigns…"

He suddenly fell silent.

"Did somebody push Pause?" Bryan asked.

The kid frowned. "It just came to me. If I can
figure all this out, wouldn't the hackers have
thought of it? And disabled the ports?"

Bryan shook his head a little. Doubtfully rather
than dismissively.

"These ports are hard-coded," he said. "They
would have had to rework the thermostat's whole
operating system."

"How about deleting the information from the
manufacturer's computers?"

"Not easy. Most companies use cloud storage."

The kid shrugged again.

"They breached the controls of one of this country's major dams."

Bryan nodded. "Don't get me wrong. They probably have the chops. But cloud hacks are complicated. And they thought they'd be on a plane before

anybody caught on to them. With Sacramento a disaster area."

Hudson's face was getting excited again. Michaels had noticed he often thought with enthusiasm.

"We can subpoena that data from the smart-therm company, right?" he asked. "There could be all kinds of info about the hackers' web-browsing patterns and log-ins."

Atta boy. Michaels smoothed his graying red beard. The session had gone well. So well, he had briefly stopped thinking about Romania.

He noticed Natasha and her trainees heading toward the door with their evidence, the connected sex toy included, and then watched them make their way over the lawn to the triage unit. They would be able to off-load data from the digital equipment, mirror the drowned phones, capture and preserve the hackers' digital footprint right here at the crime scene. If SEEKER's mobile technology had been available back in 2021, the trial of the hackers wouldn't have ended with a hung jury and five state-supported cyberterrorists walking free.

Michaels watched them enter the triage. He would head over there to observe them for a short while, then call an end to the session and check in with Morse on Scalpel.

He was stepping outside when the call came in. The beep tone sounded not through his ear but a cranial microphone.

"Professor Michaels, please excuse the interruption." Eve sounded like Audrey Hepburn very much by design; he had created the AI's voice with an audio sample from *Breakfast at Tiffany's*. "Eagle is on the line."

Annemarie, Michaels thought. It had to be urgent for POTUS to call now.

He stopped alongside the cop posted at the door. The cop didn't see him. He was invisible. A digital phantom.

"Pull me from the session," he told the AI. "But keep it running."

"One moment. Extraction in four, three, two…"

The Fair Oaks cottage, lawn, law enforcement and forensic personnel, evidence trolleys, police cruisers, crime-scene van, and even the SEEKER vehicle itself all vanished at once. So did two of the three trainees—Sherron was back home in Oregon for Thanksgiving weekend, and Way with his family in Rhode Island. They had participated in the training session as virtual avatars, using beta versions of his portable, untethered HIVE, or Highly Integrated Virtual Environment, headsets. The California cops and techs, on the other hand, were computer-controlled agents. Interactive characters created for the IR training scenario. Digital puppets.

"Establishing a secure channel to Eagle," Eve said. "Stand by."

Michaels kept his headset on for its audio feed. Across the theater-style aisle to his right, Bryan, Natasha, and Jase Hudson were physically present with him in HIVE 1, a large circular space in his Columbia University lab complex. Also wearing the stand-alone headsets, they were still immersed in the simulation. The full-surround LED wall panels that normally created the virtual environment were dark.

"Alex?" Fucillo said. "Are you with me?"

"Yes," he said. Both of them avoiding pleasantries. "What's happening?"

"I have some news out of Romania."

"Janus or up-country?"

"Both," Fucillo said. "I hope you're sitting down. We need to put our heads together and make some decisions. Because none of what I'm about to tell you is good."

Michaels nodded to himself in confirmation.

He hadn't thought it would be.

East Harlem

Adrian Soto wore three impressive career hats. He was CEO of Cognizant Systems, the innovative telecommunications firm he'd co-founded after multiple tours with the U.S. Army's Communications-Electronics Command; this was how he earned his very substantial living. Soto's second prominent hat was that of Cybersecurity Director for Net Force, a presidential appointment he had been honored to accept as his patriotic duty. But his most cherished hat was worn as founder and chairman of the Unity Project, a charitable organization he had launched in memory of his late fiancée, Malika, with a mission statement of bringing together people of different cultural backgrounds for shared socioeconomic goals, promoting cultural understanding and community growth though personal service.

Unity was his *passion*. His personal inspiration. His reason for carrying on after tribal hatreds took Malika from him in Iraq.

Tonight, the night before Thanksgiving, was one of Soto's favorite nights of the year at Unity. He had been fully briefed about Operation Scalpel, but was directing his thoughts toward the foundation, where they would be most useful. With his different and varied hats came the ability to compartmentalize. He was good at shifting priorities around in his mind to get things done.

It was around seven o'clock when his driver swung out of Third Avenue traffic and dropped him off in front of Unity's street-level headquarters. He got out and crossed the sidewalk, a little hop in his step. He could see staffers and volunteers through the storefront windows, decorating and preparing for the annual all-you-can-eat holiday dinner the foundation hosted for struggling local families. They would serve hundreds of portions of roasted turkey, mashed potatoes, stuffing, casseroles, and dessert. There would be bus rides to the festivities, prize drawings, a free photo booth, and a DJ. And there would be plenty of boxed leftovers.

Soto walked through the door. The usual reception room furniture had been cleared and several of his people were fussing with warming trays and Sterno at the serving counters. Others were laying out tablecloths, paper plates, and plastic utensils at the cafeteria tables. Gayle Robbins, his assistant director, was on a ladder hanging a huge honeycomb paper turkey from the ceiling. Slender, brown-eyed, brown-skinned, with tightly curled dark hair, she glanced down at him.

"Reporting for duty?" she said. "Step right up."

He gave her a combined nod and smile, gestured at the hanging turkey.

"My," he said, "that's a big bird."

"Wait till you see the real ones," she said.

"Do we know what time they're coming?"

"Truck's supposed to arrive at six o'clock sharp tomorrow morning," she said. "I plan to sleep here."

"Probably a few of us will have to," Soto said. Attendance had almost doubled in the past few years as the neighborhood's economy took one serious hit after another. He guessed they would have a thousand pounds of turkey and fixings, a hundred pumpkin pies…

The phone shivered in his pants pocket. It was a Cognizant dual cell/satphone, but only the satellite mode was set for silent vibrate. That meant the call was official business.

He reached for it and checked the caller ID.

Eagle.

The movable compartments in his brain shifted.

"Everything all right?" Gayle said.

Soto kept his eyes on the display.

"I hope so," he said, and excused himself.

"Madam President." Soto hurried to the back of the reception area. "Bear with me, please… I have to go where I can speak freely."

His office was a small, square room off in a corner. It had few furnishings. A U-shaped wooden desk, chairs, some standing file cabinets. The desk was clear except for a computer screen and picture frame. The picture was of Malika.

He sat down with his coat still on.

"I apologize," he said. "I was in a busy room."

"Understood," she said. "We should get right down to it. Alex Michaels is on the line with us. He'll fill you in."

Which told Soto the call had to be about Scalpel.

"Alex," he said. "Talk to me."

Soto listened in stunned silence. He'd been wrong. It wasn't about Scalpel, not really. Or about anything he would have remotely expected.

Janus Base was under attack. From the very armed security robots meant to guard it.

"Damn it," he said. "What's Colonel Howard's present situation?"

"He's rolling toward the barracks with the autons. There may be survivors down below in a shelter or safe room. That's all Duchess could tell us."

Soto paused to organize his thoughts. Instantly reprioritizing.

"The Puma command vehicle is Argos-equipped," he said after a moment. "I ordered the fitting out myself. Howard should be able to maintain contact with us."

"Do you have any idea what's going on with the hedgehogs?" Fucillo said.

"I normally don't like to speculate," Soto said. He exhaled. "They're vulnerable to a hack. Their operating systems are archaic. That's at the very least. I scheduled a trip to Romania for right after the New Year to assess whether the robots can be upgraded or need to be entirely replaced. Now I wish I'd made that inspection sooner."

"Adrian, the *world* is a busy room, to use your words. So let's be gentle with ourselves," Fucillo said. "The hedgehogs are outdated. All Janus's defenses are creaky. Funding for Net Force has been a tough fight, and I've been unable to completely zero in on it. My plate's been full. There's our recovery from the cyberstrike. And the mess in the Republic of Birhan. After three months of United Nations dawdling, we finally have a chance to push through international sanctions. I do my best, and can't feel guilty about not being able to accomplish everything at once."

Soto thought for a moment. "We have soldiers in rotation at Mihail Kogălniceanu Airfield. The Black Sea rotation—I've worked with them planning my trip. Can we send them in to help with the evac?"

"Our boys are ready," Fucillo said. "But Colonel Howard wants to wait on activating them."

"With good reason, I think," Michaels added. "Technically our troops are in-country to support Romanian operations. Not vice versa. Before they start to move, we'll have to inform our hosts."

"Who are still feeling burned by our Bucharest operation last summer," Fucillo said. "Once they get involved, they're going to have questions. They'll wonder why so many of Janus's personnel are off base. They'll wonder where they are…"

"And we're trying to keep Scalpel under their radar, at least while it's in progress," Michaels said.

Soto was quiet. He heard a trill of laughter outside his office. His crew always made setting up for the feast a kind of party.

"I can push up my trip to Romania," he said. "Leave as early as tomorrow. Whatever's necessary."

"Thank you, Adrian. I appreciate it. But for the moment, I think it's best we leave things to Howard," Fucillo said. "He's a capable man. Let's give him time. Meanwhile, we'll stay connected."

Soto heard a breath escape his lips.

"It's going to be a long night for all of us," he said.

"Now you see why I never bother trying to sleep," Fucillo said.

15

FOB Janus

The four Pumas had gone rolling and rumbling across the field in formation, west to east, and then halted in unison about two thousand feet from the large, roughly rectangular parade ground. Across it was the fiery rubble that only hours ago had been a barracks housing fifty Quickdraw military personnel.

Each of the three autonomous 4x4s was eight tons of tough-looking welded-steel armor, equipment, and onboard weaponry. There was one at the tip of the wedge, one at the right flank, one at the left. More brawn than brains, they lacked the ability to choose their own targets or engage in combat without human control and oversight. Although they did not have the deep-learning abilities of the hedgehogs, they were significantly bigger and stronger.

Julio Fernandez was banking on that crucial advantage in the six-wheeler at the formation's rear flank, where he sat watching his monitors and readouts while Wasserman spoke on the radio with a Romanian Air Force operator at Mihail Kogălniceanu Airfield. It had taken several tries to make contact, leading Colonel Howard to wonder aloud if anyone there was even awake.

But right now he wanted to see for himself what Fernandez was looking at on the displays. He started to lean forward in the jump seat, felt a sharp, stabbing pain in his side, and sank back in frustration and disgust.

"You got a visual on the 'hogs?" he asked.

"Check. Nice and clear. There's been no change in their activity status."

"Meaning?"

"They haven't budged. It's just a guess, but I don't figure they will till we come into range."

Because it would open a gap in their cordon, Howard thought. If the robots' purpose was to cut off an escape route for the people in the bunker, they would keep a tight circle around the exit. Until they couldn't. Or so Julio was theorizing.

Howard was quiet a second. Distract, deflect, and destroy. Their plan was rudimentary as all shit. And sensible. Except it didn't take the noise in the sky into account. He could hear the vibrations humming and singing through the Puma's armor like current through a transformer. Forget about it being made by a plane or a helicopter. It was drones, it had to be drones. And whatever they were doing up there, his singular objective right now was to get his people out of the bunker. Just get them the hell out while there was still time.

"What else you need to know before we move?" he said.

Fernandez was silent a moment. "*Wish* I knew exactly what adversarial machine learning's been shoved into their brains. So I wouldn't have to guess how they'll respond to our push."

"But you won't know that tonight," Howard said.

"No. And I won't without a postmortem analysis."

"Then forget about it. We—"

"Colonel?" Wasserman pulled off his headset and swung around to face him. "I've got something from MK Airfield. It answers a big question for us."

Howard saw the alarm on his face. "What is it?"

"They're missing a drone swarm. Over a hundred of them."

"How's that possible?"

"The Romanians aren't sure. They took off on their own." Wasserman paused. "It gets worse, sir. They're attack drones. Full of explosives."

"And nobody knew till *now*?"

"With the transition over to Camp Turzii, the base is down to a skeleton crew."

"But the dumb shits have suicide bots there." He frowned. "All right. What else did they tell you?"

"A mobile patrol visits the field every half hour. At one o'clock this morning, the drones were on the ground. The one-thirty patrol discovered they were airborne."

"There were no alerts? Nothing on their computers?"

"No, sir. Their monitoring systems *still* don't show a launch. But the drones were picked up in the air by their GPS sats. About twenty minutes ago."

Howard glanced over at Fernandez. "That hold water for you?"

"Maybe." The sergeant didn't take his eyes off his console. "We have a warning system in place for the 'hogs. And *that* failed."

Howard checked the time on his watch—0147 hours—and frowned.

"Those drones are what we're hearing outside," he said. "If the Romanians knew they've been coming this way for almost half an hour, why weren't we notified…or didn't they bother explaining it to you?"

"That's the thing, sir," Wasserman said. "Their GPS sats had them well north of us. Hundreds of miles north, in Ukrainian airspace. So they alerted Kiev. But nobody there could pick them up."

"So somebody fucked with their *satellite* readings?"

"Looks like it, sir. They were in the dark about the swarm's heading and flight path until I raised them."

A moment passed.

"We've been set up," Howard said. "Like tin ducks in a shooting gallery."

Neither Fernandez nor Wasserman spoke. The colonel sucked in air. It whistled slightly through the gap between his front teeth.

"Okay," he said after a second. "Wass, I need a linkup to Duchess. Quick."

"Yes, sir."

"Julio?"

"Yes, sir."

"Get ready. You've got till I'm off the com. Then it's showtime."

Laura and Mario drove toward the decimated barracks, making their approach from the left across Janus Heights, staying within a hundred yards or so of the field's southern border. Ahead of them at the extreme eastern end of the parade grounds, the high, hungry flames leaping from the buildings gave the postmidnight darkness an eerie, orange tinge.

"Laura...stop here," he said from the rear of the Jolt.

She applied the brakes, shifted into Park, and twisted around in her seat. *"Que te pasa?"*

"I want to check something out," he said. "There are binoculars in the glove box."

She opened the box, fished them from inside, then twisted around in her seat and passed them back to him.

Mario raised the binocs to his eyes. The buzzing in the sky could no longer be mistaken for anything but drones...and a lot of them. It seemed much lower and closer than just a few minutes ago, and reminded him of the cyclic, pulsating hum of a large power transformer. But louder. Exponentially louder.

He gazed out to his left, eastward and southward. The clouds had thinned and shredded after the snow petered off, and the combined luminosity of the moonlight, starlight, and flames gave him a clear view of the parade grounds.

There were two stationary hedgehogs in sight, one on the south side of the building, another on the north side. Spree and Nash, he guessed, following some corrupted version of their patrol directives, continuing to protect their specified sectors in their robotic minds. If he was right, their positions revealed something about how their programming had been manipulated and altered. Probably, Earl was out of sight behind the burning building.

Mario was still looking through the lenses when he noticed something at the very edge of their periphery. To the east. He swung them farther in that direction...and snatched in a breath.

"Mario...what is it?"

He realized he still hadn't answered Laura's first question.

"I was looking at the hedgehogs outside the barracks. But then I saw *them*." He pointed and held out the binocs. "Here. Take these. They're headed toward the barracks. See?"

She held them to her eyes.

"I see," she said. "Are they tanks?"

"Not exactly," he said. "They're Pumas. Armored battlewagons. Kind of a cross between tanks, trucks, and personnel carriers. The three up front are four-wheelers. They're moving in a wedge."

"Like an arrow."

"Right. It's an attack formation."

She kept looking through the glasses. "I see a fourth one. A little behind them. It's bigger."

"Yeah," he said. "A six-by-six. That's the command-and-control vehicle."

"Who do you think is inside them?"

He was quiet a second. Some of his earliest work at Janus had involved assisting Julio Fernandez with improvements to the master/minion configurations of his autonomous and semiautonomous vehicle systems. Logically…

"I think those first three are RCVs. Robotic combat vehicles," he said. "That last one, the C&C, it's probably manned. There could be a whole crew in it. Maybe Commander Howard if he made it out of headquarters. Maybe Sergeant Fernandez, too. He set up the system architecture. All of it. Knows it better than anybody."

She lowered the glasses.

"Mario," she said, "*hay algo no entiendo.* Why are the robots just standing outside the barracks?"

He thought about that a minute. It was a good question.

"The building has a reinforced basement. An emergency shelter," he said. "The 'hogs could be waiting. Guarding it. In case there are survivors inside."

"Then those Pumas…they must be going there to get people out."

"Yeah," Mario said. "Must be."

Laura looked at him. "We have to help," she said.

"No," he said. "I'm pretty sure there are drones in the air…and I don't think they're ours. And you're a civilian. Not a soldier. You have to get away from here."

"Mario, Mario...ese no es el punto," she said in Spanish. *"Este es nuestro deber como humanos. Pararse y ser valiente."*

He looked at her in silence.

That's not the point, she had said.

It is our duty as human beings to stand up and be brave, she had said.

Mario kept looking at her. His throat felt thick. At that moment, he knew she was everything he could ever want out of life. Laura Cruz and a thousand endless nights of holding her close. Two kids, three, maybe more. A family. Boys that looked like a combination of their mom and dad, and little girls that were miniature versions of Laura, with deep, dark beautiful brown eyes exactly like hers.

He sighed, nodded.

"Let's go," he said.

George Bush Center for Intelligence
Langley, Virginia

Morse was on her second trip back to her desk from the Keurig machine when the phone rang, her office landline this time. It was Howard again. She hurried to answer, lunging for the phone without setting down the coffee. Big mistake. Physical coordination wasn't her greatest strength. It became an outright weak spot under stress. The coffee barely missed her blazer while sloshing over the rim of her cup onto the desk.

She set it outside the spill and jabbed at the speaker button.

"I'm here," she said.

Howard gave a twenty-five second update. He told her about the drone swarms. One launching from Mihail Kogălniceanu Airfield. A second group from Camp Turzii in Satu Mare District. Then he outlined his plan to clear his personnel from the bunker.

Morse felt her pulse quicken as he spoke. She noticed coffee trickling over the side of the desk, yanked some tissues from a box on the other side, and wadded them into the spill.

"First things first," she said. "I don't see how you can launch a rescue operation without support."

"It's already done," Howard said. "We're moving in."

"Then abort and move out. It's suicidal."

"And leave my people?"

"The bunker's built to hold up under massive bombing."

"I'm not worried about the bunker. I have wounded men and women down there."

"They can have air and ground assistance within the hour. POTUS and Director Michaels have assembled a task force from BS-AST. There's a brigade of Marines at MKAF. And a joint mechanized task force is ready to deploy from Novo Selo in Bulgaria. They have a THOR antidrone unit. Don't be foolish, Colonel. Move out."

"Not till we evac the bunker, Duchess."

A second of silence.

"Goddamn it," she said. "I could turn my request into a direct order."

Both knew she wasn't bluffing. Net Force's rapid kick start had led to myriad interim command-

relationship agreements between its various compo-
nents, the intelligence community, and the military.
Under those CRAs, Morse was Quickdraw's ultimate
TACOM, or tactical command officer.

"Since when do you cuss?" Howard said.

"Since you turned into Mike Carmody."

"I'm gonna ignore that one."

She paused a beat. "Anything new from him?"

"Not that I know," Howard said. "Duchess…
what are your orders?"

Morse was silent. This one had to come from
her gut.

"Godspeed, Colonel," she said after a moment.
"You're on-site, I'm not. I won't step on you. Just
keep me informed."

They disconnected. She sat there thinking for
about fifteen seconds. Then she took the dripping
wad of tissues off her desk and dropped it in the
wastebasket. It hit the bottom of the plastic liner
with a soggy thunk.

Morse looked at her desk. The coffee was almost sopped up. She reached for some fresh tissues,
bunched them together, and began wiping away the
rest of the spill. Rubbing the tissues over the spot
in little concentric circles and thinking some more
about Romania.

She'd noticed the desk was buff and dry and was
about to toss the second bunch of tissues when her
phone rang again. The caller ID said it was Leo Harris.

She was thinking POTUS would have notified
Alex Michaels. And Michaels would have called
her ex. Medical leave or not, he was Net Force's
Director of Cyber Investigations.

The desk clock said it was ten minutes to nine at night. Not quite 3:00 a.m. But still within the time range when incoming phone calls signaled bad news more often than good. Add that this was the start of the long holiday weekend, she figured it might as well be the wee hours of the morning.

Reminding herself that the modified rule was statistically unverified—as yet—Morse took a deep breath and picked up.

Jersey City, New Jersey, USA

"I really don't care what you have to tell me," Harris barked over the phone. "I do not want to hear it!"

"Then why did you call?"

"Because I'd like to know why I wasn't consulted when you were planning this thing."

"Leo, you're ranting."

"I'm not ranting."

"You definitely are," Morse said at the other end. "You're also contradicting yourself. Either you want to have a conversation or you don't. And if you don't and are just going to sound off, I'm hanging up."

He took a breath. An abdominal breath. A belly breath. In through the nose, out through the mouth. Slow. One hand on his rib cage to remind him it wasn't supposed to move up and down. He was breathing with his diaphragm, not his chest muscles. Because his damaged, stitched-together lungs needed all the help they could get.

"Leo? Are you alive?"

He swung around in his desk chair. There were exercise machines all around him, thousands of dollars' worth of useless junk he hardly ever used. The place looked like a rehab facility instead of his living room. It made him feel pathetic.

"Halfway," he said.

"Good enough if you'll stop the crap," Morse said. "Why are you clobbering me?"

"I just heard from the prof," he said. "About what's happening in Romania."

"Before we go on…we're secure?"

"I might need a cane to walk to the grocery for toilet paper. But there's nothing wrong with my damn brain."

"Which I'll take as a yes," Morse said. "Okay, Leo. If you were briefed by Director Michaels, I assume you know the situation's in flux." She paused. "Howard updated me just now. There have been some additional developments at Janus. And not good ones."

He listened to her summary. Drone swarms flying out of two Romanian airports without the knowledge of their military operators. And in the air over Janus and the Wolf's Lair. Armed with explosives.

Harris felt his cheeks drain of color.

"Goddamn it," he said. "I was afraid of something like this."

"We all understood the risks. But we had to move."

"Why?"

"The Russian activity in and around Rosalvea. Petrovik's bluff to convince us he hadn't left the barn, complete with the most sophisticated deepfakes we've ever seen to make Zolcu appear to be *him* in our aerial surveillance images. Do you need more of a list? They're cooking something up, Leo. No one's keeping secrets from you."

"Or wants to hear what I have to say."

"That's grossly inaccurate. And unfair. It took us a while to plan things out. This mission required preparation and precision, with no time to waste, and you were on medical leave until two weeks ago. Less than four *months* ago, you almost died when that car bomb exploded."

"Tell me something I don't know." The explosive device had been in the Tesla's trunk when he opened it, and he'd dived in front of the vehicle seconds before it blew. The click of its triggering mechanism had clued him, and the protection he'd gotten from the engine block had saved him...but he'd been badly hurt.

Damaged, he thought.

Leo stared at the aluminum cane under his desk. At first he'd tried leaning it against the side of the desk when he sat down to work. But somehow or other he kept kicking it over. When his pet box turtle Mack didn't knock it down *first* while on the way to its salad bowl. So he'd started laying it flat on the floor, which is where it always wound up anyway.

"Fact is, I might've objected to the mission if anybody asked," he said after a pause. "And I definitely wouldn't have okayed Outlier staying on at Janus after the Bucharest job. She was supposed to be shipped back to the States for interrogation. That was our bargain."

"Leo, you're all over the map. Why even mention this to me now?"

"Because it was you who made the offer," he said. "We never should've let her see the inside of a classified bird like *Raven*. Never mind go along on the op."

"She's earned that much trust. Carmody requested that she accompany him, and it was my call to approve it or not."

"Yeah, well, fuck Carmody. He's the one who got us into this spot."

"Leo—"

"No, check that. It was *you* listening to his bullshit."

"Leo, stop right there. Before you get in any deeper. I won't let you punish me for your own misguided sense of inadequacy. We've been through it before, and it didn't end well."

Harris clenched the phone tightly in his hand, listening to the tunnellike silence of an end-to-end encrypted connection. "What's that supposed to mean?"

"I'm in the thick of a major crisis, Leo. That's my sole priority right now. It ought to be yours, too," she said. "I suggest you take my advice and pull your head out of your ass."

Click.

"Carol? Hello?"

Harris was quiet. He heard the odd whooshing digital silence again. Even though she'd hung up and their connection was broken. He still thought he could hear it.

Breathe in. Breathe out. Nose. Mouth. Belly.

He sat with the phone cradled between his ear and shoulder for a long while, trying to pull in enough air to somehow make himself right.

But he couldn't do it.

He couldn't.

16

Castle Graguscu

Carmody halted at the bottom of the stairs, dismounted the bike, and looked around the apron. There was enough star glow above him and artificial light spilling from inside the castle that he didn't have to flip down his DNVGs.

Schultz and the BearCat had done a whole lot of damage. The dead man on the cobbles to his right could have been mistaken for something that wasn't human. A mangled animal. The body was crushed and smeared across the snow.

He swiveled toward the castle on his boot heels and walked up the broad, low stairs outside the portico. His feet made crackling noises against the granite as he strode over drifts of shattered window glass. The sky overhead whined and pulsated.

He reached the top step and paused. The splintered wicket gate hung precariously from its hinges, and light from the Great Hall shone through the opening to wash over the overturned Rezvani. He glanced through its rear window and saw two dead men inside, one in front, the other in the rear. Their arms and legs were wildly contorted, and the interior of the vehicle was clotted with blood.

His carbine at the high ready, Carmody strode around the Rezvani to the castle's enormous main door, backed against the latch side of the shattered wicket, and leaned his head slightly past its frame to peer into the hall. He saw no movement, took a deep breath, and angled into the castle. Leading with the barrel of his outthrust rifle, his legs spread apart, his knees bent to lower his center of gravity.

He stopped, checked left and right. The hall was one of the few parts of Castle Graguscu he'd seen in Satu Mare's photographic archives, all dating back to the end of World War II. But those drab black-and-white images were of a crumbling, neglected ballroom hastily converted into a Wehrmacht field headquarters and crowded with radio equipment, maps, and military banners. There had been faded and peeling wall murals, cracked and broken floor tiles. The gigantic fireplace opposite the door had been crammed with Nazi plunder. Silver and gold and statues and artwork.

What Carmody saw in front of him now was an expensively, conscientiously restored shrine to warfare, conquest, and death. The carved stone skulls under the ceiling posts, the grisly battle scenes, the rows of swords, axes, and lances…

He knew centuries separated the Poisoner's rule from its Nazi occupiers. But there might as well have been a direct, uninterrupted line of succession.

He moved forward, stopped again, scanned the room, and listened. He saw no sign of Clinia from Cluj and heard nothing but the drones making their approach. The sound was loud and low, heavy and undulant. A pulsing oscillation in the air outside the wicket. He didn't know how fast the swarm could travel. But it was getting close.

A long moment passed. Carmody's eyes briefly came to rest on the high spiral staircase ahead of him. He wondered if they reached all the way to the tower where he'd left Clinia.

He looked up the stairs. There didn't seem to be anyone on them. From what he'd read of her emotional state, he didn't think Clinia would have stayed in the tower. She had been frightened, angry, and humiliated. No, she wouldn't have stayed. But she would have had plenty of time to come down here. So where was she?

Carmody sensed something was very wrong.

He went deeper inside. The floor was square black-and-white marble tiles. His footsteps were flat and unechoing. He studied the walls for hidden doors as he advanced but didn't see any obvious telltales. That didn't mean there were no secret ways in or out. It just meant he couldn't see them.

He neared the middle of the hall and checked around some more, glancing ahead, and up, and to his sides. Above him on the left was a balcony overhang. It was about fifty feet up, oval, and in partial shadow. In the historical photos, a swastika banner had been displayed from it.

Carmody couldn't see up onto the balcony from his angle. He took a couple of steps forward and craned his neck around for a better look and finally saw Clinia standing behind its stone railing.

She wasn't alone. A guy was behind her, holding a gun against her head. He was tall and bony with combed-back yellow hair, and wore the same kind of black uniform the security men in the hallway upstairs had worn.

"Stay right where you are," he said. "Another step, and I'll kill her."

Carmody said nothing. He didn't move. Clinia looked dazed, in shock. Her face was a battered mess.

His neck tightened up. There was a wide-open gash on her forehead, one of her eyes was swollen shut, and her right cheek was about twice its normal size. She was laboring for breath, and no wonder. Her nose was broken and skewed to one side, the blood dripping thickly from her nostrils. It ran down over her lips and chin and had streaked and spattered the front of her dress.

"She told me you would be back," the yellow-haired guy said. "Her gallant American."

Carmody said nothing. He heard what sounded like an elevator door opening to his right. In his peripheral vision, he saw a group of three men appear through a sliding panel in one of the murals.

The guy in the lead was enormous with a bald head like a cannonball. He didn't have a visible firearm, but the two behind him were carrying Kalashnikov AK-74 military rifles, the original, better-balanced version with a laminated wood stock and hand-guard. The big guy came up on Carmody and stopped slightly to his right, while his companions swung around behind him.

He felt the bore of a rifle push against the middle of his back.

"Drop your weapon," the big one said. His voice was hoarse and gritty. "Hands up in the air."

Carmody stayed very still. He did not let go of the carbine.

"Drop it," repeated the giant. "Or she's dead."

Carmody didn't move. He was six-one, and the guy towered above him. He knew he'd seen him before; a living mountain wasn't easy to forget.

But that wasn't important right now. The important thing was that there was no bluff in his voice. The guy on the balcony had done an awful number on Clinia. Savagely beaten her. He would have no compunction about killing her.

He let the rifle drop to the floor. The big man kicked it away, and it went spinning and clattering across the checkered marble tiles.

"Now your helmet. The goggles."

Carmody kept staring at the woman on the balcony. He'd told her to wait for him, wait here, and she had listened.

His lips moved. It could have been a curse spoken under his breath. Then he took off the helmet assembly and held it out. The big man grabbed it with his right hand and passed it to one of the guys behind him, reaching into his jacket pocket with his other hand.

Carmody barely had a chance to react, rolling his head to the left a split second before the giant brought his hand out of the pocket and hauled off at him, smashing a fist the size of a meat loaf into the side of his face.

Carmody saw stars. It was like being hit with a carpenter's mallet. If he hadn't sideslipped the blow, it would have shattered the hinges of his jaw. He rocked on his legs but somehow kept them underneath him.

The giant threw another punch, a sweeping right hook at his face, and he brought his forearm up to block it. Carmody had solid, powerful arms. They were built up and corded from his shoulders to his wrists. But the hit was worse than he expected, shooting a bolt of pain through flesh and muscle to his radial bone.

A glimpse of what was in the giant's thick, blunt fingers—the object he'd gotten out of his pocket—explained things. It was a weight load, with a stirrup around the knuckles and a tubular metal rod wrapped in his hand.

Carmody no sooner saw it there than the huge, brass-knuckled fist swung at him again. He bent at the knees to duck below its arcing path, then sprang up with his hands clenched together and drove them up hard under the giant's arms and into his throat.

If he remembered right about where he'd seen him before, it would be a sore spot.

The giant staggered on his heels. His growl of pain and anger sounded like wet gravel rattling inside a metal pipe. Carmody pressed in on him, and was about to ram his interlocked hands up into his throat again, when one of the guards who'd been standing behind him slammed his rifle's wooden butt into his temple.

This time Carmody didn't just see stars. This time a bright white nova blew up in his vision and splintered off in all directions. His knees going rubbery, he managed to swivel around, hit the guard with a right uppercut, and then jab his left fist into his cheekbone. The guard went spilling back onto his ass, but Carmody was just barely aware of it. He was still blinking and trying to clear his eyes of the flying, shooting shards of light, when the giant came in on him again like a maddened bull, moving faster than someone of his proportions should have, driving him backward with all his mass and muscle, slamming him up against the wall adjacent to the archway. Carmody hit it with a thud. His spine crunched. His ribs groaned. He felt his knees buckle some more and sagged an inch or so down the wall but stayed on his feet. The giant was right up against him now. Pressing him against the wall with his broad slab of a chest. His hammy, loaded fist clubbed the side of Carmody's skull again, and again, and again.

"Drop!" the big man husked.

Carmody stayed on his feet.

And then they were on him. All three of the

men who'd appeared from behind the painted wall panel, on him together. One of the guards lunged at his knees from his left like a football tackle. The other, probably the one he'd floored, pounded his head with his gunstock again.

Carmody stumbled back against the wall, off balance, blood coursing into his eyes, stinging his eyes, his vision a sheet of red.

The big man moved closer. A sudden rush, like a glacier heaving forward. The guards were both up on their feet and pinning him against the wall, one on each side, using the full weight of their bodies to immobilize him. The big man brought one foot up and kicked him in the stomach with a size-sixteen boot. Carmody slid farther down the wall but stayed up. The giant kicked him a second and third and fourth time, but he stayed up.

There were more kicks. Rhythmic. Pistonlike. Like a machine.

The air fled Carmody's lungs. The strength leaked out of his knees. The guards finally let go of him, the giant backing up a step or two. He realized they were giving him just enough room to fall flat on his face.

He didn't go down. He felt limp and boneless. But he didn't go down. His legs bent, his arms loose at his sides, he stayed up.

The big man's face was right up in his. Brutal, heavy, full of aggression.

"Fuck you, American," he said and grabbed his shirt collar with both hands and flung him to the floor like a rag doll. He landed on his back, and

ATTACK PROTOCOL   277

the massive boot came down on him again, grinding down on his diaphragm, its heel twisting and mashing into him.

"How does this feel, American? *Do you like it?*"

Carmody drew a ragged breath, blinked blood out of his vision, and looked up into the giant's eyes.

"I'm going to kill you," he said.

A second passed. The big man's upper lip twitched slightly. He hawked up a mouthful of saliva, spat wetly in Carmody's face, bent over him, and jerked his head up off the floor, holding it between his hands and turning it toward the balcony.

"Watch," the big man said. And then, raising his voice, "*Laso sa zboare.* We will see if she can fly."

Carmody heard the crack of a gunshot above him. His temples in a vice grip, he saw blood spray from Clinia's head, then saw her body spill over the railing and swan to the floor. It landed three or four feet to his right with a flat, sickening thump.

The big man snapped his head back around so he had to face him again and then looked down into his eyes, the other two security men closing ranks around him, jabbing their guns to his temples.

"No wings," the giant said. "Too bad."

Get out of here, Carmody had said over the RoIP. There was no video. No other communication. He'd activated his comlink only to speak those words. To send her the message.

Then nothing.

Only silence from him.

Kali shivered on her motorcycle. The hard, glacial cold had clamped down on her like an anvil. Above her, the sky was swollen and palpitating with sound.

Get out of here.

The time stamp on her HUD told her that was five seconds ago. Over seven minutes had gone by since he'd climbed the wide castle stairs and passed out of sight through the archway.

Long enough. But she would keep her mind in focus.

"Cas," she said. The name short for Castor, her guiding star. And for the name of the sleeper AI she had installed in her helmet computer.

"Somniator lucidus," she said. The phrase Latin for Lucid Dreamer, and her code for awakening the AI.

"Hello, Outlier." The voice was soft, male, neither old nor young. Its inflections vaguely British and somewhat West Country. "How may I assist you?"

"Are you screened from all outside systems?"

"Yes."

"Then back-door into Sentinel, code H-9-6-4-0-3-A-1. Show me its livestream. Include all positional, navigational, and timing data."

"One moment."

Exactly two seconds later, the drone flock appeared on her head-up display, the images coming from *Raven*'s high-altitude Sentinel scout, soaring above them like a hawk over a flock of migrating sparrows. There were easily over a hundred. Small, probably collapsible, probably 3-D printed. Very probably carrying explosive payloads, based on their number: one did not launch noisy drone swarms for surveillance. Their airspeed was about forty-five miles per hour, and the altimeter said they were at four hundred and twenty feet and descending rapidly. They were about two miles off.

That gave her four to five minutes before they arrived.

Get out of here, he'd said.

She had to hurry.

"Cas, export all files to Access Mundi," she said. It was the web vault she shared with only one other person on earth. "Oarsman is to receive immediate notification."

"Exporting."

"Also, activate my helmet videocam. Full two-party encryption. Should my vital functions terminate, link the recording to my biodata and archive."

"I hope that won't be needed."

"As do I."

"Will there be anything else?"

Kali gripped her handlebars. *Goddess, be with me.*

"Stand by," she said and fired up the bike.

Kali bounced across the apron, rode past the overturned Rezvani to the east side of the steps, and cut sharply back around a hundred and eighty degrees, so the steps and castle entrance were about ten yards diagonally to her right.

She braked and sat there a moment astride the bike. The main door loomed in the archway. Made of planks clearly sourced from full-grown trees, it looked solidly unmoved and immovable. But its wicket gate was smashed open.

Kali guessed it was about twelve feet high and eight feet wide. Guessed Carmody must have entered the castle through it. She'd been unable to see him from the west side of the stairs at that point; the Rezvani had blocked her field of vision. But he must have gone through the wicket. There was no other direct way in.

She tried to peer through into the Great Hall, looking up the steps. But once again she had a poor line of sight. She could see lights inside, an expansive sweep of checkerboard floor, a section of the ceiling with ribbed wooden arches large enough to be the frame of a sailing ship. The castle in all its immensity was like something out of a folktale, a Norse myth. Home of the giants.

I need you to ride like you did in Germany.

Kali let out her clutch, hit the throttle hard, and shot forward. A deep breath, and she cut sharply right toward the castle entrance, hopped her front wheel up onto the broad bottom step, and then up to the next, and the next, and past the overturned Rezvani's mangled front fender. Then up onto the fifth and last step.

The archway in front of her now, the light from inside the main hall pouring over her, she crooked her elbows, leaned low over her handlebars, and thundered straight through the wicket gate into the Great Hall of Castle Graguscu.

It was 2:15 a.m. when the Camp Turzii drone swarm reached its destination after traveling over a hundred miles from its rooftop launchpad.

The location of the target was fixed and acquired using basic GPS coordinates. The in-flight formation was maintained with a vision-based flocking algorithm that used their electronic eyes to set distances that would avoid collisions between individual fliers.

Birds of a feather directed by a set of simple underlying instructions, their simple, cohesive aerial migration had a single objective. All fifty drones held it in their brains.

In the cold, dark sky above Castle Graguscu, the swarm dove to the attack.

The two guards Matei had brought up to the Great Hall with him were named Bela and Agoston. They were tough, combat-seasoned military veterans who had once belonged to the Hungarian 2nd *Árpád Bertalan* Special Purpose Brigade, and later as freelancers, rented their services to high-level corporate and political entities around the world. They had fought in many armed conflicts, overt and covert. They had hired themselves out as bodyguards to the reputable and the disreputable. Each of them had been in violent, bloody confrontations more times than he could count. Each recognized another hardcase when he saw one.

The American they were flanking was clearly such a man. A soldier. A warrior. A survivor. They could see it and smell it and practically feel the vibe coming off his skin. Matei had unloaded on him, worked him over like they had never before seen him do to anyone. It was a miracle that he was conscious and alert, let alone able to stand upright. But neither of them was taking any chances with somebody like him. He had a tightly wrapped menace about him. A ferocious aura. It oozed from his skin, his pores, his glands. Like from a tiger in a cage.

In Bela's mind, he even looked like a tiger or some sort of predatory cat with that weird right eye. He had trained Pakistani forces on the Line of Control and seen his share of them stalking the high mountain wilds of Kashmir. Though they were supposed to be extinct there, he'd seen them. And he could tell this dude was his own fucking species of rare and dangerous beast. One could not let one's guard down with him for a minute.

The two guards had lifted him off the floor, heaving and hauling him upright, then dragging him back toward the middle of the Great Hall so he was within a foot or two of the dead girl's sprawled, bloody body. Meanwhile, Lazlo had stayed up on the balcony like a sniper on a perch. He was a Chechen, and all Chechens were half-crazy.

Both Bela and Agoston would have admitted what Lazlo did to the girl was over the line. Excessive and distasteful as hell. They understood why he'd put a bullet in her head: she was useless to them alive, and who knew what she had seen in the castle...or what the loose-lipped Zolcu might have revealed to her? Also, if you wanted somebody like the American to talk, you had to send a shock to his system, hit him where it hurt. They got that. No criticism of Lazlo there.

But beating her, doing all that unnecessary damage, it was way out of bounds. Sure, the girl was only one of a thousand pretty young women from Cluj, a short skirt and hot pair of legs who sought the thrill of rubbing up to a member of the *vampiri* elite, saw it as a possible ticket out of her monotonous, ordinary life. But the two bodyguards really didn't appreciate how Lazlo's actions reflected on their own professionalism. It went beyond his being a Chechen hothead. He seemed to have flown completely off the handle.

And the truth was they weren't too sure about Matei right now.

They stood behind the American, Bela holding his left arm, Agoston his right. Broad and hulking, Matei towered in front of him, getting right up in his face.

"There were half a dozen of you in the castle," he said. "Two armored trucks. Ten to twenty men between them, yes? And a stealth delivery aircraft. I want to know what you're all doing in Satu Mare."

Carmody stared at him. He tasted copper and salt. Blood was seeping into his mouth from the inside of his cheeks.

"We're talent scouts," he said. "Casting for big, bald, and ugly."

Matei just stood there looking baleful.

"Again," he said. "Why did you fucking come here?"

Carmody forced a smile onto his lips. It hurt like hell. They were split and misshapen from the pounding he'd taken.

"Somebody gave me your name," he said. "Can you sing or dance?"

Matei wound up, pulling his arm back to its full extension like a javelin thrower, then swinging it forward and slapping him hard and openhanded across the face. Carmody's jaw snapped sideways. He felt the plates of his skull joggle and shift. His stomach heaved with nausea. It was like getting whacked with the flat end of an oar.

"Motherfucker." The giant's voice was a harsh rattle. "I'll crack open your head and piss on your brains."

Carmody didn't think that was hyperbole. Matei was a brute, an anabolic-steroid user from the looks of him, and he was in an eruptive rage.

He balled his hand into a fist, loaded up again. And was about to strike his blow when the motorcycle came hurtling through the wicket gate.

Kali thundered into the castle at fifty miles an hour—fast, but not so fast she couldn't quickly bring the machine under control.

She throttled back, taking in the scene inside the hall at a glance. Carmody was a few yards to her left, his back more or less turned toward her. Two uniformed guards were positioned behind him like bookends, gripping his arms, their backs also turned. A third towered in front of Carmody, facing him, his fist clenched as if he was about to strike a massive blow. Above them at a right angle, on a projecting balcony, a fourth.

A woman was sprawled on the floor under the balcony in a pool of red. Kali could guess who she was and what had happened to her.

She swung around toward the group of men. They had heard the roar of the motorcycle and turned their heads in her direction and were looking at her. All of them, including Carmody, looking at her with varying degrees of surprise.

Like Carmody, she had recognized the giant immediately. Drajan's man. The one she'd brought down to the pavement outside Club Energie.

The two guards behind Carmody had let go of him to raise their weapons. But the second it took them to react made all the difference, and she sped toward them before they even got the rifles out in front of them.

Agoston was already firing, but his aim was off. His bullets chittering harmlessly past her ear, she kept hurtling forward on the bike. He had backed away from Carmody when he turned to face her, only a step or two, but it gave her another opening. She went straight at him, no hesitation.

He tried jumping away at the last instant, but it was too late. Kali struck him in his center of mass, knocking him into the air. The impact sent him flying for several feet before he hit the marble floor with a flat, thudding crash.

Then the hiss of gunfire. From above her. The man on the balcony had angled his rifle down over the rail and was trying to pick her off.

Meanwhile, Carmody hadn't stood still. As the guards released him, he had seen his chance and moved in on Bela, *close* in, all with one large stride. His right hand under the front of Bela's gun barrel, he drove it back, back, back with the heel of his palm, pushing its business end up into the air.

Bela was a seasoned operative. But his astonishment at the motorcycle's unexpected appearance slowed him down a little, and Carmody had
leverage working in his favor. He moved in even
closer, reaching out his left hand to grab hold of the
butt stock. Both hands locked around the weapon,
he twisted and pulled and wrenched it free of
Bela's grip.

Then he turned it on him.

Bela stood there empty-handed, looking confused. The gun had been taken with such swift,
sudden ease it might as well have vanished into
thin air. Except it hadn't vanished. The American
was holding it on him. All in a split second, their
situations had reversed.

He instantly knew what was coming. He had
killed a lot of men in his life and knew he was
going to die and wondered how it would be.

He stared up the length of the barrel. Staring
back, his face a bruised, pounded red mask, Carmody put three bullets into him. The freelancer's
look of bafflement deepened, blood brewing from
his chest. Then he fell dead on the spot.

A burst of semiautomatic fire sizzled past Carmody's ear before the operative's body hit the floor.
It came from the balcony to his left even as he saw
the giant charging him from a few feet away to the
right. He'd picked up one of the primitive weapons
that lined the Great Hall—a morningstar mace, its
head a spiked metal ball, the wooden shaft bound
in rawhide. He raised it over his head, brandishing
it like a medieval warrior.

In that same beat of time, Carmody heard the loud throb of Kali's motorcycle from the far end of the hall and glanced toward the sound. The space was expansive and bare, free of obstacles to the moving bike. She had made a wide clockwise loop of it without decreasing speed.

Now she was riding back from the top of the loop. Bearing straight for the giant, who incredibly seemed oblivious to her. Or maybe not so incredibly. He was fixated on Carmody. In a blood rage. His huge strides swallowing up the distance between them, he swung the weapon down from over his shoulder, down at his head in a vicious arc.

Carmody had a split second to act. He could turn his Kalashnikov on the giant, take him out before Kali even reached him. Could blow him off his feet while he was rushing him. But that would give the guy on the balcony the moment he needed to draw a bead. He had a direct, unimpeded shot on a downward plane, which made him the most critical threat.

It boiled down to reaction time, what physiologists call the twitch response.

Carmody's was exceptional. When he was recruited for the 22nd STS's superelite Group 6, he'd been tested for carnosine, a natural indicator of fast-twitch fiber percentages. Intramuscular carnosine levels thirty percent higher than normal are often found in star athletes. Levels of plus-fifty are so rare they occur in only one of every hundred million people. Carmody's plus-seventy was the only instance the Air Force project doctors had ever come across.

He stepped in toward the giant, his head low, his left hand snapping up to catch the weapon's shaft inches below its circular, descending head. At the same time he turned the Kalashnikov up toward the balcony stairs in his right hand and triggered an extended burst, firing from the hip, taking rough aim at the shooter with his peripheral vision.

His move caught both men by surprise, which was exactly what he wanted. His gun still rattling up at the balcony, Carmody planted his feet wide, grabbed the mace's handle, and wrenched it toward him with all his strength, the same stunt he'd used to disarm Bela. It had already worked once, and he was hoping twice would be the charm. Tearing it from the giant's fingers, he whirled around on his heels and brought it back behind his head and hurled it forward and up at the guy on the stairs.

The morningstar smashed into Lazlo's right leg above the knee, its spikes biting into him like crocodile teeth as he spasmodically pulled his trigger and streamed out a wildly off-target volley. The bullets going inches wide of Carmody, he stumbled back against the rail and dropped the gun. It spun down from the balcony to the floor like a detached airplane propellor.

Carmody swiveled back toward the giant, but he was no longer coming at him. He'd heard the speeding motorcycle and turned toward it in the span of a heartbeat.

Matei identified the rider at once. He did not need to see the face behind her helmet visor. He hadn't seen it the first time, four months ago. He could tell by her body type and some raw and primitive sense that went beyond mere visual recognition.

It was the demoness. The one who had nearly crippled him, laid him out on that side street in the rain.

"You!" he screamed. An exclamation of naked, semiarticulate rage, it tore up through his damaged vocal cords like a chain shaking in a lunatic fist. *"You!"*

Kali straightened behind the Ninja's handlebars.

It was at that precise moment that the first wave of drones struck the castle walls.

Seconds earlier, a group of ten Camp Turzii flying-wing drones had reached the end point of their flight. Separating from the larger swarm, they formed up into a close helical formation and made a whining, corkscrewing nosedive into Castle Graguscu's eastern battlement.

Thump-thump-thump, thump-thump. They walloped the ramparts in rapid succession. Their EPX-2R charges detonated violently on impact, chunks of rough, blasted stone spraying out into the Transylvanian night like bits and pieces of scaled, shattered teeth. They flew scattered and smoking through the high, alpine darkness and rained down to the ground in loose, fiery showers.

A second onslaught followed, a third, a fourth. *Thump-thump-thump, thump-thump.* Walls chipped, cracked, and crumbled. A drone cluster smashed into the main tower and blew a gaping hole in it.

Debris spattered from its curved outer face, smoke curling from the windows as its wooden furnishings, interior panels, carpets, curtains, and paintings burst into orange flames.

The drones kept coming in tight, directed groups. The walls trembled. Long fissures spider-veined through them as they began falling apart. Debris hailed onto the scalloped front steps, clattered and bounced off the overturned Rezvani, and went skittering across the cobbled apron below.

In the Great Hall, Kali was two seconds from closing the distance between herself and Matei when a cluster of simultaneous explosions shook everything around her. The air roared. The floor bounced under her wheels. The ribbed, vaulted brickwork overhead groaned and buckled. A mass of brick and mortar collapsed directly in front of her, the crumbled masonry spilling down and piling up in a huge, dusty heap.

Suddenly Matei was gone.

She sliced her handlebars to the left, leaning hard into the turn, her foot skidding over the marble floor to keep the bike from pancaking onto its side. A millisecond slower, and she would have been crushed underneath the pile of rubble.

She swung a wide loop around it, cut sharply to her right, and scrubbed speed, halting several feet from the foot of the balcony stairs. Where was Carmody?

She looked to her left, looked to her right. Then she looked straight ahead and up. And she saw him.

The Kalashnikov slung over his shoulder, he was

climbing the balcony stairs, taking them two at a time. On the balcony itself, the freelancer was weakly leaning back against the rail, looking down at him, his right knee gushing blood, the handle of the mace sticking straight out of it. His carbine was gone.

There were more thumping blasts. The whole hall shook. Kali felt the floor wobble and throb. It was as if the castle's very foundation was shifting under her wheels.

She kept her gaze on Carmody. Above her, he went bounding up the final few stairs to the balcony.

The hall shook.

Carmody took the last two or three stairs to the top with a single leap. Then he was on the balcony, facing the operator who'd killed the girl.

The guy leaned weakly against the rail, facing him. His right leg was hemorrhaging, the mace head buried in his lower thigh. Carmody saw blood pooled under his feet. The weapon had torn up the whole vine-like network of arteries above his kneecap.

"What is your name?" the operator said.

Carmody looked at him. Another chain of explosions struck the castle. The balcony rocked. Chunks of the ceiling plummeted down nearby.

"Your name," the operator said. "Tell me. I want to know who it is that ends my life."

Carmody looked at him.

"You first," he said.

Something else came crashing down. The operator nodded. His lips curled into a grimace.

"Lazlo," he said. It came out sounding like a curse. Full of hatred and aggression. "Now yours. *Tell me*."

Carmody nodded.

"I won't kill you in cold blood. Like you did the girl," he said. "I'm giving you a chance, Lazlo. Because we're both soldiers."

A glimmer of desperate hope showed on the operator's face. He couldn't hide it.

Carmody wanted that. Wanted to see it there. Clinia from Cluj must have clung to the same kind of hope through the beatings. Right until Lazlo put a bullet in her head and sent her flying down to the castle floor.

Carmody stepped closer. Waded right through the puddled blood, stopped, and looked at him. Lazlo was barely upright. His right leg and foot juddered uncontrollably, some sort of muscle spasm. The morningstar's shaft was sticking straight out of it.

Carmody needed to hurry. The castle was falling apart around him. And Kali was down there. Waiting.

Grabbing the mace's outthrust shaft with both hands, he jammed its head deeper into the guy's thigh, pushing hard, putting all his weight into it. Lazlo screamed and thrashed, his face contorted with pain. Fat tears sprang from his eyes.

Carmody let go of the shaft, reaching down to his sidearm holster for the Sig. The operator squirmed, his eyes widening as the gun spat three well-placed .40 caliber rounds into his good leg. They tore into his uniform pants and destroyed the left knee with an eruption of blood and bone fragments. Lazlo screamed again, and then slid limply down to the balcony floor in a sitting position, propped against the rail, his legs splayed in the widening pool of blood.

Carmody lowered the barrel of the Sig to the operator's shoulder, pushed it in, and triggered another burst. Lazlo screamed and bucked and thrashed, the back of his head slamming against the rail spindles. Carmody moved the gun to his right shoulder, dug it into the muscle, and fired again. Three rounds.

Lazlo again slammed backward against the balcony's railing. His face contorted, he was gasping and moaning in agony. Blood splashed from both sides of his upper torso. The bullets had disintegrated both scapulae and fibulae. He no longer had ball-and-socket joints. Only flesh and gristle connected his arms to his torso. He had urinated in his pants.

Something crashed nearby. Carmody lowered the gun to Lazlo's abdomen. He put three into it, aiming for the stomach and large intestine, deliberately missing his other major organs. The gut wounds would burn like fire inside him, but he would stay alive and conscious. Unless the balcony toppled from the wall or the ceiling came down on him first.

Lazlo had slid farther down the rail. His arms hung uselessly at his sides. Blood dripped and oozed from his middle.

"Yrrrnm," he said. The words slurred and unintelligible. "Rbrrnnn."

"Try again," Carmody said. "Slower so I can understand you."

Lazlo breathed through his gaping mouth. It was a wet sound, like liquid passing through a straw.

"Your…n-name," he said. And coughed blood. "Orr…*our*…fucking bargain."

Carmody holstered the Sig and looked at him.

"I'll get back to you," he said and turned toward the stairs.

Kali was on her bike facing the balcony when he came racing down. She had lifted her visor.

"Get on," she said. Her eyes were very still. "We have to hurry."

He slid onto the bike behind her. The drones kept striking. The castle shook. Stone and mortar poured from the ceiling. One of the martial panels across the hall crashed down on the row of ancient arms underneath it. Swords and maces and shields and lances clattered across the floor. The drones kept striking, the explosions loud and palpable through the gaping holes in the walls and ceiling.

Thump-thump-thump, thump-thump.

The castle shook. Carmody flicked a glance over his shoulder at Clinia's body. It was partly covered in ruin and dust. There were shards of stone in the blood that had poured from her ruptured flesh.

His promise had been good for nothing.

Kali revved the bike. Its power plant surged.

"Hold on," she said.

Carmody's hands on her hips, she opened up the throttle, and they shot out the wicket gate to the apron.

17

Castle Graguscu/The Initiation Well

Wheeler in the lead, Begai close behind him, they had slowly picked their way down the stairs of the well, for the most part in silence. There were nine landings, fifteen steps between each of them. The steps were winding, steep, and shallow, the landings barely wide enough for both men standing abreast. Every landing had a stone niche about four feet deep, every niche a rectangular LED wall sconce. Once upon a time, Wheeler guessed, they must have held torches or oil lamps.

He silently counted the steps and landings, an ingrained Delta habit that Carmody's haunted-house run-throughs had reinforced. You wanted to be able to retrace an exit route if the lights quit and something happened to the night goggles. You drilled with and without equipment so you didn't have to rely on it. So you didn't use it as a crutch.

Thirty-five, forty, forty-five. Third landing.

The electric lights gave off a diffuse but adequate radiance, but it was slow, difficult going. Wheeler thought the dimensions of the treads were subtly wrong, their breadth, width, and height off, as if the staircase was designed for people with smaller strides and different gaits than modern men...or to present a deliberate challenge.

Fifty, fifty-five, sixty. Fourth landing.

The well was like a serpent's throat. Coated with moss and moisture, its walls glistened with an oily slickness. The deeper the two men went, the more hemmed in and claustrophobic it felt. Their footsteps were flat and percussive, their echoes dying away much too quickly, as if smothered by the surrounding stone.

It took them several long minutes to reach the ninth and final landing. Wheeler stepped down onto it, waited for Begai to come alongside him.

"Notice anything?" he asked and took a deep breath.

At first he didn't. Then it clicked with him. "There's more air," he said. "And it's fresher."

"Cleaner anyway," Wheeler said. "There's an air-washing system. Like in road tunnels. They cost a fortune." He studied the well bottom with its weirdly out-of-place computer stations. "You think the Wolf takes these stairs down from the castle?"

"No way," Begai said. He motioned to the ring of arches around the compass rose. "He probably uses those for entrances. Or some of them."

Wheeler nodded. He slipped his Wally from its rig bag and held it out.

"Here," he said. "You scan the doors in case somebody's behind them. I'll take the laptops, pull everything I can from the desktop computers."

Begai took the unit from his hand. "Good luck. They've had plenty of time to wipe them clean."

Wheeler couldn't dispute that. But the contingency fell well within their game plan. Any data they got off the computers was a bonus. Their primary target was Zolcu. He was the big fish. The one Carmody wanted out of tonight. The one the deepfakes were supposed to have fooled him into believing was Petrovik.

"Doesn't matter if they did a military spec scrub," he said after a moment. "Unless they used a drive crusher—and maybe they did, who knows?—we'll be able to get something off…"

Wheeler let the sentence trail. He'd heard a faint rumbling sound. Like thunder, but not exactly.

He angled his head to one side, listening.

More rumbles, then more. They came in bursts, seemingly from above. The bursts were rhythmic, the pauses between them sporadic.

Rmm-mm-mm rmm-mm-mm-mm-mm rmm-mm…

Begai was also listening now. "What do you suppose that is?" he said.

Wheeler frowned. *Like thunder, but not exactly.* He had no answer for him.

"We should finish our shit and get out of here," he said and immediately started down the remaining fifteen stairs to the well bottom.

* * *

As Begai went to scan the archways with the TTWS, Wheeler hastened toward the computer stations in the middle of the compass rose. The rumbling hadn't stopped. In fact, it seemed to be growing louder and steadier.

He drew a deep breath to calm his nerves and turned to the computers. The laptops went right into his backpack. But grabbing info from the desktop machines would require some finesse.

Wheeler took four gumstick cloud-drive transmitters from a rig bag, popped them into the machines one by one, and booted them up. The little solid-state devices would inject and install their drive-mirroring software in under a minute. If there were cellular-signal boosters down here— and he figured there had to be for the hackers to access the internet—the gumsticks would mirror the computers and send the copied data to a dedicated vault in Net Force's cloud archive. Four months ago in Bucharest, Fox Team had used the same method to obtain the intel leading to this bizarre trick box of a castle.

He waited a few seconds and checked the tiny indicator lights on the gumsticks. They were all blinking green. The devices had successfully piggybacked onto a wireless signal and initiated the mirror-transmit. Their lights would turn solid green once the uploads were complete.

He looked around in the meantime. The setup seemed to have been vacated, cleared out, but not on the spur of the moment and not in any kind of rush. It was too neat and orderly. He had a hunch a physical search would be a waste but would take a look around anyway.

He was about to get started when he heard more rumblings. This time he was sure they were coming from overhead.

He looked straight up above him but didn't see anything. Just the old mineral-and-moss scaled walls, stairs, and archways climbing three hundred feet to the mouth of the well.

After a second, he lowered his eyes to Begai, who was standing at the rose's east-facing door.

"How's it going?" he asked.

"Okay," Begai said. He was holding the Wally up to the wooden planks. "We're alone, so far."

Rmmbrmmmbrmmmmbmmmmbrmmmrmmm-mmmmmm...

The men exchanged glances, listening, neither of them speaking a word. The tension in their eyes said everything. That had been the loudest, longest string of rumblings yet. It was like a cannonade.

Alone except for that god-awful noise, Wheeler thought. He drew a breath, motioned for Begai to proceed, and turned to recheck the computers. The gumsticks were still blinking. He hurried to get on with his search.

He found the desktops bare, the media-storage cabinets empty. There was nothing in the trash cans but their plastic liners. He crouched on the balls of his feet, looking around and under the workstations. Nothing. Not a slip of paper. Not a gum wrapper or a bread crumb.

He rose to his feet and ran his hands over the curvature of the walls, feeling for built-in drawers or panels. Nothing. He noticed a couple of narrow ventilation slots about fifteen feet above his head and decided to inspect them with his Maglite. Cool, dry filtered air whiffed his face as he got up onto a desk and shone the flash through one of the grates. He saw nothing stashed in the metal ducts behind them.

Nothing anywhere.

Nothing at all.

He stood still a minute, his eyes ranging around the walls. Where hadn't he looked? What might he have missed? He couldn't think of anything. The place was like a movie set. All crazy, surreal scenery and deafening sound effects. *Castle of the Technologie Vampiri*. It looked authentic in its own weird way. But it wasn't functional. Or at least wasn't operational. At least, not now.

Wheeler was about to hop off the desktop when his eye fell on a dark, round hole on the wall to his right, roughly between the desk he was standing on and the one in the next triangular petal of the rose. The size of a silver dollar, it was a little below the air vents. He saw at once that it was covered with nonreflective glass. And that the glass was flush against the wall.

Crap. Should've figured.

He looked around some more and noticed another circle of tinted glass. It was the same height above the floor as the first, but halfway around the circumference of the rose.

Jumping to the floor, Wheeler pushed the desk

under the first hole, careful not to accidentally un-plug the computer on top of it. Then he climbed back up for a closer look. There was a concave video camera lens behind the tinted glass. Around the lens were tiny infrared LEDs. The camera was night-vision capable.

A few strips of 100-mph tape—a SEAL's best friend—would take care of it.

He got a roll out of a gear bag, then reached into a trouser pocket for his KA-BAR folding knife. He cut a strip about three inches long with the KA-BAR and stuck it vertically on the wall over the round glass pane. Then he cut a second three-inch strip of the heavy-duty adhesive tape and put it across the first piece. *Good enough*. The glass was covered. The camera would be blind, day or night.

He blocked the other camera the same way, pushing the nearest desk underneath it, climbing up, and taping it over. When he got back down, he cut four additional strips of tape and covered the tiny camera lenses on all four computer monitors as an added precaution.

Finally, he returned to the gumsticks. The first was solid green. Wheeler pulled it out and dropped it into a shoulder bag and waited. After a moment the second stick's progress light stopped blinking, and he went to pull it from the slot.

"Sir?"

Begai. He'd moved around the circle to the east-facing door.

Wheeler turned to face him.

"Someone's coming," Begai said, his eyes wide.

* * *

At that instant, the Russian freelancer named Krask was racing toward the opposite side of the door through an underground passage, five of his men close behind him. He'd lost the livestream from the computer room in his helmet reticle, but that wasn't the thing that bothered him. The American task force was obviously top-notch. Krask had half expected they would notice the cameras.

He ran on. With or without the video feed, he still held the element of surprise. Surprise because of his opposition's unfamiliarity with their surroundings and his prior familiarity with them. It gave him a distinct edge.

But the noise…the distant, rumbling roar he'd heard almost since his descent from the castle… It was admittedly making him apprehensive. It sounded like a train wreck in progress. Or water crashing through a dam. Or something. None of the images it conjured in his mind were any comfort. The sounds gnawed at his attention precisely when he had to be at his sharpest.

He peered ahead into the dimness, keeping up his hurried pace. The passage was a slender, jagged, rough-walled tunnel hewn out of solid bedrock three hundred feet below the castle's foundations. The strip lights winding along its top and bottom provided adequate illumination for him to see his way along and gave the large, luminous likeness of Vladimir Putin inked on his neck a spectral and vaguely sinister shimmer—not that he was at all focused on that right now. The rumbling sounds were getting stronger, and the weird acoustics of the tunnels made it impossible to know where they were coming from. What if it was an earth tremor? It might be centered somewhere miles away. Too far off for him to feel its vibrations, but close enough so he could hear them. The noise might be a warning. A precursor to a full-fledged quake. How could he know? He was a security professional, not a seismologist.

Damn Matei, his orders, and most of all the Wolf's mad fixation with these subterranean burrows. Krask had no clue how many hundreds or thousands of years ago they had been excavated. Or by whom. Nor did he give a shit. He only knew that he did not want to be trapped here when the tunnels started caving in on themselves. And he only cared that this particular tunnel would bring him to the computer room and the Americans.

He would get the job done and get out.

But he wasn't about to blunder through the door. He was no rank amateur. While he did not know all the many twists and turns of this nightmarish worm's nest—did not think it was possible to know all of them—he had deliberately acquainted himself with the passages leading to the well bottom. And therein lay his advantage.

Krask ran about ten more yards and then raised a clenched fist to signal a halt. Just ahead, the passage tentacled off in three different directions. He could see the big arching wooden door to the computer room a little beyond the split. The two offshoots sprouted off to the left and right, but really converged to form a single, circular loop around the well bottom, with the other doors to the compass rose lined along them.

He turned and faced the men. They looked uneasy, and how could he blame them? Those rumblings were getting louder by the second.

"All right, listen up," he said and then sent a pair of them into each of the diverging passages with clipped instructions. He kept one with him. A tough, black-haired Siberian named Illya. He hardly seemed bothered by the noise.

Krask spun around and got back on the move, waving for him to follow.

Those rumbling sounds. Like bundles of TNT going off at a massive demolition site. Like buildings coming down. Krask felt confined and uncharacteristically threatened. Trapped, almost. The faster he got rid of the Americans, the sooner he would get out of these tunnels.

As far as he was concerned, it could not be soon enough.

It went down with lightning swiftness.

Krask led the way in. He had designated himself the number one, Illya his number two. The other pairs would enter almost simultaneously, each through a separate door.

His Kalashnikov in his right fist, his left arm leaning against the door, Krask gave Illya a nod and pushed the handle down and shouldered the door open, squeezing the carbine's trigger, pouring bullets in ahead of him. He went through the door, pivoted to the left, still shooting, his eyes sweeping quickly around the well bottom.

He didn't see the Americans.

He stood there, his carbine raised. His eyes darting to the left and right as Illya followed him in and moved to the opposite side of the door. He was keyed up. Jacked on adrenaline. The rumbling noise suddenly seemed very distant. Like it was coming from the far end of a tunnel. Like it was barely of consequence. Only the immediate mattered. The close-by. The world within the radius of the kill zone. He took in the workstations, the partitions, the entire peculiar juxtaposition of modern computers, medieval stone, and mystical symbols.

He noticed two of the desks were out of position. One of the partitions. He'd riddled them all with bullets. If the Americans had been crouching behind them, they would have been cut to ribbons.

But he didn't see them.

He stood there a second. Illya stood there a second. Flanking the door. Both of them looking around. Looking at each other. Looking mutually puzzled. They didn't see the Americans. More doors flew open around the circle. The rest of the men were entering in twos, about to pie the bottom of the well with fire.

Then a thought lit through Krask's mind like a flare-gun round. He looked up at the stairs winding around the sides of the well, saw the barrel of a rifle angled directly down at him. Behind it, a masked face. The mask adorned with fierce daubs and streaks of color.

At that very instant a 5.56 mm NATO full metal jacket round whistled from above and struck the left side of his neck, drilling into his portrait tattoo of Vladimir Putin, opening a channel dead center between its eyes and mouth. The bullet tore through his throat and jugular vein, grazed his collarbone, and punctured his right lung before lodging in the C7 vertebra of his spine to end its slanted downward trajectory.

As Krask sank to the floor with a mouth full of blood, the penultimate thought of his life was that he was drowning. His next and final thought before dying was that it could not be.

Two hundred feet up, on the third of the staircase's nine landings, Stafford Sparrow angled his Mk 12 carbine to the right, his eye pressed to its scope, resting its forestock on the rough stone handrail. He had taken off one of his gloves and slipped it between the forestock and rail to keep the gun from bouncing or pulling off.

Now the black-haired guy who'd stormed in second was in his reticle. Aiming slightly below the middle of his ribs, accounting for the kick of upward recoil, he took a breath and fired on the exhale. There was a sharp crack, and the guy staggered backward, blood flowering from his chest and splashing from his back as the bullet seared clear through him. He fell in a boneless sitting position, sliding down against the wall with his legs straight out on the floor tiles, smearing a wide, vertical trail of blood down over the wall's gray stone surface.

Sparrow's shot was still echoing in the air as Wheeler stepped from the archway on the eighth landing of the staircase, directly above the rose's north cardinal point. At the same moment, Begai emerged from the ninth and lowermost landing, just above the south cardinal point. Below them, four more freelancers had poured into the circle, two through the east door, two through the west.

They had inadvertently run themselves into a textbook cross fire.

Wheeler and Begai opened up with their MP7s in full-automatic, spraying the well bottom with bullets. All four went down without triggering a round, or even really knowing what hit them. It was over in seconds.

Wheeler looked down at the sprawl of bodies. He'd emptied his magazine. Fired a full load. Begai, too. Not a pretty sight.

He felt his legs shaking. It happened to soldiers after every battle. It happened to boxers after every fight. Jelly legs. The heart rate returned to normal, the elevated hormone levels and blood pressure dropped, the increased circulation to the lower limbs was reduced.

He lowered his gun barrel, started down the fifteen stairs to the well bottom. And then suddenly realized it wasn't his legs—or only his legs.

Before, he'd only been able to hear it. But now he could feel it. The rumbling. The rolling tremors underfoot.

The well was shaking. The whole damned well.

He reached the floor of the well, turned toward

Begai and Sparrow as they came down the final few stairs and gathered around him.

"Those passages," he said to Begai. "Did the Wally give you an idea what they look like?"

Begai nodded. "That one the first couple of guys came through…it's a main tunnel."

"How do you know?"

"It long and straight. I'm thinking it goes on pretty far. The sonar doesn't pick up where it ends."

"And the other ones?"

"They branch off it, maybe thirty yards in."

Wheeler glanced past the two dead bodies toward the open archway door. He could see only a few short feet beyond it into the passage. It looked like it had been cut through solid rock.

RMMMMMMMMMMMBMMMBBBBBMMM…

The ground shook. It made the blood around the bodies tremble.

He turned toward the computers. Saw solid green lights on the three transmitters he hadn't yet collected.

"Okay," he said. "Let's finish up. And then get the hell out of here."

Wheeler led their dash through the passage, Begai a step or two behind him, Sparrow bringing up the rear. The walls shuddered and shook as if they were about to tumble down around them.

They found the elevator a hundred fifty yards from the well bottom. It was a single stainless-steel door with an RFID/bioreader set into the stone wall alongside it.

Wheeler pulled his snoofer from its hard case and held it straight out in front of him like someone taking a selfie. The device instantly injected its software and then began running key codes and biometric identifiers.

The three men waited tensely. The walls shook. The floor shook. It felt like fault lines were about to convulsively stretch and pull apart under their feet.

Wheeler glanced over his shoulder at Sparrow. The kid was studying his smart watch. He'd switched his real-time tracker from GPS to an IPS, or Indoor Positioning System, based on ultra-wideband radio transmissions. It was the faster and more accurate option in enclosed and underground spaces.

"Location?"

"We're under the castle," Sparrow said. Then looked at him. "*Right* under it. It's like the place is coming down on top of us."

Which was unsurprising, and not good. Not if the elevator was going to bring them straight up into it.

He was about to ask Sparrow to raise Rover Two when the steel door slid open. There was no time to wait.

"What do we do?" Begai said.

Wheeler looked into the car.

"We get in, press Up, then worry about it," he said.

Behind the castle in Rover Two's forward cabin, Ray Long got some of it figured out for them.

His IPS receiver had tracked Wheeler's group to within ten feet of their physical location. He could see their avatars, and he could see his video-game recreation of the castle, and he could see they were rising from directly beneath it. Because there had been no existing references from which to simulate the castle's underground passages, the team seemed to be moving against a blank space on his dashboard screen. That was a shortfall of the model.

On the other hand, Long had been able to input some highly valuable coordinates from data that was gathered and shared by the Sentinel drone and *Raven* before she flew off.

Such as the exact position of the hidden lift Carmody and Schultz had used to exit the garage. And the lift Gustav Zolcu used to exit. And the separate lifts used by the two Rezvanis.

Which made four exits from the subterranean labyrinth that Long not only knew were outside Castle Graguscu, but whose exact geographic coordinates could be transmitted to Wheeler's team.

He turned to Reggie Fults in the passenger seat. The explosions from the drones smashing into the castle were so loud he had to raise his voice.

"The castle's getting blown apart," he said. "We can't let them head straight up into it."

Fults looked at him. "And you're thinking what, exactly?"

Long had already pulled up the coordinates of the lift exits. He pointed to the screen. "I'm thinking we can guide them to one of those exits, extract them, and move out."

Fults stared at the display a moment.

"I'll comm them now," he said.

Wheeler was stepping aboard the elevator, Begai and Sparrow piling in after him, when he heard Fults over the RoIP: "Whiskey, it's Rover Two. Do you read?"

"Loud and clear."

"Can you tell me where you are?"

Wheeler told him as the elevator door slid shut.

"That's perfect," Fults said. "Now what do you see on the control panel?"

Wheeler told him. There were four numbered buttons and an LED display. His team had entered on One, the lowermost level.

"And the castle's got two floors, right? Not counting the basement."

"Or the tower room," Wheeler said. "Right."

"Okay, got it."

RMMMMMMMMMBBBBBBBBBRRRRRMMM...

Wheeler inhaled. The elevator was amplifying the sound like a tin can. He felt the car quiver and rock.

"Rover Two, we have to—"

"Take it one level up and get out. That should be the basement—where you first split off from Preacher. We'll direct you from there."

Wheeler and his team took the vehicle lift at the base of the underground garage's Y, outside the rear gate.

Long guided them to it using data gathered

from tracking the earlier movements of Carmody's group. Of the three garage exits, it was farthest from the castle and therefore least likely to be pounded by drones and falling rubble. It was also the one Long could reach the fastest from his position at the road fork.

The group hurried onto the lift and felt it activate with a jolt, the walls of the shaft trembling around them, the platform swaying and shaking underfoot. They struggled for balance and grabbed onto each other as they rose, steadying themselves, staring up at the camouflaged mechanical door above them, breathing a collective sigh of relief as it began sliding open, retracting, the cold of the night rushing down into the shaft.

The BearCat was waiting—hatch up, platform lowered—when they reached the surface.

They climbed into the troop compartment with the rest of the men, whooping and howling at the top of their lungs.

"So, what've you three done this evening?" Long said, glancing around from the front seat.

Wheeler looked at him.

"Har!" he said.

Long grinned and lowered the hatch. "Strap in," he said. "Next pickup on this share's Banik and the furball."

He hit the gas, and the Cat jounced forward.

Joe Banik heard the vehicle speeding down from the castle grounds and assumed it was Rover Two. Long had just radioed that he'd extracted Wheeler's

team and was on his way to the gate. He'd anticipated it would take him three or four minutes.

Banik was ready. The hardest part of standing
watch out here hadn't been the cold and the snow,
the sounds in the sky, or even the thudding, rumbling explosions of the past few minutes. It definitely wasn't fending off an old man and his wife
who'd come snooping around in a rickety, sput-
tering pickup. And it *very* definitely wasn't Ellie.
Ellie was a good girl. Belgian Mals were field dogs,
and watching the flock was baked into her DNA.
If anything, he took his cues from her.

What was it the Bible said? *Blessed is he who
stands watch.* Nice words, but he didn't know about
it. He didn't think he deserved a special blessing.
Someone had to do the job. Stand post. Be the eyes
and ears. Watch and wait at the lonely gate. He'd
reminded himself of this more than once, waiting
here on the outside while his teammates were *inside*
risking their lives. Feeling extraneous and uncon-
nected and useless to them as he heard the explosions roaring over the castle grounds.

For Banik, that was the hardest part. The waiting.
Like in the old Tom Petty song. Just the waiting.

He was ready all right.

He watched the gate. He could hear the vehicle coming up to it, approaching from the castle
grounds. Its headlights shone through the hedges
bordering the access road, the beams broken to
splintery dashes by the low branches. Then the car
reached the gate, and they fanned out over the snow
on the two-lane.

He reached out to stroke the dog's massive neck. "Our ride's here," he said.

But it wasn't.

His hand tensed on the Mal's fur.

It wasn't the BearCat.

Banik watched the vehicle swing in his direction. It was no more than twenty feet away. If he'd been standing directly in front of it, the lights would have blinded him. But he was on the gravel shoulder, and they struck at a glancing angle.

The vehicle was dark. A bulking SUV.

Banik had been told there were two Rezvanis. One was down.

He was looking at the other.

"Bashim lol," he commanded, calling Ellie to high attention.

Banik stood on the shoulder, his right hand going for the MP7 slung against his side. It would do no good if they opened fire or tried to run him down. The damn vehicle was armored. But he wasn't going to stand there like easy roadkill.

He brought the gun to its ready position. Ellie had taken her guard stance in front of him and was also ready. High and wide on her legs, back straight, head slightly raised. Her ears pointed straight up. She growled, a serious, assertive belly growl.

The Rezvani sped toward them.

The Rezvani shot out the blown, crookedly leaning front gate and turned left on the two-lane. As it sped past the American with the monstrous canine, Matei glared out his window and saw the beast move into an aggressive posture.

Beside him in the back seat, one of the men had pushed the nose of his Kalashnikov into the gun port.

"Comenzile tale?"

He was awaiting his orders. Fire or pass.

Matei felt the sudden, white-hot urge to cut both of them down with a spray of bullets. A drive-by, like he might have done back in the day, working his way up the *Obshchina* ladder.

But what was the old saying? *Igra ne stoit svech.* The game wasn't worth the candles.

It was only a perfect stroke of luck that had spared him from the demon bitch in the castle. A falling pile of stone at the right moment. If it hadn't come between them, she would have smashed him to a pulp with her motorcycle. She would have killed him.

If Matei had believed in signs from the universe, that chunk of the ceiling coming down would have been one loud, crashing warning that it was time to disengage. But fuck signs. The gods of war offered no signs. He had instincts and trusted them, and they told him the same.

The castle was burning. Falling. Crumbling to the ground. A huge, fiery sacrifice to the future.

His time would come.

"Treceti-le pe langa," he said. "Pass them by."

A second later, man and dog and castle were behind him and then gone, the Rezvani's driver taking a curve and bearing east at over seventy-five miles per hour. The road ahead was dark. The trees, fences, farms, cottages, the entire countryside around him…dark. As if swallowed by the void.

The game here was played, but a new phase was already being launched elsewhere. The Russians were *master* gamesmen, and Koschei a master of masters. They owned all that was to come in the future; it had been shrewd of Drajan Petrovik to partner with them.

Matei would join him at Okean-27, the secret city, and prepare for the next move. As for the Americans, and especially the demon bitch…

A hand played wasn't game over.

He would see her again. And make sure she received her due.

Kali stopped the bike on the access road leading to the front gate. Rover One was just ahead, pulled across it. She and Carmody dismounted and walked toward the vehicle, their feet leaving vague, shallow prints in the thin coating of snow.

There was a chain of explosions behind them. Both turned to look.

Several hundred yards to the north, Castle Graguscu was being consumed by flames. The drones were still swooping down at its ravaged walls in clusters, detonating with bright flares of light. Sparks and embers danced in the sky above it like fireworks. Acrid smoke poured upward, slanting toward them on the southwestern breeze.

They turned back toward the BearCat. Max

Spencer stood to one side of the hatchway and lowered the platform to let them on.

Carmody saw the body as he came aboard. It had been transferred to a stretcher, covered with a white sheet, and strapped down flat to the floor.

"Emerick got hit coming in. We did what we could." This from Singh, the medic. He nodded toward Kali. "She made it easier for him."

The vehicle jolted into motion, backing up off the road and then angling on again with its nose pointing south. Carmody knelt over the body for a long moment, his head slightly bent, then turned toward the forward cabin. Dixon was in the driver's seat, Schultz on the passenger side.

"Wheeler's team," he said. "What's their status?"

"They're out," Dixon said. "With Long."

"Banik and the dog?"

"Same."

Carmody nodded silently. The BearCat rolled forward.

"No offense, boss," Schultz said, his eyes on the digital rearview. "You look like shit."

Carmody crouched there another second or two, then sat down on the metal floor of the vehicle. He pushed himself back against its side with his heels, brought his knees up in front of him, and wiped his lips with the back of his hand. It came away smeared with blood.

"Obviously," he said, his voice too low for anyone to hear.

18

FOB Janus

It was 2:40 a.m. when Fernandez got back on the move with the tight wedge of fighting vehicles. He was alone in front, Howard behind him in the jump seat. Wasserman had unstrapped from his seat and climbed into the aft troop section.

"We're almost in position," Fernandez said to Howard.

The colonel sat there with an H&K M320 stand-alone grenade launcher on his lap. Crisscrossing his chest were two bandoliers, each holding eight 40x46 mm cartridges.

"How long before the 'hogs engage?" he said.

"Optimum lock-on for their RPGs is probably twelve hundred yards. But I want them closer."

"I asked how *long*."

Fernandez frowned, doing a rough calculation as they chugged over the frozen grass-and-dirt field toward the parade grounds. "Three minutes," he said. "Give or take."

"Give-or-fucking-take," Howard muttered. He lowered the blooper's foregrip, popped its receiver, and slid in one of the fat explosive projectiles. Then he slapped the receiver shut and thumbed the selector switch forward. Pushing the butt plate against his shoulder, he raised it to firing position and pressed his eye to the ladder sight as if he was about to trigger a round.

After a second he lowered the weapon and craned his head around toward Wasserman.

"Where's the rest of my ammo?" he said.

The E4 clambered up from the rear and handed him a second cartridge belt. "Here, sir. Want some help putting it—"

"Shit, no." Howard grimaced as he slung it across the other bandolier. "*How long*, Julio?"

"About ninety seconds," Fernandez said.

He studied his console. The Pumas' FOG soft-kill active protection system would theoretically counter the 'hogs' antitank rockets. But he had never war-gamed the APS and didn't like relying on it. Except he would have to because if it didn't work, they were all probably dead. The 'hogs' thermobaric grenade was brutal. Right before impact, it would shoot a jet of white-hot liquid metal through armor, lancing through it like a hot needle through wax. Then the main warhead would enter the vehicle's interior and blow everything inside it to bits.

He rolled on. Another thirty seconds and the rough, bumpy ground under his wheels would give way to level pavement. He was positive the 'hogs would take a defensive posture before they got that far. They had their own system of countermeasures. Range finders that could detect the vibrations of an incoming rocket and instantaneously relay its position to their onboard computers. They could read its speed and trajectory, predict when and where it would strike.

It was a system based on evasion, not deflection. Different premise than the FOG suite, same desired result. And with good reason. The Pumas were slow and cumbrous. Hedgehogs the opposite: light, fast, and mobile. Their reaction time limited only by the speed it took for electrical commands to travel from their computers to their mechanical actuators. Maybe a trillionth of a second. Maybe less. They could dodge, swerve, do other things to elude the missiles. Their system perfectly suited their capabilities.

So, the real question for Fernandez wasn't how long it would be before the 'hog engaged. It was whether he could get close enough, fast enough, to beat it to the punch.

But how many would they be facing? One? Two? Probably not all four. Probably at least a single robot would stay on guard at the bunkers to stop anyone trying to escape.

Probably-schmobably.

Fernandez knew the robots had fairly deep decision trees relative to their actual machine IQs. They could make judgment calls. But their judgment had been twisted. Infected. Hijacked. A foreign algorithm had taken up residence in their minds like an invasive virus. It piled uncertainty upon uncertainty, and he didn't like that much at all. Uncertainty wasn't his thing.

He looked at his console. The wedge of Pumas had almost traversed the field.

"How *long*?" Howard asked a fourth time.

Before Fernandez could reply, two of the 'hogs turned away from the blaze and began trundling toward the Pumas. His readouts said the lead wagon was within fourteen hundred yards of their line.

Which meant his time estimate had fallen short by almost a minute. The 'hogs weren't waiting for the Pumas. They were racing out to meet them.

"Colonel, Wass," he said, "the rodeo's started."

Wasserman came scrambling back into his seat from the rear. On his shoulder was an M27 IAR light machine gun, an M320 blooper attached to the underbarrel in its modular mode. Once a Marine, always a Marine. That was how they did it.

Fernandez watched his screens. The 'hogs coming toward them were Spree and Nash. Spree zipping along in a straight line, Nash taking a slightly diagonal south-southwesterly path. Both heading for the border between the parade ground and open field.

"Activating FOG," he said and hit the button. "We—"

Fernandez paused. He'd heard a subaudible hum run through the wagon's interior as the unit powered up. But there was another sound, too. Outside. A loud, long, whining whistle.

"What's that fucking noise?" Howard said.

Fernandez raised a hand without turning from his console. Howard stared at the back of his head. Julio was a ball-busting hipster but probably a goddamned genius…and a good soldier. It wasn't his way to interrupt a commanding officer.

He waited. Fernandez nodded toward the screen in front of him.

"It's the drones," he said.

The fliers out of Mihail Kogălniceanu Airfield reached their precise destination at 2:30 a.m., after traveling almost two hundred miles from the scrub lot at the edge of the little-used military tarmac. Until that point, their collective behavior had been uniform and one-dimensional—birds of a feather.

But within the Monarch's more sophisticated brain was a far more complex bundle of *evolving* algorithms. In the cold, dark sky above Janus Base, these were now unpacked and distributed through the flock's group mind over a shared radio link.

The swarm of one hundred 3-D printed drones immediately divided into four smaller squadrons. Some flew this way, others that. Each squadron had a specialized task to perform within the overarching mission. Every drone within a squadron was capable of assessing and reassessing the circumstances needed to successfully execute the task, identifying likely threats and targets of opportunity on the ground, and then communicating its evaluations to the rest of its squadron so it could take action. Together the drones could suss things

out with lethal autonomy and even divide into sub-
groups as needed to execute an objective.

At 2:41 a.m., the Monarch transmitted a separate
set of algorithms to Earl the hedgehog, which had
been acting as a beacon for the flock at the east end
of the base. A subtle alteration to its programming,
and it would become a loitering munition like the
fliers—a kamikaze drone.

Within thirty seconds, Earl awoke from its seem-
ing dormancy and started out across the 'Burbs toward the west side of the base.

At precisely 2:43 a.m., the drones struck.

The motor depot near the base camp's southern
perimeter was a two-acre rectangle sectioned off
into three separate and distinct areas.

The largest was an outdoor parking lot filled with
long, even rows of JLTVs, trucks, armored wagons,
prime movers, forklifts, and an assortment of thirty
support, utility, and personnel vehicles. Beside it
was the next-largest section, a cluster of prefabri-
cated metal garages, workshops, and storage sheds
where repairs, modifications, and overhauls were
performed on the installation's entire motorized
fleet. The smallest section was the adjacent refuel-
ing area, which contained two ten thousand–gallon
aboveground diesel tanks, a partially buried twenty
thousand–gallon storage tank for heating oil, and
a large shed stacked with a dozen thousand-gallon
plastic used oil barrels awaiting recycling or disposal. Connected to the depot by a short, radial
access road was a recently completed vertiport for

Raven and other rotary-wing craft. At its western edge, outside two maintenance hangars, was a big, cylindrical fifteen thousand–gallon surface tank of Jet A-1 aviation fuel.

All together the depot contained over a hundred fifty vehicles and seventy thousand stored gallons of highly combustible refined petroleum products.

At exactly 2:45 a.m., thirty explosive-bearing fixed-wing drones separated from the main flock, whirling down on the depot. Janus's four hedgehogs had provided the fliers with up-to-the-minute data about the disposition of vehicles and storage containers. Sharing a single collaborative strike plan, they zeroed in on their various targets.

The first group struck at the two surface diesel tanks, detonating them with a roar that startled people out of bed sixty miles away in Bucharest. The underground heating-oil tank was next, ten drones twisting and turning down to destroy it with more flame and thunder. Within minutes the fuel tanks, waste-oil barrels, garages, hangars, sheds, and vehicles themselves were swallowed up in a huge, rising blister of flame. Within the burning structures, glass fused, and the water from emergency sprinklers vaporized.

Across the base, another subset of drones slammed into the trailer that had been serving as the post exchange store. Their detonations lifted it into the air, shattering windows, punching out walls, and leaving grocery items, clothes, and other assorted merchandise strewn across the snowy pavement.

Opposite the smoking ruin of headquarters, the old modular barracks in Janus Heights were blasted into scrap metal. Near the eastern perimeter, the row of Quonsets housing civilian employees went up in a fiery explosive chain. In the alley outside Laura Cruz's hut, her flat-tired ten-speed bike and the freezer where she and Mario Perez had hidden were pounded into unrecognizable pieces of bent, crumpled junk. They flew high into the air and then rained down to the ground, glowing red hot as if blowtorched.

Somewhere nearby, a cat let out a plaintive, terrified cry.

The drones struck the fences, struck the guardhouses, struck the huge diesel generators used to back up the power supply delivered from a nearby Baneasa township.

At the western perimeter, the decimated new troop barracks might have been passed over as a mission already accomplished, but the four armored battlewagons heading toward its parade grounds drew the swarm's instant attention…as did a lone JLTV speeding toward it from the northwest with two occupants, and the hedgehogs' warning that more intruders were bunkered under the fallen building.

Fifty drones, the largest group to splinter off from the flock, bore swiftly toward the barracks to stop them. Their primary directive was the protection of Forward Operating Base Janus. To execute it, they would clean up its human infestation.

Laura Cruz was swinging south onto the transverse between the two fields when the drones began their run at the new barracks.

A shiver ran through her body. As a little girl in Caracas, living on the steep hills around the city center, she had often seen bats, hundreds of them, fluttering from the caves when they awoke at sundown. They would mingle, scatter, and mass like ink spots in oil, blotting out the sky.

The sight of the bats always made her stomach feel wormy. And what she saw through her upper windshield reminded her of it.

"Mario," she said, "I'm scared."

He looked at her. "For the record, I am, too," he said. "But just a little."

She smiled thinly.

"Stop the Jolt a second," he said. "I want to take another look."

She pulled to a halt. All around them the night shimmered with unnatural orange light. To their rear, the original troop barracks was lost to sight within an orange dome of flame. Far to the left, eastward, the row of Quonsets where she had lived for the past several months was ablaze. But the worst of it was ahead of them, where the fires were burning uncontrollably, filling the entire distance, lashing up over the motor depot and vertiport at the base's edge.

"Do you know what's going on?" she asked.

Mario peered through the binoculars. First at the band of drones in the orange-tinged sky, then the hedgehogs and armored vehicles below. They were on the move. Like on a game board. All of them, every piece.

Battle of annihilation, he thought. Where had he

heard that term before? Maybe in a book or a video game or something. He wasn't sure. But he knew it meant total war. When an army threw down all its chips in a single strike. When its goal was the complete destruction of an enemy and its resources.

"I think the bots want to destroy everything here," he said. "Kill us all. Every last person on base."

Laura was silent a moment. Then she took his hand. "Mario," she said, "we should say a prayer."

He hesitated.

"I guess," he said. "But I don't know the right one."

She bowed her head slightly, then raised it. *Angel de mi guarda, dulce compañía.*

"I do," she said.

The Pumas lumbered onto the parade ground. The hard, lumpy grass and soil were higher than the lip of the quadrangle's pavement, and the transition from one to the other jarred the men in the C&C at the wedge's rear.

Fernandez watched his monitors. They showed the drones spinning and swirling against the blackness of the sky like a funnel cloud.

Wasscrman's face paled.

"Sarge," he said, "you see what they're doing?"

Fernandez nodded but remained silent. About fifty yards up ahead, a large group of fliers had poured earthward in a perpendicular column, abruptly changed direction about six feet above the ground, and come shooting at the wedge parallel to the ground. After a split second, that horizontal line divided into three, some of drones peeling off to the left, others to the right, the main column continuing to bear toward the armored vehicles in a direct-intercept course. Their sound outside the Puma was like the roar of a freight train rushing into a station at full speed.

In the jump seat, Howard leaned forward and clapped a hand on Wasserman's shoulder.

"Toy bees, kid," he said. "Julio's got our asses covered."

Fernandez smiled a slight, grim smile. He hoped he would live to remember that.

Then suddenly, a new sound through the vehicle's armor. A hissing, piercing whistle. Like a quarterback making a Hail Mary pass, Spree had fired an RPG at the lead Puma from behind the main column of drones.

Fernandez straightened in his seat. His displays showed the oncoming projectile's tail of seething propellant gases as layered bands of thermal radiation on his screen—blue at the outer margins, then green, violet, red, orange, and yellow-white.

He drew a long, deep breath as the rocket came closercloser and then veered away from the Puma at the last possible instant, as if hitting an invisible wall, as if skipping off glass, as if rebounding wildly off a comic-book force field, corkscrewing through the air like a fish on a hook and detonating far to the right a few heartbeats later.

"Woooo!" Fernandez was shouting and pumping his fists. "Wooo-*hooo*!"

He had time enough to let out a third loud, triumphant whoop before the pincering drones streaked toward the armored formation from three sides.

His heart kicked in his chest.

Come on, Foggy, he thought. *Do it to 'em.*

It did it, the FOG soft-kill jammer suite aboard all four Pumas literally creating an impenetrable, 360-degree electronic mist around them—a threat fog—its pinpoint lasers simultaneously frying the drones' guidance systems and fooling their IR sensors into locking on to phantom targets. The fliers got no closer than the 'hog's errant rocket before swerving off into the darkness.

Now Wasserman was also howling and fist-pumping with a mixture of giddy relief and exultation.

"Whoa!" he screamed. "Sarge the genius! *Genius Sarge!*"

The wedge kept rolling forward, plowing through waves of dazzled, slewing drones. They looped and curled and wheeled around the Pumas in a kind of nihilistic aerial ballet, exploding as they struck the ground. The blasts shook the vehicles' armored hulls but left them undamaged.

Fernandez felt flushed with adrenaline. It was like he was floating outside his body. He took another long breath to bring himself back down.

Then Howard leaned forward and thrust his arm between the two front seats, pointing his forefinger at the main dash display.

It showed Spree still advancing among the drones.

"Kill it, Genius," he said. "Blow the shit out of it."

Fernandez nodded.

"Pickles," he said, "enable Percy One. Striker fire control. Lock and load."

"Yes, Jules."

The lead auton's remote-weapons station was above the roof of its hull, where the manned gun turret was situated on Fernandez's Puma. Designed for a wide range of medium and heavy armaments, it had been fitted with an Mk 47 Striker automatic grenade launcher, capable of firing a dozen low-recoil .40 mm smart rounds almost identical to those carried aboard the 'hogs.

At his control panel, Fernandez triggered the auton's launcher just as Spree coughed a second RPG into the air. The projectiles passed each other flying in opposite directions, smoke trails puffing and undulating behind them like vaporous eels.

Blinded and diverted by the FOG's electronic countermeasures, Spree's grenade careened wildly off mark.

The auton's did not and hit the 'hog midway up its squat, vaguely anthropomorphic chassis. Spree rocked and teetered backward on its treads, its center of gravity shifting from the impact, the front end of its base lifting six inches up off the snow.

A thousandth of a second before the round detonated, Spree registered that it had been fooled. Lured too close to take evasive action, while an unknown defensive system aboard the Puma caused its rockets to veer off course.

A millionth of a second after that, it transmitted the data to the other three hedgehogs over their neural network. It was the robotic equivalent of a warning cry, and it went out at the speed of light via an infrared wireless connection.

And then the round blew the 'hog to bits and pieces, engulfing it in a large teardrop of flame. Fragments of its metal body sailed through the air, clanging hard against the Puma's armor panels.

Fernandez looked at his display, then half turned toward Howard.

"Shit's blown," he said.

The colonel grunted. He was staring into the displays.

"Move on at speed, Julio," he said. "We're getting our people out."

The Pumas traversed the parade grounds at close to seventy miles per hour, swinging to the right several hundred yards before they reached the barracks. The remnants of the drone swarm—twenty or so fliers—had ceased their attack for now, pulled up into the darkness, and were stalking the wedge from overhead like nocturnal birds of prey.

The whole thing felt insane to Fernandez. But he had fought in several wars. Accepted the killings, the bombings, the blood, and the terrible loss. It had given him a powerful capacity for handling insanity, even when it surrounded him.

Steady at his controls, he passed the gutted husk of the barracks on his left. The building was still burning in spots, flames sprouting from its windows and dancing in the wind. The maintenance shed was just ahead of him, around the north end of the barracks.

Howard asked, "You got a fix on the rest of the 'hogs?"

Fernandez studied the monitors. "Nash has pulled pretty far north," he said. "Same for Walt. It's backed up west of the shed…all the way to the perimeter."

"Earl?"

"Moving toward us from the civilian-housing area. Or what's left of it. The 'hogs aren't Indy racers. But it won't take them long to get there."

Howard exhaled slowly, his breathing ragged. Even talking hurt like hell. But he'd already spelled out his plan to Fernandez and Wass. At Armor School in Georgia they had called it dismounting from a stationary coil. In the cowboy movies, where they weren't so formal, it was just circling the wagons.

"Those walking transistor radios aren't as dumb as they look," he said. "They're staying far enough off so they can duck our rockets."

Fernandez nodded. "Spree must've realized it was snookered. I'm sure it sent out a red alert about the FOG to its robot brothers."

"You think they know we came here for the people in the bunker?"

Fernandez nodded. "They're able to identify and react to rescue situations," he said. "That means they can recognize and contextualize what we're doing here."

"So that's a *yes*?"

"Yeah."

"Then they're waiting for a chance to close in."

The sergeant nodded. "Probably till they think we're vulnerable."

Howard gave him a hard look and hefted his blooper up against his chest.

"We'll see how that works out," he said.

From the outside, it appeared to be an ordinary shed standing on the paved surface of the parking lot eighty yards from Janus's western boundary line, and roughly equidistant from the rubble and embers that only hours ago had been the FOB's main troop barracks. It was fairly large—spacious enough to hold a backhoe loader, snowblowers, and other equipment, along with fifteen or twenty people—with a concrete base, sheet-metal sides, and a pitched asphalt roof. Its west-facing door looked on to a wide dirt buffer between the fence and the lot, and beyond that, miles of thick black pine forest.

The Pumas quickly crossed the parking lot to the shed and shifted into a stationary-coil formation around it. Each backed up on it from a different side, leaving a dozen feet of clearance. The lead auton—Percy One—halted with its front end pointed at the north field. Percy Two faced east toward the rear of the barracks, and Percy Three nosed south. Inside the C&C vehicle, Fernandez braked with his headlights shining steadily on the western fence and his rear hatch toward the door of the shed.

Howard was already out of his straps. He leaned forward and tapped Wasserman's arm.

"You all set?" he said.

"Be right with you, sir." Wasserman tapped his earpiece. "Checking to see that the evacs are standing ready."

"Julio?"

"I'm good."

Howard unslung his blooper, waited a second as Wasserman pulled off his headset.

"Open the fucking hatch," he said.

Wasserman hopped down out of the vehicle, Howard maneuvering painfully through the hatch after him. They were a few steps from the shed's door.

The drones attacked almost the instant they set foot in the snow, whistling and humming as they bore in from the red-streaked sky.

Wasserman flinched a little. It had been easier to trust the FOG's lights and pulses inside the Puma. Now he felt naked and exposed. But its shield held up. The deflected fliers skipped away like stones across the surface of a lake, taking haphazard little hops and bounces in midair, popping off with bright flashes of light.

Howard pointed his chin at the shed. *"Let's move!"* he hollered.

They hurried over to it. Wasserman got out his key card, swiped it into the reader, and the door unlocked with the slightest click. As they pushed in, a motion sensor automatically turned on the interior light.

The shed was empty and clean, with a single small window looking to the east. There were two air-ventilation gratings in the concrete floor. Between them in the middle of the floor was a blast hatch, a three-foot-square, steel-in-steel frame. As they moved up to it, a second motion sensor opened the door on pneumatic lifts.

Howard looked down into the passage. A dozen steps descended to a small cement vestibule. The treads were textured for secure footing. In the wall facing the stairs was a gray steel door with steel compression handles and a steel frame.

Howard signaled Wasserman with a glance and led the way.

He'd only taken three steps down when the door at the bottom swung open. A man stood in the light splashing from behind it. Half of his face had been severely burned. It looked like melted wax. A bandage covering his eye on that side was soaked with fluid.

"Jeffries," Howard said. "We're here. We got you all."

The captain peered up at the stairs with his one good eye.

"Thank God," he said.

In the C&C, Fernandez was mentally reviewing weapons specs, making basic arithmetic calculations, and drawing some uneasy hypotheses.

The panel in front of him showed Walt at the edge of the lot some three hundred yards away, a clear and distinct icon on his Argos tracker, a small, squat shape to his cameras, a speck to his unaided eye. It wasn't moving from there. It was just watching—

"No, check that," he said aloud to himself. "Not *just…*"

The 'hog would be communicating with its robot brothers. Nash and Earl. Sharing data. Learning. All three, learning and planning together.

He'd been trying to think along with them—*like* them—and could pretty well suppose what their plan might be. It was in the weapons. And the math.

He sat there at his displays and controls, monitoring the whereabouts of the drones, and keeping an eye on the shed behind his open hatch.

Three hundred yards wasn't far, he thought. Not when he considered that his Striker's accurate targeting range was over two thousand yards. Many times that distance. But for the hedgehog, it was far enough to dodge a rocket fired from its barrel. Spree might have been fooled by his soft-kill countermeasures, but the rest of the 'hogs wouldn't be. They were like crows. When one was killed, the rest of the flock would gather to look at what happened, analyze the reason for its death, and use their understanding to avoid future threats to their own lives. *Social learning.*

In a sense, Spree's destruction had been good for the other robots. It was definitely instructive. They would have learned from it. Would know about the FOG system and modify their tactics. Which explained why Nash had eased off. *And* why Earl was also hanging back to the east.

They didn't want to get too close to the circle of

Pumas. They didn't have to. Because they wouldn't need to use their anti-armor rockets to achieve their objective. Not if it was to wipe out the humans escaping the bunker.

They had their M2 .50-cals for that. The Ma Deuces. The same old-fashioned, low-tech, belt-fed heavy machine gun that had torn into Doc Hughes and her Midnight Runners. The same kind of gun Audie Murphy used to hold off half a dozen German tanks and a couple of hundred infantrymen in World War II. Put a human being behind one, and its effective range was six thousand feet. Well over a mile. Plenty long enough to do the job. Mount one on a robotic gunner like a hedgehog, with its sophisticated targeting system, and its effective range extended to about *four miles*.

It was a ridiculous weapon, when you thought about it. Each bullet was five and a half inches long, the size of a dart or a pencil, and ten times heavier than the 5.56 rounds fired by most semiautomatic rifles. A single round was usually enough to kill a person. Even a person standing a mile away. The entrance wound's cavitation created a wound larger than a human head. But the force of impact alone would be enough to do the job. Would tear apart tissue on a cellular level and send shock waves into the brain. From a mile off. At a closer range—say, Walt's distance from the men and women who would be coming out of the emergency shelter—it would literally make a human body explode.

That was a single bullet.

The M2 fired eight hundred rounds a minute.

And each 'hog carried three specially designed, thousand-round disintegrating feed strips.

Fernandez took a deep breath, expanding his broad chest. The robotic tracks in the snow, and the spent cartridges near the bodies of the runners, told the whole story of what happened to them. They must have seen the 'hog gliding up and thought nothing of it. Assumed it was just making its usual patrol rounds. It had caught them totally by surprise.

Fernandez pursed his lips, ballooned his cheeks, and finally exhaled a long, slow stream of air. The 'hogs had learned their collective lesson. They weren't about to jeopardize themselves by coming any closer. They wouldn't waste ammunition on autonomous rolling stock, or even his manned battlewagon. Their goal right now, right here in the current situation, would be to take the maximum number of human lives possible. And that meant the people evacuating the bunker.

There would be walking wounded. There would be men and women on stretchers. Getting them aboard the vehicles would be slow and difficult. They would have a hard time maneuvering inside the circle of Pumas. But the hogs outside the circle would have no such problem. They could wait a safe distance from the vehicles' rockets. Then move with ease once the people appeared, and pour ammunition through the openings between the wagons, which made convenient lanes of fire. And the awful beauty of it for them was that their bullets couldn't be deflected by electronic counter-

measures. Bullets didn't need fancy guidance systems. The simplest kind of missile, they just went
where they were aimed at a barrel velocity of three
thousand feet per second.

Fernandez stared at his screens. No trace of
movement from the shed yet. Nothing from the
'hogs, either. *Sure*, he thought. *Why would they
budge?* They had their targets right where they
wanted them.

They could afford to wait.

Howard knew getting everyone out would be a
sticky proposition.

The evacuees fit into three groups. The ones who
could walk on their own, the ones who could walk
with help, and the ones who couldn't walk at all.

There were five men in the first group. Four men
and two women in the second with a variety of burns,
gashes, and lacerations from broken glass and falling debris. And a man and woman on the floor on
scoop stretchers. They were both in rough shape—
he had a shattered collarbone and a mangled leg,
and she'd suffered a puncture wound in her side that
was pouring blood. Her dazed, staring eyes made
Howard suspect shock was setting in.

That made eight out of thirteen who needed assistance. With each of the stretchers requiring two
carriers, he and Wasserman would have to help,
which would hinder them if they had to use their
weapons. But there was nothing they could do
about it.

Persevere and pick a lane, Howard thought. He

was not going to leave anyone behind for a second trip. He wasn't even sure there was time for a first trip.

"You know about the drones?" he asked Jeffries.

"Yes, sir." The captain gestured toward Wasserman. "He informed us. And we've heard the explosions."

Howard grunted.

"Those fliers might make some noise, but I think we've got them beat," he said. "The 'hogs are a problem. They're still up top. And they'll open up on us the minute we're out there."

Jeffries nodded.

"I understand," he said. And paused a beat. "Thank you for coming back, sir. Sincerely."

Howard looked at him, his eyes steady, thinking the man would need reconstructive surgery to have a face. After a moment, he turned toward the rest of the evacs.

"Keep your heads down," he said. "Once you leave the shed, don't think about anything. Don't stop for anything. Just get right inside the Pumas. We stick together, we'll be fine, okay?"

Those who could nod, did.

"Then listen up," Howard said. "I'll tell you how we do this. Then we're getting out of this pit."

Howard led the way up, helping a young E3 named Larocca, who had a badly broken ankle— it looked like multiple fractures had torn through the skin. One arm around the private's back, his blooper on its sling, he took things step-by-step, trying to ignore his own severe pain. For a moment in the bunker, he'd considered taking a morphine shot from a first aid kit. But he'd wanted to stay sharp.

Larocca managed to hobble to the top mostly under his own strength. Next came the men carrying the wounded on stretchers, then Jeffries and one of the women, followed by the rest of the evacuees, both alone and assisted. The last trooper climbed the stairs alongside Wasserman as he brought up the rear.

They pressed together in the shed and waited expectantly for Howard's instructions. He moved toward the edge of the door with Larocca, partly supporting his weight.

It had gotten quiet outside. Or quiet*er*. He could still hear the buzzing of drones, but no explosions, close by or in the distance.

"We can fit both stretchers in the C&C," he said to Jeffries. "Maybe a couple more of us if they push in tight. The rest go into one of the autons. *Which* one depends, so stay on the ball."

The captain nodded, and Howard glanced at Larocca.

"With me, son?" he asked.

"All the way."

"Like you got a choice with your ankle being so fucked."

Larocca smiled a little.

Howard looked around the shed and exchanged glances with Wasserman.

"Steady and ready, people," he shouted, grabbing the door handle. "Move out! On the double!"

Howard pushed open the door and felt cold air hit his face. He saw the Pumas around him in a circle with their hatches raised.

After a moment, he nodded to Larocca and jostled forward.

Outside the coil of Pumas, Walt and Nash opened fire.

Fernandez, waiting, leaned closer to the multipanel displays. He could hear the loud, staccato chop of the 'hogs' Ma Deuces coming alive as Howard and the rest poured from the shed.

"Pickles...engage the Strikers," he ordered his AI. *"Now."*

Two of the autons instantly released a series of grenade rounds—Percy Three's turret gun leveling on Nash, Percy One's zeroing on Walt. The guided projectiles tracked and acquired their targets in a heartbeat.

The hedgehogs were equally quick to react. Reading the RPGs' trajectories, their articulated suspensions folding to the ground, they ducked just before impact like boxers in the ring.

Fernandez watched the rockets whiz right over them, overshooting their marks. Several slammed into the west fence and detonated with brilliant bursts of light. Others popped off in the air to the north, bright as day.

He wasn't surprised. It was exactly what he'd anticipated. Trying to hit the bots was futile. They were mobile, and he was stuck in position, unable to budge until the evacuees were aboard. But maybe, maybe, *maybe* he could screw with their aim.

He turned to peer outside the open hatch. A group of evacuees was rushing up under steady fire, carrying the most severely wounded on stretchers. They pushed one, Sergeant Linda Marley, through the open hatch. A second, E4 Corey Ambler, was hustled over next. Behind them in the crowd, Howard was shouting, "Hurry! Hurry it up!"

Fernandez watched as Ambler was lifted in. So far, the defensive coil had kept everyone from being sliced to ribbons, but he could see the hedgehogs maneuvering for better positions outside it, bobbing and weaving and scuttling sideways like crabs, their guns making continual adjustments and clapping out torrents of fire.

He clenched his teeth. These were his people. His friends. Soldiers. Their lives depended on him. He would buy them some time. It was all he could do. The *only* thing. With luck they would be moving out in a few minutes.

"C'mon, Julio," he whispered to himself. "Step *up*."

He launched another volley of grenades from the autons and saw the 'hogs duck, dodge, and scamper to avoid the projectiles, their bullets rattling against his vehicle's front and sides. In the rear, the two stretchers were being strapped down, their carriers crouching over them.

That accounted for six of the evacuees, Fernandez thought. Almost half. He glanced at his screens, watched the rest climbing into Percy Two, some more slowly than others. Once they were safely aboard, the plan was to head south toward the main gate and roll through onto the Bucharest road. With Spree out of the picture, it would be the path of least resistance and the safest way off base.

The autons coughed out more grenades at his command. It didn't seem to faze the 'hogs. They swerved and jack-in-the-boxed and eluded the barrage, their machine guns hacking away without interruption. He was thinking it wouldn't be long before they got things figured out and started pouring concentrated fire through the lanes.

Fernandez waited tensely. Ten endless seconds, fifteen, thirty. Another hail of bullets rattled against his vehicle. But the good news was that most of the evacuees were finally aboard Percy Two. There were maybe a couple to go, plus Howard and Wass.

"C'mon, c'mon," he muttered.

Again he launched grenades at the 'hogs. Again they sleeted his Puma with bullets. He checked his distance displays...and frowned. *Shit and Shinola.*

It was Earl. He hadn't stayed on top of the robot's progress as it crossed the 'Burbs from the civvy-housing area. Hadn't noticed it getting so close. Too close now. He still had people out there. Could hear Howard in the thick of things, barking instructions at them.

Then he saw something completely out of the blue. An unidentified vehicle was speeding south on the transverse linking Janus Heights and the 'Burbs, almost due north of Earl's position.

Blinking in disbelief, Fernandez held his eyes on the screen. His onboards were identifying the bogey as a Jolt.

He shook his head in deepening confusion.

"So who are you…and what the hell are you doing around here?" he wondered, getting only silence for an answer.

Laura had just left the transverse and veered right onto the 'Burbs, bearing speedily toward the quadrangle, when Mario straightened with the NV binocs to his eyes. He was looking almost directly to the south.

She cut him a glance. "What do you see?"

He gazed raptly through the glasses. It was a hedgehog, moving across the field from west to east on an almost parallel course with them.

"Mario?"

"It's Earl," he said.

"What?"

"Earl."

"Ay, I heard you!" She rolled across the hard grass. "I meant how is it possible? *Como es posible?* How did it get ahead of us?"

He understood what she was asking him. They had left the bot well behind them only minutes before.

"We swung north off-road, stopped a couple times," he said. "It's light and fast. And it would've gone straight across this field. The shortest distance between two points is a straight line."

Laura considered that, her headlights gliding

over the snow. She knew from all too recent experience that the hog was a dangerous threat. She also realized it was now more or less between them and the barracks. But for her, Mario's discovery was strangely...*shockless*, she thought, wondering if that was even a real word.

They had already seen the drones dive down on the armored wedge, only to scatter pell-mell like swatted flies and blow up far off course. Then they had seen the Pumas take out one of the hedgehogs and head on toward the new barracks, followed by the noise and light in the sky *behind* the barracks.

And that was just over the past few minutes. After this whole crazy night of chaos and destruction, she was thinking it would take a lot to surprise either one of them.

"Do you have any idea what it's going to do?" she asked.

Mario sat gazing through the lenses a minute. "There's enough left of the barracks to get in the way of my view...smoke, too...but I can just make out the Pumas around back. On the north side, around the Love Shack."

"The *what*?"

He cleared his throat, lowering the binocs.

"I meant the *maintenance shed*," he said. "Looks like they're all stopped around it. In a circle."

"Stopped, why?"

"That shed was repurposed after the Romanians left," he said. "There's an exit from the emergency shelter hidden inside."

"So you think they're getting people out?"

He nodded his head. "It's where anyone down in the shelter would evac."

Her eyes suddenly met his in the rearview mirror. "The robot…Earl…it wants to stop them."

He didn't reply at first. As a specialist by training, he felt that trying to read an artificial intelligence's intent—or even *attributing* humanlike intent to an AI—was a huge stretch. But he wouldn't quarrel with Laura's basic conclusion.

"I think you're right," he said. "Earl's definitely hauling it."

"So how can we help?"

He thought a minute. Then an idea struck him. A wild one, maybe. But…

"Speed up," he said. "We need to pass the 'hog. I want to dig something out of the back."

Laura drove forward without asking any more questions.

And sped up.

Howard watched the C&C's hatch drop shut. The seriously wounded evacuees and their carriers had been crowded aboard, and the troop compartment was out of room. He and Larocca would have to squeeze in with Wasserman's group on Percy Three.

"Ready?" he asked.

Larocca nodded. "No problem."

Howard hoped not. His body felt like lead. But they were only five or six strides from the auton's open hatch.

He turned toward the auton and started to cross

the lane between wagons. Took one step, two. Larocca moving along with him.

On the western buffer, Walt glided into sight and spotted them, its machine gun firing a cascade of .50-caliber bullets into the gap. They whined through the air and struck the C&C's armored front quarter at an angle, skipping, clanging, and ricocheting off both vehicles.

Howard swore and glanced around at the C&C. They were still closer to it than the auton. He gestured at it, braced Larocca with his arm, and started to double back.

The hedgehog tracked them with its gun barrel, firing cleanly into the middle of the lane this time.

He would never know if they could have made it to cover on their own. It would have been tough for him hauling so much of Larocca's weight. But that suddenly became moot.

They hadn't yet reached the C&C when Fernandez launched several Striker rounds at the 'hog from its turret, forcing it to dip down, jump up, and skitter away from the lane as the RPGs blew harmlessly in the outlying woods.

Larocca snapped Howard a glance. "That thing almost got lucky, sir," he said.

Howard didn't answer. If its fire had been a hair closer, the machine gun would have mowed them down. But he didn't think it was a matter of luck. The 'hogs were narrowing in, getting closer to hitting their targets even while taking evasive action. *Learning on the move.*

He inhaled. His ribs crunched and jabbed under

the tight bands of his ammo belts. He figured half of them were broken and half of those were displaced and sucking and flailing in toward his lungs.

Which still left him in better shape than Larocca. Blood had soaked through the bottom of his trouser leg and was dripping from his boot into the snow. Howard was impressed that he could even stand upright.

He needed to get him into Percy Three.

Behind it, Wasserman was helping the last couple of evacuees in his group toward the hatch. Both were moving with difficulty. He saw Howard struggling with Larocca's weight and immediately started toward him.

"Sir, I'll give you a han—"

He'd barely taken a step when the hedgehog's machine gun pulsed again. Howard heard a loud, fleshy *slap*.

"My God," Larocca said. "I'm hit."

He slipped in Howard's arm, his eyes wide. Howard glanced down and realized the lower part of the young man's body was gone. His right leg was on the ground. His left hip and leg hung from his torso by a bloody chunk of meat. That was it. There was nothing else left of him below the waist. Howard could see his intestines lumping out into the snow underneath him.

He slipped some more. His eyes rolled, his face bunching up in a strange contortion of pain and puzzlement. Three seconds after the bullet tore into him, he made a sound like a cough and then shuddered and died with Howard's arm still hooked under his shoulders.

He was gone. Just like that.

Gone.

Howard's eyes met Wasserman's for a split second, the two men exchanging identical looks of shock, horror, and dismay. Then Howard let go of the body. The 'hog's machine gun was still firing. But one of the Pumas had loosed a grenade at it, forcing an evasive feint, and the bullets chewed into the ground wide of his position. He scrambled back behind the C&C to where he and Larocca had stood just moments ago.

Then the machine gun stopped firing.

Perched on his haunches, he leaned slightly past the edge of the hatch to peek into the lane between the two wagons. Walt was there in the buffer. It hadn't budged. Its gun was still silent. It was waiting. *For what?*

His answer was another burst of heavy fire. But not from Walt. It was coming from his left—the north side of the lot. Shooting through the lane between Percy One and Percy Two.

He glanced over there.

Nash.

The 'hogs had glided to roughly nine and twelve o'clock around the circle of wagons. They had lined him up in the holes. Pinned him down. And not just him.

Wasserman was crouched behind Percy Three with his two evacs. They had been outside its open hatch when Walt's machine gun cut loose. And now they were stuck there. They couldn't budge. If they moved so much as an inch away from the wagon they were done.

Like Larocca.

Howard glanced at his remains in the snow. The Ma Deuces could down an aircraft, and they had kept sheeting the private's soft flesh with ammunition. There wasn't much left that was recognizable as human.

He knew it wouldn't do any good to stay put. The 'hogs would eventually find an opening between volleys from the Pumas and shoot him where he was. Or he would move half an inch at the wrong moment, and that would be it. One way or the other, they would nail him.

As if to underscore his conclusion, the two 'hogs opened fire in unison. Bullets spat into the snow from two sides. The robots' aim had tightened in.

He was thinking he would need to make some quick decisions, when the C&C's hatch lifted back open, brushing against his right arm.

"Get in, sir!"

Howard glanced inside. It was Fernandez. Shouting across the packed rear compartment. The sergeant had swiveled around from the front cabin and leaned his head between its seats.

"Shut the hatch!" Howard shouted.

"Sir—"

"I said shut the hatch!" Howard barked. *"Keep those motherfuckers dancing. Aim high!"*

He crouched there on the balls of his feet as more .50s plowed into the snow to his left. Fernandez looked out at him another split second, then turned his head back around.

The hatch descended silently on its pneumatics.

Howard peered up the lane between the C&C and Percy Three as the Strikers pumped out round after explosive round, all going high. Walt bobbed and dipped and scrambled to avoid them, Nash doing the same evasive jig to his left.

Attaboy, Julio, he thought.

Still squatting low, he reached back for his grenade launcher and jammed it against his shoulder. Its forestock was down, and its lock sight was up.

Then he saw Walt's gun swivel toward him. The 'hog was getting a bead on him even as it dodged the Puma's shells. Its gun fired, and bullets spanged against the C&C's hatch.

It had gotten closer. But not close enough. It was off balance. And off its mark.

Howard pressed his eye to his lock sight, found his range, and waited a millisecond as the 'hog dropped down to avoid another elevated Striker round.

"You go high, I go lower 'n low," he growled.

And aiming for the lowest point of its drop, he squeezed the grenade gun's trigger. He felt it buck hard against his side, then felt a sharp and terrible stabbing pain in his chest. It was like a hot knife.

Howard didn't care what was going inside his body. It didn't matter to him. He saw the 40x46 mm round *bloop* from the barrel of his weapon and go rocketing through the lane, straight and true, smoke braiding out behind it. The projectile rushed up on the 'hog just as it bobbed below Julio's grenade, slammed into it just above its suspension. Both rounds exploded with an earsplitting bang.

Walt spun like a top. Its chassis seemed to bulge outward, fire and smoke gushing from inside it. Buzzing, whirring, and clicking, the 'hog tottered forward and back, swayed left and right, and then fell sideways to the ground.

Beside Howard, Wasserman had already yanked a cartridge from his belt, palmed it into the receiver, and taken aim at Walt. With a long-range weapon like the M320, it was equivalent to shooting point-blank.

The detonation blew the 'hog to pieces. Its gripper arm and sensor arrays went flying. Metal components rocketed into the air, fanned outward, and rained down onto the Pumas' armor, ringing and clanging like church bells.

Howard glanced to his left. Nash was still in motion, pouring fire from its machine gun and ducking rounds from the Pumas.

Getting up on one knee like a mortarman, he pivoted around toward the 'hog and slapped another round into the blooper.

"Wassy!" he hollered without looking around at him. *"Go fuckin' low!"*

He pulled his trigger, heard Wasserman's launcher discharge behind him. The projectiles swished toward Nash and connected with thudding eruptions of sound. Their combined explosive yield flung the 'hog up off the ground and propelled it backward for several feet, a bright orange-and-blue skirt of flame rippling and flapping around it.

The duo hit the robot again as it landed in the snow, their shells blasting through its armor to split it nearly in half. Smoke and flames gushed upward from inside it. Torn from its sprockets, the 'hog's right tread momentarily hung from them like a drooping, ragged rubber banner and then began melting into slag.

A few seconds passed. Howard pushed up off his knee, not caring about his pain, rising in slow stages to his feet. When he was fully upright, he paused at last, studying what was left of the robot.

"Later, shitcan," he muttered and turned toward Wasserman.

The E3 would never forget his huge, white, gap-toothed grin. The image would resurface at unexpected times for the rest of his life. There was something almost frightful about it. He couldn't have given a reason why. He just knew how it made him feel. Like he'd glimpsed something better left unseen.

After a long moment, Howard took a step toward him.

And then stopped.

He raised a hand to his chest. His other hand released its grip on the blooper so it hung loosely from its rig. The berserk smile was gone. In its place was a kind of grimace.

"Sir...are you all right?" Wasserman asked.

Howard did not answer. He opened his mouth wider and inhaled. But Wasserman didn't think the breath looked right at all. It was visibly shallow and hitching.

"Sir?"

The colonel tried to pull in air, gasping, his hand still on his chest. Then his eyes rolled back, and he tottered where he stood like a tree without roots and sagged toward the ground.

He'd passed out.

Wasserman dove forward and managed to catch him an instant before he would have crashed hard into the snow. But Howard's lurching fall almost brought him down as well. His knees bent, he tried to prop him up, stumbled, and realized he wouldn't be able to get him over to the C&C alone.

Then he realized he wouldn't have to.

He saw the door at the battlewagon's rear open again, Fernandez simultaneously jumping out his hatch and scrambling around to help.

"Come on, Wass," he shouted. "Let's get him inside!"

The sergeant got his back under Howard, and they moved him up toward the wagon with their combined strength. As they reached its open hatch, Wasserman heard the *rat-a-tat* of renewed machine-gun fire and glanced nervously at the sergeant. The sound was coming from their right—from the east side of the lot. And close by.

They held up, Howard between them, and glanced in that direction. Both knew what they would see.

The last of the hedgehogs, Earl, was barreling toward the coil.

* * *

Exactly three minutes earlier, Mario had climbed back into the Jolt's cargo section, grabbed what he wanted out of a covered storage bin, and set it down across his lap.

"Okay," Laura said, as they banged rapidly along over the hard grass. She'd managed to pass Earl up, pouring on speed. "I won't ask what you're going to do with the car jack."

Silent with concentration, he expanded the rail from its stowed length of two feet to its full forty-eight inches, making sure it was locked into place.

She flicked him an impatient glance in the rear-view mirror.

"Por favor, Mario!" she said. "Tell me what you're doing with that car jack!"

He tested the rail a second time.

"We need to get out of the Jolt," he said abruptly.

She cut him another glance in the mirror. "Are you *serious*?"

"Totally," he said and paused. "Do you trust me?"

"Of course."

"Then listen close…"

He quickly explained his plan, and they scrambled out of the idling vehicle. Mario had the binocs around his neck and the car jack in his right hand.

He raced around toward Laura's wide-open door and stood there looking south through the glasses. They were directly above the barracks parking area, around two hundred yards north of the shed. He saw the four armored battlewagons parked in a circular formation around the shed, each pointed in a different direction, with wide, open lanes between them. Laura had stopped the Jolt in an almost perfectly straight line above the Pumas facing north and west.

He could make out three men at the far end of the lane separating them. Two were Sergeant Fernandez and Glenn Wasserman, a private on Colonel Howard's HQ staff. He recognized a third as the colonel himself...and he looked in bad shape. From what Mario saw, Fernandez and Wasserman were helping him along toward one of the vehicles.

If the 'hog was going to do damage—the most damage possible—that lane would be its best, easiest lane of approach.

Mario frowned and swung the glasses to his left. Earl was about a quarter mile east, and still roughly half as far north of the shed as he and Laura were. A hundred yards, give or take.

His move would have to be perfectly timed.

A quarter mile east, he thought. *Four hundred forty yards. Okay, so...*

He estimated that the 'hog's speed maxed out at sixty miles an hour. The Jolt eighty miles an hour, tops. If Earl was going full tilt, it would be about fifteen seconds till it crossed between him and the Pumas and turned left toward the lane.

And once it made the turn...

Sixty miles an hour. A hundred yards of ground to cover. That's just under thirty yards per second.

Which meant the 'hog would reach the lane in about three seconds.

"Laura, you'd better move out of the way," he said, looking up. "In case the tires skid."

Her face anxious, she nodded and backed a few feet off to the side without questioning him.

Mario hurried. Tossing the jack through the driver's door, he dove in after it and swung the vehicle around so its front end was turned south toward the lane. Next, he shifted into Neutral, pulled up his seat-adjustment lever, and slid the seat all the way forward. Finally, he reached for the jack on the seat beside him.

His four-foot extension had been a guesstimate, and at a glance it looked on the money. He quickly jammed the jack into the footwell, pressing its heavy iron baseplate against the gas pedal, and the nose of its rail up against the bottom of his seat. The vehicle's big, loud, five hundred–horsepower engine revved and surged as he tested the jack to make sure it was wedged firmly in place between them.

An instant later he hopped out of the Jolt and peered through the binocs. Earl was now about three hundred yards to his left and a hundred yards below him, still racing forward in a straight line.

He knew the 'hog normally would have 360-degree situational awareness. *Normally* it would locate and identify him as a threat and attack. But he was betting the bank that wouldn't happen. Because its behavior was anything but normal. It had become deranged. Fixated. Obsessed.

Compulsive.

Mario thought that gave him a chance.

He watched. Waited. Earl's distance to his left—

eastward—shrank with each stroke of his heart. It was two hundred fifty yards away. A hundred fifty yards east. Seventy-five…

He shot Laura a glance. She caught it and smiled encouragingly. The 'hog was now within fifteen yards of coming in a direct line with the front of his JLTV—and the lane.

Ten yards…

He only hoped he'd gotten his math right.

He dragged in a breath, leaned in behind the Jolt's steering wheel, and slid its transmission from Neutral to Drive, tossing its electronic key fob into the front seat so the ignition wouldn't cut off. Then he let the driverless vehicle go.

It bucked forward like a stallion freed from a rope, almost ripping his arm off before he pulled it out the open door.

And that was it. He'd done everything he could. He'd soon find out if it was enough.

Mario prayed to God and the angels as Laura had shown him.

As far as malicious codes went, this one was a tiny script, a monoworm with a single purpose. Namely to turn Earl into a robotic suicide bomb and bomber, all wrapped into one.

The idea behind it was simple but ingenious.

The 'hog's RPGs fired and detonated using mechanisms that were many decades old and technologically unsophisticated. A charge of propellant fuel powered the grenade's rocket motor. The solid fuel comprising this charge was ignited by a squib of nitroglycerine, which, in turn, was ignited by a gunpowder primer when the launch was triggered.

Thus, the primer sparked the squib. The squib ignited the rocket fuel. And the fuel propelled the grenade from its launch tube on a tail of built-up gases.

Simple.

The explosive part of the grenade was its warhead. The warhead was primarily designed to detonate on impact. But as a backup, most RPGs were provided with a piezoelectric fuse that was timed to initiate the warhead's combustion four and a half seconds after launch.

There was nothing too fancy about piezoelectric devices. They used materials like quartz or certain kinds of ceramics to generate a small amount of current. A spark. They were used in everything from grill igniters to cell phones. A physical mechanism— a tiny hammer, for instance—or really anything that caused friction—would strike the piezoelectric material and create the spark. That spark could light a fire.

In an RPG, the friction that caused the spark was created by motion. Specifically, the rotation of the warhead. It launched, it spun, after four and a half seconds it activated the piezoelectric fuse. Then, detonation.

Which was where the monoworm came in. It taught the hedgehog, itself powered by electricity, how to generate a charge precisely simulating that of the piezoelectric backup fuse. Of brief duration, the charge would be directed at the onboard rocket warheads. And create sparks.

Without launch.

Without motion.

Without rotation.

Eight tiny sparks. Eight warheads, each of which was loaded with over two pounds of high-yield plastic explosive and could punch through three inches of solid steel. All set to blow at Earl's command when it reached the lane.

Ingenious.

Fernandez was thinking that if Howard was conscious, he would be pissing vinegar at him.

And probably he'd be justified.

The sergeant could see Earl racing toward him, bearing directly toward the lane between Percy Two and Percy Three.

From a soldier's perspective, he'd been dumb. There was nothing he could do to stop the 'hog from outside the vehicle. The autons wouldn't open fire without his direct command. They did not learn, and they did not make decisions for themselves like hedgehogs. They were, in reality, *semi*autons programmed to execute specific tasks assigned by a human.

And he had abandoned their controls.

Jumped out the vehicle's hatch.

Dumb.

The 'hog drew closer, its big Ma Deuce silent. That worried Fernandez more than if it had been firing away at him, though he wasn't sure why.

He and Wasserman pressed against the wagon's rear fender with the colonel slumped between them. Then he realized the four evacuees who'd carried the stretchers inside were reaching their hands out the rear entrance, doing what they could to help. Themselves walking wounded, they were reaching for *Howard*.

He glanced over at the private.

"We're lifting him in!" he shouted. "With me?"

Wass nodded. "Say when."

Fernandez took a breath. He didn't want to just shove Howard through the hatch. He didn't know how badly he was injured and worried he might do him internal damage. But they couldn't afford to be gentle.

"Okay," he said. *"Now!"*

They heaved him up. The evacs grabbed hold of Howard's sleeves, the back of his shirt, his belt, whatever they could get their hands on, tugging and pulling and hoisting his body off their shoulders. Fernandez pushed until he was all the way through the entrance, then turned to Wasserman.

"Let's move, bro," he said and started around to the front hatch.

Wasserman nodded and quickstepped behind him, shooting a cautious glance up the lane toward the 'hog.

And suddenly stopped dead in his tracks.

"Sarge," he said, "what's it doing?"

Fernandez held up in front of him. Half turned to look.

The 'hog was hurtling toward the lane faster

than he'd ever seen one of the robots move. He guessed it was about a hundred twenty yards away. At the rate of speed it was going, it would reach their position in seconds. Before they could get into the vehicle's cabin, let alone drive away.

What's it doing? He still didn't know. But he assumed it wasn't anything good.

His heart thudded. The robot kept coming. He thought suddenly about the kamikaze fliers in the sky. He thought suddenly that Earl's barreling, head-on speed reminded him of suicide drivers in Afghanistan. The two thoughts came together in his mind, and he understood that the 'hog was going to take itself out—and take them along with it.

Then he heard the noise coming from the darkness behind it, glanced past the bot, and felt his eyes gape.

"Ohhh, mama, this takes the cake," he blurted.

Sergeant Julio Victor Fernandez didn't know where the Jolt came from. But that wasn't his main concern.

He seemed to see it all in herky-jerky slow motion. The JLTV bounding up behind the hedgehog, coming on, coming on, coming on seemingly out of *nowhere* on a direct collision course with it and then vaulting up the final few feet and slamming into Earl only ten yards outside the lane.

There was a loud crackling crunch like metal in a giant compactor as they were entangled in a violent collision, the Jolt's front grill bending and warping, the 'hog buckling and twisting, the warheads aboard it exploding with a sudden burst of thunder, light, and heat. The thunder clapping out a pressure wave that ruptured both of Fernandez's eardrums. The light glaring into his eyes and leaving him momentarily blinded. The fiery furnace heat baking his forehead and cheeks.

Lifted three feet off the ground on an orange toadstool of flame, thrashing and twitching in its terminal convulsions, Earl slammed down onto the Jolt's crumpled hood, rolled back over it into the windshield, and smashed halfway through the glass to lodge between the burning driver's and passenger seats.

Wasserman stood there a moment, stunned, black smoke pouring over him through the lane. It stung his eyes and nostrils and crawled deep down into his throat.

"Holy shit, Sarge!" he said. "What just happened here?"

Fernandez looked at the private through thick ropes of smoke, more reading his lips than actually hearing him. His ears hurt and were ringing loudly.

"We can figure it out inside," he said and nodded at the C&C.

For a second Mario stared at the leaping, churning flames thirty feet away, amazed by what he'd just seen with his own eyes. Asking himself basically the same thing Wasserman had just asked Fernandez. He understood that the hedgehog had been headed toward the Pumas to do damage, understood that it was out of its robotic head, understood it had been hijacked so it would turn on the humans it was supposed to protect...

But he had not expected it to blow sky-high when the Jolt slammed into it. Get knocked off course, absolutely. Maybe, he'd hoped, get trashed in the collision. But to *blow* like that...

He was wondering how it could have occurred when Laura came trotting up to him.

"Mario!" she said. "You did it!"

"I guess," he said, unsure exactly *what* he'd done.

"You guess?" She nodded toward the fire, its reddish light playing over her features. "*Eres fantastico!* You are my hero!"

He looked at her. "Really?"

"That you're a hero?"

He shook his head. "No, you didn't say *a*. You said *my*."

"What are you talking about?"

"You said, 'You are *my* h—'"

Mario broke off. He could hear something above them   and noticed Laura did, too. They looked up simultaneously.

The fliers were gathering overhead. However many of them were left. There had to be ten, fifteen, coming together above them.

Mario's heartbeat accelerated. He lowered his eyes to Laura, saw the terror on her face, and scooped her into his arms, pulling her close, clutching her tightly against his chest.

They had nowhere to run. Nowhere to take cover. They were trapped out here in the open field.

"Laura, I want to marry you," he said.

The fliers dove.

Fernandez stared hard at his forward display as the Pumas barreled across the parking area, all four vehicles falling back into a wedge formation as they rolled toward the western edge of the 'Burbs. He recognized the uniformed kid up ahead as a 24 Delta named Mario Perez. The woman wrapped in his arms also looked familiar…from the base exchange, he thought. Why they'd driven out here in the Jolt, and how they turned it into a demolition-derby vehicle on its last romp, and when they'd gotten so *chummy* were questions for another time.

Right now he only cared about getting them within range of his FOG deflection shield before the drones dropping from the sky blasted them into the next world.

"Wass," he said, "they inside the shield yet?"

Wasserman checked his instrument console. "Not yet," he said. "We need to be closer—"

"Pickles, *speed up!* Let's get it on!"

"Handling it, bro."

Fernandez's eyes locked on the screens. The fliers were coming down in a swarming, swirling column. Those two out there in the field had seconds at most.

He rocked in his seat as the four Pumas bucked forward with a surge of acceleration. The AI was pushing their drive engines to full power, routing electricity into them from reserve batteries and nonessential systems.

The wagons went only a short distance before they shuddered to a halt. In the C&C, Fernandez saw Perez and the woman still holding each other close just a few yards in front of him, the throng of drones within ten feet of their heads.

He hitched in a tense breath, held it…

And an instant later released an audible sigh of relief.

The fliers were scattering like panicked birds. They spooled and spun every which way through the darkness, veering apart in furious uncontrolled flight. Fernandez saw bright flashes of light in his display as they crashed and detonated all across the field.

He watched for a minute, then turned to Wasserman.

"Damn, Wassy," he said. "We're hot tonight."

"Butt-puckering hot!" the private said, a smile breaking across his lips.

Fernandez realized all at once he was smiling, too. A huge, bright, daffy grin.

"Firefighter's-fart hot!" he said, not sure what that was supposed to mean.

"Devil's-piss hot!"

"Can't-feel-my-face hot!"

"Ass-in-hell hot!"

Swept by relief, the two of them sat there cackling like lunatics for a long five seconds. Then Fernandez pulled himself together and nodded toward his display. The apparent sweethearts out there were looking around like they had trouble believing they were still alive, and he could hardly blame them.

"Better pick 'em up before they catch a cold," he said and manually switched on the public address system.

His hands firmly around her waist, Mario boosted Laura through the hatch and climbed in after her. Sergeant Fernandez had instructed them to board the auton with the name Percy Two painted on its rocket tube, opening its rear door by remote command.

Mario pulled down one of the folded sidewall seats for her, and she settled into it. He was unfolding the one alongside it when he noticed her looking up at him.

"Mario," she said.

"Yes?"

"I have to ask you something…"

He stood in silence a moment, his seat halfway open as the vehicle bumped forward, heading toward the south gate.

"Uh…yes?"

"Outside," she said, "when it looked like those drones were going to…well…"

He nodded.

"I thought we might die," he said.

"I know," she said.

They were both quiet. The auton rumbled on. The monitor on the wall showed they had turned from the 'Burbs onto the south perimeter road.

"What I said to you," Mario said. "Out *there*, that is…"

"Yes?"

"I *really* thought we were going to die," he said.

Laura looked at him. "You really already told me."

"Right, right. Sorry…"

"Mario?"

"Yes?"

"What you said…"

"I know it must've sounded crazy. I mean, we haven't even had our first *date*."

"My God, I almost forgot," she said. "Bucharest, Saturday night…"

"The battle of the bands," he said. "Not that I think it's in the cards after everything that's happened tonight…"

"I would still go with you," she said. "If we can."

"Really?"

"Especially after tonight," she said. "Life goes on, you know?"

He looked at her and nodded a little. She looked at him and smiled.

And without hesitation, he dropped onto one knee and swept her hand into his, balancing there in front of her in the rocking, rumbling, shaking troop compartment. For some reason, he thought suddenly of the snowflake alighting on her nose outside the exchange. Lingering there an instant before it she brushed it off.

He noticed only now that she was wearing pink nail polish. Pale pink, her hands small and delicate, her nails short but perfectly manicured.

"I love you, Laura," he said, both his hands around hers now.

Her smile grew wider.

"I love *you*, Mario," she said.

"I mean, you're the love of my life," he said.

"Si, ey mi corazon es tuyo," she said.

He looked at her some more. She looked at him some more.

"Laura Cruz," he said, "will you marry me?"

She swallowed.

"Mario Perez," she said, "first things first."

"What?"

"Remember what I told you? Back at the base exchange?"

"About knowing when to kiss you?"

"Yes."

"So you know I'm the right guy?"

"Yes."

"But we already—"

"I kissed *you*," she said. "That does *not* count."

He looked at her. She looked at him. They both grinned and fell into each other's arms.

The Pumas rolled out the south gate onto the road, heading east toward Bucharest. Five minutes later they joined up with a Romanian military convoy that would escort them to their base.

Eyes closed, their lips together in a long, lasting kiss, Mario and Laura hardly noticed.

PART THREE

19

Various Locales

Harris snatched his cell off the dining room table on the first ring. At 7:30 a.m., he was sitting there fully dressed in a blue paisley shirt and brown plaid sport coat that had cost him an arm and a leg at a vintage clothing shop in Hoboken.

"Carol," he said.

"Leo."

"You at the airport?"

"Already heading into Manhattan," she said.

"JFK?"

"White Plains," she said. "I took an air shuttle. The detainee's already arrived at the Terminal safe and sound."

"When?"

"About an hour ago. Via a helicopter out of 84VA."

84VA being the Federal Aviation Administration's identifier for the otherwise-unnamed CIA heliport at the southeast end of the Campus.

Leo reached for his coffee, took a quick slug.

"I'll head over there right now," he said.

"As long as you're up to it," Morse said. "I gave you the option. But I ultimately want it to be your decision."

Leo frowned.

"It's my job," he said. "What other option do I have?"

"Leo, please. Not now."

"I'm just saying—"

"I know what you're saying," she said. "If I didn't want you to participate in the interview, I wouldn't have alerted you to the extradition. But I did as soon as it finally came through."

He gulped down some more coffee. *Participate.* He didn't like the sound of the word, not at all, but decided to let it pass for now.

"Where do we meet?"

"The Fusion Center," she said. "There's a small office on one side."

"I know where it is."

"Good," she said. "Traffic's pretty light on the Hutch. Fingers crossed it keeps moving, I'll be there in twenty minutes."

Harris grunted.

"Catch you later," he said, realizing Carol had already ended the call.

He frowned. Things were definitely hostile between them these days. Well, maybe *hostile* was too strong. But tense for sure.

Slowly rising off his chair, Harris went to carry his cup over to the sink. Sometimes, he found himself wishing they still got along the way they had before his injury. Though in the long run, that wouldn't have worked out. Being friends with his ex was more trouble than he needed. All it did was stir up memories in him. And it all hurt. Too much.

Better to keep things strictly business.

The New York/East Coast headquarters of Net Force was in a fortresslike, nineteenth-century building in the area between Eighth Avenue and the Hudson River known as Hell's Kitchen. Originally the city's largest commercial warehouse, the Terminal was all red bricks and iron lintels and tall casement windows, with a huge central tunnel through which freight trains once arrived along a rail spur linking it to the busy West Side shipyards. In more recent times, it had served as a regional field office for Homeland Security, but some strenuous political arm-twisting by President Annemarie Fucillo led to Homeland grudgingly moving its offices to a location about a mile downtown. In POTUS's view, Net Force had needed the space for its expanding operations, recruitment drive, and training program.

Twenty-five minutes after Leo Harris pulled his charcoal-gray Jeep Compass from its slot outside his Jersey City condo, he bumped over the old train tracks outside the Terminal and drove up to the motor-vehicle security checkpoint, his oxygen machine charging off the engine beside him. It looked fairly inconspicuous in a black shoulder bag, but he'd covered the unit with an open copy of *The New York Times* to assure the guards wouldn't notice it.

"Happy New Year, sir!" The man in the booth smiled at him. "How are you doing?"

Harris shrugged and displayed his ID, looking straight ahead. This was just his third trip to the new offices since their opening two months before, his last having been in late October, before the holidays. Now the jack-o'-lanterns were compost and the Christmas trees were out on the sidewalks. How the hell did the guy *think* he was doing?

He drove through the tunnel arch to the garage and parked. As director he got a prime spot near the elevator, and good thing, too. It would have taken him ten minutes to walk across two relatively narrow aisles in the underground lot. Like he had to labor just to get from his bedroom to his living room. Like it took him an hour to take a shower while sitting on a plastic bench.

Now he lifted the newspaper off his carry bag and set it carefully aside. The battery readout showed his machine was fully charged. Leo knew the charge would last all day. He could have used the POC in his sleep.

He pulled the charger out of the accessory socket and stuffed it into one of the bag's outer flap pouches. He took the nasal cannula from a different pouch and attached it to the outflow nozzle. Then he fitted the prongs into his nostrils and turned on the machine.

Canned breath. Oxygen on the go.

He inhaled through his nose. A long, deep breath

to inflate his lungs with purified air. The salesman at the medical-supply store had guaranteed his unit was the smallest and quietest on the market. Top of the line, at three times the cost of an average machine. The salesman had showed him a chart comparing its thirty-seven-decibel operating noise to the noise levels of bird calls and soft whispers and rain and rustling leaves. The salesman had seemed like he knew his stuff. But maybe he was just looking for a fat commission. Maybe he didn't know anything.

Harris didn't think the machine sounded like rain. Unless it was rain slamming down on a tin roof. And it sure as hell didn't sound like birds or whispers or rustling. To him its rhythmic racket sounded more like some obnoxious beatboxer on a sleepy subway platform.

Leo sat there for about five minutes, turned off the machine, and removed the cannula. Folding it into a pouch, he sat there behind the wheel a little longer and did his breathing exercises. He combed his hair, smoothed down his overcoat, slung the POC over his shoulder, and exited the vehicle, leaving his cane behind under the front seat. He would be okay without the damn thing for a while. He would have to be. He didn't want anyone to see him using it.

A wave of his palm in front of a bioscanner, and the elevator doors opened to admit him. He rode it up to the third floor Fusion Center, where cavernous, industrial-age storage rooms had been scooped out and smoothed over and transformed into an equally cavernous but brighter modern space about the size of two basketball courts set end to end. It was filled with computer workstations and large flat-screen displays.

Harris saw fifteen or twenty men and women scattered around the room, wearing the uniforms or badges of various law-enforcement and investigative agencies. There was a low hum of activity, mingled voices, chairs shifting, fingers tapping at keyboards. Later in the day, it might have three or four times as many people working cases together. NYPD, FBI, CIA, Homeland, Net Force...

It had been Leo's idea to borrow the concept of an interagency information- and resource-sharing pool from the Agency. Three decades at 26 Fed across town, you didn't leave without some takeaways.

He went up a wide aisle to an office on the far side of the room. It felt like the people who recognized him were trying not to look at the oxygen machine strapped over his shoulder. It was a long, slow hike.

The office door did not have a nameplate. Which made sense because it wasn't really anyone's office. Though reserved for high-ranking personnel, it was, along with everything else on the floor, for shared use.

Harris took a couple of deep breaths and flashed his biometric key. The door unlocked with a click, and he walked in.

The office was clean and rectangular and unadorned. No clocks, no pictures on the wall, no photos on the desk. Its only real furnishing was an institutional-gray metal desk with a computer terminal on top. There was a manila file folder next to the keyboard. An empty chair on either side of the desk, and a few more against the walls. The high casement window gave a broad but unspectacular view of Tenth Avenue three stories below.

Carol Morse stood there looking out with her back to the door. She was wearing an open pin-striped blazer over a tan sweater. Her coat was hung neatly on a hook rack. She turned to him, a Star-bucks coffee cup in her hand.

"Hello, Leo," she said.

"Carol."

"You're looking better."

Leo shrugged. He noticed that she'd darkened her hair a shade. He could tell she was spending a lot of time in the gym. Her perfume smelled like flowers.

"Where's Zolcu?" he said.

She looked at him a second.

"Is this how it's going to be?" she said. "War all the time?"

Silence. She expelled a breath.

"I'll bring you over in a minute," she said. "But we should talk first."

Harris shrugged again, took the breathing ma-chine off his shoulder, and put it on an empty chair against the wall. He unbuttoned his coat but kept it on, waiting for her to sit down behind the desk. Then he settled into the chair opposite her.

She opened the file folder on the desk between them.

"I brought two copies of his dossier from Wash-ington," she said. "I know you've seen it. But I thought we should do a quick review together."

Harris reached into the inside pocket of his coat and brought out an e-reader.

"I've got it all here," he said. "Digitized."

She looked at him. "You? An e-reader?"

"Right," he said. "You figure I read cave paintings?"

Morse didn't respond. The Leo she knew was the world's worst technophobe. Maybe there really was hope all things could change.

She slid one printout of the dossier out of the folder. It was about ten pages long and stapled together. She opened it in front of him.

"Our information about Zolcu comes from multiple sources," she said. "The Romanian Intelligence Service, Interpol, and the data Quickdraw and Mike Carmody's team gathered for us."

He nodded. "Go ahead."

"If you've read the file, you know Drajan Petrovik and Zolcu are numbers one and two at the top of the *technologie vampiri*'s leadership hierarchy." Morse lifted her coffee off the desk and sipped. "Petrovik's a breed apart, of course. Smarter, more ambitious than the rest. When he won scholarships to study in London and Madrid, he became a kind of legendary figure on the dark web."

"The Wolf."

She nodded.

"Nobody else is on his level."

"Except Kali Alcazar. She's right there on the mountaintop. Shit, she *is* the mountain. Those *vampiri* assholes, Petrovik included, are still looking for a way up."

"And thankfully she's with us now," Morse said.

Harris merely grunted and looked down at his tablet.

"Zolcu's a coattail grabber," he said. "Grew up on a beet farm. The same town as Petrovik and their partner Emil Vasile. Went to college with them for a couple years…"

"In Satu Mare," Morse said. "After Petrovik left, he and Vasile held the fort and got into increasingly sophisticated computer crimes. Later on, Zolcu branched out into other rackets. Counterfeiting, vice, drugs…banned nootropics and biohacks."

"He's a big slug in a piss puddle," Harris said. "And a whoring, gambling degenerate. Stays in his element, like an old-time mob boss who won't leave the neighborhood. Except they liked good, tailored suits, and he dresses up in stupid fucking pirate costumes."

"Cosplay," she said. "It's a thing."

Harris shrugged.

"Everything's a thing," he said. "The world's full of assholes."

Morse looked at him.

"We've got to be careful with him, Leo," she said. "Zolcu ran the fake bank-card operation that spread the Hekate bug. After the Wolf went to ground, he took over their syndicate's operations, oversaw them for months until his capture. Most importantly, with Emil Vasile dead, and Vasile's sister at large, he's our best link to Petrovik. He almost certainly knows his whereabouts. If not specifically, then generally."

Harris glanced up from the tablet. Something she'd said was getting his antennae up. The same as it had over the phone earlier.

"Why are we talking about it now?"

"Because Gustav Zolcu's no slouch. He's shrewd and confident. I just want to be sure we don't underestimate him."

"You think that's a problem? For me?"

Morse shook her head.

"No," she said. "I don't."

"Then what is it?"

She sat still for moment.

"After last November, I felt I had to take a hard look in the mirror," she said. "We weren't ready to move on the Wolf's Lair. Even knowing Petrovik wasn't there. As an organization, Net Force wasn't yet the sum of its parts. We hadn't integrated them. We weren't fully together. We were rash. It was a mistake, and we paid dearly for it."

Harris took a breath. It felt short, like he'd just climbed a flight of stairs. He could have used a hit of oxygen.

"You don't think I can handle the interview myself," he said. "That's what you were getting at before. 'Participate,' my ass. Gone a few months, and I'm washed up in your eyes."

"You're personalizing things, Leo. And you shouldn't be."

"Bullshit."

She was silent. Harris was looking straight into her eyes. She didn't blink.

"I'm sorry you feel slighted," she said. "I mean it.

I'd hoped you would understand. But you're going to have a partner in the interrogation room this morning. I think your skill sets can be complementary. Your separate knowledge bases. Especially with Zolcu."

He sat there without saying a word for thirty long seconds. Then he turned off his tablet and put it back into his coat pocket and glared across the desk at her.

"Who?" he asked.

The door behind the desk opened to an old metal skybridge spanning almost two hundred feet from the north side of the Terminal to the south side of an old bronze-trimmed office building across West 51st Street. Once upon a time, the building had been the company headquarters of Hudson Maritime Storage Enterprises—the same outfit that ran the warehouse operation for over a century. Built so employees moving between the two could avoid the pedestrians and horse-drawn carriages four stories down, the skybridge—with its curlicue pressed-tin ceiling and broad crank windows—now provided cloistered access from the Fusion Center to the Net Force East adjunct—its top floor consisting of a block of secure interview and observation rooms, the lower stories housing administrative offices and specialized equipment facilities.

Harris stopped halfway across the span.

"Something wrong?" Carol said beside him.

"No," he said.

"Leo," she said, "what can I do—"

She read the look in his eyes and cut herself short.

"I'll catch up," he said.

Carol nodded silently and continued to the door.

Harris turned to look out the window at the traffic drifting below. His back to her, he listened to the advance of her footsteps. When he heard the door slide shut behind her, he got the rubber tubing out of the bag's outer pocket and hooked it up to the oxygen machine. A couple of hits and he would be fine.

A few minutes later he was holding his biocard up at the door. It opened into a bright, wide, windowless corridor with smooth beige walls and a shiny beige-and-white tiled floor. The air was filtered and neither warm nor cool. Carol was waiting just inside the door with two buzz-cut guards wearing soft vests over black short-sleeved shirts. The letters *FBI* were printed across their chests in white. They both held MP5 submachine guns and carried Glock 17 pistols in sidearm holsters.

"The observation room is around the corner," Carol said, nodding up the hall.

He shook his head no. "Take me right over to him," he said. "I want to get started."

She shrugged. "Your call," she said.

They walked on with one guard leading the way and one behind them. The doors to the observation and interrogation rooms were closely side-by-side on the right. Another armed guard stood between them. Harris paused and slipped his carry bag off his shoulder.

"Think you can put this somewhere for a while?" he asked Carol.

She took it and nodded.

"Sure," she said. "It'll be safe."

Harris jabbed a finger at the interrogation room door, and the guard held his card to the scanner and opened it for him.

The room was a small cubicle lit by overhead fluorescent panels. A one-way mirror ran across its left wall. In its center was a long metal table. There were three molded plastic chairs with metal legs, one in a corner of the room, another pushed under the table with its back to the door.

Gustav Zolcu sat in the third chair, facing the door from behind the table. He looked like his dossier photos, thin and dark-eyed with a black goatee. The only notable differences were his shaved head and orange prison coveralls.

Harris entered alone, waiting for the guard to shut the door from behind him in the corridor. After a second he took a step toward the table, stopped, and looked directly at Zolcu, who sat there looking straight back at him.

"Before we get started, I want to inform you of your rights to an attorney and to remain silent," Harris said. "I also want you to know your answers are being recorded. Understood?"

Zolcu stared across at him in silence. Leo figured he needed a proper introduction, took a deep breath, walked around the table, and gave the side of his chair a hard, rattling kick.

Zolcu jolted up straight.

"I'm Harris," he said, standing over him. "When I ask a question, doesn't matter what it is, you answer. Got me?"

Zolcu sat there for a long moment. "I don't have to answer anything," he said. "I am an honest nightclub owner. I was attacked by American terrorists. I've been abducted from my country and am being detained illegally. Do not talk to me about my rights."

Harris took a breath, nodded to indicate Zolcu's prison uniform.

"You enjoy wearing that onesie?" he said.

Zolcu looked at him and said nothing.

"I hear you like fancy clothes," Harris said. "So happens, I do, too. But you can't pick your getups in custody. No rings and things. No buttons and bows. One guy's the same as the next. You're like Florida oranges packed into a fucking crate."

Zolcu stared at him. Harris returned to his side of the table, pulled out the chair, and sat down.

"Here's why I'm telling you all this," he said. "You've been in this country—what, three days? Before that you were in Europe. Romania, Italy… it took over a month to get you extradited and onto an overseas flight. And I bet all those weeks, close to home, you figured you'd be right back at your club in no time. Prancing around in a sailor suit, a cowboy hat and shorts. Or whatever the fuck you wear on the dance floor. Catch me?"

"No."

Harris grinned.

"I think maybe you do," he said. "You're so used to living the dream, it's hard to wake up and see it's over." He spread his hands. "You still think this shit's temporary. A little break in the action. But you better get used to it."

Zolcu shook his head.

"I don't belong here. I'm a businessman. I own a nightclub."

"You own a sleazy freak show with some of the lowest scum on earth on its guest list," he said. "Drajan Petrovik, for instance."

Zolcu said nothing. Harris studied him closely. He shifted in his chair but showed no other reaction. Harris decided to let that thread hang.

"How about we talk about your real line of work?" he said. "We can skip the pimping and drugs and go straight to forging the bank cards that spread the Hekate bug. That was some fucking hit. Thousands of innocent people died. Right here in this city."

"You're crazy."

"You didn't print up those cards? Microchips and all? Because that part was slick. Manufacturing the chip, I mean. Putting the bug on them so it would spread…"

"I had nothing to do with that."

"Which part? The cards or the chips?"

Zolcu crossed his arms.

"Neither."

"You sure?"

"Of course."

Harris shrugged. "The reason I ask—I like to put all my reasons up front—is that we're talking apples and oranges, so to speak. Apples being run-of-the-mill ATM card forgery. But the chip…that's what puts you in with the oranges. For a long, long time."

"I don't know what you're talking about."

Harris meshed his hands on the table and leaned forward.

"My feeling is you didn't make the chips," he said. "That's more what I'd expect from Petrovik. Or his Russian pals."

"I don't know anyone named Petrovik."

"How about the Wolf?"

"Excuse me?"

"The Wolf," Harris repeated, looking directly into his eyes. "His nickname."

A few seconds passed. Zolcu's arms remained crossed.

"Wolves are dangerous," he said. "I have nothing to do with them."

"Really?"

"Yes."

"Even though you were living in Petrovik's castle."

Zolcu shrugged.

"I told you, I don't know him," he said. "I rented the place through a broker."

Harris grinned. "A broker."

"Correct. A real-estate broker. I never inquired about its owner."

"And what was the broker's name?"

Zolcu said nothing.

"The name of the real-estate broker," Harris repeated. "Let's hear it."

Zolcu said nothing. Harris waited. They looked at each other.

"I don't remember," Zolcu said finally. "It was a woman."

"The same woman you were with the night we grabbed you?"

Zolcu looked at him.

"No," he said. "She was not the broker."

"But you *were* with a woman that night?"

"Yes. I met her at a club in Cluj-Napoca."

"Cluj being some little shithole Romanian town near the castle?"

"I prefer it to this big shithole *American* town," Zolcu said.

Harris grinned again. He stood regarding Zolcu for a long minute.

"Funny," he said. "I like funny."

Zolcu stared at him.

"So, funny man…what were you doing in Cluj?"

"I was there on business."

"What kind of business?"

"I want to open a new club."

"Oh?"

"In the area," Zolcu said. "I rented the castle to have a place to stay. While scouting locations."

"In Cluj."

"Yes."

Harris looked at him. "Wasn't the place a little far from there?"

"It didn't seem far to me."

"Forty, fifty miles, right?"

"I would need to check."

"Don't bother, funny man," Harris said. "I already did."

Zolcu was silent a moment.

"I scouted multiple locations. In Cluj, Rosalvea, and Satu Mare," he said. "The castle was centrally located."

Harris looked at him.

"That woman you picked up," he said. "Let's hear some more about her."

"What is there to say? We met, we danced, we drank, and we went back to the castle together. When your people broke in, I left her in my bed."

"You're some fucking champion."

Zolcu shrugged again.

"Say what you will, I don't even remember the girl's name," he said. "Is a one-night stand now an international crime?"

"No," Harris said. "The fake-card scam is. Cyberterrorism is. An innocent woman's murder... that's just what pushes a jury to vote for a death sentence."

Zolcu opened his mouth. Closed it.

"If something happened to her," he said, "I had no hand in it."

"No?"

Zolcu shook his head. "How do you know *your* people weren't responsible?"

Harris sat there looking at him in silence. Ten seconds passed. Twenty. A full minute. He knew what he would have liked to have done. If he could breathe normally, if he could go more than ten steps without the machine, he would have stood up and gone back around the table and gotten right in his face, thrown some fear into him, established his control. But he couldn't, not in his physical condition, and instead he just leaned forward over the table.

"I've got one rule in this room," he said. "And it's that I ask the questions, and you give the answers. All right?"

Zolcu looked at him. After a moment, he nodded.

"Repeat it," Harris said. "My rule."

"You ask the questions."

Leo nodded.

"And the second part?"

Zolcu suddenly smiled at him.

"There is none, you fat, wheezing old bastard," he said. "Ask all the questions you want. I won't answer any more of—"

The sentence died unfinished on his lips as the door to the room suddenly burst open, swinging back against the wall with a loud bang. Startled, Zolcu shot a look past Harris toward the entryway and saw a tall, broad-chested man dressed entirely in black burst through the entry and cross the room with a few giant strides, heading straight toward the table, coming around it, coming toward *him*...

Almost before he knew what was happening, the man grabbed the front of his jumpsuit with two large fists, bunching it up below the collar, hauling him off his chair with a violent jerk. The chair crashed to the floor, its metal legs rattling and rolling hard against the tiles. Zolcu was slammed back against the wall, his feet hoisted into the air, the man facing him now, pressing his chest against him, leveraging him even higher off the floor.

His spine jolted. His skull thumped. His molars clacked together. The man slammed him against the wall a second time, a third. Zolcu grunted in pain, his mouth gaping open, the wind knocked out of him.

The man brought his face up close to his. It was blunt and wide with flat cheekbones. All planes and no angles. His nose looked like it had been broken many times and carelessly set.

Zolcu immediately noticed his eyes. One brown, the other hazel, with faint brown lines radiating from the pupil.

"You're going to answer every one of our questions," the man said, shaking him hard. "You don't, I'll break your jaw, and we'll ask them again. And you'll answer anyway. But it will hurt a hell of a lot worse."

Zolcu stared at him in astonishment. That voice…

No man knows how bad he is till he's tried very hard to be good.

"You," he said. His face had gone pale. "From Romania. The field…"

The man grinned in his face.

Nodded.

"The name is Carmody," he said. "And I've got no rules."

Colonel John Howard was conflicted.

He was good with his housing at the airfield being double the size of his old quarters at FOB Janus. He was good with the Officer's Club, where he ate practically every meal; good with its waitstaff, full service bar, comfortable chairs, and, presently, the steaming hot lunch of spiced pork and potato stew on the table in front of him. He sure as hell didn't miss the glorified trailer that passed for Janus's chow hall, and was also good with being coddled in small doses. But he hadn't climbed the Army's promotion ladder—truth be known, it had felt more like pushing a boulder uphill—for creature comforts. The privileges of rank had never interested him. He would never forget the day a Black lieutenant came to his West Baltimore junior high school, looking about a thousand feet tall in his crisp uniform and shiny shoes, looking like he'd come down off Olympus to the seniors in the auditorium.

Or to him anyway.

Howard could still picture him. His name was Ewing, like the hoops player he idolized. Lieutenant Edwin Ewing. His skin had seemed to glow onstage. He had come to Howard's classroom after his talk, wanting to know if any of the kids had questions. Howard had asked if he was ever in battle and he said he was in the Iraq War. Howard had asked about the decorations on his jacket and he'd pointed to a couple. A Purple Heart. Somehow that made him seem even taller.

Before he left, the lieutenant had taken Howard aside and asked a question of his own, wondering if he might be interested in becoming a cadet at the United States Military Academy. There on the spot he'd said yes. Ewing told him to work hard on his grades, "stick with the curriculum," and keep out of trouble. He'd also asked what high school Howard planned to attend and promised to stay in touch. And he kept that promise.

Four years later, after graduation, Howard enlisted in the Army, and with Ewing's endorsement attended West Point Prep for the summer to bring up his grades. The following September he was admitted to the Corps of Cadets, one of only eight Black admissions in a class of fifteen hundred.

It was tough. As a plebe he caught shit from some of the white boys, but he'd played basketball in the schoolyards of Baltimore and was nobody's punk. The real slights, the ones that stung, weren't made while trash talking during drill competitions. When it came to a mouth, he had one that couldn't be outmatched. But overhearing some of his classmates calling him an affirmative action cadet behind his back...that had been something else entirely.

Howard forked some stew into his mouth, nodded with satisfaction, and followed it with a deep gulp of beer. Lessons learned, he thought. Tough was one thing. But he'd always needed to be tougher than the rest. And right now, right here...though he couldn't really say he minded being spoiled by the privileges of rank, he was ready for his recuperation to end. Ready to get back to Janus.

The satphone rang on the table and he glanced at its caller ID. *Perfect timing.*

He picked up.

"Duchess," he grunted. "What is it?"

"And a good day to you, too," Morse said. "I work with so *many* cheerful men!"

"Not sure what you mean."

"Just a stray thought," she said. "Colonel, I'm calling in part to let you know your visitor's in the air."

"ETA?"

"About zero nine hundred your time."

"Fernandez'll drive him to base," Howard said. "Where I should be."

"It's a glorified tent city right now. In the middle of winter. You'll be cleared for active duty when the doctors say you're ready."

He frowned. "What's the other part?"

"Our prisoner's in the sweatbox as we speak. I thought you'd want to know."

"Your boy in the room with him?"

"Yes. He just made a crashing entrance."

Howard was quiet. He couldn't argue with putting Carmody on Zolcu. He would have preferred the grilling take place in-country, but Morse was the CO, and she had wanted to include Harris, her investigations chief. It was Carmody's friend going stateside that had been done over his objection.

"Tell me about Outlier," he said.

"She's here."

"You trying to irritate me?"

"Never."

A pause. The silence over a secure satellite connection, like the hollow whoosh of a conch shell held to the ear.

"Outlier has been technically designated a person of concern," Morse said. "That entitles her to liberty and freedom of movement while in detention."

"Still doesn't answer my question."

"We have a close watch on her. Which in my personal view isn't necessary."

"She's got forty-one computer hacking charges pending against her in the United States alone. I stink at math, what's the total count around the world?"

"She's given us her full cooperation."

"Let's hope so."

"We're working on plea arrangements with prosecutors. Ours, other countries'," Morse said. "How many times does she need to prove herself?"

Silence bled through the line.

"We don't know who hit us in November," Howard said after a moment. "Who put the hogs on attack protocol."

"I think we agree the prisoner probably holds the key to that."

"He give up anything yet?"

"No."

"Then, I repeat, we don't know," Howard said. "Outlier and the Wolf were hot for each other once."

"A long time ago."

"And maybe the candle's still burning."

Morse exhaled audibly. "One thing's for certain, Colonel," she said. "Speculation gets us nowhere. I'd prefer it doesn't morph into unfounded suspicion. If it does, it will eat away at us from the inside out."

Howard said nothing.

"I'd better sign off," she said. "There's obviously a lot going on here."

"Sure." He eyed his beer mug. "You'll keep me updated?"

"Yes," Morse said. "And I hope you'll consider what I told you about unwarranted suspicion."

A second passed. Another.

Howard said nothing.

20

Grigor swung the blue Toyota Corolla off the interstate at the Seabrook, New Hampshire, exit, bore left off the ramp toward US-1, and continued north past the tax-free package stores and strip malls to a gas station where he pulled in to fill his tank.

He got out of the car, inserted the nozzle, and stood there stretching his back in the gray afternoon cold. His drive from New York had thus far taken four hours, almost a full hour longer than it would have if he was using the toll roads. But he wanted to avoid the plazas and their E-ZPass and license-plate readers.

Grigor was confident of his documentation and tags and knew they would hold up under close scrutiny, even in a traffic stop. The police could run a hundred different identity checks and find nothing suspicious. In their databases, he was Stephen Gelfland. But he believed in being careful. He did not intend to give anyone a way to track his movements across four states.

Stephen Gelfland.

Thirty-two, a resident of Teaneck, New Jersey, and graduate of New York Maritime College at Fort Schuyler in the Bronx. Single, no children. Two months earlier, he'd been hired as a boarding agent trainee at CloudCable's corporate headquarters in Weston, Massachusetts, starting salary $75,000 a year. One essential condition of employment had been that he agreed to relocate to New Hampshire within thirty days of his hiring. Another was that he was able to spend a minimum of a hundred twenty days at sea each year, each stint lasting three to four months...

In an abandoned barn in the Jersey Pine Barrens, the Gelfland who had interviewed for the position in early November had been reduced to biological sludge in forty gallons of clear, concentrated sodium hydroxide solution. The night before Thanksgiving, when he'd returned from grocery shopping, Grigor had waited in the darkness outside his home, slipped up behind him, and shot him twice in the back of his skull, point-blank, with his Walther .22. He'd then undressed the body, wrapped it in a tarp without leaving any traces of blood or fingerprints, and brought it to the barn in the trunk of a rental car.

Grigor had used a hacksaw to prepare his corpse for the acid bath. The head, torso, limbs, hands, and feet went into the plastic drum separately. It was an easier fit than an intact body and allowed for faster liquefaction. As an added measure to prevent identification of the remains, Grigor severed all ten fingertips at the DIP joints, burning them along with Gelfland's clothes, using gasoline and a match, at the back of the barn. He had placed the charred fingertips in the drum with the rest of the body parts, and stuffed what was left of the clothing in a compostable plastic bag. Later, he buried it in the deep woods, far from any campgrounds.

By now the original Gelfland was long gone. Within twelve to eighteen hours of his drum immersion, the hair and soft tissues—flesh, cartilage, and muscle—would have dissolved into a thin, oily fluid the color of weak coffee. Bones took longer and didn't altogether disintegrate but reduced to a white puttylike residue of slaked or calciferous lime. It was a gentle and complete biocremation that left no trace of DNA or RNA.

Grigor hung the nozzle back on the pump and slid into the car. He was thinking his work was nothing if not tidy and efficient…which suddenly brought him back to his meeting with Sergei Cosa the night he had done the job. Anyone else would have lived to regret the suggestion, however veiled, that he was less than scrupulous with the Waleks and the garage attendant. It had bordered on insult.

Grigor had almost walked out of his Chelsea den that night. Told him to find someone else for the present assignment.

It was not that he needed or wanted praise. He

knew his worth, and so did the almighty Cosa. Whether or not Cosa believed his own myth—the Deathless One, indeed—that shaggy bear was only flesh and blood. But in the end, his attitude was of no consequence. Grigor's true loyalty was to the SVR. They had literally made him who and what he was. Engineered and educated him at the *naukograd*, the secret city, a process that began under Nikita Khrushchev generations before he was born. He would see they got a full return on their investment.

He pulled onto US-1 again and drove north, continuing to follow the toll-free route. Soon the strip malls were behind him, and he was back on winding side roads, surrounded by tall New England pines and dunes of plowed white snow.

The rest of his trip took under thirty minutes. He turned west outside Portsmouth, drove along the January grayness of the Piscataqua River for about three miles, then jigged left onto a two-lane blacktop called Schooner Road and designated *partial restricted usage* on the printed map he had memorized before leaving New York—GPS being easily traceable by law enforcement and therefore dangerous. Through the tree trunks on his right, Grigor glimpsed water and, roughly up ahead, the tall structural masts that mounted communications arrays above the decks of modern ships.

The road terminated in a high gate with a guardhouse out front. Coming up to it, he saw a sign that read *Employees Only, Visitors Must Have Identification*.

He slowed down, passed over several speed

bumps, and pulled up to the booth, lowering his window to show the security man his driver's license.

"I'm Stephen Gelfland," he said with a smile. "Here for the orientation."

"Thanks, sir. Be right with you," the guard said pleasantly. He fed the license into a scanner and watched a tablet on a swing arm.

After a moment, Grigor saw the man nod to himself. He hadn't sweated the computer check. The Wolf's hacking team at Okean-27 would have ensured that all Gelfland's online records were modified, replacing the originals' likeness with his own on every archived facial and biometric scan. One of the reasons Gelfland was chosen for his new identity was that he had been a loner who shunned social media, leaving only a LinkedIn photo to be switched.

The guard leaned out of the booth to return his license.

"Here you go, Mr. Gelfland," he said. "They have everything set for you. I'll have your badge ready in a second."

Grigor waited. A small card printer in the booth issued an ID with his photo, Gelfland's name, and a bar code. The guard inserted it into a clear plastic holder with an attached lanyard and handed it out to him.

"Welcome to CloudCable," he said. "If you follow the road you're on, you'll see the administrative building up on the right. You can pull into any available slot out front. Someone from the project director's office will meet you at the reception desk."

Grigor slipped the lanyard over his neck. Then

a thought came to him. He'd glanced at his dash clock while waiting and seen that he was about half an hour early for his appointment.

"I noticed a ship while driving in," he said. "Big masts."

The guard nodded. "That's the *Stalwart*. Your home till May or thereabouts," he said. "They've been doing her refit and resupply in the yard."

"Any chance I can take a closer look?"

"Well, you can't go right up to the boatworks without clearance. Security requirements. But if you hang a left instead of a right, you'll be on Granite Harbor Lane. Take it about a quarter mile, and you'll get to a turnaround. There's a nice view of the ship. All four hundred fifty feet of her. Which happens to be the exact same length as Noah's ark, if you like trivia."

"Is that so?"

"Yep," the guard said. "In the Bible, they measure in cubits. Some historian figured out that's from the elbow to the fingertips and then worked it out in feet. But seems to me it'd depend on whether someone's got a long or short reach."

Grigor looked at him. "Tells you navy mapmakers didn't write the Bible," he said. "They say an inch can make the difference between success and disaster."

The guard chuckled. "I guess people can either trust the Bible or the experts."

"Or the facts," Grigor said. "People think the cloud that powers the internet is in the sky. But it's actually deep beneath the waves, isn't it? No matter what they think."

The guard cocked a finger at him. "Got a point there, Mr. Gelfland," he said. "Anyway, good luck. Someone gives you a problem, just show the badge."

Grigor nodded, raised his window, and drove off.

Granite Harbor Lane curved gradually up onto a craggy granite bluff at the water's edge. He saw the *Stalwart* almost at once, anchored among a group of loading cranes and tugs and service boats in a wide river bend.

The turnaround appeared on his right. The plows had been through it and pushed the snow to the side of the blacktop in low, bordering rims. The blacktop was completely clear.

Grigor pulled in and stopped the Toyota and got out into the cold. He adjusted the badge so it hung over his car coat, then stepped over to the water side of the turnaround. There he looked out and down at the ship he would be boarding within days.

The *Stalwart* was white-hulled and wide-beamed with a large, high mission bay from which the superstructures supporting the communications arrays towered many yards skyward. Her stern was flat as it was in all deepwater cable-layers. A long conveyer belt ran from the shore to her deck. On the dock was a huge drum of wound-up fiber-optic cable. Around it, men in hard hats were running large pieces of equipment that fed the cable over the belt to the ship. The cable looked as thick as a garden hose. Deep within the ship were gigantic circular tanks holding enough of it to span four thousand miles of the seafloor. She would berth a crew of eighty sailors, engineers, and other assorted workers. They would consume thousands of pounds of food, milk, and other beverages in their months at sea.

Grigor had studied and instantly memorized every available bit of information about the vessel. Every specification. He knew her inside and out without yet having set foot on her. But he had wanted to see her once, alone, as himself, before being introduced to her in the role of Stephen Gelfland.

He stood on the overhanging bluff for a few minutes, taking her in. The wind had teeth blowing over the water. His mind on what lay ahead, he reached an arm out straight toward the ship, stretching as far as possible, holding it rigidly in front of him. His hand was turned upward, fingers fully extended.

Grigor looked down the length of his arm for a full thirty seconds. Then he lowered it slightly, like a cantilever, a small degree at a time.

For a moment, the *Stalwart* appeared to rest in the palm of his hand.

He clenched his fingers tightly together, a fist.

Romania

It was 7:00 p.m. and pitch-dark out when Adrian Soto's Learjet 75 charter banked in for a landing in the cold, cloudy sky over Mihail Kogălniceanu Airport.

His Jolt parked near the runway, E4 Mario Perez at the wheel, Sergeant Fernandez watched the plane descend and felt his stomach flutter. He didn't actually know Soto but knew everything about him, or everything that was public information, and thought of him as a father, or maybe an uncle, some kind of larger-than-life patriarch. Somebody who was up there while he was down *here*. In the past several hours, he'd thought about what their conversation might be, thought of a million things to say to him. But what did you say to somebody you'd always considered a hero?

"Sir," Perez said beside him, "I'm thinking I shouldn't have done it."

Fernandez turned from the windshield and eyed him a little absently.

"Done what?" he said.

Mario dipped his head back toward the rear.

"That," he said.

"Why not?"

"It was a dumb idea."

Fernandez shook his head. "Wrong."

"You honestly don't think so?"

"If I thought so, you wouldn't have done it, because I'd've ordered you not to," Fernandez replied. "Which I didn't do."

Mario was silent. It was hard to believe he was sitting here alongside the illustrious Sergeant Julio Fernandez, someone he'd looked up to since arriving at FOB Janus seven months ago…and, really, long before that. Back at Hawthorne, Fernandez had held legendary status as a trailblazer in the military applications of AI and machine learning. The opportunity to work under him was Mario's main reason for requesting a transfer to Janus.

"So you *considered* it?" he asked.

"Considered what?"

"Ordering me not do it."

"Uh-huh." Fernandez looked at him. "But then I remembered seeing a picture of Soto at home with a couple of cats in the background."

"Seriously?"

Fernandez nodded. "Out of curiosity…did you ask your fiancée's opinion?"

"Yes, sir."

"And what did lovely Laura think of your idea?"

"What she told me—" Mario began.

He was cut off by a shrill meow.

He rotated halfway around toward the back seat. Buttons was pawing at the zippered front panel of his carrier, his face pushed up against its soft mesh window.

"Shhh, little guy. Papi's here." Mario reached a hand out so the cat could sniff it, waited a moment as he settled down, then turned back to Fernandez. "Anyway, Laura's exact words were *Si te dietienes para mirar hacia atrás cruzando la calle, serás golpeado.*"

"If you stop to look back when you're crossing the street, you'll get hit," Fernandez said. "Heavy."

Mario nodded.

"She said I'm impulsive. And that it's okay to be impulsive. But that I waste too much time questioning my impulses."

Fernandez grunted.

"And what'd you say?"

"That I just wasn't sure it's appropriate. Plus, I don't want the bigwigs at home to think we're horning in on their action," Mario replied. "By having an animal mascot, I mean."

"And what'd she say?"

"That Net Force's mascot is a German shepherd and that ours here at Janus is a pesky little cat," Mario said, "and that she didn't think they'd feel threatened."

"Uh-huh," Fernandez said. "She say anything else?"

"Yeah," Mario said. "That Buttons is resilient. And clever. You know, like we were against the 'hogs. That he *represents*. And didn't quit on the base. Or us. Hiding out for weeks, waiting for everyone to come back."

"Uh-huh."

Mario looked at him. Waited a second. "So, what do *you* say, Sarge?"

Fernandez looked outside again. The aircraft touched down. He heard the whine of the drag force around its turbines as its fans were partly closed off and it decelerated and taxied toward the apron, where a couple of guys in coveralls stood waving orange batons.

His butterflies were in a flapping, twirling tizzy.

"I say your girl's very smart," he said after a second.

Mario smiled.

"The smartest I ever met," he said.

"Bet she's the prettiest, too."

"Oh God, you've seen her. A knockout," Mario said.

Fernandez looked at him and grinned. He looked back at Fernandez. And cleared his throat, suddenly embarrassed.

"Sorry," he said. "Guess you think I've got stars in my eyes."

Fernandez was quiet, his expression suddenly serious.

"Keep those stars right where they are," he said. "And when you love somebody, don't let go." He patted a hand to his chest. "There's only one true love of your life, kiddo. That I know. Tell you *how* I know sometime."

A moment passed. The heater hummed warm air into the Jolt. Fernandez looked suddenly melancholy. After a minute he saw the plane come to a halt and the airport workers start laying down the wheel chocks.

He straightened in his seat.

"Well, company's here," he said. "Better roll up close."

Mario shifted into Drive, eased forward onto the apron, and braked a few feet from the plane, leaving on his low beams. As the airstair lowered from its cabin door, Fernandez got out, smoothed his clothes, and walked toward it. The pilot and copilot stepped down, the copilot toting a wheeled carry-on. They acknowledged him with nods, handed off the bag to him, stood to one side on the tarmac, and waited.

Adrian Soto was the next and last to exit. He descended the stairs in a hooded bomber jacket, exchanged handshakes with the crew, and approached the sergeant.

Fernandez gulped dryly and saluted. "Welcome to Romania, Mr. Soto, sir!" he said, introducing himself.

Soto offered a broad smile. Fernandez thought

he looked younger in person, somehow, than in photos and videos.

"At ease," he said. He extended his arm. "It's a great honor to meet you, Sergeant."

Oh my God, this is flipping unreal. Fernandez swallowed dryly again. Hitched in a breath. And clasped his hand.

"Thank you, Mr. Soto, sir," he said, managing to sound calm. "*I'm* the one who's honored. And privileged."

"Then we can agree the feeling is mutual." Soto glanced toward the Jolt. "Is that my ride over there?"

"Yes, sir!"

"Let's get to it," Soto said and made a kind of all-inclusive gesture with both hands. "It's brisk out tonight."

They walked to the vehicle together. Mario had gone around to open the rear passenger door, lifting Buttons's carrier out of the back seat.

Soto noticed it at once and bent to examine the large custom patch on its side. It showed the Net Force insignia, and beneath it in neatly embroidered lettering:

FOB Janus
Buttons the Cat
Camp Mascot

"Well," he said, "that's fine work."

"My fiancée gets the credit, sir," Mario said.

Soto smiled, peering through the carrier's mesh window.

"Hello there, little one," he cooed. "Pleasure to meet you."

Buttons pushed against the mesh from inside and mewled plaintively.

"Apologies, sir. He's an okay traveler. But he gets kind of claustrophobic," Mario said. "There's room for him in front…"

Soto looked at him.

"No need, he can stay with me," he said. "It so happens I have two cats of my own."

Mario did not miss Fernandez's covert glance. The sergeant stood there a second looking satisfied with himself, then nodded toward the Jolt.

"It's warm in there, and the roads are clear," he said. "I think it'll be a smooth ride to the base."

Crimean Peninsula

The submarine's hatches stood open on its upper deck, limned by the glow of the Kliegs on the long concrete pier. Of the sixteen vertical launch tubes, four were about to receive their payloads. Shore hands worked their machines, and guards in hooded parkas watched with rifles across their middles. The trial run was minutes away.

Farther down the pier, Sergei Cosa and Drajan Petrovik were two shadows approaching in the darkness.

"The boat is magnificent. Perfect," Cosa said. He paused as he spoke. "Perfection always leaves me breathless. Whether in art, music, science, technology…breathless."

Drajan paused beside him, his hands deep in the pockets of a black full-length overcoat. The wind was strong and cold, and the water slapped against the edge of the pier. He smelled the rich organic soup of seaweed and minerals and brine. Of phytoplankton bursting open in decomposition, releasing tiny bursts of gas, the smell of decay that drew the fish, crabs, and gulls upon them. The food chain beginning with the death of unseen drifters on tides and currents.

There was a splash out on the water—the wind, possibly, or some unseen creature breaking its surface.

Drajan stared into the night.

"For me," he said quietly, "it's the lunge and swipe."

"Oh?"

"I don't care about the method of the kill," Drajan said. "Magnificence is in action. Perfection hinges on the strike's success."

"Spoken like a true apex predator."

Drajan shrugged his shoulders. "I'm not sure there's such a thing."

"Really. That surprises me. You're the Wolf, after all."

"And you are feared as Koschei the Deathless," Drajan said. "The dark rider. The shape changer who strikes down his enemies as a living tornado. His soul hidden in a needle, in an egg, in a fowl, in a hare locked in a chest, and buried deep."

"You know your Russian myths."

"I know what *is* myth. And I know enough not

to believe them. Yours, mine, or anyone's." Drajan turned toward Cosa, his gaze direct. "If we aim to take down two Goliaths with one strike, I had better have my eyes open. *We'd* better."

Both were silent. They could hear a mechanical throb and clatter farther up the pier, where an operator on an elevated pedestal seat was working a giant robotic arm with his joysticks. In its curved, steel prongs was an eighteen-foot metal canister. Extended out over the submarine, the arm and canister swung slowly over one of the open hatches. Four or five hands stood topside directing the operator over radio headsets.

Cosa resumed walking toward the sub, Drajan keeping pace, his coat blowing around his legs in the fierce wind.

"You must admit, she's quite the impressive beast," the Russian said. "A hundred and fifty yards from bow to stern, electric-drive stealth propulsion…our creation is as big as a whale and quiet as a lover's whisper."

"But still, she must wear a disguise. And it's all nothing without our sleeper in the cloud."

Cosa paused a step in the wind.

"Grigor is with the cable-layer. As of only hours ago. Did I mention it?"

"Yes," Drajan said. "So you do see after all, Sergei. Deception and distraction…they're the fine points that will lift our plan to greatness. To the perfection we seek."

Cosa regarded him, standing on the concrete walk between land and sea.

"I think I can understand Castle Graguscu's

allure to you," he said. "With its trick walls and hidden passages, it must have been a wonderland."

Drajan shrugged. "It was one of many places I've rested my head in the past. Now it's just rubble."

Cosa looked at him for a moment. Then his thick lips parted, and laughter erupted from deep in his chest, the sound roaring out over the chop in the wind.

"You're a complex devil," he said and jerked his head toward the sleek form of the submarine. "But fuck all this talk. Let's go inspect our twin-giant killer."

Drajan nodded.

"Into the belly of the beast," he said. "After you."

Cosa grinned and turned toward the boat, Drajan briefly lingering behind. The incoming waves reared high, curled in, and tumbled down on themselves. He felt their pulse inside him, their beat, as if the blood in his veins had taken up their forceful, surging rhythm.

He inhaled slowly, his nostrils tingling from the sea-smells. The wind lashed his hair in all directions as his right hand went to the tattoo on his neck. The Wheel of Hekate.

Thoughts of Kali could still overtake him, unbeckoned, at any moment. He did not quite know why, but they did.

A second passed. Drajan lowered his hand from his neck, slid it into his coat pocket, and resumed his pace, moving through the radiance of the shore lights, following Cosa past the Russian guards, and then over the gangway to the open hatch.

A glance down inside, and he descended.

* * * * *

Don't miss the other books in the bestselling Net Force thriller series created by Tom Clancy and Steve Pieczenik and written by Jerome Preisler!

Available in print and digital.

Download the ebook novella!